A MARRIED WOMAN

Manju Kapur lives in New Delhi, where she is a teacher of English Literature at Miranda House College, Delhi University. Her first novel, *Difficult Daughters* (1998), received tremendous international acclaim, won the Commonwealth Prize for First Novels (Eurasia Section) and was a number one bestseller in India.

Further praise for *A Married Woman*:

'A magnetically alert, deeply readable novel, written with a profound intelligence and a deceptively light touch . . . Kapur's best and biggest triumph is Astha herself. You know her, you understand her, you just don't want to let her go. Every breath she takes, every word she utters, every feeling she experiences, every dusty scooter ride, every sari in her cupboard – – all of them are shatteringly real. Most of all, the even-handed and touching portrait of her marriage – the husband who genuinely cares and wants to be sexy and progressive, but is in fact the uneasy result of a traditional upbringing mixed with Western education – is brilliantly done. Kapur is a generous, far-seeing writer, who knows there are no answers, no conclusions to be drawn. Maybe that's what I most admire: she thinks and writes in vivid colours, but it's the grey areas – life's queasy compromises – that she furiously yet tenderly exposes.' Julie Myerson, *Guardian*

Praise for *Difficult Daughters*:

'A skilful, enticing first novel by an Indian writer who prefers reality to magic realism. Manju Kapur's sensuous pages re-create an intimate world where family groups sleep in the open air on the roof and wash themselves in the yard in the dewy cool of morning, where love-making is furtive and urgent because another wife may be listening, and women's lives move to a complex choreography of cooking, washing, weaving and mending, growing, picking, chopping and blending ... Kapur's story, structured, like *Midnight's Children*, around the moment of Indian independence and partition, has a deceptively domestic surface, unhurriedly weaving ambitious metaphors around small, believable particulars ... This book offers a completely imagined, aromatic, complex world, a rare thing in first novels.' Maggie Gee, *Sunday Times*

A MARRIED WOMAN
Manju Kapur

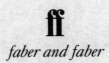

faber and faber

by the same author

DIFFICULT DAUGHTERS

First published in 2003
by Faber and Faber Limited
3 Queen Square London WC1N 3AU
This paperback edition first published in 2004

Typeset by Faber and Faber Limited
Printed in England by Bookmarque Ltd, Croydon

A CIP record for this book
is available from the British Library

ISBN 0–571–21567–X

2 4 6 8 10 9 7 5 3 1

For
my daughter
Amba

&

Ira

~

I

Astha was brought up properly, as befits a woman, with large supplements of fear. One slip might find her alone, vulnerable and unprotected. The infinite ways in which she could be harmed were not specified, but Astha absorbed them through her skin, and ever after was drawn to the safe and secure.

She was her parents' only child. Her education, her character, her health, her marriage, these were their burdens. She was their future, their hope, and though she didn't want them to guard their precious treasure so carefully, they did, oh they did.

Her mother often declared, 'When you are married, our responsibilities will be over. Do you know the shastras say if parents die without getting their daughter married, they will be condemned to perpetual rebirth?'

'I don't believe in all that stuff,' said Astha, 'and I think, as an educated person, neither should you.'

Her mother sighed her heavy soul-killing sigh. 'Who can escape their duty?' she asked, as she put in a steel almirah another spoon, sheet, sari, piece of jewellery towards the girl's future.

Every day in her temple corner in the kitchen, she prayed for a good husband for her daughter.

'You pray too,' she insisted as they stood before the shrine on the shelf, ordinarily hidden by curtains made from an old silk sari border, woven through with gold so pure that if the cloth was burnt, the metal would emerge in a little drop.

Astha obediently closed her eyes to delicious images of a romantic, somewhat shadowy young man holding her in his strong manly embrace.

'Are you praying?' asked the mother suspiciously.

'Of course I'm praying,' replied the daughter indignantly, 'you never trust me.'

To prove her sincerity she fixed her gaze firmly on Krishna, Krishna the one so many had adored. He would send her marriage, love and happiness. She fingered the rope of tiny pearls around his image. On either side were miniature vases with fresh jasmine buds. There was also a picture of Astha's dead grandparents, a little silver bell and thali, two small silver lamps which were lit every evening, while a minuscule silver incense holder wobbled next to it. Whatever meal Astha's mother cooked was first offered to the gods before the family ate. She believed in the old ways.

While her father believed in the new. His daughter's future lay in her own hands, and these hands were to be strengthened by the number of books that passed through them. At least once a day he said to her, 'Why aren't you studying?'

How much studying could Astha do to satisfy the man? Through her school years she never found out.

'Where is the maths work I asked you to do?' he would continue.

'I haven't finished it yet.'

'Show me whatever you have completed.'

Sums indifferently done were produced. The father tightened his lips. The girl felt afraid, but refused to show it. She looked down.

'You worthless, ungrateful child. Do you know how much money I spend on your education?'

'Don't then, don't spend anything,' she muttered, her own lips as tight as his.

Driven by her insolence, carelessness and stupidity, he slapped her. Tears surfaced, but she wouldn't act sorry, would rather die than show how unloved and misunderstood she felt.

Her mother looked on and said nothing. Later, 'Why don't

2

you do the work he tells you to? You can't be drawing and painting all the time.'

'So he hits me?' She didn't want her mother's interventions, she hated her as well as him.

'It's his way of showing concern.'

Astha looked away.

The mother sighed. The girl was good, only she got into these moods sometimes. And how much she fiddled with brush and pencil, no wonder her father got anxious, there was no future in art. If she did well in her exams, she could perhaps sit for the IAS, and find a good husband there. You met all kinds of people in the administrative services, and the girl was not bad looking. She must tell her to frown less. Frowns mislead people about one's inner nature.

The girl's body was nurtured by walks that started every morning at five.

'Get up, get up. Enough laziness.'

'You will thank us later when you realise the value of exercise and fresh air.'

'How can you waste the best part of the day? This is Brahmakaal, the hour of the gods.'

So Astha dragged her feet behind her parents' straight backs as they strode towards the dew and space of the India Gate lawns. Her parents arranged their walk so that they would be facing the East as the sun rose, showing their respect for the source of all life, while Astha, lagging behind, refused to participate in their daily satisfaction over the lightening sky, or the drama of the sun suddenly rising behind India Gate.

When they came home they all did Pranayam together. Pranayam, in the patchy grass surrounded by a short straggly hedge outside their flat. Inhale through one nostril, pinch it, exhale through the other, pinch that, right left, left right, thirty times over, till the air in the lungs was purified and the spirit uplifted.

*

3

At other times Astha's father took her for a stroll through the colony in the evenings. Away from her studies he was more amiable. He didn't want his daughter to be like himself, dissatisfied and wasted. You have so much potential, you draw, you paint, you read, you have a way with words, you do well academically, the maths is a little weak, but never mind, you must sit for the competitive exams. With a good job comes independence. When I was young, I had no one to guide me, I did not know the value of time, did not do well in my exams, had to take this job, thinking later I can do something else, but once you are stuck you are stuck.

Here he grew silent and walked on moodily, while Astha linked her arm through his, feeling slightly sorry for him.

After her father died and experience had drilled some sense of the world into her, Astha realised how emancipated he had been. At the time she felt flattered by his attention, but bored by his words.

~

The family counted their pennies carefully. Their late marriage, their daughter still to be settled, their lack of any security to fall back on, meant that their pleasures were planned with thrift firmly in the forefront. Once a month on a Sunday they went as a treat to the Bengali Market chaat shop. They gazed at the owner sitting on a narrow platform, cross-legged before his cash box, a small brass grille all around him. His dhoti kurta was spotless white, his cash box rested on a cloth equally spotless.

'This man came from Pakistan, a refugee,' said the father.

'Look at him now,' echoed the mother.

And the shop grew glitzier every time they came, with marble floors added, mirrors expanding across the walls, extensions built at the back and sides. The tikkis and the papri did not remain the same either, but grew more and more

4

expensive. What was in the tikki that made him charge one rupee per plate?

'The potatoes he must be buying in bulk, so that is only one anna worth of potato, the stuffing is mostly dal, hardly any peas, a miserable half cashew, fried in vanaspati, not even good oil, let alone ghee; the chutney has no raisins, besides being watery, and what with the wages of the waiter and the cook, the whole thing must be costing him not more than . . . than . . .'

Father, mathematician, closes his eyes to concentrate better on the price of the potato tikki.

'Not more than eight annas, maximum.'

'Hundred per cent profit,' said the mother gloomily. 'How much does he sell in a day? Five hundred?'

They looked around the crowded restaurant, with its tables jammed together, and the large extended section behind the sweet counters. They looked at the people being served on the road. Yes, five hundred would not be wrong.

Then they calculated eight annas multiplied by 500 made 250 rupees. And this was just on potato tikkis.

What about the papri, the kulchas, the dahi barhas, the gol gappas in spicy water, the gol gappas in dahi and chutney, the kachoris with channa, the puri aloo, the channa bhatura, the newly introduced dosas, the dry savouries, sweets, and chips that he was cunningly displaying in glass cases, what about every one of those? How much money would he be taking home at the end of just one day? To top it all, he was uneducated.

'I could make better tikkis at home,' offered the mother.

Astha stared miserably at her plate of two small swollen tikkis, buried under sweet and sour chutney. Then she stared at the fat man behind the payment counter. He sat there with his paan-stained mouth, taking people's money, opening the lid of the cash box, calmly lifting the change katoris to add to the growing piles of ones, twos, fives, tens, hundreds.

'Do you want anything else, beti?' asked the parents after they had eaten every crumb from their little steel plates.

'No.'

'Are you sure?'

'Yes.'

'Let's go home then.'

'That was a nice outing, wasn't it?' they said to each other as they started the old Fiat and headed back to their flat on Pandara Road.

~

Over these smaller worries, loomed the larger one, their unbuilt house, the place they would go to when they retired, the shelter that lay between them and nothingness. It was towards this end that they counted every paisa, weighed the pros and cons of every purchase with heavy anxiety. From time to time they drove to the outer parts of South Delhi with dealers to look at plots. Somehow, the places they wanted to live in were always outside their budget, the places they could afford seemed wild and unin-habitable.

'There was a time when Defence Colony too was on the outskirts of Delhi,' pointed out the mother. 'Let us at least buy wherever we can.'

'No, Sita,' said the father irritably. 'How can we live so far away from everything?'

How far do we have to go before we can afford something, thought Astha, who was forced to come on these expeditions, she couldn't be left alone with the servant. She herself never intended to land in any house on any tiny plot they were looking at. Her husband would see to it.

Meanwhile Delhi grew and grew, and plots they had once rejected as being too far, now became part of posh and expen-sive colonies, and not as far as they had once thought.

*

Retirement was coming nearer, the pressure to buy was growing, when in the early sixties, ministries started forming co-operative housing societies.

'Thank goodness,' grumbled Astha's mother, 'at least the government will do for us, what we have not been able to do for ourselves.'

'It's one thing to form a co-operative housing society, another thing to get land allotted to it, and still another to build a house,' said the father, born pessimist. 'In what god-forsaken corner will they allocate land to a ministry as unimportant as relief and welfare, that too you have to see.'

'Arre, wherever, whatever, we have to build. Otherwise you plan that after retirement we live in your ancestral palace?'

The husband looked pained at his wife's coarseness.

They continued to worry. When would their housing society have land assigned to it, how many more years for the father to retire, how many more working years for the mother, how long before they had to leave this government house in the centre of Delhi, so convenient?

Once the land was allotted, how much would it cost to build, how much did they have in fixed deposits, in their provident funds, how much could they borrow, how much interest would they have to pay? After discussing all this, they allowed themselves to dream a little.

'I will have a special place for my books,' said the father, 'cupboards with glass to protect them from dust and silverfish.'

'I will have a big kitchen,' said the mother, 'with screen windows to keep flies out, and a stainless steel sink, not like this cement one which always looks filthy. I will have a long counter, so I don't have to unpack the mixi every time I need it. I will have a proper place to do puja, rather than a shelf.'

'We will have a study, maybe an extra bedroom for guests,' mused the father, and then they looked frightened at the money their dreams were going to cost. Maybe not a guest room, their voices trailed off.

~

By the time Astha was sixteen, she was well trained on a diet of mushy novels and thoughts of marriage. She was prey to inchoate longings, desired almost every boy she saw, then stood long hours before the mirror marvelling at her ugliness. Would she ever be happy? Would true love ever find her?

Then the day dawned, the day Astha saw Bunty. Bunty the beautiful, Bunty whose face never left her, Bunty whose slightest word, look and gesture she spent hours nursing to death.

Bunty's family lived in one of the bigger houses of the Pandara Road colony, a duplex with a large garden, and a roomy verandah. They were on visiting terms with Astha's parents, the younger sister was in her school. The boy was away in Kharakvasala in the Defence Academy and now home for the holidays.

He came over with his father. Oh, how he stood out. He had glossy black hair which he wore in a small puff over a high wide forehead. His eyes were like soft black velvet, set in pale sockets over the faint blush of his cheek. And just beneath that the bluish black shadow of an incipient beard, framing a red mouth. As she stared, steady, unwavering, he felt her gaze, looked up and smiled. His teeth were small, white and uneven, and as she lost herself in them, he raised his left eyebrow slightly. She shuddered, and weakly smiled back.

Thus began her torture.

If only she didn't see him so often, but Bunty was restless during his holidays. Boarding school, boarding college, as a result he knew few people in Delhi. He took to dropping in with his sister. There was the attraction of her devotion.

Day and night the thought of him kept her insides churning; she was unable to eat, sleep, or study. Away from him her eyes felt dry and empty. Her ears only registered the sound of his voice. Her mind refused to take seriously anything that was not his face, his body, his feet, his hands, his clothes. She found temporary relief in sketching him, sketches that were invariably too bad to be mulled over.

Hours were spent in planning accidental meetings, how to bump into him in the colony, how to cross his father on his evening walk, how to fall into enough conversation to be invited over, how to borrow a book to prolong the stay, how to fall into a faint, how to die at his doorstep.

Once in Bunty's house she saw him pet his dog, who promptly put her paws in his lap, wagged her tail and salivated. At that moment she felt a keen shamed kinship with the animal.

She was too overwhelmed by her feelings to actually want to talk to him. To approach the site of all this wonder would be apostasy. To think that he would ever have anything to say to her was past crediting. Finally it was so unbearable, she had to tell someone.

Gayatri, school friend, eventual confidante, decided that this affair needed managing.

'What have you actually done?' she demanded.

'Done?' quavered Astha, immediately feeling worse instead of better. 'Nothing.'

· 'You are such a ninny,' scolded Gayatri, 'invite him to a movie.'

'How can I?'

'How can you?' Gayatri stared at her. 'There is a Charlie Chaplin film at the National Stadium next Sunday morning. Ask him if he has seen it. Go on. Give him a chance.'

Each day was now an exam, in which she failed daily. Gayatri was insistent. There had to be movement to the whole thing, otherwise she might as well not be in love. Astha was forced to admit the logic of this.

The day came when she stood tongue-tied before him, stammering out her request that the god come to a film with her and her friend.

'Of course he'll go, won't you, Bunty beta?' boomed his father.

'Th-Thank-you, Uncle,' stammered Astha, not looking at Bunty.

Bunty seemed stiff and bored through the film. Gayatri chattered gaily in the interval, while Astha gritted her teeth and waited for the nightmare to end. Words rushed around in her head, words that would show how clever and interesting she was, but when she actually looked at him she could not speak. She wanted to never see Bunty again. She hated him. She wished his holidays would quickly end.

They did, and Astha grew desperate. The point of getting up every morning had been the hope that she would be able to look at him, feed on a glance, a word, a smile. Now her rich inner world would become stale with nothing new to add to the store.

'Suggest writing. You know, like pen pals,' said Gayatri.

'No.' Suppose he laughed? Looked contemptuous?

'What do you have to lose?'

'Why should he write to me?'

'Why not? He does drop by, and you also visit him.'

Astha hesitated. 'That means very little,' she pronounced finally, thinking of those visits, the long pauses, she pulverised with emotion and Bunty shifting about in his seat, saying from time to time, 'So what's new?'

Gayatri pressed home her point.

'He does talk to you, and objectively speaking, you're not bad looking. You have no figure, but your features are sharp, you have clear skin, and high cheekbones. If your hair was styled instead of pulled back, it would help, but still, it is thick and curly. You are on the short side, but tall men like short girls, that is one thing I have noticed, time and again.' (Gayatri herself was tall.)

'I can't just walk up to him and say give me your address, I want to write to you.'

'It's not anything so great you are asking. Once you write, he will write back.'

'He may not.'

'Then he is no gentleman,' said Gayatri severely.

Eventually Astha blurted out the request, shoving her diary and pen at him.

She wrote, and he did reply, weeks later.

'Who is this from?' asked her mother, holding the letter away from her.

'How do I know?' demanded Astha.

She snatched the letter and tucked it into her school bag. It was from him, she knew it was. He had written.

Dear Astha,

I received your letter a few weeks back. We do not really get time to write, we are very hard worked here.

Tomorrow, I am leaving for camp. There is much work to be done; we do a lot of studies on tactics and strategy of defence and attack. We leave early in the morning, first marching 20 miles, from where we will be transported another 80 miles. At the end of it all we will land in some remote village. After lunch, which we carry, we will 'dig-in' for the night to carry out a defence exercise. Digging trenches in the Deccan plateau isn't quite as easy as you might think. Each one takes 3 to 4 hours. We shall also have to climb Simhagarh, Shivaji's famous fortress, and incidentally the highest one. At night we shall ambush and patrol, the sole difference between this and a real war being that we shall fire blank rounds at each other instead of live ones.

And so on. It was a soldier's letter, what else had she expected? If the reality of Bunty was a little flat after her image of him, her love could take it. She re-read it all day and the days to come, till she got his next.

11

It turned out Bunty liked corresponding. Through the year Astha heard about his friends, the war with Pakistan, Lal Bahadur Shashtri, his academic subjects, his service subjects, his feelings about the Indian Army in general, and cadets in particular.

And Astha, Astha was witty, clever, chatty, all the things she could not be when he was in front of her. Her writing was laced with little drawings which he found ingenious and talented. She started flirting. Letters were safe.

As the correspondence established itself, so did the mother's suspicions.

'Why is he writing so much to you?' she asked every time a letter came. By this time there were two people waiting for the post, Astha and her mother.

'Is it a crime?' Astha replied.

'You are too young to be indulging in such goings-on.'

She made it sound so sordid. What words could Astha use to a woman who saw the world in terms of goings-on?

'There is nothing going on,' she said, lying with great dignity. There was no need to explain the pulpiness of her heart, the wretched and permanent knot in her stomach. No doubt her mother would consider that a going-on too. How she wished she could really be gone, gone in the arms of Bunty, who would hold her close, whisper his love, confide that her letters had made him realise she was his soulmate, they would marry after he graduated, could she wait for him.

'You have got your exams coming,' went on Astha's mother, staring hard and penetratingly at her daughter.

'I know,' said the daughter, staring back just as hard.

Astha's mother sniffed, a tight cold sniff.

Astha paid no attention. She was living in a world of her own, waiting for the holidays to come, so that she could see Bunty. It would be different now, no awkwardness or shyness. They were closer, they had shared their thoughts and feelings. Hopefully they would kiss. Where and how? She imagined the places, grew lost in her fantasies.

The holidays came. The minute the mother knew that Bunty had come, she went to his house and from then on Bunty refused to have anything to do with Astha.

For a long time she didn't know what had happened, nor could she bear to find out. She lived in pain and anything that touched it was too much for her.

The night before, on the phone, she had fixed to see him, this time she would not need Gayatri. She had spent many hours thinking about her hair, her clothes, should she wear casual or formal, new or old? How should she do her hair? Up or down? Loose or tied?

Dressed in her newest churidar kameez, tight around the hips, loose around the waist, Astha went to Bunty's house, at eleven o'clock as planned. His father met her at the door.

'Bunty is not at home, beta,' he said politely, without asking her in, a slap in the face for Astha, standing awkwardly in her new churidar kameez, so tight around her hips, so loose around her waist.

'When will he be back, Uncle?' she managed, dread making her voice heavy. Did Bunty's father hate her? Had Bunty said something to him? On the train home from the Defence Academy had he decided to loathe her instead of like her? Was this his way of letting her know?

'I don't know, beta. It is his holidays, he has so many friends and relatives to see. You can phone him some time. Bye now.'

The door was closed before she was even down the steps. No seeing her off, no nothing.

She walked home, feeling sick. The year of writing to each other, he had said he wanted to see her, had he been lying, seeing how far she would reveal her feelings in those stupid letters before he showed them to his father? How could she have forgotten the little interest he had shown in her when he was actually in Delhi? He was amusing himself, that was why he had written, now when it was time to meet he intended to drop her. How Gayatri would laugh. Was there any way she could stop being friends with Gayatri right that minute? Dump her for ever, and never see her again?

Astha had not been in the house ten minutes when Gayatri called. 'What happened?' she asked breathlessly, as though she had been the one waiting all these months to be kissed.

'Oh nothing,' said Astha airily, through gritted teeth.

'Nothing? What do you mean nothing?'

'It's very sad. One of his uncles died, and he has to go to Bombay immediately with the whole family.'

'But why didn't he tell you?'

'There wasn't time to write.'

'Odd,' said Gayatri after a pause. 'He might have met you for a few seconds alone. After all those letters.'

'I'm telling you there wasn't time,' said Astha her voice rising.

'Oh Asu, poor you.'

'Not at all. I found I didn't like him so much when I actually saw him. He looked very silly. All he could say was "So what's new". One tends to build people up through letters.'

'I suppose,' said Gayatri, sounding dissatisfied.

The holidays passed. Astha suffered daily. Neither drawing nor reading could engage her. Her heart felt like lead, her mind like stone. She couldn't get Bunty on the phone, he was always out. Shyness, reticence, some shreds of self-esteem forbade her from persisting beyond politeness. No matter what had happened, he should also want to see her, if only to clear any misunderstanding. And so pride carried her through each miserable day.

A year later, when the pain was less, and college had made her feel more a woman of the world, she wrote, a light casual letter, 'What happened?'

He wrote back, 'I thought you knew. Your mother visited us the very night I arrived and told my father that I was distracting you from your studies. At the same time she asked him what my intentions were. My father thought it better if we had nothing to do with each other. Why create complications? I wish you well in life. Yours sincerely, Bunty.'

Can one die of shame twice? Astha did. How dare her mother interfere in her friendships? But then Bunty too had given in so easily, not bothered to find out how she felt, no word, no sign.

Where was the man whose arms were waiting to hold her? Till his arrival, she would walk alone, alone in college, through corridors of happy, independent, bustling girls, through classrooms devoted to the study of English Literature, alone in the colony through the dreary lanes between the houses.

She tried to put Bunty from her mind, though once or twice when girls huddled together, heads bent in the canteen, she brought out his name experimentally, to show she too had lived and knew what love was.

'Yes, these boys—'

'Yes, there was someone, only last year—'

'Yes, he was handsome—'

'Oh, he doesn't study here. The Defence Academy at Kharakvasala.'

'Yes, we still meet during the holidays, nothing special from my side. I thought it better not to have a long-distance relationship, you know how it is . . .'

The girls listened sceptically, how could they believe in the reality of one who was never seen hanging out at the back gate? Still, they teased her sometimes saying, 'Astha, tell us more about Bunty,' and Astha cursed her need to feel part of a group by making light of something that still tightened her chest with grief.

~

Five years after its inception the housing society of the Ministry of Relief and Welfare was awarded a piece of land across the Jamuna.

The habitual gloom on the father's face became even more pronounced as he conveyed this news to his family. 'Other ministries, where the bureaucrats have pull, managed to get allotments in South Delhi. But what do we get? A site across the Jamuna, where there is no water, no electricity, no markets, no bus services, no amenities, no proper roads even.'

'Never mind,' consoled his wife, concealing how bitter the blow was for herself as well, so much had depended on the promised piece of land. 'Once construction starts, things will change. Everything has to have a beginning. How much are the plots going for?'

'How much can they go for?' replied the father. 'In the middle of the jungle with thugs, dacoits, and wild animals. 7–8,000 rupees.'

'Size?'

'225, 280, or 350 square yards.'

Their future home was going to be small and relatively cheap.

The lots were chosen by draw. On the appointed day, the mother said to her daughter, 'I hope he draws a 350 plot, in the corner. There is very little difference in price.'

'From?' asked the daughter languidly. She had been paying insufficient attention to the family fortunes knowing that wherever they built a house, she would not be in it.

'Don't you ever listen? After we are gone it will be yours.'

'I don't want it.'

The mother trembled with annoyance. 'Don't you see our lives?' she hissed. 'Have you still not realised the value of land, that once you have it, there is always something solid to fall back on?'

Astha looked at her mother, at the sallow skin with liver markings, at the carelessly dyed hair, black and white, at the hands gnarled from a lifetime of housework, the veins standing out on the backs, only fifty, despairing, shrivelled, and old. Her dream of a house was coming true in a way that made that dream for ever unrealisable. Her thoughts were now of 225, 280 or 350 square yards, of whether it would be near a park, or near the main road, near a market or bus stop, whether her husband would be happy there or not, because she of course could be happy anywhere.

Slowly she took her mother's hands in her own. 'It will be all right, Mama,' she said beginning to rattle off what she had heard so often. 'Trans-Jamuna will grow, South Delhi too was once like this, it will be different once the new bridge is built. Just imagine, we will have our own house at last. A garden too.'

The mother looked at her daughter's young hands holding her own loose-skinned bony ones.

'Yes darling, at last,' she sighed heavily.

The father came home.

'Well?' asked the mother, taking his briefcase.

'280.'

There was silence as the family digested this. 280. They were going to live on 280 square yards. But still, that was more than 225, of which there were so many.

'There were only four 350 ones.'

'Only four? Then naturally we won't get one.'

The father paused before continuing, 'One of them the President drew.'

'I'm sure it was rigged,' flashed the mother.

'God knows. It seemed fair enough. It was done in front of us all.'

'Of course it will seem fair. These people are not children.'

They consoled themselves over tea with reflections of the general perfidy of the world, and their own inabilities to succeed in the games that were demanded of life's players.

Now that they had their plot, they drove out in the direction of the wilderness to see it. Along with them was the President of the Ministry of Relief and Welfare Group Housing Society, needed to show the way.

'Behenji,' he turned around to address Astha's mother, sitting in the back seat with the reluctant daughter, 'in ten years time this area will be really built up. The future of Delhi is here. How far can Delhi spread south?'

'It is a long way around,' murmured Astha's mother.

They were heading north, towards the Red Fort, beyond the ghats for burning the dead, towards Shahadra, across the old British-built double-storied bridge for cars and trains, the lone bridge across the river to east Delhi.

'When the new bridge is completed the journey will be quicker, Behenji,' consoled the President. 'Twenty minutes and you will be in Connaught Place, heart of Delhi.'

Astha's father drove without responding to any of these remarks. The privilege of owning a plot in this godforsaken place would come as a result of belonging to a ministry in which he had felt wasted all his life. The bitterness of this kept him silent.

The roads they were now passing were potholed and badly kept, establishing kinship with the dirt roads of villages. From time to time they caught sight of a brave house standing alone.

'People are already constructing,' pointed out the President.

The road got narrower and bumpier, the trails of dust bloomed larger.

'Nirman Vihar, Swasth Vihar, and there, Preet Vihar,' said the President, waving his hand at the bare expanses around him. A gloomy silence filled the car, they were too old and too young to regard with excitement this particular future laid out before them.

'Here, turn here,' indicated the President. They left the narrowness of the main road for an indistinguishable little lane, bumped along, turned once, and there they were. The land was dry, dusty, bare, treeless and nondescript. Asman Vihar. Sky Colony.

What had they imagined? Neat plots, lined with trees, and

little lanes, waiting for owners to come and build houses? For 8,000 rupees? Were they crazy?

'What's that?' asked Astha's father pointing to a village they could see in the distance.

'Oh, that will go, we are dealing with them,' said the President. 'They think they have a right just because nobody has dislodged them so far. The land is vacant, so these villagers use it to farm. And the odd group of Gujjars roams around.'

'Is it safe?' trembled Astha's mother.

'The more people come, the safer it will be.'

'And water, electricity connections?'

'For water we have to dig our own tube wells. And they have promised a temporary line for electricity. It is only a matter of time when this will be like your Golf Links, Jor Bagh, or Defence Colony.'

After this trip they did not talk about their dream home anymore. They heard stories of how, in one of the lonely houses there, dacoits had broken in at night, stolen everything, and injured the owner so much that he was in a state of semi-paralysis.

When the future was taken out and aired they concentrated on the difference the new bridge would make, the changes in infrastructure that would come about once the area became more populated. When the prices went up, they could sell their plot and buy a little flat in south Delhi. They had to trust in God and wait, though with the father's retirement only six years away, the period they could wait was limited.

~

Now that Astha was in college her mother focused anxiously on their primary parental obligation. Every Sunday she scanned the matrimonial pages meticulously, pencil in hand, circling ads. Later on she would show them to the father.

'You have to take her to the studio to get nice photos taken. One full standing, one close-up of the face.'

'She is only in second year, Sita, for heaven's sake. Let her finish her education at least.'

'In the time it takes to finalise a match she will have graduated. Good boys are not to be found so easily.'

'She has just turned eighteen. Let her be.'

'You want her to turn out like us? Marrying in her thirties? And everybody wondering what is wrong?'

'Let her settle down to a career, then we will see. I can't go around begging people to marry my daughter.'

'There is a time for everything,' went on the mother. 'The girl is blossoming now. When the fruit is ripe it has to be picked. Later she might get into the wrong company and we will be left wringing our hands. If she marries at this age, she will have no problem adjusting. We too are not so young that we can afford to wait.'

Astha, eavesdropping, wondered where this stream of logic would lead. She herself had tasted love and wanted nothing of an arranged marriage, but what did her father think?

Her father refused to answer and refused to take Astha to the studio.

The day the mother found a suitor, was a day when Astha came home from college, tired, stinking of sweat, her bag heavy on her shoulders, her red pointed ballerina shoes pinching her feet. All she wanted was to quickly bathe, get lunch out of the way and then lose herself in the Georgette Heyer she had borrowed from a friend.

Her mother was sitting in the drawing room with a young man dressed in khaki.

'Beti,' she called. 'Come here.'

'Coming,' Astha shouted back, but she didn't like the tone of her mother's voice. She hid behind the curtain dividing the room and listened.

Mother: 'That was my daughter.'

Young man: 'Does she like sports?'

Mother: 'Very much.'

Dread filled Astha. Her mother was lying. She had some-how found a groom without a studio photo. Did her father know? She locked herself in the bathroom.

'Astha.'

No answer.

The door rattled. 'Come out beta. Hurry up.'

'Why?'

'There is someone here to meet you.'

'Who?'

'Someone.'

'First you tell me.'

'O-ho. A boy.'

'Why are you so interested in a boy meeting me *now*?' asked Astha bitterly.

Bang, bang, bang – the wooden bathroom door shook against the onslaught of the mother's rage. Astha watched the towels hanging from the hooks shudder, she heard the tap next to the toilet dripping into the tin can below it.

'I'm not coming,' she shouted.

'You don't object to seeing boys otherwise. Suddenly you become so high and mighty, and refuse to even be polite to someone who has come all this way.' The mother dropped her voice to wheedle, 'Now come, what is the harm? It is just a meeting, nothing else.'

Astha stared at a tiny crack in the old wood of the bath-room door. She was about to humiliate her mother in front of a stranger. She took a deep breath. 'I can't,' she whispered hopelessly, 'I can't meet anyone like this.'

The mother finally gave up, leaving Astha collapsed against the bathroom door, tears falling, crying, crying for Bunty, crying for the lack of love in her barren life, crying because she didn't want to see a dull stolid man in the draw-ing room who advertised for a wife and asked about sports.

She remained in the bathroom long after the suitor left. The bathroom represented her future; she had better start getting acquainted with it now.

Hours, years, later her mother banged irritably on the door, 'He has gone, fool that I was to try and arrange anything for you, you are just like your father, thinking everything is going to happen on its own. The food has gone stone cold, you can reheat it and clear up everything after you have finished.'

~

One month after this the boy appeared. In his final year of college, he was a bit older. They had been introduced by friends of friends at the University Coffee House. Like everybody they knew, they were missing classes in order to haunt these hunting grounds, their gaze sorting through the tables speculatively.

Astha began to be included in groups that included him, at cinemas, restaurants, appointed meetings at the Coffee House, instead of casual ones. A boy was interested in her. With every visit he made to the back gate, her stock grew in college.

She began to lie at home about where she was going, and what she was doing. Most of the girls she knew who were seeing boys lied. It was the routine, self-protective thing. And how necessary, Astha had already seen.

Now every evening Astha took a walk in the colony, announcing her intention of dropping in on old school friends on the way back. My head gets so tired with studying, she complained, I need a change.

Go, beti, go. Take some exercise, and remember, walk briskly, swing your arms, and breathe deeply from the stomach, said the mother, glad that her daughter was at last beginning to understand the value of fresh air.

And Astha would dash out of the colony, down the main road to the corner where Rohan was waiting in his old

Vauxhall. A quick check to make sure no one was looking, then she would jump in and they would roar off.

It was the first time in the old Vauxhall, side by side, in the front seat. The car was parked in a narrow empty lane, next to a Minister's house in the Lutyens part of New Delhi. Rohan had shut the windows, and locked the doors. It was late November and dark. The car smelled of Old Spice, Rohan's aftershave lotion, and the musty scent of ancient leather.

Astha glanced at Rohan sideways. He was twisting the car keys in his long slender hands with the hairy fingers, tapping them restlessly on the steering wheel. Finally he turned and reached purposefully towards her.

'Do you want to marry me?' she asked breathlessly, anxious to get this thing out of the way.

'What?' he asked distractedly.

'Marry me. Do you want to?'

He took his hands away and stared at her. 'Isn't it a bit early to decide that?' Astha felt she had offended him.

'Well, you know, otherwise—' she trailed off, trying to look as cute and disarming as possible.

'Good God, is that what you are worried about? I'm not the type to let a girl get pregnant, what do you think I am?'

Astha realised she was sounding very un-hep, but she couldn't help it. She had to know how safe she was. 'Marriage,' she persisted, 'you know—' She inched a little further away from him.

'Oh God, all right. We might get married. One day.'

His mouth closed on hers, his tongue was exploring, while Astha choked and wriggled frantically.

'What's the matter?' he asked letting her go. 'Don't you like it?'

'I don't know,' she mumbled non-committedly.

'Well, let's find out.' Rohan was beginning to sound impatient.

Astha had volunteered to go with him in the car. Her body had registered excitement when he had parked in the dark lane. When he bent close to her, she had been overcome with dread and longing. There was no going back. She offered her lips, trying not to shrink into the seat.

'God you're so stiff,' said Rohan shaking her a little bit.

'Sorry,' she mumbled.

'This is not some kind of torture you know.'

Astha didn't know what to say. Rohan let her go, also silent. Finally he said, 'Give me your hands.'

She held her fists tensely out. Slowly he moved his thumb around her wrist, stroking the closed hand open. He kissed the fingers, nails, palms, he felt the small hair on the back with his closed lips. Astha felt something flow inside her as she stared at his bent head. She had never been so aware of her body's separate life before. After a little more of this he dropped her at their secret corner.

She got out of the car reluctantly. Something hadn't happened. But then again, something had. On the whole the encounter left her anxious for more.

When Rohan at last slid his tongue into Astha's mouth she was putty in his hands. Her neck, her ears, her throat, eyes, chin, lips, all had been explored, and this time her strongest feeling was gratitude.

This was the start of numberless kisses in the car. The only problem was in finding a place sufficiently isolated.

To Astha all places looked the same, but no, muttered Rohan, his eyes scanning various deserted spots, his fingers kneading the palm of her hand, not that one, not there, that's not safe, while Astha burned with impatience. Finally before rolling up the windows he always put out his hand and locked the door from outside.

'Why are you doing that?' Astha asked.

'Precautions.'

'Against what?'

'Just.'

Astha was not really interested. All she wanted was for

him to start, so that the world could fall away, and she be lost. This is love, she told herself, no wonder they talk so much about it.

One evening, they had parked in their usual dark corner in a by-lane off Akbar Road. Rohan liked Akbar Road, he considered it among the safest places he could find.

Astha had slid as far down the seat as she could go without dislocating her hip. Rohan was lying as much as he could on top of her without dislocating his own. Their eyes were closed, their breathing audible. Absorbed in what they were doing, they did not hear footsteps approaching, did not see faces pressed against the windows on either side, eyes peering down at them.

The car shook, hands banged violently on the glass, rattled the handles. Astha and Rohan jerked upright, the whole car was swarming over with threatening bodies trying to get in.

'Oye, oye,' they shouted, leering and grimacing, furiously working the handles. Rohan frantically turned the key in the ignition, pressed the accelerator, the old Vauxhall shook and roared. The men fell off as he sped in reverse down the dark lane, lights off. They ran after the car for a while, then couldn't be seen anymore. Some distance down the main road, Rohan stopped.

'Who were they? And why—?' stammered Astha, shaking with fright.

Rohan took her hand. 'Some fools. I'm sorry,' he said.

She started to cry.

'Calm down.'

'Take me home.'

'Calm down first. Look, nothing actually happened.'

Astha felt worse and worse. Those men had wanted to attack. Suppose they had managed to break the car window, gang rape her because of her shameless behaviour in a public place, and beat up Rohan when he tried to intervene? And all the while her parents would be thinking she was breathing in fresh air. If her mother knew she would first kill her and

25

then herself. Astha's tears grew copious and she began to choke in her dupatta, while Rohan took sly glances at his watch. 'Come on,' he said at last, 'it was bad, but now it is over. Don't cry, for heaven's sake. We won't go there again.'

'Hoon,' sniffled Astha.

'You are all right, so what exactly is the problem?'

Astha only knew she felt terrible. Finally when Rohan dropped her off, she sensed eyes hidden in every bush, eyes that saw and condemned. She pulled her dupatta around her head, and hurried home trying to concentrate on the various lies she would have to tell as to why she was so late.

~

The day Astha's mother read her diary dawned cool and clear, beautiful like all winter days, with the flowers blooming in the garden, and the promise of basking for hours in the sun.

She was deep in a book when her mother called, 'Come here, I have something to show you.'

Reluctantly Astha marked her place, and went inside. When she saw her journal in her mother's hands, she wanted to instantly erase herself. There she was, with her skin ripped off, exposed in all her abandoned thoughts and deeds.

'Is this you?' the mother's voice quavered, her grip like iron on Astha's arm.

Astha shook her head nervously.

'Then, what is it?'

Desperate silence while she tried to think of something plausible.

'Answer me,' screamed the mother in a whisper.

'I–I don't know,' stammered the daughter, 'I mean, I don't remember.'

But she did, of course. All her secret fantasies, the things she did with Rohan, painstaking details of the furtive, exciting moments in his car.

'Well, look at it,' the mother waved the offending notebook in front of Astha's nose, an innocuous old brown paper covered thing with *St Theresa's Convent School* in a half moon on top. It had been hidden behind her college books, how had her mother discovered it? It looked awful in her hands, soaked in sin.

'You have no right to read my diary,' she weakly muttered in self defence, averting her eyes.

The mother ignored this remark and continued leafing through it gingerly.

'Here, what does this mean?'

The usual scene of passion. Astha went through puzzled motions of glancing, page turning, furrowed brow.

'These are notes for a story I am writing,' she said, inspired at last.

The mother's body sagged as some of the tension went out. 'This is your imagination?'

'Yes. Yes, it is my imagination.'

The mother was silent for a moment, then sighed heavily and held the tender young body of her innocent daughter close to her. 'My child is too sensible to do anything like this,' she whispered. The girl remained rigid, arms by her side.

They avoided each other for the rest of the day.

There were three consequences to this.

One was that Astha stopped being able to write in her journal. She tried a few entries in an elaborate code, but an audience was now branded into every page, and she could inscribe nothing beyond a casual account of her day in college.

The second was that Astha's parents took an annoying interest in her reading matter. Her father began diligently to bring her books of moral and intellectual substance. 'You need a sense of your cultural background,' said the bureaucrat. 'Of what made this country great. Know your artistic heritage, since your interest lies there.'

Her mother decided that the virtues of tradition needed to be made more explicit. 'Our shashtras teach us how to live.

You will learn from the *Gita*, the Vedas, the Upanishads.'

'I can't read them,' protested Astha violently. 'My Hindi is not good enough, you know that. It is your fault for sending me to a convent school.'

'Your father happened to think that a convent gave the best education. That doesn't mean we can't broaden your base now,' replied the mother. And she began getting Hindi books and magazines from her school library, so that Astha's Hindi could improve and the sacred texts of the Hindus be made available to her.

The third consequence was that the parents tightened their surveillance. Getting to meet Rohan proved more and more difficult.

She didn't want to tell him of what she was going through. He was preoccupied with his final year exams and seemed to have less time for her.

'Why do you keep phoning all the time?' he complained one evening when they met. 'I have to study.'

'I don't phone you all the time. Once or twice a day to ask how's it going.'

'It distracts me.'

'If you don't want to talk to me, just say so. Don't look for excuses.' Astha's voice shook. Rohan sighed and put his arms around her. Astha snuggled into him and slid her hands under his shirt.

'Baby, don't be unreasonable. A man has to do well. Get a scholarship. Go abroad.'

This was the first time he had talked of going abroad so definitely. Astha shifted herself out of his arms.

'Hey, little one,' cooed Rohan, reaching out for her. 'What's the matter?'

'Nothing,' she said forlornly.

'Do you think I'm going to forget you?'

Astha did think exactly that, but how could she admit it?

'Let me just finish my exams, little one, and then—'

Rohan's words helped bolster Astha's illusions, it was all right, she was still safe, their affair was going to end in marriage. But the cold feeling did not go away, though each time Rohan spoke, Astha clung to his assurances.

Rohan did very well in his exams, and on that stepping stone began the process of his going away. Away to the West, where ordinary mortals cannot go, where even the words PPE and Oxford showed Astha how great the distance was between them.

'Oxford,' she breathed in awe. Suddenly her life seemed very small.

Rohan looked nonchalant. 'Might as well follow in the family tradition, keep the old folks happy. My father is an Oxford man, you know.'

No, Astha had not known. 'How lucky you are, Rohan,' she said.

'Well, my father is keen,' continued Rohan, his gaze centred on the middle distance.

'When are you going?' she asked, and then hated herself for being in a situation where she was forced to prise answers from the man she had been so intimate with.

'Soon.'

'Doesn't it cost a lot of money?' asked Astha tentatively.

'Lots,' said Rohan, lighting a cigarette and breathing the smoke sexily out. 'But we are trying to manage something.'

Astha thought it might seem rude to ask for more information, and waited for Rohan to tell her. Rohan did not. He looked at her briefly and smiled. 'Come, let me drop you home,' he said, 'There are a lot of things I have to do.' He hadn't touched her once. As he turned the key in the ignition, Astha thought, he was going to Oxford, he had the resources, his father was an Oxford man. What was her father? A minor bureaucrat, who had never studied abroad, whose sole possession was 280 square yards in the wilderness beyond the Jamuna.

'Wait, Rohan,' she said, 'I hardly get to see you nowadays, you are so busy, and it is still early.'

Rohan continued drumming his keys against the steering wheel.

'How come you never mentioned your family traditions before?' Astha went on carefully, scratching and poking at the leather so hard, she could smell the car on her hands long afterwards.

'Well, there was no point talking about things, until things got certain.'

'Yes, but you might have told me that there was a possibility of your going away.'

'You knew that,' said Rohan coldly, not looking at her. 'I never tried to hide anything. There is no need for me to hide.'

'No, no, of course not. That is not what I meant,' floundered Astha. 'But you just mentioned once or twice, like people do, you know, about going abroad, and I didn't know . . . Why, your results are just out, and you must have been trying since last year if you are going so soon.'

'Sending applications is not something to make a song and dance about. I would look very stupid afterwards if I got neither admission nor funding.'

Astha felt hopeless. She sat in silence, next to this boy whom she had thought she knew. The hands that he had used on her body were now clenched around her heart, slowly squeezing, slowly hurting.

'What about us?' she asked abruptly, drawing a deep breath.

'We will see,' said Rohan briefly. He was waiting to take her home, waiting to get rid of her. He started the car, while Astha stared out of the window all the way to the edge of her colony.

'Bye,' she said, closing the door carefully, feeling it would be her last time in the Vauxhall, which was just as well. Old cars were so ugly, so useless, so slow, why did anyone bother with them?

'Bye,' said Rohan. 'Be seeing you,' he added, a remark which her dignity threw back silently, with all the coldness and contempt her falling to pieces self was capable of.

'Where have you been? Dinner has been getting cold,' came her mother's voice, as Astha tried her usual unobtrusive entrance.

'Nowhere.'

'Nowhere has a name or no?'

'No,' said Astha, going to lock herself in the bathroom, free from voices, free from everything except the terrible things she was feeling, because Rohan didn't love her, Rohan had lied to her. Rohan was what her mother had been warning her about since she was old enough to be warned, and how pleased she would be to know she had been right all along.

In the days to come Rohan neither called, nor sent the usual secret messages through her girlfriends.

It was over. Over. Over.

Astha entered her third year with a desire to get her education over as quickly as possible. Every day was painful to her. She was constantly reminded of Rohan, in the Coffee House, at the back gate, at their secret corner of the road, every evening at home. As for old black cars, they made her physically sick.

~

Rohan went abroad and Astha enrolled in MA, bored and unenthusiastic. Three years of an Honours course in English Literature had given her all she wanted to know of the subject. Not for her did the excitement of intellectual discovery lie ahead, only more of the same. After two years were over she supposed she would drift into teaching, that is what women like her did. School or college, remained to be decided.

All through third year her classmates had been busy preparing for competitive exams, or like Rohan, applying for higher studies abroad. Those not in this category had married and disappeared, to be heard of occasionally, moving around with husband, and later baby, stamped with the marks of confirmed adulthood.

Now in MA, her friends were few.

II

Astha was in her final year when the proposal came. The MBA, foreign returned son of one of the bureaucrats who lived in the larger houses bordering Lodhi colony, had seen her and wanted to meet her. His father dropped in on them, and acquainted the parents with their good fortune.

'I don't know him,' objected Astha when they told her the news.

'He also doesn't know you, Madam,' said the mother crossly. 'That is why he wants to meet you.'

'Give her the details, Sita,' reproved the father. 'This is a question of our girl's happiness. There is no hurry.'

'With you retiring in one year, there is every hurry.'

'That is no reason to marry.'

The mother fell into despairing silence. Retirement, father's uncertain health, finances in a meagre state, the bridge to the plot unbuilt and their dearest daughter still to be settled.

'How many times can I meet him?' demanded Astha, a little excitement rising in her. Somebody found her desirable and had gone to lengths to find out who she was.

'One, two times, what is the need for more?' said the mother. 'You cannot tell about a person before marriage, no matter how many times you meet him.'

Astha sat silent, twiddling her thumbs, staring down at her flat feet in their bathroom slippers. Had she known Rohan? Not really, and the soiled feeling she now associated with that interlude came over her again.

'Papa?' she quickly asked. 'You think this is a good thing?'

'I'm not sure,' said the father uncertainly. 'The plus side is that he is the only son and both his sisters are married. The younger one, settled in the US, wanted to sponsor him, but he

33

decided to return to his parents. He is twenty-six, five eleven, he works as an assistant manager in a bank.'

'Clearly a good, family-minded boy,' said the mother complacently.

'And Vadera's ministry was allotted land in South Delhi. They will be able to build on it, they won't have to wait for bridges and water and electricity connections, they won't have to worry about thugs or gypsies,' continued the father bitterly.

'Isn't that a good thing for our daughter? She at least will have a decent home. God has heard my prayers,' added the mother piously.

'Sita, are your prayers that the girl be married to a plot in Vasant Vihar? Why don't you go and do the pheras there?'

'What's wrong, Papa? You don't like the family?'

'I have heard things about Vadera.'

'What things?'

'He is in the commerce ministry. Nice place to be if you want to keep a certain standard of living, and licences are needed by every manufacturing unit, big or small, for anything they do.'

'So?'

'He travels abroad, gives his daughters big weddings, buys a car, a *new* car every three or four years.'

This did indeed seem very bad; such high living had to have some dark reason behind it. 'How does he do it, I ask you?' went on the father. 'Must be taking bribes. Will you be happy in a house that doesn't share our values?'

'Papa, you don't think it is a good idea, I won't meet the boy.'

The mother collapsed into rage. 'Everybody is corrupt, are they? Throw out nine tenths of the government, run the country yourself with your high blood pressure. Expect the whole nation to be like Gandhi. Send your daughter to an ashram, because we have neither the means nor the money to get her properly married.'

'I will look after myself,' said Astha bravely.

No one paid attention.

'Their sole interest is the girl, her looks, her education, her qualities. That is something,' said the harassed father.

'It's more than something,' insisted the mother. 'How many people do you know like that?'

'Big dowries are being offered for Hemant. He is known to be quite smart.'

'Is that his name?' asked Astha.

'Yes.'

A nice name. Hemant and Astha. It had a certain ring to it.

'Why aren't they going in for big dowries?' inquired the prospective bride.

'The boy does not believe in dowry. Must be the foreign influence, couldn't be his father.'

Astha felt an even greater interest in the boy. 'Let me meet him, Papa,' she declared. 'After all, the father came with the proposal, they must be thinking alike to a certain extent.'

Hemant came to the house. The parents left them alone for half an hour. Astha was so nervous her palms were sweating. He had only gone by her face, she knew that was passable, but what about the rest of her? Should she tell him about Rohan, but what to tell? That though she had kissed a boy, her hymen was intact? That he had broken her heart but she hoped to find happiness in marriage? How could she say this to someone she didn't know? She looked up at Hemant and smiled tentatively, he smiled back, asked about her hobbies before continuing to talk about his experiences in the USA.

A few weeks later the engagement between Astha and Hemant Vadera was decided upon. The wedding was to be held in June. By then Astha's MA exams would be over, Hemant's elder sister's children would have their holidays, and his younger sister would be able to come for a month from the States. With all this settled, Astha and Hemant began to date.

~

The day of Astha's wedding was like any other day in June. The heat rose and rose, dust gathered, and all activity struggled against a dull and heavy lassitude. In the morning Astha's mother brought her tea and gazed at her approvingly.

'Today you are getting married and leaving for your new home,' she murmured, tears in her eyes, while relatives clustered and consoled, speaking of the necessity of this moment, the pain of a mother at parting, the joy of a mother at her duty successfully completed. These murmurs fluttered around Astha, who, restless and ill at ease, waited for the action to begin.

Outside, the tent wallahs had started converting the central common ground into a wedding hall, enclosing it with shamianas, covering the stubbly parched grass with durries. In the afternoon the caterers came, putting up tandoors near the garage. Five hundred invitations had been sent out. Both the families lived in the same colony, worked for the same government, had lived for years in the same city. A huge guest list was unavoidable.

In the evening there was a havan, during which Astha's red and white wedding bangles, with the dangling chura, were put on. She sat before the fire, tossing the samagri in, feeling dazed and unreal.

After this it was time to get ready. Her wedding sari, fresh from the ironers, was laid out. She contemplated the thick red and gold silk in which sweat and discomfort were guaranteed. Normally summer brides wore thin tissue woven with gold, but with the wedding costing so much, she had to wear the heavy bridal temple sari bought years ago at a special price by her father on a government tour to South India. Now Astha hoped Hemant would not find her dowdy or unfashionable. She hoped he would not mind that she had little jewellery, she hoped he would like her without beauty parlour bridal make-up, and that he would hate, like she did, those assembly line creations, pink and white, with black-lined eyes.

*

Night came, the barat arrived. Astha was called to garland her groom to the taped music of shehnais. At the auspicious hour they sat down next to each other under a small rickety pandal, with a fan trained on them. The hot air from the fan, the smoke from the fire, the sight of her father waiting to do the kanyadaan, the feel of her hand in the hand of her bridegroom, in a trance she realised this was the beginning of the life ordained for her.

The pundit was chanting. They were taking the seven steps around the fire, the steps that meant they were legally married. It was stifling, perhaps she was going to faint. Her cousins clustered around her, fussing with her jewellery, adjusting her palla and teasing the bridegroom.

This time tomorrow she would be in Kashmir, surrounded by mountains, trees, and lake, where waters rippled gently around gliding shikaras, where a book would not be her companion, but her husband bending tenderly over her, her companion for life.

~

On the plane to Srinagar Hemant held Astha's hand, while she looked shyly out of the window at the mountains they were flying over. A deep seed of happiness settled in the pit of her stomach, she was married, she didn't have to be the focus of her parents' anxieties any longer. She was now a homemaker in her own right, a grown woman, experiencing her first plane ride.

Throughout the journey, Hemant kept touching Astha, a finger slid inside the sleeve of her blouse, a hand pressed on her knee.

The consummation took place in a houseboat on Dal Lake. Hemant undressed her slowly, gazing at her steadily, while Astha nervously looked at his stomach.

'Now you undress me,' he said.

She shook her head modestly, wrapping the sheet around herself, tucking one edge in.

'Come on,' he urged.

She bent her head still further and stared at his shoes planted next to her smooth, freshly waxed bare legs and pedicured feet, their mehndi patterns still a deep orange.

He took her hands and put them on his chest. She undid the buttons, and slid his shirt off. As he lifted his arms for her to remove his vest, the hair of his underarms sprang out at her, along with the smell of him. She pulled off the vest quickly and stopped. He drew her hands again to him, unzipping his pants himself in his impatience to guide her to the right spot.

'There,' he whispered, jamming her hand into his underwear, swelling bulkily, 'it's yours. Do you like it?'

Astha hardly knew. She snatched her hand away, and rolled face down on the pillow, while Hemant excitedly finished his own undressing.

Afterwards they found a spot of marriage blood on the sheet. They both peered at it.

'Did it hurt?' asked Hemant fondly.

'A little,' confessed his wife.

Later, in the privacy of the bathroom, Astha allowed herself to wonder whether she had been misled about the magnitude of the act.

Sex. There was so much of it. The pain Astha felt between her legs was never quite absent. She could only thank God they never spent that much time actually doing it. Hemant attacked the whole thing with great urgency, gazing at her a little anxiously after each time, while she uncertainly smiled back to a look of satisfaction that came over his face.

Unbidden thoughts of Rohan came. How slow his kisses had been, how infinitely long, how thorough. Then she scolded herself. Rohan had abandoned her, Hemant had married her, he valued her, he thought her pretty. The question of whose lovemaking she preferred did not arise.

During the day they wandered around the tourist spots of Srinagar, hand in hand. People looked at the bangles on her wrists and smiled. She was a bride, and her grip on Hemant's hand grew more certain, and the blush on her face more conscious. Hemant's attention was constant. He took endless photographs and never let her read.

Astha wanted to record what she felt. This was her honeymoon, a one-time thing. She tried writing in her journal, but as usual the words didn't come. She tried sketching her surroundings, but the beauty was too overwhelming. She drew Hemant instead, his face, body, torso, arms, legs, it was the first time she had had so much nudity to work with. And when she was tired of art, she attempted writing.

One evening, sitting on the roof of the houseboat, drinking her evening tea, looking out on the lake, she wrote a poem about the sky, the shikaras, the sound of the birds, the sun behind the mountains reflected in the water. She wrote that she, the watcher, was part of that harmony, and it was fitting that her new life begin in beauty. As she put down her pen, tears filled her eyes.

Her husband saw. 'What's the matter, darling?' he enquired, leading her downstairs to the bed, where they had made love last night, this morning and afternoon.

'Nothing,' gulped Astha, her head laid out on the pillow. Hemant scooped her legs up, and lay down next to her.

'I don't like to see my baby crying,' he said softly.

Astha pressed her face into his shoulder, and laced her arms around his back.

'Are you missing your mother?'

She started to laugh, the idea was so absurd. 'No, silly,' she said.

'Then what? Tell me, I'm your husband,' urged Hemant. 'Tell me, wife.'

Astha didn't know why she had been crying. Nothing in her present life seemed to justify tears. Finally she mumbled, a little sheepish, 'It hurts.'

'Where?'

Astha's hand vaguely danced over her middle. Hemant put his hand firmly between her legs. 'There?' he asked. She nodded.

'Why didn't you tell me? You must tell me these things, I will never know otherwise. We are one, you know. Now promise.' He bent to kiss her.

Astha responded more warmly than she had in her entire marriage. 'I didn't know what to say,' she went on whispering in the ears of her lawful wedded husband, her husband who would take care of all her hurts like he was taking care of this one.

'Poor baby,' murmured Hemant, 'we won't make love till it stops hurting, all right?'

'Hemant?' asked Astha, a week after they were married.

'Hum?' replied Hemant sleepily. Astha's head was on his shoulder, his arm was around her, and he had spread her hair across his chest.

'Why didn't you marry an American?'

'Why do you ask?'

'Well, you were there a long time, you must have gone out with girls. Fallen in love, thought of marriage.'

'Never.'

'Never had women?'

Hemant side-stepped this. 'I was always sure I wanted to marry a girl from here.'

'Me, you mean.'

Hemant's grip tightened around his wife, while Astha felt thrilled and wanted. 'Besides,' he said, playing dreamily with her hair, 'I had responsibilities to my parents. I am the only son, and I wanted someone who would fit in with our family life. American women are too demanding. Their men have to cater to all their whims and fancies.'

'Is that true?' demanded Astha, visions of American women waited on hand and foot, basking in love, flashing through her mind.

'You bet,' said Hemant with great certainty. 'Besides you can't be sure they won't be up to something.'

'Like?'

'Other men. It's not so unthinkable for them as it is for an Indian girl.'

Astha fell silent. She was wondering if she liked this conversation. She turned to kiss him, but Hemant was not to be distracted. This was a topic he had considered deeply. 'I wanted an innocent, unspoilt, simple girl,' he went on.

There was a pause.

'A virgin,' he elaborated.

'Suppose I had not been one?' asked the wife carefully.

'And the blood on the sheet, what was that? A mirage?'

'Some women don't bleed, even though they have had no sex, you know,' said Astha. She had read this in a magazine.

'Since that didn't happen in our case, why talk about it,' said Hemant.

Rohan's face bending over hers arose before Astha's eyes. Had she been a virgin? Unlike Hemant, she was not sure. She decided to forget the whole business, after all now she was definitely not one, and what was the point of thinking about the past?

'I see you are a writer', said Hemant, looking through her notebook, 'as well as an artist.'

'Not really,' said Astha modestly, and waited for him to draw her out.

'What are you doing now?' he asked.

Astha showed him the paper on which she was writing a poem.

'They say a picture's worth a thousand words,' he read, then looked up and frowned. 'But this is not a picture,' he objected.

'I know,' said Astha, quickly. 'I was just looking for a way to start. Whenever I sketch the scene, it ends up looking like a post card, so I thought I'd try words instead.' She reached out to take the page, 'I'll work on it more and show you.'

'No, no, let me read. Maybe I can help you. I used to read a lot when I was in college.'

'Really?' asked Astha interestedly. 'What?'

'Harold Robbins. Erle Stanley Gardner, Somerset Maugham, Agatha Christie, P. G. Wodehouse, all kinds of authors. I was quite a reader, you know.'

Astha was silent, while Hemant's eyes quickly scanned the page. 'You certainly have a nice imagination,' he said, 'You put things well.'

Astha looked pleased.

'And for being so clever . . .'

He leaned towards her, and reached under her blouse. Astha pressed him close, and breathed my husband into his waiting ear.

'My baby,' responded Hemant.

Astha heard him with satisfaction. Her husband was going to encourage her writing. Maybe she could become a poetess as well as a painter. Her life was opening up before her in golden vistas.

'Do you think there will be golden vistas in our life, darling?' she asked, taken with the sound of the words.

'Of course, baby,' he replied. 'Golden like your body in the sunlight when it comes through the window touched by the water of this lake.'

'Oh, Hemant,' laughed Astha, 'I didn't know you were a poet!'

Hemant looked modest. After they had kissed, fondled and not made love, Hemant told the bearer to take the drink tray upstairs to the roof.

They reclined on deck chairs facing the lake. The ice tinkled in Hemant's glass, bird sounds tinkled in their ears, water lapped around the boat. They were too high to see the sludge that had gathered around the houseboat, too high to notice the slight smell that came from the stagnant edge. Upon the roof, hand in hand, Astha's heart was as full of love as the lake was full of water.

Back in Delhi, Astha submerged herself in the role of daughter-in-law and wife. The time spent in the kitchen experimenting with new dishes was time spent in the service of love and marriage. Hemant's clothes she treated with reverence, sliding each shirt in his drawers a quarter centimetre out from the one above so they were easily visible, darning all the tiny holes in his socks, arranging his pants on cloth-wrapped hangers so there would be no crease. With her mother-in-law she visited and shopped in the mornings, the memory of the night past, and the expectation of the night to come insulating her from any tedium she might otherwise have felt.

Every evening her father-in-law remarked, 'How nice it is to have a daughter in the house.'

Hemant looked as though it were all his doing, while Astha's mother-in-law sighed and talked of her absent daughters; Seema, so far away in America, and Sangeeta, well, now that Hemant was married, he and his wife were responsible for Sangeeta, whose troubles with her husband and in-laws were always hinted at rather than spelt out.

Astha, proud that she was considered responsible enough to share the family problems invariably replied, 'Don't worry Mummy, she has us,' though she was seven years younger than Sangeeta, and had only seen her at the wedding.

After they had had tea Hemant and Astha dropped in on her parents. 'I do not want them to feel they have lost a daughter,' Hemant insisted, as they walked through the colony to Astha's old house, while Astha thought how nice he was, and how lucky she.

'Why do we have to drink tea twice every day?' she complained occasionally, for the pleasure of hearing Hemant say, 'And disappoint Mama and Papa, who are waiting? And when Mama makes snacks especially for us, no fears.'

'Especially for you, you mean,' said Astha.

'It is the same thing,' said Hemant drawing Astha's hand through his arm even more tightly.

In the kitchen, Astha's mother would hiss 'Happy?' and Astha would give the slightest non-committal nod, wanting to keep her happiness to herself. To share it or voice it might encourage its departure.

Meanwhile Hemant immersed himself in sex manuals. He hid them in his cupboard under rows of shirts.

'Mummy might see,' Astha objected nervously. Her mother-in-law frequently visited their room, examined all the items, and straightened the covers on the bed.

'So what?' laughed Hemant. 'We are married, what can anybody say?'

The number of sex manuals increased. All the books had graphic illustrations.

'Why do you have to read these things?' Astha demanded for form's sake.

'They are interesting. Look.' Hemant tried to show her, but Astha turned away her head, and Hemant did not persist. 'I will show you in other ways,' he murmured in her hair.

Astha blushed and said nothing, too diffident to tell him that she had already noticed a change in his lovemaking, he was less in a hurry, and his focus had widened from the single point of her vagina.

New positions, timing the length of intercourse, variations on a theme. There seemed no end to what one could do with two bodies. At the suggestion of sexy clothes she balked.

'What do you think I am? A whore?'

'There is nothing to be ashamed of darling,' said Hemant caressing her. 'It is to increase married pleasure.'

Astha looked at the lacy black thing he was offering her. 'What is it?' she asked suspiciously.

'A teddy.'

'So I am to be your teddy bear?'

Hemant was not interested in double meanings. 'I went to a lot of trouble to get it for you,' he said.

'For me?'

'Who else is the woman in my life?' asked Hemant, pushing her towards the bathroom. Thank God their room was slightly separated from her parents-in-law's bedroom, thought Astha, and they had a bathroom to themselves. Otherwise there was no way she could do these things. She locked the door and looked at herself in the mirror, clad from throat to ankle, neck to wrist. Diaphanous, lacy, and a soft pink she had all along thought this nightie made her look quite attractive. Slowly she took it off and looked at her body. She was in her hairless condition, the way Hemant liked her, with legs, arms, and underarms freshly waxed, shining smooth, with not an unsightly black stump in sight, only a series of pink bumps where the wax had pulled too hard and left its protest. She raised her arms and anxiously sniffed the wet place underneath. Hemant didn't like the smell of sweat, or vaginal fluids, he was a little squeamish in that respect, and she now washed and dusted herself with powder before turning her attention back to the thing. Single piece, lace and satin, slinky, with holes and slits, she could crumple it in one fist, its only stiffness the wires in the cups.

She put it on, and there from below her chin, a deep cleavage appeared with black laced mounds on either side, the dark nipples straining through black net hearts. She almost didn't recognise herself, with the sexual parts so emphasised. She raised her arms to take out the pins from her hair, watching as her breasts rose and thrust forwards, feeling an excitement that embarrassed her.

Astha wrapped a dressing gown around herself, and slowly went into the bedroom locking the door quietly. Hemant was lying on the bed with the small bedside lamp on, his arms and chest shone brown and shapely. He kept his eyes on her, as she took off the dressing gown and walked self-consciously across to him, desire rising still higher, trying not to think of what she was wearing, what it was doing to him, to her. She sat next to him, and he grabbed her tightly encased body.

'Sit on me,' he said hoarsely, pulling her on to him, twisting the little bit of lace aside.

Astha sat on him, her breasts tight and forward, falling over him, over my husband, she thought, as they rocked together, while sensation took over, drowning thoughts even of husbands.

The days passed. Astha had not imagined that sex could be such a master. Slightly ashamed, she kept hidden that she longed to dissolve herself in him, longed to be the sips of water he drank, longed to be the morsels of food he swallowed. The times he was away she was focused on one thing, the moment of their union. When he came through the door, she wanted to jump on him, tear his clothes off, thrust her nipples into his mouth, and have him charge his way through her. One with him, one with all that mattered.

I haven't really lived, thought Astha, till now I did not know what life was all about.

She felt a woman of the world, the world that was covered with the film of her desire, and the fluids of their sex.

~

A few months and dullness began to taint Astha's new life. What was she to do while waiting for Hemant to come home? Her in-laws were not demanding, for the housework they had help, and supervision, no matter how painstaking, still left her with enough free time to be restless in.

'You need to work,' said her mother.

The teaching job she had never considered with interest loomed large. Now that she was married, Astha could see that its hours qualified it as the ideal job, a fact her mother was even now pointing out.

'As a teacher you will earn some money, but you will only be out half the day so the home will not suffer.'

Astha looked resentful. Her future suddenly seemed very pedestrian.

It was some evenings later that Astha's mother brought up the subject with Hemant. 'She needs to be occupied, beta.'

'Yes, Ma, I know,' said Hemant. 'I myself was thinking.'

'What about your painting and writing?' asked her father. 'You can make use of these talents in journalism.'

Mother and husband expressed scepticism.

As they walked back through the colony to their own house, Hemant repeated, 'Journalists have to stay out late, they have very odd hours. We must see about a teaching job. You read quite a lot.'

'I don't think that alone will equip me,' said Astha, briefly wondering whether all women were destined to be teachers or nothing.

Hemant laughed. 'You will probably know more than anyone,' he said.

With the newly introduced 10+2 system, it was not difficult to get a job teaching elective subjects to classes eleven and twelve. In answer to the combined wishes of Astha's relatives one of her college teachers phoned with news of a vacancy at St Anthony's School, and if she was interested she should go and see the Principal, Mrs Dubey.

Astha's in-laws approved. 'It is a good time pass.'

'It's near enough. You won't have to spend much time on the road,' commented the mother.

Her father merely said, 'It will do until you decide to develop yourself in other ways.'

Her husband said, 'With a job you won't be so fidgety if I am a minute late.'

'Oh, I am to work so you can do what you like?'

'Who says I want to do what I like? It will benefit you to

leave the house in the mornings. When the children come we will see whether to continue this.'

At the interview Mrs Dubey made it clear that a teacher at her school needed to show commitment to the institution, foster students' interests in extra-curricular activities, and make sure they did well in the tenth and twelfth board exams, the reputation of a school unfortunately depending on results. Astha agreed to everything and was hired. Later she thought that since the job fell into her lap, her destiny must be teaching.

Being a teacher meant the languor of her days was over. No longer did she have the luxury of leisurely brooding over her love, she had to get up early and go to work. She had exercises to correct, and lessons to prepare. She started a reading club, a writing club, a painting club, directed by the principal's suggestions and followed through with her encouragement. The peripheries of her world now stretched to include many schoolgirls. Life was shaping up nicely, with her mind and heart gainfully employed.

Hemant dropped her occasionally when she was getting late for morning assembly. Both families exclaimed at his devotion as a husband.

A day, as usual, with Hemant coming in late. Astha had been waiting the whole evening, and now took this opportunity to gaze at him, her soul in her eyes, the soul that she was waiting to hand over on a platter.

'How are you, darling?' he asked, looking at her affectionately. 'How was your day in school?'

'They have asked me to edit the school magazine,' she managed, but even those few words were difficult, so heavy was the passion weighing her down. Her tongue felt useless in her mouth, unless it was activated by his.

He sat down on the sofa, and Astha knelt to take off his shoes. She unlaced them, and pulled off his socks, gathering the day's dust in her lap. At that moment she loved Hemant so intensely, that every fetid, stale, sweaty smell that came from his foot was a further nail in the armour of her love.

'How was your day?' she asked. 'Why are you so late? I have been waiting hours.'

'The director called a meeting,' replied Hemant looking disgruntled.

'At this time?'

'What does he care? Slow, pompous, ass-licking fucker.'

'What has happened now?'

'The latest directives for distributing loans. Our target has been increased, and he is worried we might not make it. Then his head will be on the chopping block.'

Oh dear, this was not going to be a happy subject.

'This percentage for cottage units, that for farmers, this for small scale units, that for backward classes, and without any security! No collateral, no third-party guarantor, because the government has to look good in the next election while we bear the losses. How can any bank function in this manner? This is what happens when you nationalise banks, constant meddling and interference.'

How long would it take for him to notice her? 'I kept thinking of you in school,' she started, but Hemant hadn't finished.

'How are we encouraging any initiative, if these buggers get money for free? And how do you make sure someone is scheduled caste, for fuck's sake? Just a few months ago I had a branch officer complaining that the local bigwig was demanding a larger than usual cut for supplying the bank with certified scheduled caste people. He was falling short of his target and he had to give in. Bloody country, this is why we never progress. In America such interference would be unheard of.'

'Well, this is India, dearest,' said Astha, not wanting Hemant to start on the subject of America versus India. 'This is the way things function. If you get angry, you will only harm your health. My father got blood pressure because he hated his job. Fire burns itself,' she added, a saying she had grown up with.

Hemant deflated. 'When I think of how my classmates are doing, how much money they are making – with an American MBA you can do anything, but there are no opportunities in this bloody country, none. Sometimes I wish I had never come back.'

'Money isn't everything darling. Look, you have your family, me, our parents.'

'Maybe we all emigrate, huh? Seema's husband keeps calling, he's willing to sponsor me.'

Live abroad? 'Yes, let's go,' she said excitedly.

Hemant sighed, 'No, Az, I came for Papaji and Mummy, I have to stay. Papaji knows I am being wasted here, and he tries his best to make me happy, but still, what can he do about the job? This is not satisfying work, it is a clearing division, clear this loan, that loan, deal with union demands and government meddling, nothing is allowed to become efficient.'

Astha's desire receded. She felt cold, dreary, and distanced from him. She had been waiting for him all day, thinking of their being together, but nothing of this was reciprocated. He was a criminal, destroying her anticipation, ruining her happiness.

Her subservient position struck her. She had no business kneeling, taking off his shoes, pulling off his socks, feeling ecstatic about the smell of his feet.

'What's the matter, darling?' said Hemant as her hands stopped moving. He reached out and ran his fingers through her hair. 'Leave my shoes, I'll do it.'

He got up, put them away, and catching her by the elbow sat her down next to him. Poor man, thought Astha softening, he must have had a hard day in the office, was that anything to mind? She must make his home a haven for him, not a place of recrimination.

'So what were you saying about school?' he asked, passing his hand down her back, gently pressing the dividing line between her haunches.

Astha sidled closer to him, and the pressure became a little firmer. 'I kept thinking of you,' she whispered. 'I missed you every minute.'

'Baby,' he murmured, accepting this as his due. 'And school, how was that?'

'Well, they have asked me to help with the school magazine, as I am the teacher for the senior elective English classes. And I thought, why not?'

'Do they know you write?'

'Of course not. Anybody with reasonable English is enough for this job. My class XI girls got really excited, they want to organise a creative writing competition. We can publish the best poems and stories, maybe even send them to the children's page in the newspaper.'

Hemant wasn't really listening. Astha stopped talking about creative writing as he got up to lock the door.

'They are waiting,' objected Astha.

'Just a quick one,' said Hemant.

'They will know what we are doing,' said Astha, already imagining what was to come, even if it was a quick one.

'Let them know. We are married.'

Astha lay back, aware of every inch of her skin, aware of every thread she wore, now about to be dislodged. The day, with its petty vexations flowed away from her. This, what was going to happen, was the central thing in her life.

～

The last year of Astha's father's service drew to a close. They would have to leave their house soon. Hemant threw himself into their plans, politely suppressing his surprise at their unworldliness.

'Az,' he said frequently to his wife, after visiting his in-laws, 'how come Papa didn't plan more for his retirement?'

'He was planning,' said Astha hopelessly, 'in fact they were always planning.'

'Then, what happened?'

'They kept trying to buy, but it was always too expensive. Then this housing society thing came up and they were allotted land trans Jamuna. They thought once the bridge was built and prices went up, they could sell the plot and buy a small flat this side.'

To Astha now, this seemed like not very much planning.

'As an investment, Az, this is not good strategy,' said Hemant, banker. 'The bridge is nowhere in sight, you can't depend on government promises.'

'Well, I don't know, that is what they did,' said Astha pettishly.

'They can still live on it, though. People are building, after all. Then when prices rise, their property will be worth even more.'

'How can they? It's still so undeveloped it's not safe. No infrastructure, no nothing. You should see it, it's just a patch of mud. In one of the nearby colonies, the owner was alone in the house when dacoits broke in, stole everything, and beat him till he almost died. You want this to happen to them?' Astha's voice rose slightly.

'Now, now, baby, don't get upset, of course they shouldn't go if it is not safe. We'll help them all we can.'

'OK,' said the wife, feeling momentarily soothed, pushing away the knowledge that it is one thing to offer help, another to give it, still another to take it, and that her father was a very proud man.

Astha's father retired, and in six months they had to vacate the house in Lodhi colony. It had been central and inexpensive, the rent 10 per cent of the father's salary. Now they were thrown to the outside world. While the mother was at school, the father trudged around various colonies with property dealers. The private colonies near Lodhi Colony were all too posh, there was no question of trying Sundar Nagar, Golf Links, or even Defence Colony, where army officials had bought plots for a song not so many years before. Finally he found a small two-room apartment in Jangpura. Its advantage was a large terrace, its disadvantage that it was on the first floor.

'You will have to go up and down everyday,' said Astha, 'are you sure your health can take it?'

'Climbing stairs is good exercise,' said the father.

'When you have high blood pressure?'

'I will be all right.'

What choice did they have? The flat was comparatively cheap, the location comparatively central. The landlord was kind, only demanding three months' rent in advance, not insisting on a company lease.

Dismantling the house in which they had lived for fifteen years was not easy. They took the furniture the new flat could accommodate, the rest they sold. The father's books were put in boxes which were then placed so as to make two beds and a living-room divan. They would still be with him, that knowledge would have to replace the pleasure of seeing them every day. The bed linen, the small pieces of bric-a-brac that Astha's mother had stored through the years were given to the daughter. 'I don't need them anymore,' she said.

'But these are brand new,' said Astha looking at the carefully preserved things, wrapped in soft, old saris. 'Why don't you use them?'

'No, no, I do not need,' insisted the mother.

Hemant helped them to move. 'I don't like asking him to do so much for us, beti,' said the father.

'He is your son-in-law, Papa. It is all right,' said Astha.

Again they had no choice.

In the small flat, near the highway, noisy, confined, far from tree and grass, alone for half the day while his wife was at work, eating things he was not supposed to, the father wandered through his life, looking at what was left behind and what lay ahead, and decided there was no use living. Other people decide that with less success.

They had been in the new flat a little over a year when one evening after dinner he complained of a slight chest pain. That night he died in his sleep. Through the period of shock and mourning, Astha and her mother clung to each other.

'It was the move,' the mother kept sobbing. 'He was never the same after he retired.'

'He was a saint,' said the relatives. 'Never liking to trouble others.'

'I kept telling him, do not strain, do not exert yourself, but no. He was never careful. And now he has left me and gone.'

'You have me, Ma,' said Hemant.

'Yes, Ma. We are all with you.'

As consolation to the widow, now all alone, the relatives said, thank God he saw his child settled, he will rest in peace.

In the months that followed the father's death, the mother became listless and withdrawn. The evenings Astha spent with her she would desperately try and cheer her up.

'You are still young, Ma, still working. Think of all the things you can do.'

'You don't worry about me, beti,' said the mother dully.

'You can travel, you can do social work, you can do something for the children of the poor, you always said you wanted to help other people. Now you can.'

'Han, beti. You don't worry about me.'

'But I do worry. Why don't you come and live with me?'

'You live with your in-laws, and besides where is the room in these government flats.'

That was true enough.

Astha tried to interest Hemant in the problem of her mother. He was a good son-in-law, everybody said so, his own parents in particular, closely echoed by the mother-in-law herself. If there was an illness he would call the doctor, if she needed money he would offer it, if she needed help in shifting he would provide it. But appeals beyond this irritated and annoyed him.

Then the mother met a swami. She informed her daughter of this casually.

'A swami?' repeated Astha, puzzled. 'How did you meet him?'

'One of the teachers in school took me. Often she has mentioned him, but when your father was alive I never felt the need for anything more in my life. Also he was suspicious of this kind of thing, your father always thought he knew best.'

'With reason, Ma. Swamis are known to take advantage of women, especially widows,' said Astha.

Her mother ignored this. 'Why don't you come?' she went on. 'He lectures on the *Gita* at Gandhi Bhavan. He teaches you how to accept things, how to look inside yourself, how to deal with your wants and desires. There are lots of young girls there.'

'I don't want to look inside myself,' said Astha.

'Well, I am learning a lot from him. Through him I understand the *Gita*, it is something I have wanted to do all my life.'

'Really? How come I didn't know?'

'Where was the time or place to say I want this or that?'

'And now you have a swami? Is that what you wanted time for?'

Astha's mother looked offended. 'Why don't you come and see before you start your criticising?'

That evening Astha said to Hemant, 'Ma has found some swami. She wants me to go to him and look inside myself.'

'Rubbish. These people just try and sound clever.'

'That is what I said.'

'Who is this man?'

'I don't know.'

Hemant looked alert. 'One has to be careful around swamis,' he said. 'Thank God I am handling her money.'

'I know,' said Astha, her wretchedness increasing. 'But what can I do?'

'Somebody is putting ideas into her head. People think old women are easy targets.'

'She doesn't listen.'

'Don't worry sweetheart, once we have a child, she will forget all this nonsense. There will be a new interest in her life.'

Astha smiled her agreement.

~

Loving Hemant as she did, Astha longed to get pregnant. During sex she imagined his seed spurting into her womb; later she would gather his wet shrivelled penis, adoring it strong, thick and hot, or wet, limp and woebegone. 'I want to have your baby,' she would murmur.

'You can't be so old fashioned,' remonstrated the progressive husband. 'This is like villagers, marry, impregnate wife, pack of children. No, no sweetheart, we need to be by ourselves. Time enough for these responsibilities later. With a young wife one can afford to wait.'

Astha looked at him in admiration. Everything about him was so masculine, his decisiveness, his hairy blunt fingers, his tall heavy set figure, his muscled limbs, his moustache that tickled, the bitter tobacco taste from his tongue.

'These ideas are all from America,' said his parents, refusing to see the value of bonding time for the young couple. They had married, now they should get on with it.

It was two years before Hemant relented, two years before Astha could stop using birth control, two years before his seed found its home.

Astha and Hemant drove to Jangpura on their weekly visit, full of the good news.

'Ma,' said Hemant, 'You are going to be a nani.'

Tears filled the mother's eyes. 'If only he had been here,' she said.

Astha thought of her father and felt sad. He had sent her forth, and then left, duty done.

'Ma, this is a time to celebrate,' reproached Hemant.

'Beta, you are right. May it be a boy, and carry your name for ever. A great son of a great father.'

Astha thought her mother was overdoing it.

'But Ma, I want a daughter,' said Hemant.

'That's true, Ma,' repeated Astha, 'He wants a girl.'

'In America there is no difference between boys and girls. How can this country get anywhere if we go on treating our women this way?'

There was no mistaking the admiration in both women's eyes.

Astha enjoyed every aspect of her pregnancy. As it advanced, she became more and more bucolic. Teaching was an effort, and she had no energy for any extra activity. At home she slept most of the time.

Hemant adored what was happening to her. 'My wife is becoming a woman before my very eyes,' he said passing his hands over her belly, large and full, over her breasts, certainly larger and fuller than they had ever been. 'I hope they remain like this,' he said holding them possessively.

'What'll happen if they don't?'

'Another baby, what else?'

'You'll get tired earning for all these children you plan to produce.'

'With you looking like this, never,' declared Hemant passionately. 'A real woman rather than a girl.'

Astha had heard men were revolted by the way women looked when they were pregnant, but not Hemant. He loved touching her belly and breasts, her breasts especially, sucking on them experimentally, drawing a little milk when he sucked long enough.

'It's very sweet,' he said with surprise.

'It's called colustrum,' she informed him knowledgeably. 'It comes for the first three days, and is full of nutrients to prevent the baby from getting sick.'

Hemant smiled, 'How full of information my wife is,' he said. 'Where did you find that out from?'

'Books.'

'Our baby will be the best looked after baby there is,' said Hemant, caressing the taut stomach, gently stroking the raised belly-button, following the linea niger down to her pubic hair with his fingers, before inserting them into her vagina.

Anuradha. Born in March, after fifteen hours of labour at a private nursing home. Six pounds, eight ounces, nineteen inches. Long delicate nails, a head of thick black hair, pink, wrinkled, foetus like.

'Oh,' chorused the new grandparents. 'Just like Hemant. Same nose and forehead.'

'Such a straight little nose,' detailed Astha's mother, 'such big eyes. Handsome like her father. Girls who look like their fathers are lucky.'

Hemant leaned over the tiny baby and kissed her cone-like dome enthusiastically. Astha thought with amazement, he doesn't see through my mother's flattery, before tightening her own hold on the child.

The first time Anuradha put her mouth to her mother's breast and started pulling, Astha was astonished. Hemant's own pullings were nothing in comparison, mild as the winter sun. Anuradha meant business. She tugged ferociously, and Astha's womb in response obligingly contracted, spurting out blood into the pad she wore.

A month of wet before the blood ceased to come, before the womb had contracted all it was going to. A time of swollen aching breasts charged with milk that dribbled constantly, soaking the towel inside her nursing bra, staining her clothes, a time when she had to beg Hemant to drink from them to relieve the pressure.

Hemant always willingly obliged, putting a gentle mouth to the tight breast with its blue veins now clearly marked. 'It's very watery,' he said the first time, surprised once more.

'Is it?' asked Astha, 'Let me see.' She cupped a hand under her nipple to catch a drop of the still-oozing milk, and tasted it. It was sweet and watery, bluish-white in colour. 'I guess we are used to cow's milk, which has more fat. That is meant for calves, this is meant for humans,' she explained pedantically, her new-found knowledge still burgeoning in her mind.

Anuradha yawned in her sleep, and made wuffling baby sounds while both parents gazed at the little variations in her movements, with a joy that spilled into each other.

'Darling,' said Hemant one night.

'What?' said Astha preoccupiedly. Anuradha was six months old now, and had just begun to sleep through the night. Astha was looking forward to sleeping through the night too, something she felt she had never appreciated before.

'Where's the teddy?'

'What on earth for?'

'I wonder how it looks. It's been a long time since you tried it on.'

'It's been a long time since I had a figure,' retorted Astha.

'You have a figure,' said Hemant, gazing upon his wife's fullness appreciatively. 'Go on, try it,' he urged, pushing her stubborn form towards the bathroom.

'No, no, I don't want to,' expostulated Astha.

'Why? You think because we've had a baby, our life is over. I haven't touched you in months.'

'I know, I'm sorry. Soon it'll stop hurting. And our life isn't over, if by that you mean sex, but it's not necessary to have sex with that thing on, is it? What'll happen to Anu's subconscious? She might grow up with a problem.'

'Look at her. She's totally unconscious. How do you think half the country fucks? You think they have separate rooms?'

Astha knew they didn't. She didn't like the leer on Hemant's face, but she could think of no more reasons for objecting. What could she say? That she was too old? She was twenty-five. That the early days of their marriage were over? They had been married three years. That Hemant should want her without her prancing around in a tight black cut-away garment? But she had worn it before, she had been turned on herself, wasn't she being rather prudish now? She threw a glance at the baby, maybe she was waking? But no, Anuradha slept peacefully, while her mother made her way slowly to the drawer where the teddy was hidden en route to the bathroom.

She pulled it on. Her breasts spilled over the top, and looked more voluptuous than they were. That was all very well, thought Astha, but the sight of her stomach bulging through the shiny stretchy lace see-through stuff, that sight was not pretty. Also she hadn't been so regular about her waxing, there was hair growing all over her limbs.

This'll put him off teddies for ever, thought Astha, surveying herself in the mirror, a little regretful that her body should have this deterrent effect. Finally she wrapped his dressing gown around her waist and emerged complaining, it's so tight, look darling it doesn't fit, I'll never be my old self again.

Hemant saw her point. The teddy was put away and never mentioned again.

～

'Once we build our new house, we can start planning for our next child.'

'Um,' said Astha absently, handing her husband the baby oil. Hemant poured a little into his palm and began carefully rubbing it on his daughter, her bath part of his Sunday morning ritual. He insisted on doing this, ideas about fatherhood are so antiquated in India.

'I want to have my son soon,' declared Hemant, looking emotional and manly at the same time. 'I want to be as much a part of his life as Papaji is of mine.'

'How do you know we will have a son?' asked Astha, feeling a little scared.

'Of course we will have a son, and if we don't we needn't stop at two.'

Astha silently took the oil bottle from him and closed it.

'Is the water ready?'

His wife hastily tested the water in the bath-set crammed into a corner of the bedroom. 'Yes,' she said.

The father gently lowered his daughter into the water, while the mother stood ready with the shampoo, rubber toy, and soft towel.

After the bath Astha called the servant to mop the floor and throw out the water while she hung the towel, disposed of the oil, comb, powder, toy, dirty diaper and night clothes. She then settled down to nurse the baby while Hemant went on discussing their house and their future.

'Hemant?' said Astha after a while.

'Yes?' replied Hemant engrossed in the soft feet and tiny legs of his child.

'I thought these things didn't matter to you. What if we don't have a boy?'

'Of course they don't matter to me. I was so pleased Anu was a girl. But that doesn't mean we should not try for a boy. I am the only son.'

'It is not in our hands, at least not in mine. It is the man's chromosome that decides the sex, and with two sisters in your family, it may be a girl. I have read about these things.'

'You are always reading,' said Hemant coldly.

'I am sorry. Does it bother you?'

'It fills your head with unnecessary ideas. Let us first not have a son and then we will see. Keep it simple. All right?'

Astha looked dissatisfied but could think of nothing to say.

~

In the family she had married into Astha had ample opportunity to witness how the business of building a house and planning for retirement should be gone about. Papaji's ministry's housing society, Papaji's rank, Papaji's draw had achieved for them 633 square yards in Vasant Vihar. And for the next ten years the family watched in amazement, satisfaction, and smugness the rate at which their initial investment of twenty thousand rupees multiplied five hundred times over.

Astha's marriage entitled her to the same emotions. This is what my parents hoped would happen to them, she thought wistfully every time the latest price of their plot was discussed, and it was discussed many times.

Vasant Vihar too was once wilderness, home to rabbits, peacocks and deer, but by the late seventies almost a third of it was under construction, a boom which the Vadera family now joined.

For the plans Papaji contacted the chief architect of the New Delhi Municipal Corporation, who enjoyed the same secretary level status he did. A senior teacher of the Delhi School of Planning and Architecture was recommended, drawings were made, their relative living convenience minutely examined.

The house was going to be double storied, the ground floor for Hemant and Astha, the one above for Papaji and Mummy. Each floor would have a drawing-dining, kitchen, two bedrooms with attached baths, and a small study to double as a guest room. In the centre, overlooking a patch of lawn running on the side of the house, would be an open informal area where the family could congregate. There would be one large verandah beyond the drawing-dining, and small balconies outside the bedrooms. On the roof would be the servant's quarters.

A puja was done at the site, and the building started. Steel and cement could only be obtained on quotas, and construction on the house lasted nearly two years, despite Papaji's contacts, as thirty tons of rolled steel bars and thousands of bags of cement were released in dribs and drabs by the concerned ministry.

Periodically Hemant and Papaji would go shopping along with the contractor. To GB Road for cast iron and galvanised iron pipes, toilets, taps, stainless steel and ceramic sinks, wall tiles and marble chips; to Bhagirath Palace for mild steel conduit pipes, electrical cables for light and power, switch boxes, switches, fans, hinges, door locks and door handles; to Paharganj for wood and plywood; and last of all to Kotla for glass and paint, Snowcem for the outside, oil bound distemper for the inside, lime wash for the ceilings.

Two to three times a week Hemant visited the site, he was a junior officer, and he didn't have the pressures Papaji did. Sometimes Astha accompanied him, audience to Hemant's sense of himself as the child of fortune. 'This – this,' he said waving his hand at their plot, 'this is worth over a crore today.'

'A crore?' breathed Astha. 'So much.' And she warmed with the pleasure of being part of a family that was in tune with the ways of the world. Now and for ever she would be looked after.

To avoid death duties, the five Vaderas were registered as co-owners, with a letter of intention signed amongst them as to future rights. Hemant was to get the ground floor; Seema, who had contributed dollars towards the construction, was to get the first floor; and Sangeeta, who had contributed nothing, was to get the terrace, which allowed a built up area of 25 per cent. Should either of the sisters wish to sell they had to give their brother first offer.

After the house was built, it was given on rent to an embassy, at over a hundred times the rate they paid for their Lodhi Colony government accommodation. Astha's mother listened to the details of the increase in the family finances with glistening eyes, sighing heavily, blessing her daughter, remembering her departed husband, a very simple man, with no sense of this world.

~

The two-year excitement and absorption of building a house over, Hemant began to get bored. On his way home from work he took to frequenting the club where, swimming, playing tennis or drinking, he met men like himself.

They were a new breed, these men. Their fathers had opted for the security and prestige of the civil services, but the sons wanted challenge and money. Educated abroad, their idealism had been exercised in their choice to return to India, now they wanted tangible returns for that sacrifice. Certainly Hemant did. He decided to try his hand at business.

'Isn't it terribly risky?' asked Astha nervously. 'Business is full of bribes and corruption, headache and uncertainty.'

'Az, this is the thinking of the past. Maybe a government job was all right for our parents, they wanted to serve their country after Independence. And perhaps it once was the place where you could make a difference, but no longer. The inertia, red tape and small-mindedness kills you. Now people sit on their asses and push files around all day. As an entrepreneur you can see the result of what you are doing. And it generates work.'

'But we are comfortably off, you have a secure position, your work is not demanding. Even now, we spend so little time together, what will it be like with longer hours?'

'I miss you too,' said Hemant absently. 'But I am not starting the business immediately. I can get a loan more easily if I am at the bank, and the company, my dear, will be registered in your name.'

'And what will I be doing?' inquired Astha.

'Making TVs.'

'TVs? What market is there for TVs? All you get are rubbishy programmes, like *Krishi Darshan*, *Chitrahaar*, and half an old black and white Hindi movie on Saturday with the other half on Sunday.'

'You wait, Az, TVs are the thing of the future. In developed countries, TV has taken over the culture, and here too, when

64

colour comes to India . . .' He paused and, stirred by his vision of the future, put his arm around his wife.

His wife had less imagination. 'What will happen?' she asked.

'Do you know how much profit margin there is on a colour TV?'

'No, I don't know, and what's the point, there is no colour, even if we do make the sets.'

'You wait and see.'

Well, thought Astha, at least we have the security of the house if anything goes wrong.

Hemant applied for a plot of land with the Uttar Pradesh Industrial Development Corporation, and he was allotted one in the ambitiously called 'Electronic City' of Noida, Sector 16. For this as yet undeveloped piece of property he had to pay nine lakhs in installments, with ten per cent down payment. His connections in his bank made applying for a loan easy, a few trips to Lucknow, and the loan was routed through the Noida branch. He registered his wife's unit as a small-scale industry, something that Papaji's position in the commerce ministry facilitated.

Along with other erstwhile factory owners, Hemant waited for Noida to develop, in the meantime hiring a factory. He made his parents board members, and started his unit with a thousand black and white TVs a month. They had the standard 20-inch screen, sold at 1,850 rupees a set, with a profit margin of 20 per cent.

All this took a year to accomplish. Hemant now left the house every morning at seven to first visit the factory, and then make the long drive to Parliament Street. 'My family comes first,' he would say, as he juggled factory, bank and home.

Astha watched Hemant in his new avatar and felt moved by his grasp of the rules of getting on, by his ability to exploit situations rather than be defeated by them. Because he was her husband this meant that she too would not fall between the wide cracks of the world like her parents had done.

Somewhere along the way Hemant's attitude to Astha changed. She told herself it was only slightly, but it oppressed her. Occasionally she tried addressing this directly.

'Hemant, why is it that we never talk anymore?'

'We talk all the time.'

'About the business, the house, or Anuradha. Not about ourselves. Like we did before.'

'Grow up, Az, one can't be courting for ever.'

'Is it courting to be interested in the other person? Their feelings?'

'Why are you so childish? I work hard all day, and when I come home I want to relax. If you are feeling something, tell me. I have no time for all these games.'

'I want to be close to you, have a better relationship—' faltered Astha, knowing she had lost the argument before she had been able to define its parameters.

'There is nothing wrong with our relationship.'

'Are you saying there is something wrong with me?'

'You said it, not I.'

'But I'm not happy, so how can you . . .' She bit back words that might seem to indicate some insensitivity on his part.

'You think too much, that is the trouble.'

Astha stared at him nonplussed. 'I love you,' she said lamely, but she meant something else.

'I know, baby, I know,' said Hemant, drawing her to himself, caressing her. 'Maybe we should go out together more? Would you like that?'

'What about Anu? I don't like leaving her with Mummy so much. She looks after her when I am at school as it is.'

'We'll take her, you are the one with all the scruples. Come on, darling.' He slipped his hand under her sari, undid the first two hooks of her blouse and slid his hand over her breasts.

'Poor little things,' he cooed, 'Have I been neglecting them?'

'It's not that,' murmured Astha.

'Cheer up, baby. Make it nice for me to be with you.'

Baby. That is how he liked her. The look on his face became focused as he pulled her sari palla away and yanked at the rest of the hooks on her blouse, drawing it down from her shoulders and arms. Now he would bury his face in her breasts, pressing them against himself from either side, suck on her nipples, and they could both be babies together.

She found this soothing, and later scolded herself for being so demanding. Hemant was busy, Hemant was building their future, she had to be adjusting, that was what marriage was all about.

~

When Anuradha was four, Papaji retired. The tenants left, the family moved into their Vasant Vihar house, and Astha conceived again.

'God willing it will be a boy,' said her mother. 'I have asked swamiji's advice as to what offerings to make.'

'Nonsense, Ma,' retorted Astha uneasily. 'These people are not like that.'

'You are still such an innocent. What people say and what they do are two different things. Besides why is Hemant working so hard? For whom, if not his son?'

'It doesn't matter to Hemant,' said Astha valiantly.

'I hope for your sake you are right.'

A few nights later. Hemant laughing, 'Mummy is so sweet.'

Hemant often found the things his mother said or did sweet, so Astha paid not much attention. 'She is hiring a pundit to come every day and do some special pujas.'

'Why?'

'To ensure a grandson.'

'But puja may not make a difference, it may still be another granddaughter,' objected Astha in alarm.

'Don't worry, sweetheart, then we will try again, it's perfectly all right. Why do you get so tense for nothing?'

'But Hem, I do not wish to go on trying and trying until we get a son. It's very difficult with the teaching as it is.'

'Oh-ho, what is there in teaching? Hardly a serious job, you just go, talk to some children about poems and stories, organise a few clubs, and come back. If you do feel it is important, all the more reason not to mind if Mummy does some puja. Who knows it may yield good results?'

But Astha did get worked up, she couldn't help it. She tried to stay calm for the baby's sake, she took to meditation, she concentrated on peaceful thoughts. But she was not allowed to forget that everybody, her colleagues, her in-laws, her husband's friends' wives, her mother, the cook, the gardener and the part-time help all had an opinion about her baby's gender, and that almost universal opinion was that it would be a son and heir.

'Baby, it's you they want to be a boy,' Astha would whisper sometimes, 'are you a boy or a girl? I'll love you no matter what,' and she soothed the foetus she imagined so troubled with her troubled hands.

When Astha's son was finally born she felt a gratitude as profound as it was shamed.

'The family is complete at last,' said Astha's mother piously, feeling her own contribution.

Hemant's mother agreed, too happy in the birth of her grandson, carrier of the line, the seed, the name, to respond with her usual reserve to someone she increasingly felt was her social inferior.

The naming ceremony of the boy was carried out on a much grander scale than that of Anuradha's. Caterers were called, and they came early in the morning, setting up their fires in the narrow driveway. The priests arrived for an elaborate puja and havan. The letter taken out for the baby's name was 'h'. An auspicious sign, same letter as his father said everybody, and he was christened Himanshu.

Astha was given gold jewellery and a new sari. Anuradha and the child's aunts were given gold necklaces. The new-born was given gold guineas.

Astha was officially declared the mother of a son. Her status rose, and she pushed from her mind thoughts of what might have happened had she been unable to do her duty.

Himanshu was two months old when he raised his wobbly head from his mother's chest to smile at her, wet pink lips stretched over little toothless gums. Astha thought, he recognises me, and she smiled back, silently, across her chest, this human being and her connected. The baby, trying out the strength of his neck, began to laugh, which made Astha laugh too. Happiness flowed through her like a river, lapping at her mind. She never forgot this first exchange, it lived on in her memory, a link between a male and her that was joyous, simple, and unproblematic. So what if it was with her two-month son.

Astha often looked at her family, husband, daughter, son. She had them all. She was fulfilled. Her in-laws frequently commented, 'Woman is earth,' and it is true she felt bounteous, her life one of giving and receiving, surrounded by plenty. Visitors to the house would say, 'A mother's love' and then trail off, words collapsing into significant silence, which in turn washed over Astha and made her feel that she had partaken of the archetypal experiences marked out for the female race.

III

Between Anuradha's birth and Himanshu's, Hemant changed from being an all-American father to being an all-Indian one.

After he came home the last thing he wished to bother about was taking care of a child.

'It's your job,' he said.

'That's not what you thought when we had Anu,' replied his wife. 'I can't do everything myself. It's tiring.'

It was also boring, though this was not acknowledged.

'It's woman's work,' said Hemant firmly. 'Hire somebody to help you, or quit your job.'

'This is our son, the one you wanted so much. It's nice if we look after him together.'

'Send him up to Mummy if you can't manage.'

Astha was struck dumb. Were Mummy and he inter-changeable?

'And,' continued Hemant, 'my son is going to be very lucky for us.'

'Oh Hemant, how?' asked Astha with an effort that wasn't noticed.

'Wait and see.'

~

Hemant had invested in the future with his TV project, and was now about to witness the fruits of his foresight. Three months before the Asiad of 1982, the Minister for Information and Broadcasting declared that India would go colour: we have a certain dignity to uphold, an image to project. The games will be beamed internationally, conveying the pomp and splendour, hopes and aspirations of a developing nation. How can all this be done in black and white, when colour technology is prevalent worldwide? It is a question of marching with the times.

The Left protested: such a priority is elitist, false and a waste of precious foreign exchange. When the nation is still poor and backward, when electricity, water, roads, education and basic health care have yet to reach hundreds of villages, why should we develop a totally useless technology that will neither feed nor clothe?

But whether the technology was useless or not, whether it would help the nation or not, it was there to stay. Hemant now needed to travel to South East Asia; the indigenous black and white TV was possible to piece together locally but colour expertise was still not available in India. He resigned from the bank and security, to devote himself full-time to risk and money.

Hemant placed his first order in South Korea, for twenty thousand colour TV kits. Along with the order came a manager to train the workers. Local contribution involved the assembly of the TVs, the wooden cabinet, testing, selling and service. The final product was advertised as manufactured under foreign supervision, long after the initial foreigner had left.

Four times a year Hemant travelled. The glamour of international references entered the house, as he flew to South Korea and Japan looking for the best deals. He always went alone, always made sure his trips included at least two weekends, which he claimed he needed in order to establish personal contacts. He invariably came back in great good humour, with generous presents for everyone: perfume, chocolate, sweaters, jeans, toys, Japanese dolls, games for the children, underwear for Astha, toiletries, soaps, creams, shampoo, kitchen and electronic equipment. Gradually their house acquired the gloss of a house with money.

Astha was now virtually a single mother. Beleaguered by job, small children and house, she sometimes toyed with the idea of resigning from school, but between her marriage and the

71

birth of her children, she too had changed from being a woman who only wanted love, to a woman who valued independence. Besides there was the pleasure of interacting with minds instead of needs.

At school she had grown to be her principal's right-hand woman, appreciated and valued for one tenth the work she did at home, and paid for it too. Her salary meant she didn't have to ask Hemant for every little rupee she spent. With two children, family obligations, entertainment and holiday costs, the travelling involved in a new business, the uncertainty of business itself, rising prices, she knew Hemant would prefer her to bear her small expenses herself. As it was he spent enough on her clothes and jewellery that she always looked well turned out.

And so the once looked-down-upon job had become dear. She couldn't leave it. Nor could she go on relying too much on her mother-in-law for help with the children, it led to remarks from mother-in-law to Hemant to Astha which left her seething with anger and resentment.

Thus began the search for a maid. A succession of women filed through their flat, but they either came with large families, or they had insufficient references, or they stole, or they were lazy.

Hemant felt Astha was guilty of mismanagement, it could surely not be that no ayah was right? After all he managed a factory with four hundred workers.

'Why can't you train these servants properly?' he demanded.

'I do try,' she said, not liking to acknowledge how inadequate she felt with all of them. 'I was all right with Bahadur, (their cook) and the two part-timers.' (To wash clothes, clean the dishes, swab the floor, and dust the rooms.)

'Then don't hire one.'

'I need someone to help me,' said Astha bitterly, wondering how much her husband really knew of her life.

'Have all the help you want,' went on Hemant carelessly, 'only learn how to manage it.'

The search continued till Bahadur, their cook, went home to Nepal on annual leave, and brought back a widow.

'My sister,' he said, introducing her laconically. 'See if you like her.'

Astha looked at the woman. She had a broad flat face, slitted eyes and a wooden expression.

'Have you done domestic work before?' asked Astha, beginning with the standard questions, while wondering whether this woman was Bahadur's blood sister, cousin sister or village sister, and whether they were sleeping together.

'Mala knows everything,' said Bahadur interrupting. 'Try her.' There was something about the woman's straight gaze that appealed, and she was employed. Mala's appeal grew when Astha discovered how quick and capable she was. She was fast, she was clean, she needed to be told nothing twice. When Astha and Hemant went out she made sure the children had their meals on time, and that they were in bed by nine. She even made sure Anuradha finished her homework, and this while being illiterate.

Mala had some bad qualities. She stole food and clothes, she answered back, she took her time coming from her quarter upstairs, she became deaf when it suited her, and on Bahadur's days off she tended to develop illnesses from which she did not fully recover till he came back.

Unfortunately for Astha this usually happened on weekends, when Hemant was around.

'I am going to fire that bloody woman,' ranted Hemant the last time Mala had fever.

'She can't help it,' defended Astha.

'She is shamming.'

'How can we prove that?'

'She is like this because you encourage her.'

'How do I encourage her?'

'I saw her going out with Bahadur.'

'He said he was taking her to the doctor. Do you want me to take her to the doctor instead?'

'She thinks she can get away with anything.'

'I'm sure she'll be all right soon.'

'Where's Mala?' whined Himanshu, who was listening.

'See? You make the children too dependent on her.'

'She helps look after them, it's natural they should like her.'

'You treat her as though she was one of the family. You have to know how to handle servants.'

'I can't behave in any other way.'

'She's shamming,' Himanshu piped up insistently, wanting to be heard.

'She's sick darling, don't you get sick sometimes?' said Astha.

~

It was in this two children, husband, servants, job scenario that Astha started to have headaches. Years after she would remember the first time it happened, thinking that as a herald of what was to come, it might have announced its arrival in her life a little more gently, allowing her time to get used to this pain in her forehead, this throbbing at her temples, this stretching of the skin around her eyes.

She had laid the table for dinner, and they had all sat down to eat when she discovered she had forgotten the water. She rose from her chair, and in that moment, between getting up and standing, in the moment that hung between a bent body and a straightened back, it appeared. Just above her nose, at the inner corner of her eyebrow. She pressed the spot, and the pain promptly shot off in neat lines across her eye socket. It will disappear as suddenly as it came, she thought, carefully pouring the water into everybody's glasses.

The heaviness in her head increased as she ate. If she didn't lie down soon, she might fall headlong into her plate, banging herself against the table, startling the family.

'I'm going to lie down,' she managed.

'Are you ill?' asked the husband, looking at his wife's wrinkled eyebrows and drawn face.

'I'll be all right. Just a little headache.'

How the children were put to bed, when Hemant came to the room, Astha did not know. Through the night the pain grew worse. Nausea came upon her, she could no longer stay lying. She got up and sat outside, maybe the cooler air would help. It didn't.

As she bent to retch in the toilet, she hoped that now she would feel better. But though the queasy feeling gradually subsided, the throbbing was still there. Her limbs were shaking, she had to lie down again. Sometimes it seemed, if she lay on the hurting side, that felt better, sometimes she felt that no, the other side was better, and she kept gingerly turning her head trying to pin the point of meagre comfort.

Gradually towards morning, when the sky lightened, and the pain began to recede, she fell asleep.

The next day, the whole world seemed new. She was still in one piece, that terrible thing had gone. Her head felt delicate, it had gone through some bad times and needed to be treated gently.

'Are you all right now?' asked Hemant, looking concerned.

'Yes, I'm better,' she replied.

'What happened to you?'

'I don't know.'

She took leave from school and sat around the whole day, not using her eyes to read, not using her mind to think. She dusted and tidied, mindless labour that soothed and kept her busy. She hoped that what had happened to her the night before was a one time thing.

Soon it became clear that her headaches had arrived to stay. Stress made them worse, going out in the sun made them worse, sleeping too little, too late made them worse, eating the wrong kinds of food made them worse. Slowly her life changed to accommodate her headaches. She learned to dread each small twinge, was it going to be bad or medium? Maybe she was tired, should she lie down and rest? Or maybe it was anxiety, should she meditate, shut her eyes, ignore the throbbing, clear her mind of images, and focus on a spot of light between her eyebrows? The last was the most difficult, but her GP had said there was nothing physiologically wrong with her, it was all in her mind. He prescribed some painkillers, but they only gave momentary relief, making her dull and drowsy, with greater chances of having a headache the next day.

Her mother took her to a homeopath in her neighbourhood in Jangpura. 'My daughter is not well, doctor, she suffers from tension. Little things upset her, and she gets a headache.'

The homeopath, a well-known one in that area, looked concerned. 'Tension,' he stated, 'the disease of modern life. The secret of health is a balanced mind.'

'I try and be calm,' said Astha earnestly, 'but still I have headaches, and the pain lasts quite long.'

'Right side or left?'

'Usually right.'

'Front or back of the head?'

'Eyebrows. One or the other, never both.'

'Morning or evening?'

'Any time. Occasionally I wake up with a headache, at other times it comes in the afternoon or evening.'

'Which season?'

'All.'

'Hot or cold suits you?'

'Cold.'

'Sun or shade?'

'Shade.'

Etc. etc. etc.

Astha left the homeopath clutching Sanguinaria and Belladonna, 30x. Four times a day, alternately. Come after two weeks.

She dutifully took the Sanguinaria and Belladonna four times a day alternately. She kept a diary of her headaches. Once to twice a week. Hemant felt homeopathy was mumbo-jumbo, and took her to an ENT specialist. The specialist looked up Astha's nose and informed her husband that with such a deviated septum, it was a wonder that Astha could breathe properly, in fact if you notice, her mouth is open.

Astha shut her mouth quickly.

And of course she is going to have headaches. Time will not improve her condition.

At the thought of everything going from bad to worse, all power of decision left Astha.

The family took a second opinion, and surgery was decided upon.

Astha was in hospital four days. Her nose was heavily bandaged and hugely swollen. She could hardly breathe. It was not a good beginning to a life of easy breathing, and a head that didn't pain.

Hemant spent a part of every evening with her, while Papaji supervised in the factory.

'Poor little baby,' he murmured as he stroked her hand, 'does it hurt?'

Astha nodded, and tears rolled down either side of her bandaged nose. She tried to talk, but then her nose moved, it hurt more, and the tears came faster.

'Baby, don't talk,' said Hemant tenderly. Astha wished to capture his expression in her heart for ever. She looked more beseeching, more piteous, and Hemant pressed a soft kiss under the swollen lump, lingering long on the salty lips.

'How are the children doing?' croaked Astha.

'Do not worry,' said Hemant, head of the household, the type of person his wife could depend on, poor little thing. 'Mala is very reliable when you are not there. She knows she can't try her funny business with me. Besides they love being with Mummy, she thinks they are not dressed well enough, and has bought both of them new sets of clothes.'

After he left, 'How good Sa'ab is,' said the day nurse with a sigh. 'Coming to see you every day. Not every husband is so nice.'

77

'Yes, he is,' said Astha.

'Love marriage?' asked the night nurse.

'No.'

'Arranged is best,' said the night nurse with an even larger sigh, and then proceeded to tell the story of how her husband had first seduced and then married her sister. She could hardly bear to speak to him when he came home at night, that is why she had taken up this job, otherwise she came from a respectable family where the women didn't work, but now what else could she do, it was very bad madam, her sister looked after all the children and ran the house.

After her operation, Astha came home, waited for her headaches to go and life to become pain free. But the headaches continued, and Hemant was naturally not as attentive as he had been in the hospital.

If that nurse could see her now, her envy would be greatly diluted, thought Astha as she fretted over absent husband, and often absent children as well.

Where were they? Upstairs. Five days had been enough to establish this pattern. When she called them down, this was seen as objecting to their being with the grandparents. She tried talking to Hemant about this.

'It upsets the children's routine if they are up for so long,' she protested. 'And if they eat so much junk, their appetite is ruined for dinner.'

'You fuss too much. Besides their Dada Dadi are lonely. They complain they do not see enough of the children.'

'I send them up whenever I can, Hem, you know that.'

'Yes, but you know how it is with old people, they think they have little time left, all rubbish of course, but if it cheers them to have the children, why not?'

'What about me? As it is when I am in school Himanshu is upstairs. When I come home I want the children. I hardly have you, I should have them.'

Tears came to her eyes. More tears for Astha, poor thing.

She was climbing a mountain, and when she reached the top her face sweating, her heart going at its fastest, all she could see was another mountain. As she gazed at the jagged edges, her head began to ache, and the blood that was pounding in her heart obliged by moving to her head and pounding there.

Hemant rolled his eyes, and drew out a handkerchief to dry her face. 'What rubbish,' he repeated. 'It is all your imagination. When don't you have me? You are the one who keeps wanting to stay at home with the children, or your school work, or your books when we are invited to parties, or when I want to go to the club.'

'How can you say that? I always come with you.'

'And hate it, don't deny it. Half these invitations I refuse because of you. I am the one who is lonely, and without company.'

By what sleight of hand had their problems become identical?

~

She continued with her sketching, but found herself scribbling poetry, her father's encouragement more firmly in her mind now than when it was first given. She wrote about gardens and flowers, the silent dark faces of gardeners tending plants and never getting credit. She wrote about love, rejection, desire and longing. The language was oblique, but it was her own experience endlessly replayed.

Writing alleviated the heaviness within her, a heaviness she found hard to deal with. Discussing her feelings with Hemant usually led to argument, distance, and greater misery. In the struggle to express herself she found temporary relief.

After Astha had written about two hundred poems, she felt she needed to go somewhere with them. Publication would make her work seem less futile, but how to get there? She started revising them, typing them out on the small portable typewriter Hemant had brought back from the States.

After she did twenty she showed them to Hemant. As a man of the world, she trusted his sense of how to do things.

'Poems?' he remarked, looking pleased. 'I didn't know you were still writing.'

Astha smiled and said, yes, she was still writing.

The last he had seen her poems had been on their honeymoon, he reminisced, while Astha smiled some more. 'That was about a lake,' he went on.

'I don't write about things like that now.'

'You don't?'

'I've lost interest in Nature. I'm older, I think differently,' said Astha.

'But you look as young,' responded Hemant automatically. He put his arm around her for a moment before turning his attention to her writing.

Astha waited nervously. It was the first time anyone was seeing her poems. Hemant frowned, shuffling through the twenty typewritten sheets. To his wife's horror he started reading one out in a puzzled voice:

Changes

The eventual release from pain
In the tearing relentless separation
From those in habit loved

Can come so slowly
It seems there will never be a day
Of final peace and tranquillity

Who promised me, that if I
Did gaze upon reality
Accept it, embrace it, befriend it

I would never suffer again
But no matter how many times
I heave the doorways of my soul

To let the chill light in
The darkness grows silently
To hide me in the break of day.

Hemant stared at her. Astha cringed. 'Actually, forget it,' she said. 'They probably need more working over.'

'But I am here to help you,' said Hemant genially. 'I personally thought the one you wrote in Srinagar was very good. I said so at the time, didn't I?'

Yes, you did, you did, you did. But now it's all changed, and I want to bang my head against the wall because you never understand anything. 'I thought you might help me in deciding what to do with them,' she said tense and calm.

Hemant continued riffling through the papers, sparing her the embarrassment of more loud reading.

'You don't like them?'

'I don't know what to make of them. Look, I am no reader, but they sound rather bleak, don't you think?'

'Do they?'

'Good heavens, Az, they are all about cages and birds, and mice, and suffering in situations that are not even clear. There is not one happy poem here.'

'Poems are about emotions,' defended Astha. Maybe now he would ask her why she felt sad and they could really talk.

'What kind of emotions? This person sounds positively neurotic.'

'I don't think so.'

'If others read these poems, they might actually think you weren't happy.'

'No, no, they are not about me,' said Astha quickly.

'I know that. But people are so quick to put two and two together and come up with five, quick to gossip, you know Az.'

'Perhaps I should test that by sending them somewhere,' said Astha looking down, not wanting to see his face.

Hemant looked doubtful. 'Well, I don't know, it's up to you.' He held out the poems and she took them forlornly.

That night she thought long and hard of 'Changes'. How self-indulgent it had sounded when Hemant had read it out. And this was one she had considered her best, evocative and moving. Maybe he was right, they were all too alike, she would be exposing herself to the world.

She gave up writing and continued rather sadly to draw, sketching with the soft pencils and coloured charcoal that Hemant got her from Japan. Nobody could put two and two together about painting, say it was negative rather than positive, say she should paint lakes in Kashmir instead of mice, birds and cages. Maybe one day she could do something with her art, but for now her school and herself were audience enough.

~

That summer Astha's mother announced, 'I am going to Rishikesh for a month.'

'Why?' asked Astha.

'Swamiji is giving a course.'

'So? You listen to him here, don't you?'

'His ashram is by the banks of a river. It will be a different experience.'

'I think you should stay here,' said Astha uneasily.

'In my stage of life one is free from places. Soon I will be retiring. I have to think of what to do – where to go.'

'You can stay with us,' said Astha, who had not learned the futility of making this statement.

'Why don't you come too?' asked her mother with equal futility. 'It will help your headaches.'

'I'm all right,' said Astha. She looked at her mother, who was smiling benignly. Astha became suspicious, it was not like her mother to smile, and that too at nothing in particular.

*

'Ma is going to Rishikesh,' said Astha to Hemant that evening.

'Why?'

'She says she is free of places.'

'Very foolish of your mother.'

'Talk to her.'

'I will, as soon as I find the time,' said Hemant.

Which turned out not to be before she left.

From the banks of the Ganga in Rishikesh Astha's mother sent her a parcel containing a letter, a commentary on the *Gita*, and a small booklet entitled *The Purpose of Life*.

Dearest daughter,

How are you?

The air here is pure, and the scenery is beautiful. Hemant, you and the children should come. I will book a room. Everything is on me. It will do you good to meet Swamiji. He is so wise, just seeing him is satisfaction. He is also asking you to come. Everything is on me.

I am sending you two books that Swamiji has written. Read them every day. In ourselves alone is peace. Even when we know how difficult it is to change ourselves, still we expect others to change, and are unhappy when our expectations are not met. Remember that. It will help with your headaches also.

If you were to hear Swamiji you would realise that to keep a relationship going I should ignore the dark side, i.e. weaknesses of a person. Accept without condition if you want to live in peace. Any relationship can be beautiful if you nurture it. In time of difficulty don't lose heart. Freedom from all complexes is essential. Don't assert your ego – don't argue. Employ wisdom to solve the problem. You are committed to ME says Lord Krishna.

Accommodation and acceptance keep families together. What you cannot change accept gracefully, cheerfully as prasad for the Lord. Create a home where you are. Such a person is free from sorrow. Every understanding requires composed mind. Worst thing in life is anger. Read the *Gita*, especially chapter xiv.

With a thousand blessings for a long and happy life,
Ma

Astha stared at this communication. Where did these thoughts come from, what was happening to her mother, a helpless widow, with her child too caught up in the web of daily life to go and free her parent from another web. If only Hemant had talked to her mother, but then why should she rely on Hemant every time.

When the mother came back after her month in Rishikesh, she made it a point to have her stay over often. The mother prowled around, pointing out the wasteful habits of the servants, the dirt in various corners of the house, the children's thinness and bad eating habits, and Astha's neglect of her in-laws.

Reduced to a nervous wreck, Astha took her anger out on the children. 'Don't scold them,' her mother's soft voice filtered unctuously through her shouts, making the children behave worse than ever. 'They are only children.'

How come, thought Astha resentfully, this thought never occurred when she was young?

'Swamiji has taught me a great deal,' continued Astha's mother, reading into her daughter's silence. 'In the old days I was ignorant. Now I know better. If I made mistakes with you, I do not want you to make them with your children. All too soon this time will go. Let them enjoy their childhood.'

Astha felt hunted. Nothing she could do was right.

Her mother introduced her to Mrs Reddy, short, plump, grey hair pulled back, widowed colleague and original introducer to Swamiji. 'Tell her,' she ordered, 'how much going to the classes will help her.'

'Behen, it is all right. When the time is right for her, she will come herself,' said Mrs Reddy.

'Tell her,' insisted the mother, concerned about her daughter's happiness.

'The Hindu religion,' opined Mrs Reddy, 'is wide, is deep, capable of endless interpretation. Anybody can get anything they want from it, ritual, stories, thoughts that sustain. But first you have to realise your need.'

'She is always so tense and angry,' complained the mother.

'I don't need religion, whatever I am,' said Astha firmly, while the two older women looked sorrowful.

The time came for Astha's mother to retire.

'I must leave this flat, beti,' said the mother. 'It is too expensive for me.'

'Of course you will come and live with us, Ma,' said Astha.

Tradition reared its obdurate head. 'What'll his mother think?'

'What'll she think? Nothing. She lives upstairs. It is not as though you are taking away her space. Besides Hemant is doing well enough for one mother-in-law not to be considered a drain on his resources.'

'It doesn't look nice.'

'To whom? To whom doesn't it look nice?'

'To me.'

'I wish you wouldn't be so stick in the mud, Ma. Why didn't you have a son to look after you when you were old, if you cannot take anything from a daughter? Why did you stop with me?'

'I have talked to Swamiji,' responded the mother. 'He also thinks one must be independent.'

'What does Swamiji know? Parents belong to their children.' By now Astha was grinding her teeth with impatience. When had this swami become so important that all Astha was saying meant nothing.

'I am thinking of moving to Rishikesh.'

'Rishikesh? You are going to live there all your life?' Astha was appalled.

'Arre, who knows how long one is going to live? The atmosphere should be pure, one should lead a life of virtue and truth, where and how does not matter.'

'What if you fall ill? Who will look after you? Swamiji?'

'One cannot live in fear,' said the mother severely.

'Nor in isolation. You will be lonely.'

The mother was silent. So was Astha, what could one say about loneliness?

'Swamiji is insisting that I take my time and think about it,' said the mother finally, 'he is not agreeing for right now.'

'And a good thing too,' said Astha baffled. She felt that in some way she had been tested and found wanting. She envied Hemant his relatively straightforward relationship with his parents. They demanded from him material care – which he gave, grandchildren – which he gave, emotional concern and physical presence – which he gave. Duties, responsibilities, obligations, all seemed clear.

A few weeks later Astha's mother gave up the lease of her flat, and got rid of most of her belongings. 'Material possessions are a burden,' she informed her daughter.

Her daughter did not feel the same way. She loved the pretty things that decorated her home, her books, her lamps, her carpets, her cutlery, tableware, linen, furniture, everything that Hemant and she had bought together. Now she wanted to add the twelve boxes of books that had formed the beds and the divan at her parents' place.

'Are you mad? We don't have the room,' declared Hemant.

'We do, we can build shelves.'

'Come on, Az, donate them to a library. We can't clutter up our house with a lot of old books. And you know you don't read them.'

'That's not the point.'

'What is the point? Books are meant to be read, and in a library they will be of use. Better looked after too.'

'Please, Hemu, my father's books.'

'Don't be so sentimental, Az. I will talk to Ma, you will see she will agree.'

Astha's mother agreed to such an extent that the books were donated to a library before Astha even knew about it.

Astha was devastated. 'Why did you do that?' she screamed at her mother. 'They were mine as well. I loved them.'

'But you never showed any great interest in them when you were growing up,' protested the mother.

'That was then. This is now. Don't you care about Papa's memory? How could you do this to him, to me?'

'People do not live in their things, beti. Besides,' added the mother, 'it is Hemant's house, and he said there was no room.'

'Then who am I? The tenant? We could have found room, we could have built bookshelves, done something, we could at least have discussed it.'

'You know how much work they were. Every year take them out, dust them, and then they get infested by silverfish, accumulate dust and space. In a library at least they will be read.'

'You sound like him. At the very least I would have kept a few, or do you think I too should not be weighed down by material possessions?'

The mother sniffed, looked martyred and misunderstood. What was the use of saying anything, thought the daughter, the books had gone, and all the screaming in the world was not going to bring them back. But together her husband and her mother had deprived her of the dearest part of her father, and continued before her eyes to be oblivious of their crimes.

Astha's mother was now free to leave for Rishikesh.

'When will you be back?' asked Astha anxiously, as she dropped her mother at the station.

'I don't know beti, let me see how it goes.'

'I wish you hadn't turned to religion, Ma,' said Astha feeling as though her mother had cheated on her, manifesting a strange turn of mind that her daughter could neither follow nor understand.

'We are all looking for peace of mind,' said her mother. 'Swamiji will guide me.'

The train came and she left. Astha stood on the platform and watched her mother leave the city where she had spent all her working and married life. Now with just a bedroll and a trunk she was embarking on a pilgrimage, searching for a community she could call her own, with no possessions to weigh her down.

The months passed. Astha's mother showed no signs of returning. Her letters, about love, peace, renunciation and knowledge, revealed nothing.

Dear Beta,

Perform action with the full understanding that you have no control over the result. Success and failure have to be faced by everyone. By being thoughtful, reflective and prayerful we can overcome the spirit of 'I'ness that dominates all our actions. This approach keeps families intact and we don't become insecure. We have a set up to relax in, this paves the way to security, and to self understanding.

The meaning of life is struggle. There are challenges in all walks of life, how to tackle them is the question, not to run away from home, work, society and obligations. Perform your duties with detachment. Learn to give and not take. When you develop the spirit of giving intelligently, there is peace in the mind. Most of our problems are due to discontent with what we have.

Give my love and blessings to dear Hemant, Anu, little Himanshu, and to your mother and father-in-law.

With many more blessings to my dearest daughter,
Ma

Once or twice Astha asked Hemant, 'Won't you go and see her, convince her that her place is with us?' but Hemant was clearly not concerned enough for action. Astha's suspicions hardened, maybe her mother was right, it would not be so good for her to live with her daughter. She wished she had a house that was more clearly hers.

'I need to go and see my mother,' she finally said to her husband. 'She might end up staying in Rishikesh. She probably feels neglected.'

'That's absurd,' said Hemant, 'why should she feel neglected? Old people turn to religion. It is natural.'

'It is not,' said Astha indignantly, 'only when they have no other choices.'

Hemant looked at her. 'Religion is a choice as much as any other thing,' he said. 'If she decides to stay in Rishikesh, it must be because she is happy there. Besides I have told you I will talk to her.'

'Like when?'

'When she comes.'

Astha paused. She felt her mother's condition was partly Hemant's fault. Had he shown more concern . . . Tersely she pointed out, 'I know you had no time, but this cannot be left any longer, I need to see if she is all right.'

Hemant took umbrage. 'If that was the way you felt, you should have gone before,' he said. 'I have enough things on my plate.'

'And so I will. As soon as the children's exams are over.'

It was five o'clock on a Saturday morning of the following week, when Hemant took his wife and two children to the New Delhi Railway Station. He bought his wife a *Femina* and *Stardust*, for his children chips and chocolate, and sat with them in the compartment till the train left. 'Bye-bye Papa, bye Papa,' said his children. 'Why aren't you coming with us, Papa? See you soon, Papa.' Papa wrapped his arms around them, gave Astha a brief pat and jumped onto the platform.

The children passed the five hours to Haridwar having their breakfast, playing games, fighting, eating rubbish, dozing, and going to the bathroom, while Astha was divided between looking after them, and looking out of the window. The fields on either side had wheat growing in them. Her mother must have looked at this scene and felt alone. If she were not weighed down by children, husband, job, she too might become nothing, no different from the dots of people they were passing, lost on the flat plains of northern India.

At Haridwar they got down, and walked across the road to the depot, from where they were to catch a bus to Rishikesh.

'Bus to Rishikesh?' said Information. 'Half an hour. I will announce.'

Astha and her children settled on one of the benches watching the others sitting, squatting, or sleeping on the floor. The hall was large and spacious. Already the air felt cooler than in Delhi, the breeze less polluted.

They sat and sat and watched bus after bus leave. Finally after twenty-five minutes Astha asked Information, 'When will you announce the bus that you said was leaving for Rishikesh in half an hour?'

'It is already leaving,' he said languidly pointing to a bus lumbering away.

There was no time to get angry. 'Quick,' shouted Astha, grabbing the one suitcase, and shoving the smaller bags at her children.

They ran towards the slowly moving bus, their feet slamming the dust while the passengers stared at them curiously. Astha banged on its side, 'Stop, stop,' and the passengers hands echoed theirs in the banging, and the bus did in fact stop as it turned towards the exit.

Feeling stupid and incompetent – you can't even catch a bus – Astha pushed her children up the steps and clambered on. Inside she distributed Anuradha and Himanshu where she found space on the hard shiny rexine seats, each packed with three to four people. The suitcase she manoeuvred in the crowded aisle, the packages she held in her lap, and with her attention wandering between her children, the green trees, the butterflies, the narrow road slowly rising, the mountains beyond, the tightly oiled plaits and shiny magenta nylon ribbons of the little girl in front, she passed the hour to Rishikesh.

They finally stopped in a small and dusty square, which appeared to be the depot. Lugging their baggage to a group of waiting scooters, Astha gave the address of the ashram, and they bumped their way through narrow roads, lined with refuse and running sewers, the scooter wallah blaring away at every pig, cow, mongrel, rickshaw, two-wheeler and pedestrian in his way.

'What's that?' asked Himanshu pointing to some enormous black creatures, rooting in the profuse garbage, ugly as sin.

'Pigs, darling.'

'But they are not pink,' he objected.

'That is just in books, stupid,' said Anuradha. She herself was seeing a black pig for the first time, but her grasp of the difference between reality and theoretical knowledge was infinitely quicker than her brother's.

It was late afternoon by the time they reached the ashram doors, set in the middle of high walls. As they stepped into the compound, it seemed another world, clean, green, spacious, its long low buildings hidden by trees and shrubs on either side of a central open space. At the far end they could see benches, more trees and a paved terrace overlooking mountains across the river.

Astha's mother was waiting with her arms open to receive her children, to show them her place, peaceful, serene, and at its centre a swami who contained the clues to life.

In the ashram Astha could see how her mother had changed. Her movements were confident, her smile less tentative. She had made friends, she spent a lot of time walking around the terrace, and many hours reading the notes she had taken during Swamiji's lectures. 'Look,' she said, showing her notebook to Astha:

Sleep, the state of being most pure. In sleep there is no thought, no emotion, no subject, no object. Sleep is the state where there is no 'I'. The state in itself no different from death, or previous lives in which we are in identical states – we need sleep not only to survive (you can't be awake if there is no sleep) but in order to understand reality.

'What on earth does all this mean?'

Astha's mother looked conspiratorial. 'Ask Swamiji, he will tell you. He's a very learned man, he studied fifteen years before his own swami sent him into the world.'

'But when he lectures he does so with a mike,' criticised Astha. 'That is not very unworldly.'

'If you live in this world, you make it serve your aims. It is hard for him to speak continuously and loudly to such large audiences,' pointed out the mother protectively. 'So we insisted he have the mike.'

'A present from one of his disciples?' inquired Astha, thinking in an idle way, that as a teacher she too could do with a mike, and she never talked as much as this man.

'A present from me,' said her mother smiling that little smile again.

'He asked?'

'He never asks.'

That evening Astha spent a lot of time staring at the swami upon the dais, who, after his lecture was immediately surrounded by his devotees, many women, some men, some resident and some from town.

They were sitting in the pleasant lecture hall, next to the river. All sixteen fans were whirring. Groups of people, while waiting their turn with the swami, were comparing notes on what he had said: today he explained very well, today he used a lot of Sanskrit words, difficult to understand, but then really you need ten years to understand. What was it Swamiji said, when that man asked a question about the mind – to answer will take me six years, to comprehend will take you twelve. Swamiji was in form all right, how he makes you laugh sometimes, and how my life has changed since I started coming to the lectures, yes, you get mental peace, no doubt about that.

One man in so many lives. Certainly in her mother's. She turned to look at her. 'Don't you want to ask him anything?' she asked.

Her mother shook her head shyly. 'These people know so much more than me. Let them ask.'

As they came down the steps a breeze was blowing, and a pink tinge on the water reflected the sunset.

'Let us go to the temple,' said the mother.

Astha stared at her. 'Since when have you started going to the temple?' she asked. Her father had not believed in going to temples, and as a consequence nobody ever went.

'There is arti in the evenings, and one of the women here is a very good singer,' said the mother as Astha's question slid by her. 'Come,' she said, calling to the children, 'Anu, Himu, come, we are going to the temple.'

The temple was in another compound, small, white, with pink decorated columns and roof, facing the river front, lit with tube lights, and floored with marble. It was exquisitely clean with devotees waiting quietly for the evening prayers to begin. The mother sat at the back, Astha sat next to her, the children fidgeted and looked around.

The service lasted for forty-five minutes. Bhajan singing, praying, arti, offering bhog, receiving prasad, drinking holy water, and smoothing wet hand over head and eyes.

In the queue to receive prasad Anuradha asked, 'How come we don't do this at home?'

Astha didn't know what to say. We don't believe was not

strictly true, I don't have the time trivialised religion in a way that might be bad for her children, saying only old people prayed like this suggested that religion was only useful when you were feeble and decrepit. Instead she said, 'God is in our hearts, beti, and some of us do not believe in ritual. Maybe when Nani comes to Delhi, you can pray with her.'

'We will all do it together,' said Nani firmly, her eyes gleaming with the prospect of inducting her grandchildren into puja, ritual, Vedanta, and the sound beginnings of a Hindu life.

It was towards the end of Astha's visit that her mother said, 'I'm thinking of selling my land, and building a set of rooms in the ashram. Swamiji has agreed.'

'Live with us, Ma,' Astha said hopelessly, 'it is the best solution.'

'It doesn't look nice. Mother-in-law comes and never leaves.' Here the mother sighed, and looked at the waters of the river with a melancholy eye. 'It is so beautiful here, so peaceful,' she went on.

'You must be lonely, Ma,' said Astha. They were sitting on one of the benches overlooking the river. The children were running up and down the steps. The heat of the day had gone, the light was gentle, the water below them was turning dark.

'It is a lonely life,' said the mother, filling Astha with a dreadful sense of guilt.

'It is my house too. If people mind it is just too bad. I don't believe in all this shit about parents being the responsibility only of the sons.'

'After all Hemant's parents are staying with him, aren't they, not with their daughters.'

'His parents can't stay with the daughters, one is in America, and one—' Astha was going to say and one is staying with her in-laws, but changed it to, 'and one has a bad marriage, with a small house.'

*

94

Next morning at the lecture Astha again looked at her mother's teacher carefully. His beard was grey, there were little white spikes sticking up from his shaven head. He wore glasses, and the eyes behind them were gleaming, sharp, intelligent, she supposed compassionate – he was a swami after all – and how does one describe a swami's eyes? His legs were crossed, his foot waggled, his clothes all saffron. His voice was deliberate and quiet:

'There is pain and suffering in every life. When the burden becomes intolerable, we seek distractions, which in turn trap us. We develop a craving for pleasure and sensation, till finally we are at the complete mercy of our desires, which out of ignorance we have encouraged to grow into monsters.

'With desire comes dissatisfaction, and a dissatisfied man is full of misery, even if he has at hand the pleasures that the world can give him.

'We mistake gratifying our senses for living in the world. We act in order to be happy, and then we are surprised that the happiness does not last, and we look for other things, and the same pattern is repeated. Discontent is the cause of restlessness.

'All our pleasures are connected with our deeds. They have a beginning and an end. The fruits of our actions similarly have a beginning and an end. They are transient and can therefore never quench our longing.

'We breathe to live, but every breath draws us one step nearer to our end. In our body is our decay. We cannot alter this decay, the richest man in the world shares the fate of the poorest.

'Against the world we are weak. Hunger, thirst, cold, heat, flood, famine, storms, all these things create fear. We run seeking protection here and there, but the strongest protection against the world comes from knowledge that comes from within.

'It is only in a state of self-realisation that we can draw from the reservoir within to gain happiness. If we find contentment within ourselves, we will find good in all things. As the sun shines so shall the contentment within us light our lives and the lives around us.

'We protect our feet with shoes, we protect our body with clothes. We cannot be harmed by the stones in our paths, nor by the sun or the rain that falls on us. Similarly, those who have achieved self-realisation are contented in all circumstances. The troubles they encounter on their journey through life cannot hurt them.'

Astha listened, caught up in his words, like everybody else in the room. The swami looked beyond time, because he was bowed down by nothing. If examples were what one had to go by, he was a good example of what he preached. His face shone with non-attachment, though his disciples hung on to every word he uttered with fierce attachment.

All these people here were looking, looking for shoes to protect them from the rough paths they had to tread. She wanted shoes as well. She sat in front of the swami trying them on. For a wild moment she wanted to go up to him and beg, tell me what to do.

And he would tell her, what? She already knew. Misery springs from desire, desire springs from attachment, and that if she gave up all these things, she would be happy.

The weight in her chest increased. She had come to rescue her mother, and yet seeing her mother in that place, the person who seemed to need rescuing was herself.

She tried no more to prevent her mother from living in Rishikesh, or from selling her plot of land. Clearly her mother needed quite a bit of money if she were to live respectably in the ashram. It seemed crazy to sell a piece of property, whose value, now that the bridge was built, doubled practically every year, but when one gave up material possessions, one also gave up speculation in the future.

Another three days and Astha left.

In October that year, the sale of the plot went through.

'Dear child,' said Astha's mother, who was in Delhi for the signing of the papers, 'I have given Hemant part of the proceeds of the house.'

'Why? The money is for you, Ma.'

'I don't need so much. You can consider this your father's legacy.'

'They why give it to Hemant?' asked Astha bridling.

'Why not? He is a man, he knows about money. He will invest it for you and the children. I have discussed the whole thing with him.'

How had this happened? Hemant had found a buyer and checked the legalities of the sale, but even if he was the man of business, she wanted to participate in any decision concerning the money her mother chose to give her.

'Really, Ma, don't you think women can be responsible for their own investments?'

'Of course, but this was a lot. Are you suggesting I hand the whole thing over to you?'

No, Astha wasn't. The sad thing was that she herself would have felt nervous handling a large sum. Suppose she did something foolish, and it did not multiply fast enough, it would be through her arrogance that the money had not functioned in the optimum manner.

'Hemant is very clever, look at the way he does business, with no background,' went on the mother. 'You yourself have said he manages everything financial. It was the same with your father, I only did the household accounts.'

'You were earning too, Ma.'

'Yes, yes. But he looked after my tax saving, my provident fund, decided how much we should spend, how much to save, all that. After him, Hemant took over.'

'Yes, Ma.'

'He has promised to double the amount in a few years.'

Could Astha ever have made such a promise? Never, not even if the gates of hell opened and the stock market collapsed in her lap. She had better stick to her job, and what it earned her. Nobody thought it was anything. Nobody discussed it, speculated with it, promised to increase it at fantastic rates. She could do with it what she liked, take it to bed, chew it, shit rupees in the morning and nobody would bat an eyelid.

Her mother had delivered her into Hemant's hands. If her mother was at fault, so was her father, for managing the money, and teaching his wife that this was normal behaviour, so was her mother-in-law for bringing up Hemant to never regard women as beings to be consulted in their own lives, so was the Swamiji for teaching that only in detachment lies happiness, which lesson can be read in as many different ways as there are people and attachments.

After Astha's mother left, the money was discussed briefly and bitterly.

'Darling?'

'Dearest.'

'You know Ma's money?'

'I have several plans for it. It will be well invested, don't you worry. Long term for the children, shorter term for you.'

'Thank you darling. But I was wondering, you know, whether I could also have a say in what you do with it.'

Hemant began to frown. 'Don't you trust me?'

'Of course, of course, I trust you. It's not a question of trust, surely. You are my husband.'

'Exactly. So what's going on?'

'I wish to feel—' Here Astha paused and treaded carefully among the thickly laid minefields of income, expenditure, rights, responsibilities, knowledge, power, and dependency. 'I mean if I wasn't so ignorant about things concerning money, I wouldn't feel so stupid.'

Hemant relaxed. 'When I have finished I will explain everything to you. In fact I am glad you have brought this up. I have been thinking you should know what is going on. That way if anything happens to me, you will not be left in the dark.'

'But Hemu,' said Astha, 'I don't wish to be enlightened only because you might die, which I hope will not be for a long long time, and certainly not before me.'

Hemant smiled, 'We will die together in old age, huh?'

'Yes,' she replied, 'yes,' she repeated, 'yes,' she faltered. 'We will die together, I hope, but meanwhile, I feel so clueless about our financial situation. I know that in business things can be uncertain, so I thought that now that I have some money, it would be useful if I looked after it. That way I will gain experience.'

'Your mother gave me this money to manage, I didn't ask for it,' said Hemant coldly. 'She trusts me even if you don't.'

'That's not what I mean. I know she trusts you, certainly much more than she trusts me, but is it such a bad thing if I know how much is in my name and how I can have access to it?' Astha was pleading now, begging Hemant to understand. She meant nothing personal. She didn't want to feel dependent, that was all. Surely equals could relate better than master and slave?

'What has gotten into you I don't understand. I will tell your mother to give the whole thing to you, you will handle it yourself. She should have consulted you first, before she handed anything to me. In fact why didn't she ask you to look for a buyer and get a lawyer to check the sale deeds? You have been missing out on so many things that life is not worth living, isn't that so?'

Astha sat stunned. What kind of fool had she been to expect Hemant to understand? She had a good life, but it was good because nothing was questioned. This boat could not be rocked. She should paint that on a canvas and put it up on the wall, and stare at it day and night, so that its message burnt its way through her brain into her heart. This boat cannot be rocked.

Besides if the boat could not be rocked, what need did she have of money, or knowledge of investments? Hands that had grasped money, and felt it pass through their fingers were the ones capable of rocking boats. Hers were not.

The next morning, quickly she got her children ready and sent them off to school, quickly she had her tea, packed her breakfast to eat later, jamming an omelette between two slices of fridge cold bread and dripping violent red chilli sauce over the insides. Quickly, quickly she did all this, smiling, smiling all the while, so that no distress was palpable.

It was only in the staff room in school that Astha could be alone with her thoughts.

'Why so silent?' they asked? 'Are you ill?'

Astha shook her head. She looked at her colleagues, women she met every day, women whom she liked, whose lives ran smoothly, women who had no shadows between their husbands and themselves, whose husbands were 'him' and 'he,' and whose in-laws were 'they'. Whom among them could she tell that she had not been able to sleep? What reason could she give that they would not think self-indulgent?

'I'm fine,' she repeated, and opened the usual stack of brown-paper covered notebooks that laced each day's work.

IV

It was early in the year 1987, that the principal of Astha's school invited The Street Theatre Group to hold a workshop on their premises. The workshop would be held in the break between the final exams in March and the opening of the new school year in April.

The staff were not pleased.

As usual the Principal wants to attract attention to herself.

Just because she is interested in theatre, we are forced to be interested too.

They'll want staff volunteers, wait and see.

We have to correct exam scripts, prepare report cards, see to the merit lists, file an account of each child's progress in the school records – where is the time to do all this extra-curricular activity?

A gloomy silence descended. The Principal was not known to respect the convenience of her teachers.

Astha wondered whether she would be asked, she did not relish working in the holidays while her children were at home. She was very fond of Mrs Dubey but sometimes she felt that their special relationship caused her to be exploited. She had done enough for the school, the Principal should look elsewhere, she decided, readying herself for a tussle.

In which she lost.

'You need someone with more experience if an outsider is coming,' she tried objecting.

'With Aijaz you don't need experience,' said the Principal. 'For him any place is a stage, any person an actor. He has performed at factory gates, outside offices, at bus stops, in front of shops. He has dramatised issues like unemployment, atrocities against women and urban poverty. Indeed he is the voice of the underprivileged. That is his genius.'

He can take his genius elsewhere, thought Astha, why is he bringing it here.

'He is my brother's friend and is coming here on my personal request,' went on the Principal, somewhat coyly. 'This is a great opportunity.'

'It's my children's holidays.' The woman-to-woman approach.

'Bring them, they will benefit. Aijaz is a wizard. He is actually a history lecturer, but his knowledge of drama is immense. Besides writing his own plays and songs, he has adapted Brecht, Shakespeare, and Greek tragedy into Hindi. People grumble about the lack of activity in the school, but when it comes to giving our students exposure they come up with all kinds of objections. Where is the school spirit?'

Astha had no option but to agree.

Hemant was not pleased. He timed his trips to be free for his children's holidays.

'Why can't you stay at home? And why drag the children into this?'

'I had no choice,' said Astha. 'Anyway it will be good for the children to see schools not as elite as theirs. Anu was actually asking when were we taking her to Disneyland. All her school friends have been, she says. I don't believe her. Disneyland! Imagine!'

'Nothing wrong with wanting to go to Disneyland,' said Hemant.

'At this age! Why, I haven't been abroad yet.'

'We are not talking about you. If parents can afford to show their children the world, why not?' said Hemant. 'This is the eighties. We are not deprived Indians any longer.'

Astha felt there was something morally wrong with getting things without struggling for them, but she knew this view irritated Hemant. He was making more money at his age than their combined fathers at their retirement, and he didn't seem to have any intention of letting his children struggle. She turned the conversation to the topic at hand.

'Apparently Aijaz Akhtar Khan, the founder of The Street Theatre Group is very well known. He teaches history, and during the holidays he performs in slums, factories, streets, villages and small towns.'

'What's the point of that?'

'Create empathy, generate social awareness by having workshops that involve workers and students, bridge the class divide,' said Astha glibly, replicating that morning's exchange with her Principal.

'Culture-vultures,' snorted Hemant, 'why don't they do something real about the class divide, like creating jobs?'

'Not everybody can be a factory owner.'

Himanshu was delighted. His face broke into a slow and gleaming smile that went straight to his mother's heart. He was always wanting to come to his mother's school instead of his own.

Anuradha registered her brother's pleasure and loudly protested against the injustice being done to her.

'Why should I spend my holidays going to your school?' she demanded. 'Don't I go enough to my own?'

'I can't leave you here alone the whole morning. It's not classes, it's a drama workshop. You'll be doing fun things.'

'I don't want to do fun things. Besides Papa said he was going to spend fewer hours at the factory and take us out.'

'Well let him actually make the programme and then we will see,' said Astha with some irritation.

'I won't,' said Anuradha her eyes flashing, getting ready for a confrontation that would continue till collapse or victory. 'You can't make me. I'll spend my holidays with Dadi upstairs.'

Himanshu looked on piously, while Anuradha waited for the next round. 'Please beta,' said Astha, 'your Dadi then complains to me that she gets tired. You have so much energy she doesn't really know how to keep up with you. Come for a few days, if you don't like it you needn't continue. Promise.'

Once it was established that Anuradha was doing her mother a favour, it was easier to take her.

~

At first Astha did not pay much attention to Aijaz. He seemed quite capable of managing thirty-two children without her. He sat them in a circle on the stage. Do you know why people sit in a circle – so that there is no hierarchy – all of us have something to offer from backstage to front – what is the theatre about – communication – what kind? – drama – older than the written word – what did they think was the subject of drama – where did they find it . . .

How pedantic, thought Astha, is he giving the history of drama, are they going to do an exam, or is he going to get on with the workshop, which is why we are all here in the first place, I'm sure all the children are bored. And her mind wandered, till it came back ten minutes later to Aijaz explaining that the way man lived in society was politics and this affected everybody, literate, illiterate, powerful, powerless, poor, rich. He read out sections of the newspaper and asked how they would translate what was happening into drama for people who couldn't read? For example what would they do with the Babri Masjid–Ram Janambhoomi controversy?

The spot where Ram was born thousands of years ago some say is the exact spot where a masjid stands today. Is this fact or faith? If it is faith, is it sacrosanct? Are there ways in which faith can be motivated and played upon by political forces . . .

His voice faded, and Astha's mind turned to the religion consumed at home on one of her husband's TVs. Ever since the Ramayan was serialised, viewing it had become a ritual, insisted upon by the grandparents, strongly supported by Hemant.

And so, every Sunday morning, the family gathered upstairs before a ClearVision TV, twenty-inch screen, manufactured by the son of the house, and watched the story of the Ramayan. Week after week they agreed, this was the golden age of India, this is our noble heritage, now thoroughly debased, when justice flourished, when Hindus had pride, when a king showed responsibility towards his people, when duty, honour, devotion, truth and loyalty had a place in Ram Rajya. And today the birthplace of this king, our Lord, is occupied by a mosque, the shame of it, dismissing as nonsense the protest that it was not possible to really place the exact spot of a man's birthplace so many thousands of years ago.

Suddenly Astha saw the long arm of history twisted and refracted, till it popped out of a TV box, took them to Ayodhya and planted them on Ram Kot in front of the Babri Masjid.

She was sitting at the back of the stage, her arms around her knees, thinking all this, when she looked up and saw Aijaz looking at her. Uncertainly she smiled. 'What do you think, Astha?' he asked.

How had he found out her name? And from being indifferent to Aijaz, the single use of her name, created a pleasure in what she, unused to the ways of men outside marriage, saw as interest rather than a communication strategy.

'Do you think you can write the script?' he went on.

'Um,' Astha hesitated, 'I don't know anything about the Babri Masjid.'

Aijaz leaned towards her and said, 'Just a working script. Your daughter has volunteered your name. She says you write.'

'I am not really a writer, just a few poems,' said Astha surprised, her eyes on her daughter's back, with the hair curling down the white shirt.

Aijaz was used to persuading people. 'Just a simple working script which we can improvise on, Astha.'

He was focusing on her. She blushed.

Himanshu frowned. Was his mother being forced to do something unpleasant, but no, she was agreeing, she was participating in extra-curricular activities, doing the bit that wasn't necessary, volunteering despite her uncertainty about her capacities, because everything was worth trying.

Aijaz smiled, showing his even pearly teeth. Why does he smile like that, he knows he is charming, thought the newly appointed writer of scripts.

Going back in the scooter, Astha thought of the India International Centre, where her parents-in-law were members, and the library that only she was interested enough to use. There was bound to be something on the Babri Masjid there. As if reading her thoughts, Himanshu piped up, 'I'll help you, Mama.'

Anuradha snorted. 'You? You are so stupid. What can you do? Do you even know what the Babri Masjid is? Do you know where it is?'

Himanshu turned around and hit Anuradha in the stomach. Anuradha hit him back twice as hard, then once on the back for good measure. Astha slapped Anuradha's hand. Anuradha glared at her mother. Himanshu began to cry. Just then the scooter took a wrong turn inside the colony, and in the middle of shouting at her children, Astha had to break off and redirect the scooter wallah through the maze of Vasant Vihar. He insisted on charging ten rupees more, and that was the end of their first morning at the theatre workshop.

Later Astha had a talk with Anuradha. 'We are going to be together for fifteen days,' she said. 'And in that time I forbid you to call your brother stupid.'

Anuradha looked cunning. 'And after that?'

'Even after that. You can't go on calling someone stupid. It hurts their feelings.'

'But he is.'

'Even if he is.'

Anuradha looked victorious. 'See, you also think so.'

Astha stared at her daughter, 'Anu, what's the matter with you? Four years younger, what comparison can there be?'

'You are always taking his side.'

Why was it, thought Astha wearily, that love always had to be balanced by its opposite? She had a secret tenderness for Himanshu that her daughter targeted unerringly, battering her mother, shouting out her dislike, making even the love and hate in the world. She looked at Anuradha's contorted face, and angry eyes, and cajoled, 'I need help in writing a script. Himanshu can't help me.'

Anuradha looked wary. 'Don't try and flatter me,' she said.

'You mean what I'm saying is not true?'

For a moment Anuradha was out-manoeuvred.

'So, it'll have to be you,' continued Astha.

'When do we start?'

'This evening. We'll go to the library and get some facts first.'

'And leave Himanshu behind.'

'Absolutely. I'll send him upstairs.'

That evening Astha and Anuradha made for the library. As Anuradha looked at magazines, Astha quickly browsed through the books in the history section. There seemed to be no end of fuss around this mosque. Had there been a temple on this site, claimed to be the birthplace of Lord Ram? Had Babur ordered this temple destroyed? Had he compounded the arrogance of conquest by building a mosque bearing his name using materials from the temple? Zealous historians, pursuing evidence and rationality had gone into its structure, pillars, stones, inscriptions, had investigated Babur's diary, his religious and building habits, had cited examples of British divisive policies, but nothing had been able to quiet the controversy.

Astha stared at the picture of the Babri Masjid. What was it about this monument that had created so much bloodshed and fighting over two centuries? It was not even remarkable, squat and three domed, surrounded by trees. How could she effectively present its history, long and tortured, in a manner that was simple without distorting?

Over the weekend as she read through books and photo-copies she had made in the library, she thought that controversies need places, disputes need sites, not the other way around, and the Babri Masjid was one of them. Babri Masjid–Ram Janambhoomi. The amount of blood, hate, and passion for ownership these words evoked bathed each stone with a corrosive mixture, slashing through the surface so that it was no longer an old mosque. It was a temple, a birthplace, a monument to past glory, anything but a disused nesting place for bats. Despite all this it had endured for over four hundred years.

It was too much to handle as a play. She felt like giving up, but the thought of not having anything to show Aijaz drove her on. She gripped her pen, took a deep breath, and plunged.

She was still plunging when Hemant returned from the Sunday tea spent upstairs with his parents, bonding over business and politics.

'Back already?' she asked.

'It's been two hours,' he replied.

'Oh, I hadn't realised. This whole thing is very complicated,' said Astha.

'People make it so,' replied the husband. 'Otherwise what is there in an abandoned mosque? The government is too bloody soft on these Muslims, that is the problem.'

'Surely that is not the issue. Power seekers – on both sides – use religion quite blatantly. How can beliefs about god be compatible with violence?'

'You don't know *their* religion.'

'As though ours is so much better. Ram would have hated what was going on in his name – a man who sacrificed everything to keep his father's honour, who left his home, his palace, his kingdom in order to make sure his brother inherited, he would be the last to appreciate the fuss over his birthplace.'

'Times have changed. We are preserving his honour as it needs to be done now.'

Astha stared at her husband. Was he agreeing that people

should be killed in the name of God? She didn't want to know what he thought.

'Wasn't Aijaz going to write this play,' continued Hemant. 'Didn't you tell me he was a history teacher? Surely this is his area of expertise, not yours. How have you got so involved?'

'He wants everybody to participate,' said Astha thinking quickly. 'Besides you forget I am the teacher volunteer.'

'Volunteer, not donkey.'

'Translating history into theatre is hardly work a donkey can do.'

'Nor can you. What is your experience?'

'I don't need experience.' She felt she was being denied something, not understood, throttled, and choked. And yet it was just a play. He was right, she had no experience. Though Aijaz was in a better position to write about masjids and controversies, still she would hold her own, paltry though that own might be. 'Aijaz doesn't think experience is necessary,' she went on in defence.

'Oh pardon me,' he said, and his wife hated the mockery in his tone, 'he clearly knows how to get work out of you.'

'Can I speak to you a moment?' Astha asked Aijaz on Monday during the fifteen-minute break he allowed the kids.

'Trouble with the masjid?' he smiled.

Astha nodded briefly.

'Shall we go to the canteen?'

In the canteen she opened her bag and took out flurries of photostats. 'I don't know where to begin,' she started. 'It's such a tangled history, and leaving one piece out makes it lopsided. Besides it is used for many different political purposes in the present as well.' This Astha had only realised yesterday. So far the Babri Masjid had been something mentioned in the news with the irritating air of a problem that wouldn't go away. 'I do wish you would write it, or conceive it. I am sure you are far more knowledgeable.'

Aijaz looked at her clutching her photostats. 'Do you think it is only the so-called experts that should be allowed to deliver opinions? You are looking at it from the outside. Your perspective is fresh, it is invaluable.'

'But I am very ignorant and I cannot possibly do it justice,' she said, quick as a flash putting herself down.

'It doesn't matter, Astha,' he said. His voice was coming at her, his eyes were looking at her, any second and his teeth would glow at her. She was married, she should not be registering these things. She shifted uneasily on the hard canteen bench, clutching her bag in her lap. 'The thing is,' he went on, 'we have to create awareness. There may be differences of interpretation, it doesn't matter. If our players and our audience think for one moment about this issue, we have done our job.'

'You have already created awareness in one,' she mumbled daringly.

'And you will create it in many.'

'I don't know,' she replied, 'I have no experience.'

The smile, the teeth, the hand that lightly touched the phototstats. 'What is all this?'

'Material I gathered. I sketched out a few ideas, though I am not sure—'

'Let's see,' he interrupted, leaning forward. She could smell him, a faint sharp smell. She shifted uneasily again, clutching her bag still more firmly to her stomach, riffling through her papers.

'I thought of starting in 1528, you know when Mir Baqi decrees that a mosque be built at the highest point in Ayodhya in the name of his most noble ruler Emperor Babur, a brief two-line scene. We could have a boy with a placard announcing dates and locations. Perhaps the same boy could double as the mosque, a mosque that just wants to be left alone thinking each fight will be the last.'

'Himanshu would be good for the part. He is the youngest.'

Her own thoughts exactly. She looked up and smiled, he smiled back, she quickly looked down, he must think she found her paunch fascinating, she looked at it so much. 'Do go on,' he said after a moment's silence.

'Then a short scene set in 1855. The Muslims think the Ayodhya ruler is showing favours to the Hindus. They claim that the temple at Hanuman Garhi is built on a mosque, they march towards it, the Hindus retaliate by saying the Babri Masjid is built on a temple and they march upon it—' she paused. 'Actually there was more but I have pared it down to the essentials, everybody thinking they have been done in, and asserting their power through temples and mosques.' She looked at Aijaz anxiously. 'I hope I have got it right?'

'Absolutely. Then?'

'A lot of people were killed during this time, Hindus as well as Muslims, and the whole thing became openly political. There was an enquiry committee consisting of Hindus and Muslims, presided over by the British Resident. But after 1857 power equations changed, and two years later, the British declared that access to the Babri Masjid would be bifurcated. The Hindus were to enter from the east, and the Muslims from the north.'

'Then?'

'This state continues till the British leave. Then in 1949, some idols appear. The Hindus claim this is a miracle, while the constable on duty states that about fifty to sixty people broke into the masjid on the night of December 22. The next day the District Magistrate declared the area disturbed and locks are put on the masjid. At this point I stopped.'

'You haven't written more?' Aijaz sounded disappointed.

'Well last February the district court ordered the locks open. Rajiv Gandhi is probably involved, but I don't know how far to go in showing the masjid as a tool in modern political equations,' said Astha, pleased at his tone.

'We'll work something out.'

Aijaz took out his wallet, while Astha groped around for change. 'If you don't let me pay for one sweet and overcooked cup of tea I'll be very upset,' said Aijaz as they rose to go.

*

The appreciation that Aijaz had shown moved Astha so much she couldn't help talking about it at dinner.

'Aijaz liked the script,' she started.

'He told us it was a wonderful script,' put in Himanshu 'but we could change it any way we wanted because we are to bring our own – own – what, Mama?'

'Interpretations.'

'Yes that – to our parts. And I'm to be the mosque and carry placards. I have to keep crying and getting hit. Everybody wants me.'

His parents looked at him indulgently. 'Really beta?' said Hemant. 'I must come and see you.'

'Yes, Papa. We are going to do it the last day of the holidays. All our families and friends should come, Aijaz said.'

'Aijaz Uncle,' corrected the father. 'He is older than you.'

'No Papa, Aijaz does not believe in hi – hi—' He looked at his mother again.

'Hierarchy.'

'The girls in Mama's school don't call him anything,' said Anuradha. 'They are so shy, can you imagine? It is a very good thing that Himanshu and I go, otherwise poor Aijaz would have a hard time with them.'

'Anu,' reproved Astha, 'they are not that bad.'

'Oh, Mama, you don't know.'

Only later did Astha realise that Hemant had not actually said anything about her script. Well, it didn't matter, he would see the play performed, and recognise his wife's hidden talents. At night, lying in bed, she drifted off to sleep with thoughts of Aijaz and the days ahead.

Astha loved looking at Aijaz on stage, allowing herself frequent covert glances. He was of mediun height, his body compact. His face was the clear delicate luminous brown of freshly rained-on earth. His lips were a darker brown than his skin, and his eyes were black and narrow. While working he rolled up the sleeves of his shirt, allowing Astha to view at her leisure his round strong arms, hairless, smooth and muscular. He had prematurely grey hair, which, thick and springy, fell about his face and neck in ways that suggested a good barber. He must be vain of his hair, thought Astha, knowing how attractive the grey made a young face look.

Through those fifteen days, Astha saw the little thing she had penned transformed, and her admiration for him grew. Song, dance, mime, action, improvisation, actor involvement, he fused all these elements effortlessly into a fast-moving, absorbing piece.

She and her children talked of nothing but the play, the rehearsals, the way everybody was acting, who was good, who was bad, who came late, who not, who had team spirit, who not, and what Aijaz had said. Every day Astha was called upon to add a bit of information, to corroborate some piece of evidence, suddenly she was the Babri Masjid expert, and this she felt was Aijaz's doing – he who was the history teacher, allowing her to parade her knowledge when surely his own was greater.

He looked at her, he wanted her opinion even when it wasn't necessary, he smiled when there was no occasion. Perhaps she shouldn't think of him so much, but soon it would be over, where was the harm, it made her happy, and that in itself was worth something?

Sometimes as Astha sat on the stage she absently sketched the scenes before her, wanting to capture her son as the mosque, her daughter as a rabble rouser, and Aijaz as their teacher. By now she knew by heart his perfect teeth, his full lips, the smoothness of his cheeks, the deep dimple near his mouth, the curl in his hair, the glint in his eyes. She tried to translate these things on paper, but only registered pale copies. Her activities attracted his attention.

'What are you doing?' he asked during one break.

'Nothing much.'

'No let's see,' and he gently tugged at the papers she had turned face down on her lap. For a moment his curled fist rested on her knee.

Hastily she shoved the drawings at him, repeating the mandatory, 'It's nothing much.'

Aijaz turned the papers over. Astha drew fast and there were ten sketches in all. 'For how long have you been drawing?' he asked.

'On and off since I was young. Mostly off.'

'You should continue. You capture whatever is going on well.'

She found his immediate presence too disturbing for conversation.

'Why don't you come to my place sometime, you can have a look at what I do.'

Paralysed silence on her part. After a second he dropped the papers back into her lap and shouted 'Time's up', clapping his hands to get the children's attention.

What did it mean, did he like her, did he want to have an affair with her, why had she been so startled by his hand on her knee, why hadn't she responded, but she was a married woman, with two children and those right before her eyes.

'What was Aijaz saying to you, Mama?' asked Anuradha, the sharp eyed one, in the scooter back home.

'Nothing much, beta. He was looking at my drawings, that's all.'

'Did he like them?'

'There is nothing much to like,' said Astha, teaching her daughter how to devalue her work, and passing on the tradition from woman to woman.

Anuradha lost interest. Himanshu having just grasped their topic of conversation demanded, 'What? What? What did Aijaz say to you, Mama?'

'Nothing much beta.'

'Then what was Didi saying?'

Anuradha cast him her usual you're so stupid look.

'She wanted to know what he said about my drawings, that's all.'

'What did he say?'

'Nothing.'

'What did he *say*?'

'He said they weren't bad, that I should continue, continue to draw,' repeated Astha quickly before Himanshu could say what again.

That night, lying awake in bed, Astha went over everything Aijaz had said, she relived that touch on her knee, his head bent over her drawings.

In a few more days the workshop would end. Would he repeat his invitation? Had it been a spur of the moment thing, or was he attracted to her? Why was she so shy? Maybe she should phone him, call him over, but how, with everybody watching, it was so difficult, after this would she ever see him? How could they meet again?

She tossed and turned, trying not to disturb Hemant. If an accidental brush against her knee was so dislocating what would anything else be? And then she felt stupid, had Aijaz asked her to elope with him? No, he had merely asked her over to look at his drawings. What connection did that have with her marriage? She was a fool, a fool, a fool.

One thing was clear though, he liked her drawings, he thought she had something. He was also an artist, he must know what he was talking about. Suddenly she glimpsed possibilities, suddenly her life seemed less constricted.

She sighed, and closed her eyes, willing sleep to come, pressing herself firmly against her husband, hoping for the comfort of habit.

The auditorium was dark. The parents in the hall fidgeted, making allowances for the twenty-minute delay in the rise of the curtain on *Babri Masjid: Fact, Fiction and You.*

'It sounds like a bloody political tract,' said Hemant.

'Don't you like it?' asked Astha, sitting next to him in the front row. 'The title was mine. Aijaz thought it was a good one.'

'Darling, you would hardly go and see a play called *Babri Masjid: Fact, Fiction and You* if your children were not in it.'

'No, I wouldn't, but maybe I should. There are too many people like me in this country who are not paying attention to what is happening.'

Hemant raised his eyebrows. 'What is happening?'

'The locks on the masjid were opened to appease Hindu sentiments. Then the Muslim Women's Bill was introduced twenty-five days later in Parliament to appease Muslim sentiments. Basically both communities were pandered to as an election ploy.'

Her husband stared at her. 'Are you all right?'

Astha looked self-conscious. 'Of course I'm all right, why shouldn't I be?'

'You sound like a parrot.'

'To have an opinion is to sound like a parrot?'

'Please. Keep to what you know best, the home, children, teaching. All this doesn't suit you.'

The play was over. Himanshu came rushing over to them. 'Did you see me?' he cried. 'I was under the sheet.'

'Beta, you were the best mosque anyone has ever seen,' said Hemant swinging him up in his arms. 'No wonder everybody was fighting over you.'

'And me?' cried Anuradha tugging at his sleeve, 'Did you see me?'

'Of course I did. You were soooo good, sweetheart.'

'Come and meet Aijaz, Papa,' went on Anuradha dragging him to where the director stood, surrounded by parents congratulating him, telling him how their children had enjoyed the workshop, how they could talk of nothing but their play, and when was he going to do another?

Astha watched as Hemant met Aijaz, watched as they shook

hands, exchanged a few words, as Aijaz ruffled Himanshu's hair in a parting gesture, watched as he turned towards other parents. A few months later she heard he was going around with a woman working in an NGO.

~

Her name was Pipeelika Trivedi. She lived alone in Delhi, sufficiently isolated from conventional society to believe her choice of partner concerned only herself. Her mother was horrified when she learnt of her engagement.

'You can't do this,' she told her daughter.

'Why not? You're the one who is always going on about me getting married.'

'But not to a Muslim.'

'He's sweet. So what if he's a Muslim?'

Her mother clicked her tongue. 'They marry four times.'

'How do you know?'

'It's part of their religion.'

'Do you, you personally, know any Muslim who has married four times?'

'How is that relevant?'

'It shows you are speaking out of prejudice. Meet him and then decide.'

'It has nothing to do with meeting him. You like him, he must be nice. But everybody knows that all they have to do is say Talak, talak, talak, and the girl is out on the streets.'

'She is not.'

'How do you know?'

'The Qu'ran says.'

'How do you know?'

'Aijaz says.'

'It's not true. He is lying.'

'Does he know more about the Qu'ran or do you?'

'I know more about the world,' said the mother, tight and tense.

117

'Well I know more about Aijaz.'

The mother looked at her stubborn daughter. 'You kept saying no to any boy I suggested for this? For this I struggled after your father died, so that you throw yourself away?'

'He is not a heap of dung, you know. Besides I am almost twenty-nine, you've always said you want to see me married, now is your chance. I'm not going to find anyone else. He's intelligent, sensitive, socially committed, a history lecturer, a theatre activist, but all you can see is a Muslim who is going to both divorce me and marry four times.'

The mother stayed silent, hating to be so opposed to her daughter. The daughter wondered at the unreasonableness of her mother. They had always been so close.

Mrs Trivedi, the mother, had been a widow for much of her adult life. Her parents' apprehensions about their daughter's marriage to her Delhi University teacher, twenty years her senior, were fully justified when he dropped dead one morning in front of the blackboard in his classroom. The widow was left with two small children.

She tried for a while to manage in Delhi, but it was difficult. She was too gentle, too pretty, too meek, too young and her circumstances too straightened. Her parents called her to live with them in Bangalore.

Mrs Trivedi went. Gentle and meek though she was, she had also been a wife, and she found it galling to fit into the daughter mode again. Added to this was her parents' obvious sense of her doom. The years with Jyotin had been the best in her life, it was an insult to his memory to be treated like a cornucopia of tragedy. She made enquiries about a teaching job in a boarding school where she could live with her children.

'I am moving to Shiksha Kendra,' she announced. 'Board, lodging, and the children's education all will be taken care of.'

The parents were opposed to further movement. 'You have not suffered enough?' they asked. 'These poor children have not been knocked around enough?'

'We will manage. Their home is with me, their mother, not in a place,' said the widowed daughter, showing all the signs of marriage to an intellectual husband.

'On what money?'

'At Shiksha Kendra I won't need to spend on the essentials. My salary will pay for the extras.'

Shiksha Kendra, set in a forest, miles away from nowhere, the brainchild of the philosopher S Swaminathan, a school which emphasised harmony with nature, respect for every form of life, and the all-round development of body and mind. All this the brochure said, and all this Mrs Trivedi felt when she visited the school. A home for herself and her children was what she was looking for, and at Shiksha Kendra she found it.

'This school will not equip Ajay and Pipeelika for the competitive world,' warned the grandparents. 'They need to get ahead. They have no father, they are starting out with a disadvantage.'

'Swaminathan got ahead,' said their daughter, somewhat elliptically, 'if fame and reputation are anything to go by.'

Ajay, the son, showed his determination to succeed from a very early age. No need to tell him the disadvantages of his situation, he felt them all himself. A boy with competition in his blood, he stood first all his life, in school, in IIT, making straight to the US as soon as he possibly could with a wonderful scholarship to MIT. His success evoked tears of joy in all concerned. The widowed mother's sacrifices had borne fruit. He departed amid great jubilation, and never came back.

Pipeelika, the daughter, was left to fulfil the hopes of her mother on native soil. After school, she moved up North, to Miranda House, college and hostel, to do an Honours degree in Sociology. After that an MA from the Delhi School of Economics.

Her brother thought she should come to the States and do a PhD, increase her market value, he would sponsor her, but I do not wish to join the diaspora, and what about Ma, said Pipee, morally the superior. Instead, after a brief teaching stint, she joined an NGO run by three women, dealing with alternative education for slum children.

Pipee had been working in Ujjala for four years when she met Aijaz Akhtar Khan, at a conference. She was reading a paper on the effects of communalism on the education of Muslim children in the basti. They were discriminated against, made to feel stupid and backward, were told their loyalties were to Pakistan, and looked upon with suspicion. Aijaz was reading on the use of street theatre in the dissemination of social and political awareness in educational institutions. Clearly their interests were similar.

After the sessions were over, he sought an introduction, inviting her to a nearby dhaba for a glass of tea if she were free. She looked at him, the clear warm reddish light brown colour, the long thin nose, the gleaming even teeth, the thick grey hair, and then she smiled, her mouth turning in, making dents at either edge. Yes, she was free.

They talked for hours, it became dark and Aijaz insisted on escorting her back to her flat. She lay awake at night thinking of him. He seemed so gay and lighthearted, with many interests besides teaching. Not only did he manage and encourage drama activities in his college, but he was the prime mover and shaker of The Street Theatre Group. Drama was an effective way of addressing communal issues and dealing with social evils, if she liked he could bring the group to her basti. Pipee liked, and she was sure Neeraj, her friend and colleague would also approve. Ujjala was already involved in introducing drama to their children through the helpers, it would be a wonderful opportunity.

*

The courtship took six months. Now Pipee wanted to marry him. Mrs Trivedi tried an old tack.

'Your father would not have liked it,' she said.

'He would have. My father was a secularist,' said the daughter firmly. 'Any father who names his daughter after an ant proves that.'

(Pipeelika? That's not a proper name, that's a word. What does it mean? How do you spell it, pronounce it?

Is this a real name? Never heard of it.

Isn't that the Sanskrit for ant? How can you be named after an ant?

And so on through the years.)

Pipee saw her mother momentarily at a loss and pursued her advantage. 'You can't deny it,' she said, 'my father didn't want his daughter's life cluttered up with references to goddesses, and now I am going to live up to his legacy. He married whom he liked, so did you, now it's my turn.'

'You don't know what you are letting yourself in for. It is only later that you will realise.'

'We'll wait for that day. Right now we are getting married.'

'What does his family say?'

Pipee hesitated.

'See. They are not happy either,' her mother quickly pointed out.

'You are all the same. We don't care.'

'Oh, Pip, everybody else will care,' sighed her mother.

'Neeraj doesn't. She likes him, he is so charismatic it is hard not to like him, you would too if you gave yourself the chance.'

'I keep telling you it is not him.'

'So much the worse for you, Ma. Besides *Neeraj* thinks, even if *you* don't, that I will be happy with him, she encouraged me.'

Mrs Trivedi was silent for a moment. Neeraj was somebody she respected, whose interest in her daughter she had been hitherto grateful for. Now she said bitterly, 'You all work in your own NGO, and think you don't have to answer

121

to anybody. My child you are swimming in a very small pond.'

'Small pond! When I've been working with women for five years, going to all kinds of slums, seeing all manner of injustices done to people I have actually met. If we help them too overtly we alienate the community, and lose whatever influence we have. It's so frustrating. Ma, you haven't even seen a slum.'

'I hope my daughter will not judge her partner by the men in slums,' said Mrs Trivedi crossly. 'And don't tell me what Neeraj thinks. I had no idea she would encourage you to go against your family and religion.'

This was not the time for Pipee to point out that she didn't give a shit about religion. 'Come on, Ma,' she said instead, wrapping her arms around her mother's neck, 'the world has changed, you don't realise it living in this tiny place. When you meet Aijaz you will love him, you'll see.'

'At least make sure my grandchildren are Hindus. Once you marry God knows what he'll make you do.'

'Ma! They will be his children too. He's not that sort of person, and do you think I would love him if he were? He never mentions religion, except politically, never suggested conversion, nothing. In fact you are the one obsessed with the whole thing.'

Aijaz to Pipee in Delhi, 'Was it bad?'

'It could have been worse.'

'Poor thing, it must be very hard for her,' said Aijaz, shifting Pipee's head more comfortably on his shoulder. They had finished making love, and were talking about their marriage.

'When she sees you, she will come around.'

'The whole world may not have your faith in me.'

'But my world does, and she is a big part of it.'

'You are very close to her, aren't you?' asked Aijaz wistfully.

'Of course. She is all I have. My father's family don't like my mother, we are not in touch with them, my grandparents disapprove of my lifestyle, and Ajay shows no signs of coming back. What's the use of having a son and brother if all he does is write patronising letters from the States?'

'Well, you have me now, and so does your mother.' Aijaz pulled Pipee on top of him, and pushed his hands through her hair, pulling her head back so that he could look at her milky skin, and pink mouth with its indented corners that smiled in a peculiar way. She smiled now, loving the feel of his hands in her hair, the way he massaged her scalp.

Pipee had a lot of hair, it sprung up all around her head in waves and curls and frizzes. Aijaz loved it, loved it almost as much as he loved her breasts, large and full of give. He shifted his hands to them, and Pipee squirmed a little. She was still not used to how much sex Jazu seemed to need, but men were like that, and all the time before and after was the stuff of happiness, when they were talking, wrapped in each other's arms.

Afterwards Aijaz cast a nostalgic look around, 'I will miss this room,' he said.

'I won't,' said Pipee. 'The landlord is an extortionist. This must be the smallest room in all of Delhi.' In fact it was one of six tiny ones, built around a spiral staircase in the back spaces of one of the larger houses of Greater Kailash II.

'Our love grew here,' pronounced Aijaz.

Pipee laughed, 'Well it can flourish somewhere larger.'

'Yes,' said Aijaz thoughtfully. 'Sometimes I wish I had my own flat – but out of the house all day, teaching, travelling, theatre – being a paying guest was the most convenient thing.'

'Soon both of us will have a proper home. I am sick of living in hostels and rented rooms. It's been almost ten years, but now all of that is over.'

Pipee flung an arm out, the future glinting in her eyes. Aijaz smiled and kissed the waving arm.

'You have to promise to spend more time with me,' went on Pipee. 'I refuse to be a nagging wife. You have to promise and keep your promise, and never break it, without my saying a single word.'

'Of course. Why do you think I am getting married?'

'Sex every minute, seems like.'

'You think one needs to get married for that?' laughed Aijaz.

Pipee remained silent.

'What's the matter?'

'Nothing.' But the number of women Aijaz had had bothered her sometimes.

'I want to settle down, I want a home, I want you,' said Aijaz turning to Pipee impatiently again.

Pipee pushed him away, 'Really Jazu, sometimes I think you just have one thing on your mind.'

Aijaz looked proud and manly. 'Wait till we are living together – then you will really see.'

'Yes, let's see if marriage will cool your ardour.'

'My ardour, as you put it, will never be cooled. And we must really start looking, it's very difficult without a company lease, or months of rent in advance.'

'I've a surprise for you.'

'You've found a place!'

'In a way.'

Aijaz looked wary. 'What way?'

'Now listen – listen properly—'

'I'm listening, I'm listening.'

'You know what Premlata said to her father, when he was going to marry her off? She said thirteen was under-age and against the law, and if necessary, she would call the police! Wasn't that brave of her?'

'Very. But what's the connection?'

'Our efforts are bearing fruit, that's what. After three years of going to our centre at Salempuri, more children have reached literacy level, more girls are going to school, and you wouldn't believe how some of them have changed! They always worked hard, these girls, they cook, wash clothes, look after the cows, buffaloes, younger brothers and sisters, send them to school, help in the family business, they embroider, make envelopes, necklaces, sew sequins on, but are often made to feel worthless. But at the centre they develop self-confidence, look at Premlata! We want to open more centres.'

'I still don't see what that has to do with us,' repeated Aijaz patiently. He had heard Pipee about her work many times.

'Since we are expanding, we are going to apply for permission from the home ministry for foreign funding. Then Ujjala will hire me a flat in lieu of a raise in pay. They know I'm getting married—'

'I take it they don't disapprove of me, no don't tell me, our marriage is a strike for communal harmony.'

'What's wrong with their approval?'

'Your mother hates me because I am Muslim. Your friends love me because I am Muslim, I don't know which is worse.'

'How does it matter? Look what they are doing for us, isn't that nice of them?'

'Very,' said Aijaz with reserve. 'And I am sure they will extract their pound of flesh. Make you work ten times harder, demand your presence so much you will hardly be in your precious flat.' There were times when he resented the women in Pipee's life, especially Neeraj.

'You don't know how women operate. Just think, we will have enough space to have my mother visit us in Delhi during her holidays, and of course your family too.'

Aijaz yawned and turned away. Pipee tried to suppress her annoyance. Why was the man so unwilling to discuss his family?

'Have you told them yet?' she demanded.

'I'll tell them, I'll tell them, what's the hurry?'

'They're your family, I want to meet them, know them.'

'You are so idealistic,' remarked Aijaz.

'It must be nice to have so many people belonging to you.'

'It's a total pain in the ass. You can deal with one person's expectations, but here there is the whole community.'

'So?'

'So they all take my father's side. He has never accepted my theatre activities. If his eldest son wanted to be a lecturer, the least he could do was help with the mango orchards in Shahjehanpur during the summer, instead of getting involved in some silly drama-shama. It doesn't even pay, which makes it that much harder to understand.'

'We can both help with the orchards from time to time,' said Pipee enthusiastically and ignorantly.

'That's not all. They wanted me to marry my cousin Azra. My mother was especially keen since she had brought Azra up after my aunt died. I suppose they were trying to make sure I eventually returned. They don't understand my life, they don't realise I have no time for all this fuss.'

'I am sure they will hate me,' said Pipee in a small voice.

'We'll take it as it comes. Why worry now?'

It took six months for the grant to come through. The accommodation they ended up with belonged to Neeraj's sister's husband settled in the States. He had bought a flat in Vasant Kunj as an investment, and was now looking for a reliable tenant (i.e. one who would leave when asked). Neeraj convinced him that Ujjala and Pipee were what he was looking for.

It had two bedrooms, two bathrooms, a kitchen with built-in closed shelves, a dining area at right angles from the sitting area. Outside the sitting-dining there was one big balcony, outside the bedrooms there were two smaller ones.

'I'm going to have a potted garden here,' said Pipee, stretching out her arms to the hot white sky above the verandah. 'I'm going to have everything. I can't wait to show it to my mother.'

'Look at all the space! How clever you are, darling,' exclaimed Aijaz, putting his hands under her shirt, and unhooking her bra as she walked about.

126

'Well it was really Neeraj. She always manages to find solutions to problems.'

'I prefer to think it was you.'

'Are you jealous?' laughed Pipee. 'You shouldn't be, she loves you.'

'She hardly knows me.'

'I talk to her sometimes.'

'About us?' Aijaz looked appalled.

'One can't be talking of work all the time,' temporised Pipee, and then to change the subject, 'Oh, I never told you, we will also have a phone, think how nice that will be.'

'We could have got that on our own.'

'We would have had to wait years.'

'I have connections too, you know, I could have got us a phone. Now stop moving.'

'Jazu, do you ever think of anything else?' murmured Pipee, as she so frequently had to.

'No,' said Aijaz pinning her against the wall, seriously this time.

~

It was in September 1988 that the marriage between Aijaz Akhtar Khan and Pipeelika Trivedi was solemnised in Tees Hazari. The bride and groom paid for their own wedding, the whole thing came to five hundred rupees. No relatives were present from either side, a colleague of Aijaz's and Neeraj acted as witnesses, while the theatre crowd, a few of Aijaz's colleagues, and the staff of Ujjala, later gathered at Karim's to complete the celebratory aspects.

Pipee had arranged her work so that she would be free the two weeks of Aijaz's autumn break. They were going to Shiksha Kendra, and as Mrs Trivedi's winter holidays started in mid October, they would all come back together.

'I think we will avoid my grandparents, they needn't really know we are coming. Besides they are very orthodox, and

127

will fuss like mad over the Mozzie issue.'

'I can pretend to be a Hindu if you wish.'

'I wouldn't dream of it, why should you? You are not a pariah, after all.'

'It's not a question of pariah, what difference does it make? Old people need to be treated carefully.'

Pipee needed only a second to realise the possible personal application of this remark. 'Will your family look upon me as a pariah? Shouldn't we visit them so that they get to know me?'

'No, let's give them time to get used to it first,' said Aijaz. 'Besides your mother is coming back with us, and we can't complicate matters.'

'If your mother came too, they could be company for each other,' said Pipee, showing how little she knew of the science of in-laws.

'Another time.'

'You have to travel quite a bit to this school of yours, Pip,' said Aijaz on the second day of their train ride to Bangalore.

'It's the best school in India,' said Pipee proudly.

'And like all shrines, difficult to reach,' replied Aijaz looking deadpan.

Pipee smiled in the way Aijaz loved to see, the corners of her mouth turned in, the deepening dimples. She pinched his side several times in the crowded second class compartment. 'You'll see,' she said loftily, 'I will say no more.'

'Promise?'

This time Pipee pinched him so hard, he cried out, and everybody looked at them with curiosity and disapproval. Young, alone and enjoying themselves.

In Bangalore they took a bus to Madanapalle. 'From there we will take a taxi,' said Pipee. 'It is sixteen kilometres.'

As they drove away in the taxi towards Shiksha Kendra, Pipee grew thoughtful, the dimples and the smile went.

'Why so quiet, dearest?' asked Aijaz, 'I'm not used to it.'

'Nothing much.'

'Come on, tell me.'

'It was in school that I first fell in love, and now I am coming here on my honeymoon. I feel strange when I think about it, that's all.'

'Your first love! You never told me.'

'There was nothing to tell.'

Aijaz ignored this. 'Who was he?' he went on.

'She.'

'She?'

'Her name was Samira.'

'You were in love with a woman?'

'Woman? Hardly that. Schoolgirl really. She was only seventeen.'

'That's not so young. In my village girls marry at sixteen, how old were you?'

'Well Shiksha Kendra is not Shahjehanpur,' said Pipee a little coldly. 'And what does it matter how old I was? It was so long ago I do not remember.'

'Did your mother know?'

'What was there to know? We were schoolgirls,' said Pipee withdrawing from the conversation.

'Where is she now?'

'She married,' said Pipee shortly. 'We lost touch after college.'

Aijaz fell silent. Pipee was so unlike her usual self that he didn't know what to think. It must have been like those crushes that girls had on filmstars or their teachers. She was young and inexperienced and imagined her feelings to be love.

He looked sideways at her, she was still looking remote. Did she think he was narrow minded enough to disapprove of a schoolgirl crush, he who knew of the strong ties that existed between women in the zenana? He reached for her hand. 'Don't feel sad, Pip. I am here. After all this is our honeymoon.'

Pipee smiled at him and thought there were some things that could not be shared, no matter how understanding the other person. All said and done she was lucky to have found him. So many of her acquaintances were still struggling, looking for love and companionship, rejecting arranged marriages, only to experience a series of heartbreaks on their own.

At the gates of Shiksha Kendra, Pipee stopped and paid the taxi. 'I want to walk,' she said to Aijaz. 'I want you to see it slowly, take it all in.'

The path leading inside was wide with thin trees lining the way, shady, green. 'The school planted these,' said Pipee gesturing around her. 'This is a drought area, even now the leaves are drooping.'

Aijaz looked carefully and could see that indeed the leaves were drooping. 'They have their own dairy, bakery, their own gardens, fruit trees, imli trees, mango trees, which they lease out,' continued Pipee.

'U-huh,' said Aijaz.

'We were not allowed to touch any of the fruit because it wasn't the school's.'

'But of course you did.'

'Of course.'

'Where are we going?'

'They will be eating now,' said Pipee looking at her watch, 'It's one.' And she started to walk faster, though laden with bags, afraid to miss her mother in the dining hall, anticipating the surprise and pleasure on her face.

The din in the dining hall was deafening, though Pipee didn't seem to notice. Aijaz hung back as she scanned the rows of tables and benches.

'There she is,' she said, making unerringly towards a particular back.

Her husband remained in the doorway watching the reunion.

Later in Mrs Trivedi's two rooms in Peacock House. 'Mama, don't you like Aijaz? Isn't he all I promised?'

'Very much beta,' said the mother. 'He is your husband after all.'

'Let's show him where I grew up,' Pipee went on.

'What is there to show? These two rooms.'

'And where Ajay didn't grow up.'

Mrs Trivedi shot a glance at her son-in-law, who was careful to look as bland and harmless as possible. 'My son stayed at the hostel,' she said. 'It was better, he could participate more in the activities, and of course he came every day.'

'For fifteen minutes,' said Pipee.

'And every weekend.'

'Just to eat.'

'Pipee thinks he should have stayed with me like she did,' went on Mrs Trivedi. 'She doesn't realise boys need to be with their own kind. He had a housemaster who was like a father to him. And I had Pipee.'

Pipee pressed her cheek against her mother's, 'And now you have Jazu.'

Jazu looked charming.

'Indeed,' said Mrs Trivedi.

They spent ten days at Shiksha Kendra. Pipee took Aijaz over the entire campus, the banyan tree, the rocks they had to climb, the place where they watched the sun rise every morning, the art, music and dance rooms, the playgrounds, the senior school, the library, the lab where she had sat for her exams.

'It's a whole world in itself, isn't it?' wondered Aijaz.

'Some parents are not happy about how cut off it is, they think their children will not be able to survive outside. But look at me. I've survived perfectly well.'

'Indeed you have,' said Aijaz kissing her. 'A perfectly untouched specimen.'

Pipee was right, once Mrs Trivedi came to know Aijaz, she loved him. They had been in Delhi two weeks when Pipee said triumphantly, 'Well Ma, what do you have to say about Muslims now?'

'He is a very good boy, beta,' responded Mrs Trivedi.

'Then?' said Pipee sharply for she knew what was coming.

'I am sure his family like you equally,' said Mrs Trivedi smoothly.

'They will when we go to meet them in the holidays. They are a very large family, and his mother is old and cannot travel easily,' said Pipee, with a guile to match her mother's.

Later to Aijaz, 'I've told her that we are going to meet your family in the holidays.'

'What was the need to do that?'

'She happens to think the lack of your family presence in our marriage very strange. Don't mind, she is just an old worry pot.'

Aijaz said nothing. Pipee felt a pang of guilt. What did it matter about his family anyway? Let them think whatever they wanted, she should not make it more of an issue than he did. Besides Aijaz had been so sweet to her mother, coaxing her from her prejudice, never seeming to mind her oblique references to Muslims, four wives, large families, instant divorce, inter-community marriages, the religion of babies from such unions. The more she relaxed with him the more she wanted to know.

'There is a limit to your questions,' Pipee shouted one day. 'Is he your son-in-law or the whole Muslim community dating from Babur's time to now?'

'It's all right,' said Aijaz soothingly. 'Let her ask. After all I am the first Muslim she has had anything much to do with.'

'Still.'

'I'm used to this. She is not alone.'

Such gentleness deserved to be rewarded by total belief. Pipee vowed that she would never mention Aijaz's family unless he himself brought them up.

After Mrs Trivedi left, the young couple settled into the joys of living on their own.

Pipee's hours were flexible, and she tried to be home by the time Aijaz arrived. This was usually not difficult. After a morning of teaching Aijaz was often at college rehearsals, or working out programmes with The Street Theatre Group. And, thought Pipee indignantly, everybody imagines academics to have nothing but free time.

Ujjala was by now in the process of establishing a community centre at another basti. This second place had a greater number of facilities. It had sewing machines for women to acquire a skill to increase their earning potential, it had a library, toys, and art and craft supplies for the fifteen to twenty children who came every afternoon from three to five.

Soon they extended their activities by organising trips outside Delhi. The results were encouraging. Girls, helpers and administrators bonded, and the girls' sense of themselves strengthened. Each of them wrote a piece on how she had experienced the trip, what she had felt being away from home with others from the basti, for the first time not part of a family structure. Pipee put these together in a series of booklets called *Yatra aur Vichar* that she spent many hours over. She was filled with a sense of achievement, all day with Ujjala, every other moment with Aijaz, she thought life could have no more to offer.

It was almost a year after their marriage that Aijaz made a casual announcement. 'We have to go to Shahjehanpur. They want to see you.'

Pipee, lounging on the cushions of the cane double-seater they had recently bought, looked up, astonished. In all this time Aijaz's family had shown no signs of her existence.

'That's nice,' she said carefully.

Aijaz stared moodily at the balcony. Pipee gazed at him, and for the thousandth time thought how she loved the way he looked. His wavy grey hair, his clean brown colour, his sharp nose, his warm eyes. 'You know my mother also had her reservations,' went on Pipee encouragingly.

'Mine would have too, had she known,' muttered Aijaz.

'What? What did you say?'

'You heard me.'

'Do you mean your mother – family – didn't know we were getting married.'

'Something like that.'

'You didn't tell them?'

'How could I tell them?' demanded Aijaz. 'You knew the problems.'

' Still, you could have *told* them. They must be feeling awful now, much worse than if you had *told* them.'

'For God sakes, Pip, stop going on.'

'You hide things from them, from me, and you accuse me of going on,' shouted Pipee. 'How do you think I feel?'

'You have to take me as I am,' shouted Aijaz back. 'Me, alone. If I didn't tell them it was to spare them pain, and you trouble.'

Pipee tried to tell herself that Aijaz was an exemplary human being, socially committed, personally tender, but this palliative irritated her further. He had no moral right to behave in a way that didn't add up.

All the things her mother used to say about Hindu-Muslim marriages came unpleasantly to her mind. For a moment she stared at him with revulsion. What was the use of him looking like a dream if he could behave like a nightmare?

'What the hell, Aijaz,' she said, 'you have a poor idea of trouble. You have not been fair to your family or to me.'

'I'm sorry, Pip, I really am, don't be angry. My family is not like yours. There are so many, and they all want to be part of things, they would never have tolerated a Tees Hazari wedding, we would have had to go there and get married amid five thousand people at least, God it's enough to put anyone off. And then there might have been fuss about the conversion thing – I didn't wish to put you through all that.'

'Or yourself,' said Pipee dryly.

'Whatever,' said Aijaz, looking charming.

'Well, why now?'

'They heard rumours. Made enquiries.'

'So I am going to meet them with the guarantee that they will hate me.'

'They'll adore you.'

'With this background?'

'You don't know my family. Once they know they can't change things, they just accept them.'

This time Pipee kept her reservations to herself. 'When are we going?' she finally asked.

'We are on the waiting list. As soon as I can get confirmed bookings.'

'What about my work? We have a big meeting with the community helpers from both centres next week. Neeraj, the others, won't like it.'

'Tell them you are going to visit your Muslim in-laws. They will love it.'

Their reactions were reserved, which was just as I expected, thought Pipee, and shows how little Aijaz knows of families in general.

'I hope they like me soon,' she said to him on their first night in Shahjehanpur.

It was summer, and their beds were spread on the terrace, in deference to their married status, a little separately to one side of a storeroom. As soon as it was late enough they squeezed together in one under a mosquito net.

Aijaz yawned. Pipee poked him. 'Do you think they will?' she asked.

'Give it time, Pip, now let me sleep.'

'I told you they wouldn't like me.'

'They are so glad I'm married, they would have liked anyone.'

'But they would have preferred a Muslim?'

'Come on, Pip, be reasonable. After all your mother would have preferred a Hindu. Anyway who has the time to worry about such things?'

'I suppose,' said Pipee forlornly, thinking of his mother and the jewellery box she had pushed in front of her.

'For my eldest son's wife,' she had said.

'No,' said Pipee, embarrassed, yet dying to look at what was inside.

'Take,' said Ammi, with a trace of reproach, her hands busy with the lid. Pipee gazed at the plump, rounded fingers, studded with gold rings, the short nails which gleamed with clear nail polish, the kurta sleeves long and fitting, and the many bangles that tinkled at her wrists. She looked very sure of herself, unlike her own poor mother, who lived in two rooms at Shiksha Kendra, with no one to boss over except some very small children.

Eventually, since she would not take, she was given a heavy gold necklace, thick gold bangles embossed with flowers, and a set of jhumkas set with pearls and rubies.

She held them, admiring their beauty, marvelling at their heaviness before returning them, I have no locker, I will have to worry about their safety, keep them for me please.

In the days that followed, Pipee realised for the first time she had married a Muslim. Everything was strange, the large haveli, the dishes they ate from, the food they ate, their paan making, the way they dressed, the way they greeted each other, As salamalaikum – Wa Alaikum Assalam, their manner of speaking, the kh's that made her Hindi tongue seem crude and unsophisticated.

And then there were so many relatives. How many people lived in that house, till the end of her visit she did not know. They were a world complete unto themselves, so different from anything she had known while growing up. Occasionally when eating in the long dining hall, she would gather as many as she could within a single glance and feel a great longing for the day when she would be completely accepted as one of their own.

~

It was the year 1989, and bricks were being collected for the Ram Mandir – collected, worshipped, and escorted out of towns, wrapped in silk and saffron, on their way to Ayodhya. If communal disturbances occurred in the wake of these processions, that was not the fault of the bricks, but the fault of the narrow-mindedness of minority communities, who couldn't bear to feel that their domination in this country was over.

It was in this atmosphere that Aijaz and The Street Theatre Group travelled to Rajpur fifty kilometres outside Delhi to put up a play.

'I wish you wouldn't go,' said Pipee, 'Rajpur is a sensitive area. It is not safe.'

'If I only went to places where it was safe, I would never go anywhere,' said Aijaz. 'Theatre is a limited medium, but what else do people like us have?'

'Then don't go,' said Pipee, 'don't go if it is no use.'

Aijaz looked depressed. 'One has to do what one has to do,' he said. 'Of course it is so much easier working with people from schools and colleges, they even write the scripts, and do the research.'

'Well stay here, and go to schools and colleges, instead of dashing out on weekends to some town or mohalla, or factory, god knows where all. Now you are married you have a responsibility to me, to us,' said Pipee, and then felt guilty. Here she was sounding like a nagging wife. Would she like it if Aijaz stopped her from going to the bastis? Or decided that her work with Ujjala led her into dangerous situations?

'What is the use of confining oneself to the middle classes where it is safe – safe and cowardly,' went on Aijaz reflectively.

'At least wait till the whole fuss about the bricks is over,' amended Pipee. 'I will come with you next time. I've never travelled with you. Besides you will be leaving me alone on New Year's Eve.'

Aijaz looked at her in astonishment, 'I never knew this day meant anything to you, Pip. It's just a capitalist device for making money.'

'If it can keep you home, then I am a committed capitalist.'

'You are being totally neurotic. When I go somewhere nice, then you come. The mohallas of this township are dirty and crowded, there is nothing much to see or do. I'll be worrying about you, instead of concentrating on the play and the group.'

'I can take care of myself,' said Pipee with great dignity.

'So can I,' said Aijaz ruffling her hair.

~

'Didn't you know this man?' asked Hemant looking through the papers three days later.

'Which man?' asked Astha indifferently, her life an arid desert so far as men were concerned.

Hemant flapped the papers in front of her. There, in the middle of page three were the headlines, THEATRE GROUP BURNED ALIVE IN VAN, and below the story:

A horrendous incident took place here last night, in the township of Rajpur. Aijaz Akhtar Khan, noted theatre activist, and his troupe were dragged from the site of their performance, and taken away in a Matador. Later the charred remains of the Matador along with the bodies were found near the river. The culprits are still absconding.

It is surmised that rising tensions between two communities led to this action. Aijaz Akhtar Khan, leader of the well-known Street Theatre Group was in town to perform in the mohallas. The issues dealt with were of a sensitive nature, and it is surprising that in this time of communal unrest he got permission to stage a piece involving the Babri Masjid-Ram Janambhoomi controversy. The

District Magistrate says he was deliberately misled about the contents.

According to our sources, a procession containing bricks for the proposed Ram temple in Ayodhya was routed through a gully adjacent to a minority community mohalla earlier in the afternoon. Despite the presence of the police, slogans were shouted. Untoward incidents were then avoided, but that evening violence, possibly premeditated, broke out during a performance by The Street Theatre Group. Unruly elements in the crowd started heckling the actors. Other elements responded. In the confusion the members of the group were driven away in a van, ostensibly for safety. This seems to have been a ploy.

Aijaz Akhtar Khan has left behind a wife.

There followed a list of the other members of the theatre group, along with their survivors, but Astha could not read further for the tears in her eyes. What a way to die, what a horrible, horrible way to die – and for what? Because the man was trying to reach people and do some good. She hadn't even known he was married. She turned away her head to cry some more.

Hemant, watching her, immediately lost his temper. 'Why are you crying?' he demanded. 'What was he to you?'

'Some murderers trap and burn a whole theatre group in a van and you ask me why I am crying?'

'This kind of thing happens all the time, I don't see you wasting your tears.'

'I can't weep for the whole world, only when it means something to me. Maybe I am deficient, but I knew him, he was always working for everybody's good, even the children loved him. And he has been burnt to death. Isn't that reason enough?' she sobbed rocking to and fro with rage and grief.

'Don't get me wrong, this should not have happened. But if you meddle in things that do not concern you, you have to take the consequences. He was a Muslim, he should have kept to the issues within his own religion.'

Astha stared at her husband in revulsion. Ten men had died in the most ghastly way possible, and this was all he could say. Did he have no feelings?

After Hemant left for work she started phoning. Identification of the bodies was being done at Willingdon Hospital, they would probably be released the next day. A condolence meeting was being held that afternoon at the Constitution Club. The next day there would be a funeral procession that would start at the Club and go all the way to the electric crematorium.

Numbly Astha put on a white sari, she would go straight from school to the meeting, at least she would be with people who felt as she did. She would meet his wife, what would it be like to be her at this moment, and to have your husband dead like this. Could you ever get over it, should she arrange for the driver to bring her children there after school, they had known Aijaz, they would grieve with her, they should be exposed to the political realities of this country, but then to be exposed to such violence, such mindless hate, how could she explain it, she could barely deal with it herself. Political realities could wait, Mala would look after them, if she was late they could go upstairs.

At the Constitution Club mourners were gathered on dusty lawns, standing on sidewalks, dressed in white, with black armbands, sombre faced. There were many speeches:

We are witnessing crimes deliberately stoked by the forces of communalism. Neutral voices are seen as threatening, the voice of secularism is not tolerated. Can ten men be burned alive, taken from the mohalla in full view of everybody without connivance from the authorities? What has the State done so far, what have the police done so far to apprehend the criminals? Is this the message for the citizens of this country, live in fear, do not raise your voices for they will be stifled by fire, murder and violence.

This is what the state provides, *this* lawlessness, *this* disregard for life, *this* brute force. *This* is its protection for its citizens.

To speak and be heard is the freedom that is at the heart of a secular nation, this is the right for which these brave young men gave their lives. Now we must carry on as though they were in our midst, forcing us to resist repressive fascist forces. This is the struggle that lies before us.

Astha saw Mrs Dubey, her eyes damp and swollen, she went to her and touched her on the shoulder, they stared wordlessly at each other, and then Astha's own tears, soaking her hanky, her nose running.

It grew dark. Candles were lit and passed around. They started singing. Songs of protest, songs that Aijaz had penned, songs that many had sung in different circumstances. They ended with *We Shall Overcome* in Hindi. Word went around about the funeral arrangements. Tomorrow they would start at noon from the Club and walk all the way to the Crematorium with the ten bodies. Let the city see the atrocity that had been committed, let the traffic come to a standstill, let the line of death be visible in slow motion.

Next day there was a crowd of thousands waiting for the bodies to be released from the hospital. Many had not known the ten men, but it was not necessary to have known them. They came to protest an outrage, to arouse similar protests from an anaesthetised public. Artists and innocent men have been murdered without any provocation during a performance in broad daylight. Today them, tomorrow us. How can this happen? What can we do?

Finally the procession started. On and on they walked, blocking traffic, creating havoc, silent, disciplined and determined. The police tried to stop them, they did not have permission, they would have to turn back. The news spread – they are trying to stop us, we are going to defy them, nothing can turn us back, we will fight if necessary and then the police had to give in, escorting them instead, as they walked down the streets of Daryaganj, past the Jama Masjid, turning right towards Ring Road, then on to the electric crematorium, where thousands more were waiting to receive them.

It took six hours to reach their destination. The vast room quickly filled while the rest of the crowd waited outside. The families of the men laid the bodies out, and two by two their charred remains, indistinguishable from one another, were slid into the massive fires and the doors clanged shut. They had been together in life, and they were together now. Silence occupied the hall. Astha watching from a squeezed-in place near the door remembered the Aijaz she had known, and that once she had thought he smiled too much.

Four days later a massive protest rally was organised from the Red Fort to the Prime Minister's house.

'I shall be late coming home from school today,' said Astha to her husband that morning. Her tone was cold; she had still not forgiven him.

'Why?' he asked busy with his own preparations for the factory. 'Where are you going?'

'To a rally to protest the circumstances of ten men's deaths.'

Hemant looked at Astha. Astha returned the look.

'Whenever did rallies do any good? Goondas hire people from neighbouring villages at ten rupees a day to come and make trouble, block traffic and show their muscle.'

'It's not the political, made-up kind of rally. We want to draw attention to what has happened. How does one speak so that one is heard? You tell me a better way.'

'Rallies!' snorted Hemant ignoring the question. 'No matter how big – who cares – who remembers what they are about?'

'Besides, we don't want their memories to die.'

'I'm sure you don't.'

Astha left the house without a further word.

*

By the time school had finished and Astha reached Red Fort, the air was thick with banners. Some of the marchers were carrying posters with Aijaz's photograph hugely blown up. Some were carrying banners with Leftist slogans. Black arm-bands were being passed around.

The rally set off. Down the road, shouting slogans, they marched, blocking traffic in a way that Astha found most satisfying. Cars were standing still, motorists were fuming, and people were getting late because of her. She shouted with the others:

Sampradayakta
Down Down
Down Down

Communalism
Will not succeed
Will not succeed

The Street Theatre Group
Martyrs All
Aijaz Akhtar Khan
Remembered Forever

Why did they have to die like this, thought Astha, trapped in a van, what were his last thoughts, he who had lived for others. How was there any fairness in the world when such a man could be murdered so brutally? Tears came to her eyes, but tears were not an adequate tribute to Aijaz, they were too ephemeral.

He had seen talent in her, what was it like to live with a man who saw you as having something to offer? If only there was some cause to which she could devote herself, maybe she would not feel so lost and dissatisfied, but what, and how? Knowing what to do was so difficult, and brooding over her life she continued to shout and raise her fist with the others. Down Red Fort Road, past the Asian Circus, past the Centre for Tibetan Refugees, past the Kashmiri outlet for woollen shawls, past the police chowki, past water sellers, lemonade

143

sellers, past bhelpuri wallahs down Connaught Place and Janpath marched the procession. Compressed into half the road, cars were inching along, staring at them, curious, sympathetic, frustrated, annoyed.

They reached the boat club. Astha sank under one of the trees, extremely hot and tired. She had not realised her clothes were unsuitable for marching in the sun, she was wearing a thick black polo neck sweater, with Hemant's vest on underneath. This meant that though damp and hot, she couldn't possibly take it off and be exposed in her underwear.

The speakers on the stage were beginning to talk about state atrocities, an endless list. After that were impassioned recitals of Brecht's poetry in Hindi. Fists were clenched, defiance was hurled towards parliament looming above the tree tops behind the boat club.

An hour later the procession set off towards the prime minister's residence. Three roads away they met a police block. 'No further,' said the policemen. 'Question of security.'

They handed over their memorandum, and were forced to disperse.

As Astha was leaving, her principal stopped her. 'Astha meet Reshana, she used to be a singer for The Street Theatre Group. She was especially close to Aijaz.'

Astha stared at the direct eyes, the face still with sorrow. Especially close – how close was that? What about his marriage – was she close before or after?

'I am trying to meet all those who worked with him,' Reshana was saying through swollen lips. 'We have to make sure his memory does not die, are you interested?'

'There is nothing I wouldn't do for him,' breathed Astha.

'Good,' said Reshana. 'I will inform you of our first meeting.'

As Reshana left, Astha turned to Mrs Dubey, 'Who is she?'

'Reshana Singh. She is a classical singer from an old and

established family. She has many connections, it is good she is taking such an interest in this cause.'

'Is Aijaz's wife not here?'

'Poor thing, I only saw her at the funeral. I don't think she is able to cope with the shock of it all.'

'I would have liked to meet her.'

'When she recovers, we can arrange something.'

In the evening Hemant asked somewhat testily how it had gone. Astha was too full of the day to continue angry with him. If he was limited, that was his misfortune, she could be generous. Where should she begin, the crowd shouting slogans, the palpable determination to do something, singing *We Shall Overcome*, the sense of togetherness, her excitement at Reshana asking her to be part of the new society.

'The traffic arrangements were terrible as usual,' said Hemant, not realising she had an answer. 'I had a meeting with the distributor in Connaught Place, and getting there was totally impossible. Why do they allow rallies in the middle of the day, in central Delhi, I'll never know. Arre, you want to protest, protest, who is stopping you? Let the ordinary tax-payer lead his life, that's all I ask, but no.'

Astha's generosity was not required, her sharing could keep. She could not enter into his frustrations, he could not share her enthusiasm.

For the rest of the evening, they talked of the children, Hemant's concern about his mother's arthritis, his father's blood pressure, his forthcoming trip to South Korea, and maybe they could all go abroad next year for a holiday, and finally something that was beginning to bother him more and more, the increasing competition in colour TVs.

In Noida alone where Hemant had his factory, eight others had come up. He was making 1,500 black and white, and 1,200 colour TVs a month, but the market had become so cut-throat that he was forced to reduce his profit margin to maintain his position.

Never mind, Astha tried to console, dragging her mind to business concerns, now that the government has allowed religion on TV, there will be no end to the shows that will have the same kind of popularity as the *Ramayana* and the *Mahabharat*. There was a captive audience of millions, with a big enough market for all.

Hemant grunted. That very day he had heard that a rival factory was trying to instigate a strike amongst his workers. He had managed to bribe the men in question, but the general atmosphere of suspicion made it difficult to go on bribing. He would discuss the problem with his father in the morning.

V

A few days later at the meeting of the Sampradayakta Mukti Manch, a forum set up in memory of The Street Theatre Group, it was decided that painters should donate a painting for an exhibition devoted to worker unity and secularism. Astha was busy staring out of the dirty windows, where was his wife, was she still getting over her grief, how come she wasn't there, would she never get to see her, when she heard Reshana address her.

'Astha, what about you?'

Astha panicked. Why was Reshana asking, had Mrs Dubey made claims about her talent, but she was no good, she was a beginner, a drawer, a sketcher, nothing serious, her support was absolute, but she could do nothing on her own.

'I'm not sure,' she managed.

Reshana smiled warmly, 'Just try,' she suggested.

Astha felt the disapproval of the gathering at her delayed consent. There were too many people looking. She nodded, and sank back into her chair.

Her anxiety over her task was so great, she had to start immediately. After school the next day she sketched crowd scenes, patterning them on Rajasthani miniatures, trying to choose between a funeral and a procession. Finally she decided there would be more colour and interest in a procession.

She painted a broad road, on one side lines of figures, dots of black hair, holding banners, on the other side, rows of cars, scooters, taxis, cycles, and bordering this the white shops of Connaught Place, the trees in the central section, the massed pedestrians, the large blue sky.

She could think of nothing but her painting. When she was

teaching, her mind was on her figures, the spaces, the colours of her canvas. At home, after lunch, she painted, and as a result there was no time to take the naps she had been used to. Her headaches became worse and often in the evening, after the children's homework, she lay on the sofa, balm smothered, dopey with pain killers. When the pain was very bad she threw up. She tried to keep this from her husband, to participate enthusiastically in his social life. But he did notice, and he did mind.

'Why are you doing this to yourself?' asked Hemant one evening, when it was obvious she was in pain, the smell of balm all pervading, eyes drooping, brow furrowed, face contorted. 'You can't paint and teach, every time I come home you are lying on the sofa. You are suffering, we are all suffering.'

Certainly suffering was involved, it was true. Astha remained silent, her shoulders hunched. Assent and helplessness.

'Your body cannot stand the strain. Mummy said you are neglecting the children, you do not sleep in the afternoons, you are exhausted in the evenings, you are spreading mess in the house, everything smells of turpentine. And all for what? Some dead man.' He never mentioned the nine others.

'It's not for some dead *men*,' flashed Astha, 'it's for a cause. And I'm sorry your mother found it more convenient to complain to you instead of me.'

'What is it to her? She has your interests at heart.'

'I have a better idea of my interests.'

'It seems not. You can't do everything. Leave your job if you insist on painting. It never brought in enough money to justify your going out of the house.'

'You were the one who thought I should work.'

'But now you need not, dearest, I am making enough money.'

'I want something of my own,' murmured Astha.

'What?'

'My own money,' though she knew it was contrary to the spirit of good marriages for a wife to hang on to things and say they were her own.

'You make me sound like a stingy husband, Az,' said Hemant in some hurt.

'No, no, that's not what I meant,' she said weakly.

'Then? Quit for heaven's sake.'

But she was not yet enough of a painter to risk giving up a job she had had for ten years. It represented security, not perhaps of money, but of her own life, of a place where she could be herself.

Reshana phoned frequently, inquiring about the progress of the painting, once dropping by, flattering Astha by her interest and her praise.

At this visit Astha asked, 'Reshana, how come I never see nor hear anything of Aijaz's wife? She must still be really devastated, poor thing,' she added in case her remark was construed as criticism.

Reshana made a face, 'Just between you and me Astha, some people have a problem working with others. I do not wish to say more.'

'Oh.'

Six months after the massacre, the exhibition was ready to be held.

'Ten thousand rupees,' said Reshana.

'Ten thousand!'

'We need the money.'

'But will people buy? I'm not known.'

'It's a large canvas. It is good. If you were known I would have priced it at fifty thousand.'

Ten thousand rupees – the outrage among spectators, each one saying, I wouldn't take this canvas if you *paid* me ten thousand. She would be tested, tried and rejected. But the money was for the Manch, she couldn't protest too much.

Reshana was right. The painting sold on the second day. The crowd was large, many people wanted to help the anti-communal cause, especially if they could get something in exchange.

'I have told all my friends that my mother has sold a painting,' said Anuradha, looking important.

'Only one, darling,' said Astha.

'So what? They were very impressed. None of their mothers is painting.'

'Well don't say too much about it, it was not because of me. People bought it to help those harmed by state violence.'

Anuradha's face darkened as she stared at her mother, and Astha knew she had ruined her satisfaction. She wanted to say yes, I have done it, I have sold my first painting, I have achieved something, let us celebrate, but the number of 'I's' involved ensured that the words refused to leave her mind.

The Manch was anxious not to lose the impetus it had gained and efforts were made to chalk out a long-term plan of action. Unfortunately the Manch also had its fair share of members who could not agree, and valuable time was spent in arguing. Some talked excitedly of the international recognition their cause could get with a film that would document communal atrocities in the villages of North India. It could end with the murder of The Street Theatre Group so that the middle class could also relate to the theme.

Some wanted to start at a more grass roots level, doing the kinds of things Aijaz had done, street plays, slogans, posters, meetings, pamphlets, consciousness raising.

Some wanted to bring anti-communal activists and academics together to exploit the forum of the written word, maybe start a journal. Others thought this was too elitist, too far from the spirit of the theatre group.

Some wanted to concentrate on bringing out a collection of the writings of various members of the group, while objectors felt that since Aijaz was the main person who wrote, it would be like bringing out his writings, and such individualism was inimical to the spirit of the Manch.

Some felt that all their energies should go towards bringing the killers to book. Not a single arrest had been made so far, and this just mirrored the complicity of the police in communal riots and murders.

Most felt this would only end in frustration, and with the rampant corruption of the government they might as well bang their heads against a brick wall for the rest of their lives. The need of the hour was for positive action.

At last a sub-committee was formed. They would present a report, everybody would meet again.

Astha sat silently at the back, her head bent steadily on the moving hands of her watch, and as the hour advanced so did her alarm. It was getting late, the children were upstairs, their homework had to be attended to, Hemant would be coming home.

As she got up to go, Reshana, near the door, put up her fingers. 'Five minutes,' she mouthed. Astha sank back in her seat. She felt the familiar pain marching across her temples to the tune of what were five minutes.

It took twenty-five. Astha was in agony. Reshana turned to her once in the middle, winked and smiled, enclosing her in a conspiratorial glance from which Astha was powerless to escape. She thought of the dinner, they could order some chicken from the neighbourhood restaurant. Rice, a salad, potatoes fried in cumin and coriander, it would only take a minute, there was the dal from the afternoon.

The meeting over, Astha made her way to Reshana. 'I have to go,' she whispered, 'it's getting very late.'

'Stay a moment, I want to introduce you to someone who really liked what you did.'

'His wife?'

'No. This man is a film maker.'

Pyjama-kurta, grey beard, grey hair, 'I loved the emotion portrayed in your painting. I wish I could have afforded it, but Reshana here had priced it too high.'

'Very funny, Arjun,' said Reshana distractedly, 'If we start buying our own work we might as well kiss the Manch goodbye. And here, Astha, meet Kabir, he was a good friend of Aijaz's, they used to perform together. He is on the sub-committee.'

Kabir blew smoke through his cigarette, and smiled at Astha, 'Tell me about your other work.'

'I have not exhibited anything else.'

'You must do more.'

'Thank you,' said Astha in some confusion. She could barely keep her voice from trembling.

Reshana looked at her. 'Are you all right?' she asked.

'I have a headache,' said Astha, clenching her teeth, and carefully enunciating her words.

'Oh you poor thing. Why didn't you say? Come let me walk you to a scooter stand.' On the road Reshana gave Astha a brief hug. 'Take care.'

Astha replied, feeling foolish, 'You too, see you, bye,' and turned to a scooter man who was cleaning his teeth with a neem twig.

'How much to Vasant Vihar?'

'Thirty.'

'Too much.'

'That's what it costs.'

'I'll pay by the metre.'

'Metre not working.' The scooter wallah spat on the road to emphasise his point.

'Twenty-five,' argued Astha, 'I pay twenty-five every time.'

'Thirty. At this time I won't get a fare back,' he added to make the defeat easier for her.

Astha sat inside. The scooter wallah, galvanised into action, threw away his neem twig, and jumped vigorously up and down on the pedal. It didn't start. He flung open the seat, took out his tools along with a rag, fiddled with something underneath, carefully wiping his hands every five seconds.

'I can take another auto,' Astha pleaded. She didn't dare look at her watch.

The scooter wallah glared at her. 'I'm fixing,' he stated. 'Nothing wrong. Just fixing.'

Finally the vehicle coughed and shuddered. Astha's head throbbed along with everything else.

At the next red light more stalling. With cars furiously honking behind it, the scooter was reluctantly pushed to the side of the road, and tinker, tinker, on and on before it sputtered into life, only to collapse on the bridge over the tracks of the rail museum. Astha could stand it no longer. She jumped out, opened her purse defiantly, and thrust fifteen rupees towards the man's hand.

'What's this?'

'Your fare. Or don't you want it? This is the worst scooter I have seen in my life. You have made me late, very late.'

'What can I do? The scooter is about to start. Just fixing.'

'No. Here.'

'Twenty.'

'You make me late, and now you are arguing about the fare.' Astha was almost beside herself.

The scooter wallah was not impressed. 'I'm a poor man,' he insisted, scratching his balls. 'What can I do? The fare is twenty till here.'

Astha lacked the courage to throw fifteen rupees at the poor man and walk away. She thrust another five towards him, and walked down the bridge towards the next stop light, where there was a cab stand. She was coated with dust. The sound of traffic roared in her ears, there would be the problem of dinner waiting for her and the children's homework which would not have been touched.

It was clear from the moment she stepped inside that she was in trouble. Hemant received her frostily, no question as to how was the meeting, you are looking tired, are you all right, I will look after things, you go and lie down.

Instead there was silence through the hastily put together meal, silence as she went through the children's notebooks after dinner.

Himanshu wrinkled his nose at the balm on her forehead. 'You smell, Mama,' he complained.

'Sorry darling, my head is hurting,' murmured Astha.

'Shall I press it?' he asked. Himanshu liked pressing his mother's head, and she liked having him do it, the touch of his small inept hands soothing to her.

'All right,' she allowed. He scrambled into her lap, and put his face next to hers, managing to jab her eye with his finger. The discomfort was slight, but the tears still came. The day had been too much.

The homework was finished at last, the school bags packed and the children asleep. Before sinking her head onto her own pillow and blanking out the whole horrible day, Astha had to try and make amends with Hemant. He had come home, she had not been there, he must have been surprised, wondering, maybe even worried.

From the passageway she could see him in his reclining chair, with his newspaper, feeling lonely. She was his wife. Still she looked, feeling exposed in her thin nightie, breasts hanging loose and obvious, eyes watering with fresh balm. She lifted her feet to go towards him, but found herself walking to her bed. She was tired, her feet were telling her, and tired women cannot make good wives.

That night as the pain receded and she fell asleep, she dreamt. She and another person were riding close together in a scooter – rickshaw. The person turned, it was Aijaz with long silky hair, which brushed across her face. Astha leaned closer, the corners of their mouths met and pressed, alone against the commotion of the street. Slowly Astha opened her mouth, and bit on the hair. She didn't let go, even when the scooter stopped, and they got out, her mouth firmly clamped on the rich, long, black, thick, sweetly smelling, dusty hair. This made her dumb, she

154

could not argue with the scooter wallah, who was charging too much, but Aijaz took care of him. Aijaz took care of everything. Together, they walked into a room full of doors and windows, with a huge double bed in the centre. Blue and white curtains waved in the breeze, sunlight came flowing through, the bed was covered with soft, printed Rajasthani quilts. Doors opened, people walked in and out, but they were invisible.

Slowly they fell on the bed, kissing all the while, when Aijaz, entwined around her, turned into Reshana.

Reshana?

She woke. It was early morning, the sky was lightening, she could hear the birds beginning outside. Deeply unsettled, she turned to Hemant, opened his pyjamas, gave him an erection and climbed on top.

He forgave her sins of the evening before by responding.

The disturbance lingered with Astha all next day, the vividness and strong emotions of her dream demanding some kind of recognition. Hesitantly she started making sketches. Two women faced each other in a scooter, their noses covered because of the pollution, only the eyes visible. The scooter wallah was a dark Sardarji with a striking red turban. Perched next to him was a young man, taking a ride. Around the edges of the canvas, traffic, buildings, road, but in the centre the scooter with its passengers bent towards each other, the devouring eyes, the Sardarji and the young man.

'How's it going?' Reshana phoned to ask.

'Fine,' said Astha briefly, not wanting to engage with Reshana when her head was full of other things. She would think about the Manch canvas when she had finished this one.

Now that Astha was devoting practically all her afternoons to painting she found it difficult to work inside the house. There were too many interruptions, the servant, the children, the phone, the kitchen, her own restless mind. Besides which she was continually observed by whoever happened to be around, watched intently as she made preliminary sketches, prepared canvas, squeezed paint, mixed and applied colour, cleaned brushes. She could not say go away, that was rude as well as selfishly withholding of herself.

The canvases also meant that when they entertained guests, certain conversational sequences were invariably set in motion – who paints, my wife, oh really, very good hobby for a woman, my daughter also paints very nicely, or my sister, or wife's sister – you name it, there was always somebody who knew somebody who painted. Each time this happened Astha was forced to make her work the subject of idle gossip, a thing she hated doing.

She mentioned this to Hemant one weekend. They were in the bedroom lying off a heavy lunch eaten upstairs.

'I need more space.'

Hemant drew her close. 'The whole house is yours, Az.'

'I was thinking of something more specific. You know, a place to work in peace, spread my stuff about.'

She knew it sounded presumptuous and unfamily-like to want space that was hers and hers alone. Hemant clearly thought so too, as he said, 'You don't need more, you have all you can use here.'

'Not quite. I get in everybody's way.'

'Many women would die to have the space you do. We could never afford anything like this now. If only your father had done the same—'

'Maybe I could have the other room on the barsati?' Astha interrupted in a rush, a room so uncomfortable, distant, remote, and undesirable that she could ask with equanimity, and hopefully be given without hesitation.

'What?'

'Nobody is using it.'

'But it belongs to Sangeeta, she may feel insecure. You know how touchy she already is.'

A wave of anger hit Astha, Sangeeta sitting in Meerut was to be given greater consideration than herself.

'I will vacate it whenever necessary, besides the servants are already there, and presumably she tolerates that.'

'But darling, it has no electrical connections, how can you use it?'

'I'll get it wired, all we have to do is extend the connection from the servants' room.'

'It'll kill you, with your headaches, that's for sure.'

'Please, please, please.'

Hemant looked distinctly annoyed. His wife on the roof, next to the servants' quarters, painting.

'What is wrong with working down here? I let you work – I don't stop you – I say nothing about the smell, about the canvases all over.'

'The smell, the canvases, the inconvenience are exactly why. Please, darling.'

Hemant talked to his parents. They did not agree. Sangeeta would be very sensitive to a family member encroaching on her territory, servants were different.

Astha vowed bitterly to earn enough money to rent her own studio one day. In the meantime if there was no area available to her, she would try and make do with the wide ranges inside her head. Constantly reminded of the space nobody thought enough of her to give, she became very bad tempered during interruptions. Finally she steeled herself, she shut the door, and if disturbed too often locked it. In this way a certain uneasy privacy was granted her.

After *Women Travelling*, Astha's imagination increasingly worked in pictures. For the Manch painting she decided to experiment with an issue she felt strongly about. She would deal with the Rath Yatra, with the journey a Leader was making across the Hindu heartland in the name of unifying the nation. Like the religious leaders of old, he drove a chariot, identical to Arjun's in the serialised *Mahabharat*, familiar

157

to millions of viewers. That the chariot was really a DCM Toyota was a necessary concession to the 10,000 kilometres to be done in thirty-six days. His journey was to start from Somnath, one of the first places to be destroyed by Muslim mauraders (Mahmud of Ghazni) in 1025, and end in Ayodhya, where Lord Ram was born, the hallowed spot that needed to be reappropriated to assuage the feelings of 700 million Hindus. It was also a journey to political prominence.

To portray this Astha chose a large canvas, four by six, and again drew inspiration from Rajasthani miniatures. On one end was a temple, on the other was the Babri Masjid, on its little hill. Between the two the leader travelled, in a rath, flanked by holy men, wearing saffron, carrying trishuls, some old, some young, their beards flowing over their chests. Besides the rath on motorbikes were younger men, with goggles and helmets, whose clothes she painted saffron as well, to suggest militant religion. She sketched scenes of violence, arson and stabbing that occurred in towns on the way, people fighting, people dying; she showed young men slashing their bodies, and offering a tilak of blood to the Leader; she showed young men offering even more blood in a vessel; she showed the arrest of the Leader as he approached Ayodhya.

The day Astha finished her Manch canvas, called simply *Yatra*, she took a deep breath and stared at it for a long time. This was good, she felt it was. The Manch had promised her half the money for the painting, she wondered how much that would be.

This time Reshana priced Astha's painting at 20,000 rupees. 'It's very strong. A bit bloody, but the scale is so small it is not offensive. And it certainly adds to the colour.'

'Thanks,' said Astha, feeling warm and glowy.

'I had no idea you were doing the yatra. A controversial issue will be noticed in the reviews.'

Astha saw respect on her face, which pleased her, but unfortunately it also made her remember her dream. Desire for Hemant darted through her, the safe, solid, stable, secure thing in her life.

'Come back tomorrow and see where we have put it,' continued Reshana, and Astha returned from the exhibition hall with an empty feeling in her chest. The canvas she had worked on and thought about all these months was gone.

Again Reshana proved right. Astha's painting was mentioned in the reviews, one paper even printed a photograph of it, and it was sold before the end of the exhibition.

Hemant said, 'Congratulations, you must be really pleased, I am happy for you,' as though they had met at a party, instead of sharing the same bed for years.

Astha said, equally politely, 'Thank you, Hemant.' She put out of her mind an idle romance, that he would be the one to buy it, give it pride of place in house or office, and tell everyone that this was an example of his wife's work. She knew this was impossible, and that people who expect the impossible are setting themselves up for misery, and Astha would rather die than be such a pathetic woman.

Instead she hugged the vision of herself as a woman who had sold two paintings in one year, sum total thirty thousand rupees, of which ten thousand was hers. She felt rich and powerful, so what if this feeling only lasted a moment.

One day she would get so famous that Hemant would feel obliged to display something she had done, and somebody, friend? banker? associate? would see it and, impressed, would ask to meet her. Unlike Hemant, he would find her fascinating. Would he want to have an affair with her? What would he be like in bed? Here Astha firmly drew a line across the remaining part of her fantasy, it exceeded anything remotely credible.

～

Summer holidays. Everything that was touched or breathed was dust laden. The heat was its usual, intense and unbearable.

There was no question of Astha painting, her children were all over the place, she was busy with things to occupy them, summer workshops, the transportation involved, and the impending visit of Sangeeta with her children.

'Will you show Sangeeta Bua your paintings, Ma?' asked Anuradha.

'Right now I have nothing to show.'

'You have the picture of it from the newspaper, and the mention in the review.'

'Let it be, babu, she might think I am showing off.'

' So? Shefali is always boasting about all the things she has.'

'Poor thing. Sweetie, there is a lot of trouble in Shefali's house, her parents fight, and maybe she talks like that because she is insecure. Let's not say anything about my paintings it might make Sangeeta Bua feel bad.'

'You mean jealous.'

That was what Astha meant, but this was the child's aunt they were talking about. 'Painting is not everybody's cup of tea,' she temporised.

Through the summer, and the trials with Sangeeta, Sangeeta's children, Shefali and Samir, and her own children, her painting remained with her, at the back of her mind. She yearned for the moments when her hand, her eye, her brain fused into one, and her daily life was blocked out. She had experienced this increasingly with the second and third canvas, and she was impatient to experience it again.

Meanwhile the six of them shopped, went to the zoo, went to films, went to restaurants, went to Appu Ghar, went to the science museum, went to the crafts museum, went swimming. For a week the nine of them went to Nainital, where Hemant rented a cottage. Here they boated, roamed around the lake, took long walks, had pony rides, and Astha was wife, mother, sister-in-law, daughter-in-law.

Hemant was happy with her. He found this easier when his relatives were there, and Astha spending so much time with them. When their anniversary came, he bought her a ring, an emerald surrounded by tiny diamonds. The quality was excellent, and the ring looked well on her hand.

'Brings out your colour,' said Hemant turning the hand around in his own, smiling at her.

'Such a husband,' murmured her mother-in-law in the background. Sangeeta looked on registering each gesture.

There was no need for Astha to say anything.

The summer over, Sangeeta and her children departed, school about to start. Astha stood on the verandah over-looking her tiny garden, thinking her forced exile from paint, turpentine and linseed oil was at last over. She looked at the scene in front of her, wondering how she could catch even a fraction of it on canvas. The sky was heavy with dark clouds, the air had a grey yellow quality to it that made the grass and trees more luminous, the red flowers of the gulmohar tree more vivid, the waxy white flowers of the champa tree more arresting against their large dark green leaves. There was so much moisture in the air, that as the breeze blew, it brushed her face with dampness.

Mughal miniatures were full of monsoon scenes, lovers on the roof, the man's hand fondling the woman's breast, while the woman leans heavily against him, a grey sky above with white birds flying in a V-formation against the clouds. How about a monsoon urban scene, children splashing in puddles, kites flying, jamun, bhutta and phalsa sellers squatting in front of their baskets on pavements, and on the roof, a solitary woman looking towards the heavy darkness above. Melancholy filled her. After the deadness of summer, the monsoon was a time of awakening and desire, but what was one to do with one's longing?

She wished she could share her feelings with someone, but with only Hemant to fall back upon it was certain that her loneliness was secured. Still he was all she had, and she made an attempt when he came home and settled down to his drink.

'It was really pretty today.'

'I suppose. I didn't have time to notice.'

'That's why I am telling you. I want to share it.' But already the tone was edgy, and Hemant responded promptly.

'Yes, it's nice when you have time to admire nature.'

The offensive implications were clear. Astha forced a sketchy smile to her lips, then turned to study the label on the whisky bottle. More than this she could not lie.

'I have a surprise for you,' he said.

She was grateful, 'Oh, really? What?'

'We are going to Goa.'

'Goa! Why Goa? The monsoon has begun there.'

'Arre! You were the one who wanted to go.'

'That was in winter. In season.'

'Exactly. And do you know how expensive it is in season?'

'Not if we had stayed in a cheap place. There are plenty of those.'

'Why go if we have to slum it. Now I've got an excellent package deal.' His eyes softened and he squeezed Astha's arm. 'It's been fifteen years since we married. It's an anniversary present for you.'

'Our anniversary is over.'

'O-ho, May–July same thing. Either it's hot or it's raining. And the rates are off-season. I've got reservations for the Taj. When one goes to a five-star, the hotel becomes the destination then you really get your money's worth.' Hemant looked pleased with himself. 'Off season rates,' he repeated as they settled down to dinner.

'But Hem,' said Astha, managing to get excited at the idea of staying in a five-star hotel, if it was raining outside, so what, five-star was five-star. 'It will take two days to go there, two days to get back, almost as long as the stay itself, is it worth it?'

'We are flying,' and pride swelled his chest, and filled the room.

'What? Have you won a lottery?'

'I have to go to Bombay to see a dealer, the children's tickets will cost half, yours is the only ticket we have to pay for. We will spend the money you earned for your painting.'

'But darling, you could have asked me if I wanted to spend the money on a plane ticket, and that too when it is off season.'

'You have a bee in your bonnet about seasons. I am telling you it will be very nice, you don't trust me.'

'I do, really I do.'

'Then show it.'

It was fair, she told herself later, that her money should go towards paying for a family holiday, after all why should Hemant have to pay for everything. There was no question of any choice in the matter. Everything was already decided. They reached Goa in the rain, they drove to the hotel in the rain, the children ran towards the beach in the rain.

'Why don't we go too?' asked Astha. 'It might never stop raining.'

'No, you go.'

'I don't want to go without you,' said Astha. There was a possibility he would remind her they were on holiday, and why did they holiday if not to be together? She glanced wistfully outside. In the distance was the sound of the sea, and she could make out a thick grey and white undulating line.

'You are such a child,' said Hemant indulgently moving to her. 'Remember this trip was to celebrate our anniversary?' He started tugging at her sari.

'What are you doing? The children may come in any minute.'

'Just a quickie. They won't come for another fifteen minutes at least.'

Quickies. It seemed that was all they ever were. They completed the act within the specified time, the sound of the rain and the more distant noise of the sea mingling with Hemant's breathing in Astha's ears.

The next day it was clear in the morning.

'I have been talking to reception and they say that we should sight-see now as it will probably rain in the afternoon. I have hired a taxi.'

'Where are we going?' demanded Anuradha.

'Mapusa, and then some beaches.'

They set off. Husband, wife, two handsome children, riding in a taxi, sightseeing in Goa.

The town of Mapusa was small and barring a few traces of Portuguese influence, not very interesting. The Mediterranean colonial style of architecture could be seen here and there in old houses surrounded by lush green gardens, colourful bougainvillaea and hibiscus spilling over boundary walls, or flinging themselves with abandon on the houses.

After driving them around a bit, the taxi stopped in front of a hideous shopping arcade with concrete circles plastered all over for decoration. The traffic was chaotic and noisy, taxis, cars, cycles and motorbikes driven by scantily clad foreigners whizzing around.

'Cashew nuts, Goan wines,' said the driver firmly as the family hesitated inside the car. 'Antiques, silver, jewellery,' he continued gesturing at the dark spaces behind open doors.

'Might as well see what this town has to offer,' said Hemant.

Perhaps that was a mistake. Because one of the things the town offered was an antique silver box, priced at five thousand rupees. It was so beautiful Astha fell in love with it immediately – old, blackened, intricately carved, and totally useless.

'Please, can I have that box?' she asked Hemant.

'You must be out of your mind,' said Hemant.

The tone, the refusal both hurt her. She was an earning woman, why couldn't she have a say in how some of their money was spent? She never said anything when he chose to squander money on airline tickets, why couldn't she buy a box she liked? Maybe it was too expensive, but she was sure if they bargained, it would become cheaper. Besides silver was silver.

'It's so pretty. It would also be a memento of Goa.'

'It's too expensive, these people are all cheats.'

The shopkeeper sensing indecision, urged the box upon them, very nice, old box, old price, now it will be twice as expensive if you go to buy.

'See?' said Astha. 'Old prices.'

'How can you believe him? They all lie.'

'I also earn. Can't I buy a box if I want, even if it is a little overpriced?'

'You earn!' snorted Hemant. 'What you earn, now that is really something, yes, that will pay for this holiday.'

I have earned for my ticket she thought, but this was not the place to bring it up. The children pottering about in the shop had fallen silent. Anuradha went and stood at the doorway staring at the traffic. Himanshu was fiddling with the cashew nuts they had bought to take back to Delhi.

Astha let out her breath in jerks so that nothing was audible. 'Let's go,' she said almost to herself.

They went to see the other beaches, and on the way back from Vagator, Hemant put his arm around her for a conciliatory moment in the taxi. She could feel the solidness of his body next to hers. She felt limp, attacked and baffled. She didn't want his touch, his nearness to compete with the pureness of her despair.

She got through the rest of the day somehow, sick and wretched. The beaches were lovely, and she felt resentful of their beauty, resentful at being forced to register anything besides the pain within.

Back in the hotel, the children beat against her mind, forcing attention from her through their shells. 'Look, look at this one – you're not looking – see, mine, put it to your ear, can you hear the sound? – not like that, you have to put it like this, can you hear the sea now? – I want to take all these shells to Delhi, they will look so pretty – I'm not putting sand everywhere, they are perfectly clean – that's my shell – she took my shell – it's mine – I saw it first – no he did not – she's always taking my things – you are always taking his side . . .'

Another hour and Astha's head was splitting. By the time the children had eaten their dinner and changed she was ready for the waves of pain that submerged her consciousness.

The night passed. Twice, thrice she staggered to the bathroom, clutching the walls for support to retch into the pot. Each time she hoped the pain would lessen, but it didn't, and her nausea continued until the birds started chirping, and the dark sky turned silver with the day. Finally with nothing left in her stomach, nothing left of her, she managed to close her eyes and sink into a calm exhaustion.

Once or twice she was aware of Hemant asking from his side of the bed, expressing concern in a strained voice, 'Are you all right?'

She acknowledged its tokenness by replying in a voice hoarse from vomiting, 'I'm fine.'

'Are you sure?'

'Yes. The pain will soon go.'

It was late next morning. Hemant had given the children breakfast, and he was now sitting with Astha on the verandah, in front of a tray of tea and papaya. Astha looked over the undulating grassy patches to the sea line. She could hear the thundering of the waves. Above, the sky was rolling with heavy grey clouds. She couldn't remember seeing a miniature of the sea. Maybe miniature painters traditionally lived inland.

'Feeling better?' Hemant asked. She nodded. He held out his hand, and she put her own in it. The feel of it was dry and warm. There was a certain comfort she associated with this hand.

'I had hoped that with the sea air your headaches might become better, not worse,' he continued, a careful, mock blame in his voice.

'That would have been nice,' she managed just as carefully.

Inside, the children's voices could be heard trading shells, with a few brief snatches of argument.

'I think the children really like it here,' remarked Hemant, letting go of her hand to pour her a cup of tea.

It was tepid, but Astha sipped it gratefully, aware of the residual heaviness in her head with every motion.

The bill for five days and four nights was nine thousand five hundred rupees. Hemant was triumphant.

'That was money well spent,' he said as he came back to the room after settling all the accounts at the front desk.

Nine thousand five hundred rupees spent on one of the worst weeks of my life, thought Astha, as she stepped into the hotel bus for the airport. She thought hopelessly of all the things she could have done with that money, of the beautiful silver box she could have possessed and admired for ever. But their money spending was decided by him, not by her.

~

'Oh, God, you look terrible. Have you been ill?'

Thus was Astha greeted by her colleagues on the first day of school.

'The holidays were tiring,' she replied. 'My maid was away.'

Everybody understood what this meant.

'I tell you, after one's servant takes a holiday, it should be understood that we get a holiday too. Look at Astha, poor thing, it is obvious she needs a break.'

Take a break, how they all said it like a mantra, as if taking a break would make any difference when you always came back to the same thing.

Colleague two was talking of her sister-in-law, settled in America, who had discovered that her husband was cheating on her, and who now wanted a divorce. This brought about the usual virtuous reactions centring around Us and Them, East versus West.

'There they go on divorcing – marrying till the age of 60–70.'

'They do not understand the concept of family. They only think of themselves.'

'The divorce rate is three out of four.'

'They don't know what it is to be a woman, what it is to sacrifice.'

Well, Astha was a woman, and she was sick of sacrifice. She didn't want to be pushed around in the name of family. She was fed up with the ideal of Indian womanhood, used to trap and jail. Excuse me, stop the juggernaut and let me off. I have had enough.

'It may not be a bad thing,' she said tentatively. 'If a marriage is terrible, it is good to be able to leave.'

Everybody stared at her. Astha fiddled with her notebooks. They would be wondering whether her marriage was all right. 'Take my sister-in-law, for example,' she added quickly. 'Her only time off is with us in the summer. She is not allowed to work, rather her in-laws make her slave inside the house, she is nothing but an unpaid servant. If she complains, her husband sides with his parents. If she were in the West she could contemplate divorce without the social and economic death that would follow here.'

The bell rang. Astha got up carrying the forty notebooks of her students and headed for class. She had a job, there was no doubt as to that, but she doubted whether that made her any less trapped than poor Sangeeta. She should have kept her mouth shut about divorce. Its sole result would be speculation about her.

Meanwhile Anuradha turned thirteen and started menstruating. She did not take kindly to this, and Astha grew to dread her periods, interspersed as they were with bouts of rage, pain and depression. She could not remember ever attracting so much attention to herself during these times, even when it had hurt unbearably.

'It is a woman's lot,' she explained.

'Why, why is it a woman's lot, it's not fair,' moaned Anuradha, as she clutched her hot water bottle, tears flowing from her eyes, wetting the corners of her face, disappearing into her hair.

Where does fairness come into it, thought Astha. It hurts, you bear it. That was the end of the matter. 'It happens so you can have children,' she tried again.

'I'm never going to have children, I'm going to adopt.'

'We'll see when the time comes. You might want your own children.'

Anuradha glared at her mother and did not deign to reply.

'What's the matter with Didi?' piped up Himanshu, who was watching his sister wail and scream with great interest.

'She's got a stomach ache. Go and see what is on TV, beta.'

'Nothing is on TV. Why can't we get a dish and watch the Gulf War?'

Astha turned to stare at her son. Anuradha forgot her pain long enough to point out how spoilt he was.

'What's wrong with *Chitrahaar*? You have always liked it.'

'I want to watch the Gulf War. In school everybody watches the CNN and the BBC.'

'I doubt everybody in school has a dish. You can talk to your father when he comes.'

'How was the day?' asked Hemant when he came home that night.

'Terrible. Anu has her period.'

169

'Oh? Poor little thing. Was it very bad?'

'Yes. I had to give her two Brufen. I hope she doesn't become dependent on them. How will she bear pain in later life?'

'She's still a little thing. Why should she have to suffer so much?'

'She's not so little, and it's part of nature.'

'Where is she now?'

'In bed with a hot water bottle, reading Nancy Drew. And she has a test tomorrow.'

'Poor baby, let her be,' repeated Hemant quickly, pouring himself a drink and making for Anu's bedside.

'Oh Papa, I want some chocolate,' murmured Anuradha in a babyish voice, snuggling next to her father.

'Tomorrow, all right?'

'All right.'

He never sounds or looks like that when I have a headache, thought Astha, and then struck that thought from her consciousness. The father–daughter bond could not be compared to the rocky terrain of a marital relationship.

A few weeks later a dish appeared on the terrace. Astha was informed of this casually the night before.

'A dish? But it is so expensive.'

'It is good for the children. They will see the BBC, the CNN, they will know what is happening in the world. Who can watch Doordarshan? Two channels, I ask you. Now at least they will have competition.'

'But such a lot of money, to have a dish in our own house. We are not a hotel, or something.'

'Arre, I am in the TV business, I have to keep up with these things.'

Astha's mind travelled to the little silver box in Mapusa, only five thousand, while the dish was at least eight times that. But it was useless to say or feel anything, the children and the business ensured the non-comparable nature of any argument. If she knew how much money they had, she might be on surer ground, but she never did.

~

31 December. Constitution Club. 6.30 p.m. A slight mist was beginning to add to the general chill. Astha had not realised it would be this cold, and she stood shivering in her sweater and shawl. Nearby was a peanut seller, roasting his peanuts over a small fire but she didn't dare advance towards him, in case it looked as though she thought more of her appetite than the cause.

It was the anniversary of the massacre of The Street Theatre Group. It was also a protest against the Hindu Samaj Andolan decision to construct a temple at the site of the Babri Masjid.

'Come and help me, Astha,' said Reshana, approaching with two big plastic bags. Squatting on the pavement, they poked candles through tiny foil-coated plates to prevent wax from dripping onto the hands that carried them. Absorbed, Astha could forget the scene she had had with Hemant before she left.

Ten days ago, Hemant had asked, 'What shall we do this New Year's Eve?'

Astha looked wary. Last year they had spent over two thousand to go to a five-star hotel with friends, and Astha had disgraced herself by getting a headache and throwing up at one o'clock in the morning with the discomfort of everyone's concern directed towards her. 'Leave me at home,' she had pleaded when Hemant had taken it up with her. 'I can't help myself.' But that was not socially acceptable either.

'I don't know,' she now said. 'What did you have in mind?'

'I'm not sure,' said Hemant leafing through brightly coloured invitations sent by various hotels and clubs about Xmas Nite, New Year's Eve Nite, dinner and dance. 'The Delhi distributor has invited us, they have booked a hall at the Sayonara club.

But it's not very personal, they call all their clients, and it is one big tamasha,' said Hemant looking disgusted.

'Can't we stay at home,' asked Astha tentatively. 'That's really personal.'

'Stay at home on New Year's Eve? No thank you.'

'Tell me then, where are we going?'

'We've got several invitations, let's see how many we can take in,' said Hemant, his pride at being socially sought after showing in his voice.

'All right,' said Astha, not bothering to ask who the invitations were from. Some friends, some place. Eating, drinking, laughing, talking. It made no difference to her. Her mind was always not quite there.

She didn't tell him about the demonstration, also planned for New Year's Eve. She felt this information would not be well received.

Now she was about to be proved right. Hemant saw her getting ready to leave and demanded, 'Where are you going? I am free, you know that.'

Astha thought of all the evenings she had been free and waiting, and wondered if there would ever be a day when she could feel the same right to complain that Hemant did. Now she tried to be conciliatory, she didn't want tension on a night of heavy duty partying. 'I am not going to be away long, just an hour.'

'Where are you going?' Hemant repeated.

'To a demonstration outside Rashtrapati Bhavan. It is the anniversary of the massacre.'

'You seem to forget that your place as a decent family woman is in the home, and not on the streets. You also forget that this is New Year's Eve, and we are going out.'

'No, I do not forget. I will come back in time, what does it matter what I do one or two hours before?'

Hemant's face assumed its shut-in aspect. Astha knew she was equivocating. It mattered because going out with her husband must be the highlight of the day, not something she was squeezing into the rest of her activities, unregarded, unimportant, done for the sake of doing. She left the house, hoping the anticipation of parties would do its bit in removing Hemant's ill humour.

Back at the Constitution Club. By 7 p.m. about three hundred people had gathered. 'Good turnout,' said Reshana to Astha as they finished with the last of the candles, and gathered themselves up from the pavement. 'And that too on New Year's Eve. We did contact everybody but you can never be sure.'

'Many might think this is the best way to spend it,' said Astha with feeling. 'To do something you believe in makes other things a little easier.'

Reshana drew back. Astha flushed. There she was trying to give Reshana her heart and soul, behaving inappropriately. She must remember that everybody was here for the cause, and if the cause also had a personal impetus, discretion demanded this be shrouded in silence.

Down Rajpath they marched, candles glowing. They carried placards that declared they were for a united India, that secularism was part of our Constitution and traditions, that communalism was the scourge of the nation.

They chanted as they went:

Raise your voices – We are one
We will fight injustice – We will fight together
Communalism will – Never succeed, never succeed
These are false weapons – Of the true god Ram
False Ram-lovers – False weapons
Temple, church – Mosque, gurudwara,
All the same – The same for all

Up towards Raisina Hill, candles dripping wax on the paper plates, holding a memorandum, on which they had been gathering signatures for the past month, protesting the attacks on the Muslims, protesting the bid to demolish the Babri Masjid.

Around them swirled cars and pedestrians, irritated at having to stop in front of aggressive placards and glowing candles, while the procession marched across as many roads as it could, hindering traffic, drawing attention to its message.

Towards Rashtrapati Bhavan, home of the President, home of previous Viceroys. Huge, mammoth, it towered in the distance, far from the high and massive wrought-iron gates that barred unauthorised entry. There the processionists halted, lit by TV cameras that dimmed the candles they were focused on. From Raisina Hill Astha could see the lights of cars swishing up and down Rajpath. How few we are, how many indifferent on this one road. She looked towards the former Viceroy's Lodge. Designed as a regal sandstone testimony to British glory, it had served its purpose for only seventeen years, before becoming a testimony to illusion.

The protest songs and slogans continued. Finally an official arrived, and a side gate opened a suspicious crack. The memorandum along with two spokespersons squeezed in; two people and a thousand signatures of mainly school and college teachers, artists, painters, and film people. A lot of the marchers had brought their children, who looked as convinced as their parents as to the justice of their cause and the usefulness of their protest, never mind how few they were.

While they were waiting a letter was read out. Worded in English – objection – it should be in Hindi. The writer, an English academic, quickly explained in Hindi that the letter would be in both languages, and sent to all the leading newspapers. For now he begged their indulgence, he would read the letter in English, pending its immediate translation.

The letter proclaimed that the Sampradayakta Mukti Manch, and the teacher and artist community were united in condemning both the BJP and the Congress in encouraging

Fascist forces in the country, and in failing to take quick action against the threats to the Babri Masjid. Were these threats actualised, secularism would be at grave risk, and communal hatred unleashed on a scale that would be difficult to control. To take no action was tantamount to encouraging social divisions along religious lines. Weaker sections would suffer. This was not to be tolerated. We appeal to the government to do something before it is too late.

Signed—

A resolution was then formed to establish a core group that would see to further action, the first being to circulate more petitions.

This done, the songs resumed:

For how long will they loot my village?
Taking a torch I will go
Through the world I will wander
To make my village safe for me.

Half an hour passed without any sign of the spokespersons. The last night of the year was wearing on. Astha kept surreptitiously looking at her watch.

'Arre, will we ring in the New Year here?'

'Let's go, they can come later.'

'No point hanging around.'

The TV crew began to pack up. The candles had burnt down. As the procession started back towards the Manch office, Astha lagged behind, keeping a sharp look out for an empty scooter. She had to be home by eight-thirty, or things would be worse with Hemant. At one point where the procession had stopped the traffic she found one, and by quickly agreeing to pay his price, bumped her way home.

～

It turned out they were going to at least three of the parties they had been invited to. Senior bank manager, dear friend, and American NRI come to visit his parents.

Astha hurried towards a thick dressy silk sari, peeling off her woollens. The sari was green with a broad red and gold border with woven flowers, hearts and peacocks. A matching deep green blouse was dotted with tiny gold paisleys. Her ordinary jewellery would have to do, she hadn't had time to go to the bank locker to take out some of her heavier stuff. Hopefully Hemant wouldn't notice. She threw her mother-in-law's maroon pashmina shawl casually over her shoulder, and thus guaranteed to freeze in the manner of women partying in Delhi winters, she was ready.

Ready to feel cold, ready to drink, dance, smile, laugh, talk, ready for anything the last day of the year might bring. She had made a gesture of some significance before Rashtrapati Bhavan, it made her more amenable to the evening now. Having something of your own makes you strong, she thought.

'All set?' asked Hemant picking up his wallet and car keys.

'Yes,' replied Astha. She was pleased that he had put the unpleasantness over her involvement in the demonstration behind him. They were going to have a nice time.

'You look very nice,' he commented admiringly.

'Thank you,' said Astha, feeling a small flush of pleasure.

'I thought we would go to the manager's house first. It is bound to be the dullest, we can leave quickly.'

The senior bank manager lived in a large house in the older part of South Delhi. Clearly he believed in doing things big. The little front lawn, shamiana draped, the verandah, the drawing, dining room, all were devoted to the party.

'Gosh,' said Astha, as they were bumped constantly by people, avoiding glasses, and lighted cigarettes, 'there must be five thousand people here.'

'More like two hundred,' said Hemant smiling indulgently.

Astha could see his mood had further lightened. It had taken two hundred people but still she was glad.

She put out her hands to warm over an angeethi and tried not to breathe the thin spirals of acrid smoke coming from it, the coals were obviously wet. Other women holding soft drinks and glasses of juice were also standing around the angeethi. Astha smiled at them uncertainly, noticing the jamawars and pashminas flung over their shoulders, their smooth white waxed arms, glittering jewellery, and beauty parlour done hair. They looked perfect, perfect in a way she could never hope to look, lacquered and finished. She wished she could say she despised that look, and she did despise it, in theory, while crumbling wordlessly before it in practice, never able to hold her own.

She took a deep breath, turned to the woman next to her, and remarked, 'Cold isn't it?'

The woman smiled her agreement, 'What does your husband do?' she asked in her turn.

'He manufactures television sets. And yours?'

And so the phrases flowed on, till Hemant, one double whisky down, gestured to her that it was time to leave.

The next party was at the house of the parents of the NRI. The place was full of men slapping each other on the back, counting the years they had been acquainted, walking down memory lanes, those lanes always so evident at this time of year with the foreign returned, the come back for two-three weeks when the weather is good and the kids can stand it, returned.

The food was mostly chaat and snacks. There was all kinds: papri, gol guppa, and for those who couldn't eat cold things in cold weather, hot tikkis, with green sour chutney and red sweet chutney, fat and swollen bhatura served with spicy channa, laced with halved green chillies and onion rings, dosas, idlis and vadas, and finally jalebis floating in hot oil, crisp, sweet, inviting to be crunched up ring by ring. There was even tea in earthen mugs which all those who weren't drinking sipped gratefully.

'Oh, can't we go home, now?' moaned Astha, who thought she would burst if she had to eat another thing.

'One more party, darling,' said Hemant over his whisky glass. 'Chin up.'

I hope he is not too drunk to drive, thought Astha, the glow the food had given her fading, as she thought of the drive to Greater Kailash II where Hemant's closest school friend resided.

Ankur's party was on the terrace of his two-roomed barsati. Ankur had divorced after ten years of marriage, and was now discovering the joys of an affluent single life in an emphati-cally male environment. He fancied himself a cook, and with flushed face offered earthen mugs of mulled wine, mulled wine going ethnic, he said genially. On one side of the terrace a barbecue was set up. Seekh kababs, paneer, mutton and fish tikkas were being served with thin romali rotis, folded into triangles, on flimsy silver paper plates. There were four dead-looking salads, all smothered in shiny glutinous mayonnaise: pink (thousand island?) green (herb?) two whites (garlic? yoghurt?). As Astha jabbed at bits of paneer, it was easier to seem to eat than to argue with her host, she wondered it was only five hours ago that she had stared at wax dripping onto an identical foil plate.

Inside the music was loudly drowning everything out.

'Come, darling, let's dance.' Hemant's alcohol-aided spirits were high.

Astha obediently swayed, her sari palla slipping, looking covertly at the others doing their stuff to popular numbers pounding through the dimly lit smoky room.

'Are you OK?' shouted Hemant above the din.

'Yes,' she shouted back, automatic response-cum-smile.

'Good,' he said, his voice slightly slurred, and in the dark he came towards her and pecked her cheek. His breath smelt of whisky, and she let her head tilt towards him, imitating reciprocity, before a couple bumped into them and forced them apart.

'Now, now,' they shrieked, 'no kissing between husbands and wives.'

How stupid they all are, thought Astha. No kissing between husbands and wives. As though we were something besides conservative, strait-laced, middle-aged Indians. Should an unmarried couple kiss, I would like to see the reaction, I would just like to.

Early next morning Astha rose, made herself a cup of tea and went out. It was another year, and she wanted to mark it in some way special to her. New Years should be private affairs, she thought, thinking of all the partying she had done last night. They had screeched Happy New Year, hugged, kissed, danced, eaten relentlessly, drunk this and that, and finally at 2 a.m. made their way home, Hemant slow and careful because he was trying to appear in control, and Astha silent, because she knew Hemant had drunk more than he should have, and there was no tone sufficiently neutral in which she could convey this.

It was cold in the tiny garden. Astha grabbed the mali's jhaaroo, and began to sweep the dead leaves into a pile. She wanted to make a fire. A fire was a good New Year's thing. Burning all the old year debris away.

As the flames smoked through the wet leaves, Astha cupped her hands around the mug of tea. It was Flowery Orange Pekoe, a delicate and flavourful smell. She smiled, thinking of the year ahead. She had found what she really wanted to do, something she was good at, she was lucky. She now felt established enough as a painter to give her art the time and energy that was its due. She was ready to leave her job. She had been teaching almost fifteen years, staying because it had been a good occupation for a woman.

She finished her tea, and went into the spare room. It was early, but she wanted to begin the first day of the New Year with work important to her. She took out her file and started visualising scenes for a March for Justice. The idea had grown last night among the candles. The canvas would be dark, with a group of people huddled before the gates of Rashtrapati Bhavan, which loomed remote and massive in the background. The bright spots were going to be the candles the marchers held, the yellow of the halogen street lamps and the red and white lights of the cars on Rajpath. The rest would be in shadow. Astha hummed as she worked. There was no one to tell her how tuneless her singing was.

VI

Pipee stumbled into the New Year alone in her flat, staring at the two-rod heater, nursing a small rum and coke. It had been a year since Aijaz's death, and as every day in the past year, she had been fierce in her desire to be alone, turning down well-meaning invitations that friends, colleagues, relatives and acquaintances showered her with.

Her mother-in-law had phoned from Shahjehanpur asking her to visit. But she couldn't. Not yet. The one time Pipee went, she had hardly been able to stand the memories that swept her every inch of the way. In every face she saw traces of Aijaz, and their sweetness to her had made it even harder.

She and her mother-in-law had cried and cried together, but conversation had been difficult, everything they had in common was in the past. She only stayed a few days, and as she was leaving, the mother-in-law gave her a cheque for one lakh. 'I didn't spend on your marriage, now you take this.'

'I don't want it,' Pipee's voice trembled, there seemed no limit to the number of times they could cry together.

'Please, for him,' replied the mother. 'He would not like to think we did not look after his wife. I want you to know you will always have a home with us.'

Dully, and with Neeraj's help, Pipee bought a flat in Vasant Kunj. She had the money from Shahjehanpur, life insurance, and dollars sent to her by her brother.

It usually takes a lifetime to possess a place of one's own.

'You can't go on like this,' Neeraj had remonstrated on New Year's Eve at the office. 'It is not healthy. You are still young.'

'I don't feel young. I don't feel anything.'

'Make an effort, you are not even trying.'

Pipee turned away. What did Neeraj think, that she liked feeling the way she did? In fact she would give anything to be free from the thoughts that haunted her. Only since Aijaz's death did she realise that how you die is as important as the loss itself, and can make all the difference to the ones left behind.

There was no relief from the pain of his final moments. She couldn't get rid of the thought of him trapped in the Matador, suffocating with the heat, burning bit by bit, screaming for help perhaps, trying to break the windows, wrench open the doors, and then the terrible moment when he realised he was going to die, him along with nine others, those nine there because of him. What had it felt like? Had he been able to think of her, their love, their lost future?

Till now not a single culprit had been brought to book. Perhaps if the assassins had been identified and punished, a bit of the horror might be stilled; she didn't know, she only knew it wasn't likely to happen. As for that Sampradayakta Mukti Manch, she hated it more than anything. What had they done to ensure justice? Had they worked on bringing pressure on any government organisation? No, they had a platform in his name which they called freedom from communalism, and all they did was hold exhibitions, raise money, and indulge in cultural nonsense. She hated them, each and every one of them individually, but above all she hated Reshana Singh, who had surfaced out of the woodwork, from god knows where, after Aijaz's death and taken over his memory. She managed to imply that theirs had been a deep connection, she was practically masquerading as his wife. How well had she known Aijaz, she was so much older than him, that any attraction on her husband's part must have been a purely passing phase.

What should she do, should she leave Delhi? Her mother had tried to get her to relocate in the south, you can find an NGO in Bangalore or Madras, there are slums here as well. You need to put the past behind you, start a new life, you will be near me, come, come, she persuaded in letter after letter. Pipee now looked at the last one:

My darling daughter,

Every day I miss you, think of you, pray to God for your well being, and the courage that will see you through this crisis. Aijaz was a wonderful man, a loving husband, and you were lucky in your marriage. I say this despite the terrible tragedy, because what you two had can never leave you. You have been a wife, you have been loved, and this will stay with you for the rest of your life.

I know what you are going through and darling I would have given my right hand for the same thing not to have happened to you that happened to me. But it seems we cannot escape our destiny, whether our husbands are young or old.

Maybe it is a blessing in disguise that you have no children. When your father left me, I had my Pipeelika, and my Ajay, I needed no one else, but you with your youth, your intelligence, your personality, you need other outlets. Aijaz would not want you to be unhappy or alone. I know that. Life has its own laws that will be heard and felt.

You are always, always in my heart,

Your loving Ma.

Maybe, she thought, staring at her mother's letter, she really should make more of an effort to go out. Although it had been a year she didn't feel any better, perhaps she never would. But to go on refusing to meet people, always to be alone, that was not the answer either. Her life stretched before her, long and dreary. What her mother was advising was to form a new relationship. But how? Aijaz had been hard enough to find. And there had been Samira when she was young. She had never loved anybody else.

Perhaps she should go to the States, leave Aijaz to the Reshanas of this world. The whole of last year Ajay had been calling her insistently for a Ph.D. programme, you will be surprised what a difference a complete change of place will make.

Yes, she would be surprised. Ajay had no imagination, but still she, who had lost everything and had nothing more to lose, could give it a try. In the meantime she might travel with Ujjala.

With these thoughts, in front of the heater, eating her dinner of scrambled egg on toast, Pipee passed into the new year.

~

Waving saffron flags, Hinduism marched across the country in the following months, marched in time to film songs converted into bhajans, to Leaders trying to convince the masses that the glory of an ancient land could be resurrected by their united hands. Young men, show your manhood, rescue mother India from the influence of the Muslim invaders, whose long shadow falls over us even now. The wrongs of the past have to be righted.

These hoards, gathered mostly from the Hindi heartland, become the face of militant Hinduism, armed with tridents, swords, and a determination to die if necessary for the cause entrusted to them. This behemoth turns it head towards Ram's Janambhoomi. A temple needs to be constructed on the sacred soil of Ram's birthplace, burdened for so many years by a mosque. A date is fixed for the event.

As they converge upon Ayodhya, a cordon is drawn around the city, roads are blocked, trains and buses denied entry, any leader suspected of creating trouble is carefully watched.

But there are always the fields and villages, always people to give food, water, rest, and show the way.

And likewise there are leaders to hide in the lanes of Ayodhya to mastermind the breaking of the cordon around the city, there are officials in the state police who feel it their duty to personally assist all those similarly inclined.

The kar sevaks declare that neither guns nor bullets can stop them. They prove this when in defiance of all barriers they climb the mosque, plant a saffron flag on the highest dome and claim it for their own. They are fired upon by the police, hundreds of them are injured, many are killed. Videos are made of this, and are later shown around the country as an example of the threat to Hinduism.

The government falls, and for the time being further crisis is averted, but only for the time being, promise the forces for Hindu Restoration in India.

Give us three places in India, that is all we want, Ayodhya, Varanasi, and Mathura where the Muslim invader built mosques on our sacred sites. If necessary we will bathe these mosques in blood. Why should Hindus give up their position of dominance in the only Hindu country in the world? If it is mosques the Muslims want, let them go to the many countries where Islam is the official religion, we are not stopping them.

The Sampradayakta Mukti Manch were doing what they could in the face of resurgent communalism. They prepared pamphlets, organised marches with other Left groups, and decided to go to the banks of the Saryu to talk directly to the people of Ayodhya to counter the growing rhetoric of religious fanaticism. As they planned their trip, Reshana suggested that Astha also come. 'Between you and me I wonder if academics sometimes have the impact we desire. How I wish Aijaz was with us today. He could capture a crowd like no one else.' She sighed and continued, 'If you could give a small five-ten minute speech? I think it might make a difference to the women. If they realise they have some kind of voice, it will be a useful counter thrust to violence and aggression. After all they stand to lose the most. It's worth a try.'

Astha agreed. Now that she was no longer teaching she welcomed brief respites from the house. And yes, any contribution to the cause was worth a try. In her association with the Manch she had been exposed to detail after detail of atrocities perpetuated in the name of religion. She had made paintings for this cause, she had been part of debates that worried about the far-reaching implications of fundamentalism, she had seen the spread of the worst kind of jingoistic rhetoric and it gave her both a platform and a focus around which she built her work. When she looked back it seemed amazing that she had come such a long way in two years. The detour she had taken between home and school had now become the road she travelled.

'I hope it won't be a problem, leaving your children,' Reshana ended.

It was a rhetorical statement, but Astha responded with a dry laugh, 'Since when has the personal been allowed to interfere with the need of the hour?'

So far her mother-in-law had not commented about her activities. But Astha's going to Ayodhya was a different matter.

'You know I never interfere in whatever you decide to do. Today young people feel they must live their own lives. But there are times when it is necessary to listen to the advice of elders. What is the need to leave your family, and roam about like a homeless woman on the streets of some strange city?'

'To protest.'

Mummy looked nonplussed. 'But why go to Ayodhya?' she returned after a pause. 'You want to say something you write a letter to the newspapers. That is much better. People get to hear. You used to write.'

'Long ago.'

'This is all politics, you should not get involved. Besides have you thought about what you are going to protest? Lord Ram's Janamsthan is in Ayodhya, is there any country in the world where the birthplace of their god is not honoured? Hindu tolerance does not mean you accept everything and anything. Is this the pride we have in ourselves?'

'But Mummy, if the temple is constructed, thousands of people will die agitating over it. Why they could feed hun-

186

dreds of poor children on the money they are collecting for the bricks.'

Her mother-in-law looked at her. 'It is not a woman's place to think of these things,' she said firmly.

Astha remained silent, her mind full of her husband. She had mentioned her trip as a possibility in a casual conversation with Hemant. Was this his way of letting her know he did not want her to go? He did not even have time for a discussion with her.

Meanwhile Mummy was repeating, 'You know I never try and stop you from doing anything. Even when you neglect the children, and are busy in your paintings and meetings, I do not say anything. I am not the type to interfere. I am glad my daughter-in-law does not feel she has to sit at home. Till I have the use of my hands and feet I will help you, but it is my duty to point out that you are going too far.'

'You won't have to help with the children this time, I will take them,' said Astha wildly thinking of Anuradha's sulky face, and Himanshu's bewildered expression. 'It is good if they are exposed to such things early.'

'Exposing them to what? Filth and crowds? Don't you care about your children or husband? But he is too good, he will say nothing. If you were living in the conditions Sangeeta is, you would better value what you have. I hope you never regret this.'

Astha was struck dumb. Her mother-in-law had never spoken so openly before. And where did Hemant have the time to notice what she was doing, let alone mind? But he had noticed, he had minded, and so had others. Mumbling something non-committal she retreated downstairs shaking with rage and hopelessness. With a mother like that, what chance that Hemant would ever support her? She dreaded trying to convince him and the possible scene. And because she dreaded these things, she became all the more determined to go.

*

The argument started that night when they were getting ready to go to bed.

'I have decided to go to Ayodhya,' she said.

'As my wife, you think it proper to run around, abandoning home, leaving the children to the servants?'

Astha went into familiar distress. As his wife? Was that all she was?

She tried to interest him in the issue, pulling out a pamphlet from her bedside drawer, 'Look at the stuff they are publishing. It's so inflammatory but people fall for it.'

'You should see the stuff they publish against India and Hindus in Pakistan. Why don't you protest against that?'

'I do protest. I happen to think that any religion that incites violence is bad, ours, theirs, everybody's. Listen to this:

This is not a 'new' political struggle. It is the 77th attempt in the history to restore the Ramjanambhoomi, our heritage. Thus far over 300,000 kar sewaks have laid down their lives in the 400 years.

Pseudo-secularists want the mosque declared a national monument forgetting that Ram was an Indian and Babur an invader. It is a national dishonour if a symbol of invasion is so declared:

'Now Ask Yourself!'

Can even the most tolerant, most reasonable and peace-loving Indian run away from his pride – the reason for his being? The time has come to fight for our threatened faith.

'Hindus unite! Act as one.

Not against anyone!

But in defence of our motherhood.'

She watched as Hemant reached out and turned the Ramjanambhoomi Nyas pamphlet over in his hands. She liked his hands. They were so square, so competent, they smelled nice, they felt nice on her. His palms were soft and pink, his nails always short and clean. Why was it like this between them? She sidled next to him, and put her hands under his kurta, rubbing his soft stomach. 'I do so wish they hadn't planned it around New Year's. I hate to leave you alone, but darling what to do?' Plaintive, appealing, emphatic.

Hemant grunted. 'Say no, what else is there to do?'

'But I have committed, it'll look bad.'

'They don't own you.'

'Just for two days. I'll be back so soon, you won't realise I have gone,' said Astha trying to be playful.

'I won't be here.'

'Why?'

'I have to go away.'

'But you never said.'

'I only knew of this today.'

She did not believe him. How would she leave the children? She would have to move them upstairs, and that too after her dignified statement of taking them with her. He was doing this to punish her.

'Where are you going?'

'Bombay. To see a dealer. It's important.'

Astha did not ask how and why, and nor did Hemant elaborate. 'What about the children?' she asked a little forlornly. They had never been without both parents before, without her really, Hemant was frequently away.

'That's your responsibility,' he replied. 'I have work to do, a factory to run, I can't be both mother and father.'

She would have to be conciliatory with Mummy, she would have to sit down and explain why she was going instead of getting angry, she would have to tell the children she was leaving them with their grandmother, and hope the grandmother would not bad mouth her while she was away. She might as well have spared herself the worry of what Hemant was going to do, he was going to manage just fine.

That night she couldn't sleep. Her mind refused to rest, roaming restlessly among the things that made up her life, her home, children, husband, painting, the Sampradayakta Mukti Manch. Was it too much for a woman to handle; was her mother-in-law right? But why? Her children were well taken care of, she had trustworthy servants, she had someone who cooked better than she, she had left her teaching. And yet she was chained.

Her thoughts grew darker and darker. Restlessly she tossed to and fro, looking for a position that would force her mind to imitate her closed eyes, and free her into sleep. Hemant snored next to her, and his impenetrability irritated her further.

Next morning, tired and bewildered, she got up, looked at her husband, who appeared fresh and lovely. He glanced at her, and she smiled, her lips stretched across her face, cracking her skull, but still her lips would stretch, and her eyes would look up at him.

Hemant left for Bombay, departing one day before she did, destroying the fantasy she had had that he might drop her at the station, and they could part tenderly with many expressions of I will miss you, hurry back, phone me when you reach.

'You are also leaving?' Himanshu asked, round eyes.

'Yes darling, only for two days.'

'But why?'

'I have some work.'

But this explanation did not resonate the way the father's did, and both mother and son felt a little unconvinced.

Next night, the train to Ayodhya from Old Delhi at 9.30 p.m. Both children insisted on accompanying her to the station. Mala was taken to escort them back. They left the house at 8.00 and at 8.30 were caught in a religious procession starting from a gurudwara.

Mother, son and daughter watched the green dial of the dashboard clock tick the minutes away as they waited and waited. For the first time Astha felt the impatience Hemant did in traffic, but there was nothing she could do, blaming the

190

government did not come so easily to her, nobody to blame in fact, but God above who had made them Indians in an over-crowded land.

People darted in and out of the traffic, bumping against rickshaws, cars, buses, weaving in and out all over the road. From time to time cars, scooters and scooter-rickshaws inched forwards squeezing themselves wherever they could, but they could not squeeze themselves as small as people did.

'Will Mama miss the train?' asked Himanshu interestedly.

'Don't be stupid,' said Anuradha.

Astha clenched her fists. 'I think I can see the traffic lights now,' she said after the car had crawled along for twenty minutes.

It was five to nine. There were the traffic lights visible at last, the end of the intersection was almost in sight, it was the last major light before the station.

Finally they reached. Station. Parking lot. Platform. They might as well have saved themselves all that anxious clock-watching. The train was one hour late. They hung around the platform, surrounded by standing, sitting, squatting, lying, waiting people. There was hardly any room to move. By the year 2010 standing room only in India. Make way, make way, squeeze in more, that year is lurking around the corner.

'How long do we have to wait for that stupid train?' com-plained Anuradha, while Himanshu clung to her. Astha felt his body through her sari, felt his arms around her waist, his hand resting on the bit of bare back between her sari and her blouse.

'Do you want an orange?' she asked.

He nodded. Astha reached into her sling bag and started peeling one.

'I also want,' said Anuradha indignantly. Astha handed her half.

Announcement. The train was delayed another hour. The people on the platform stirred, rippled, and then settled down to waiting again.

'Go home,' said Astha, 'Mala take them home. It is getting very late.'

'No, I'm not going, I'm waiting with you,' wailed Himanshu.

'We will wait, it's all right,' said Anuradha gruffly. She demanded some money to buy *Stardust*, and settling herself on her mother's suitcase, began to read. Himanshu picked his nose, and looked vacantly at the train tracks beyond his feet.

At last the whistle, the clang, the arrival. The platform woke, and a huge beast sprang into motion. It pushed, it shoved, it jostled. Sharp cornered boxes and heavy suitcases were lugged onto the heads of coolies while the parcels and bags slung from its arms jut, poke, obstruct, protrude, and threaten with injury. Astha clutched Himanshu with one hand and dragged Anuradha along with the other, trying to keep up with the coolie looking for her compartment.

There was her name and berth number, pasted outside a second class AC coach. More squeeze and push till they reached the berth.

Finally. The coolie was paid, and Mala and the children sat around in a listless sort of way, listening to more announcements of delayed trains, before they all agreed that the family had seen Astha off and now they could go home.

'Bye darlings, bye dearest ones,' she said, 'I'll be back before you know it, and I will phone, all right. Be good, don't give Dadi any trouble.'

The children jumped off and led by Mala fought their way out of the crowd.

Eventually, three hours after it was supposed to, the departure whistle blew, and the train gave a little jerk.

Astha sank back into solitude. She laid out the pillow and sheets that an attendant had thrown at her, and settled down for the night, rocking with the quickening rhythm of the train, not yet wanting to close her eyes and go to sleep.

Next morning, and the U.P. landscape through the purple film plastered over the train windows. The land on either side was flat and dry, with patches of green fields. Uttar Pradesh, home to eighty million people, many of them leading poor, illiterate, and harsh lives, but ready to leave their fields, villages, and towns to converge upon the Babri Masjid, to protect their faith and motherland, something that would not have occurred to them before.

Faizabad, Ayodhya's twin city, 11 a.m. The Sampradayakta Mukti Manch had made arrangements for the women to stay at a guest house they frequently used. Astha got into a rickshaw and gave the address.

'Have you come to do Ram darshan at the masjid?' asked the rickshaw wallah, as Astha put her feet on her bag to prevent it from falling on the road.

'Yes,' she answered cautiously.

The rickshaw wallah nodded, it was the expected answer, Astha could see.

The guest house was a large white washed bungalow set away from the road, in what used to be the Faizabad Civil Lines. A middle-aged lady came out to greet her.

'Astha Vadera? The others from your organisation are out. They will be back soon.'

She was taken to a high-ceilinged, dark drawing room and served tea. The lady launched smoothly into a brief history of her life, she owned the house, she didn't really need the money, running a guest house was a time pass, one must be active, her son and daughter were in America, she didn't want to burden their lives. See, here they are, gesturing at pictures in ornate silver and wooden frames on the massive Burma teak sideboard.

A house, thought Astha, if my mother had a house, she too could have done something like this, instead of going to Rishikesh and losing herself in an ashram.

The widow got up, adjusting her sari palla around her head. 'Your room is upstairs. Come.'

The uncovered staircase was next to the outer wall, and led up to five small rooms in a row. There was a verandah running the length, a nice view of the garden, in one corner were the bathrooms, in another, a bit of terrace to sit on.

'Food to be ordered two hours in advance,' said the widow, unlocking the door of a small room, one little window, red floor, one bed, chair, table and cupboard.

As Astha sat there, eleven forty-five in the morning, the sense of adventure she had experienced in the train fell away. The room was neat, clean, without character and totally remote from everything that made up her days. She felt strange and dislocated. What would her children be doing? She missed them, she hoped Anuradha wasn't fighting too much with Himanshu, she hoped that their grandmother wasn't feeding them too much rubbish, but it didn't matter, it was just two days, she hoped they weren't watching too much TV, but then that didn't matter either, it was just two days.

Tonight will be better, she thought, trying to argue away her depression, tonight at the function she would be where the action was, she would make her speech, feel the purpose of her visit more.

A little later, when Astha washed and went down she discovered that in the widow's estimation there were seven thousand temples in Ayodhya.

'Seven thousand? Are you absolutely sure?' she demanded incredulously.

The widow looked at her sternly. 'It's Ram's birthplace. There is a need for so many. When there is a festival like Ram Navmi, lakhs of pilgrims visit. Many temples double as dharmsalas. They charge one rupee to ten, and the pilgrims sleep wherever they can.'

'So many temples. And they want one more.' The figures startled her into being naïve, she knew the agitation had nothing to do with numbers.

'Of course,' said the widow. 'Ram was born right on the exact spot where the Babri Masjid is. You can even see from the pillars inside that there was a temple there. Eight pillars with Hindu carvings, mango leaves, goddesses, apsaras, kalash in black stone. Where did they come from? They built the mosque around them to mock us.'

'Mock us?'

The widow glanced at her pityingly, and spelt it out. 'To remind us that they have the power to destroy our temples.'

'I don't think it's quite like that,' began Astha when the widow interrupted. 'Even now, Muslims living here really have their allegiance somewhere else. You will see during cricket matches they want Pakistan to win, this is not their soil.'

Astha knew it was useless to protest. Opinions like this, based on preconceptions, did not change. What did it take, a lifetime? A whole new history? What?

The widow seemed nice, even educated, she would not condone violence, no. Hers would be the gentle voice declaring 'they' were all the same, and these were words that would have a longer reach than any missile thrown.

Was it like this in Pakistan, Astha wondered. Did Muslims look upon Hindus with suspicion? Ah, but where were the Hindus in Pakistan? All dead or gone, leaving scars that rankled even now.

Reshana came, 'Have you been waiting long?' and didn't wait for an answer. 'They are escorting a fresh lot of bricks into Ayodhya, bricks wrapped in saffron, silk, cotton, with tikka on them, stamped with the name of Ram, as though they were an object of worship, bricks to build the temple, high hysteria around the whole thing. We have been trying to make sure our function tonight is well attended, but—' her voice trailed off, a little hopeless.

Astha understood. As an artist the visual and symbolic appeal of saffron clad bricks would be far stronger than any appeals to reason and history. Still one had to do what one had to do.

Afternoon shaded into evening, as not far from the banks of the Saryu, on a platform in front of a mike a thin academic gave the history of the Babri Masjid.

The audience spread before him had been gathered through posters and advertisements, with the promise of entertainment and songs. Despite Reshana's fears the turnout was large, though it was debatable whether they had come for the spectacle or from a willingness to be converted to a historical point of view.

There is no evidence, thundered the academic, punctuating the air with an excited fist, no evidence that Babur, busy fighting the Afghans, ever came to Ayodhya, let alone destroyed a temple.

Do you think Babur, founder of an empire in India, would have come here to build this little mosque? Yes, there is an inscription inside saying he ordered it, but the close set writing is of a much later style, carved to strengthen rumours of imperial destruction. The wooden beam below the arch is not a remnant of a temple, but put there by local masons, using local materials, unskilled in building arches. There are others like it in Jaunpur.

Brothers and sisters, I have not come from Delhi to bore you with historical details, only to show you that for every bit of evidence used to prove there was a temple to Lord Ram here, there is a counter-argument to prove there wasn't.

History can be used to build or to destroy. We choose the lessons we wish to learn from it. For years Muslims and Hindus have lived peacefully together. It is the British who suggested that an ancient temple was destroyed so that Hindu would turn against Muslim. Brothers and sisters, we have seen what the British succeeded in doing. They believed in Divide and Rule. They ploughed rivers of blood through our country. The same dark forces threaten us now. It is politicians who are creating religious insecurities to get votes. Do not let them succeed.

*

Astha was sitting in front, nervously waiting her turn, clutching in her cold palm the piece of paper on which her rehearsed points were written. She looked around to see the reaction of the audience. He may have been passionate, but he was still an academic. 'Do you think they understand what he is saying?' she whispered to Reshana.

'It's all we can do, though I doubt we are any match for organisations that have been working the fundamentalist rhetoric at the grass roots level for years.'

'I think this speaker should appeal to their emotions, instead of talking about beams, arches and inscriptions,' said Astha.

'He's a very respected historian,' replied Reshana stiffly. 'And he is showing the relevance of beams and inscriptions.'

Her tone annoyed Astha, Reshana was so easily offended. How come love for the people did not translate itself into tolerance for individuals? She looked around for a more congenial sight.

They were in front of a canal, next to a bridge. Across the modern park on the other side of the water lay the old town, its interspersed domes and spires clearly conveying its mixed heritage. It looked old and fragile in the yellowish rose of the falling light.

Finally the academic finished. 'It's your turn now,' whispered Reshana.

Astha got up. Her irritation had given her energy. When she spoke her voice was firm and clear.

'Brothers and sisters,' she started, 'In essence women all over the world are the same, we belong to families, we are affected by what affects our husbands, fathers, brothers and children. In history many things are not clear, the same thing that is right for one person is wrong for another, and it is difficult to decide our path of action. We judge not by what people tell us, but by what we experience in our homes. And that experience tells us that where there is violence, there is suffering, unnecessary and continuous suffering. When we look to righting wrongs committed hundreds of years ago, we look to the past. But that past cannot feed us, clothe us, or give us security. History cannot be righted easily, but lives are lost easily, pain and trauma to women and children come easily. Tomorrow your sacrifice will have been forgotten because the duty of life is towards the living.'

She saw some people nodding, and she ended by repeating that nothing except misery and suffering were to be gained by violence.

A song, followed by a street play, and the evening concluded with an invocation to Gandhiji:

Gandhiji was a devout Hindu – none more devout than he. But he knew the true meaning of religion. All men are brothers. Hatred between communities led to his death, and in listening to the voice of hate we kill him all over again.

The speaker was speaking in terms everybody could understand – Gandhiji, father of the Nation – love – hate – oneness. But were these strong enough to drown out – exploited for centuries – awake – defend – protect – Motherland – Ram – God, faith, and Love of Him?

In the middle of all this Astha looked up and saw someone staring at her. The woman caught in the act, went on staring instead of looking away. Then she smiled slowly, squirrel front teeth advancing slightly from the rest.

I wonder who she is, thought the one being stared at.

Later. 'I really liked your speech.'

'Oh, thank you. It was nothing much.'

'It made sense. The basti women who are with me related to it.'

'It was my first. I am not used to making speeches.'

A pause.

'What is your name?'

'Pipeelika.'

'Pipeelika? Ant?'

'Yes. My father's legacy. He liked the sound and he had a sense of humour. It does mean I have spent my life explaining it. Maybe it has affected me, I don't know. What's your name?'

'Astha.'

'Faith?'

'Yes. I don't know if I have been touched by it. The faith in my family centres around my mother and her swami.'

'Don't you have faith in anything?'

'I don't know. Perhaps my brush.'

'You paint?'

'Yes.'

'Can I see?'

'Any time.'

They arranged to meet the next morning. 'Do you know the place?' hinted Astha at parting. 'I thought I'd see something of Ayodhya before my train leaves tomorrow night.'

'Of course I know the place. I'll show you around.'

She thought about her later. Her hair was like a halo round her face, springing away from it, black, brown, red, orange, and copper, her skin was a pale milky coffee colour. She liked the way she smiled, but she looked sad at the same time, why was that? Had she herself sounded interesting, why hadn't she brought something nicer to wear, suppose she didn't come to the park at ten like planned, why hadn't she asked her where she was staying?

She tried shaking herself, if she didn't come, she would see Ayodhya on her own.

The next day as she hurried in a rickshaw to the meeting place, she saw her waiting under a tree. Immediately she felt stupid. A stranger she had hardly spoken to, to bother about her clothes, what was wrong with her? They would meet, they would part, she would catch the evening train home.

'Hi.'

'Hi.'

They said nothing much as they walked through the small town. In every lane were shops crammed with representations of gods, pictures and figures, small, medium, large kalashes, bells for doing arti, prayer beads, green, yellow, black, blue with pearls, and the mandatory rudraksha in every possible size and colour from pale blonde to dark brown. This was a town of serious religious buyers judging from the number of shops.

'We are near Hanuman Garhi, it's on the way to the masjid, do you want to see it?'

'If you think it's worth seeing,' said Astha, humble in her being guided mode.

'It's one of the biggest and richest temples here. Hindus and Muslims fought over it too, though that is not so well publicised.'

They climbed steps lined with beggars, mostly old people dressed in white or saffron, begging bowls in front, in which people were dropping money, coconuts, sweets, prashad. Overtaking them were eager pilgrims bounding up, shouting, 'Jai Shri Ram, Jai Siya Ram'.

'This is supposed to be the temple with the most steps,' said Pipee, as they passed an old lady bent over her cane, her eyes on her bony, bare brown feet, with their spread-out toes. They could hear her murmuring Ram, Ram, with every step she took.

Inside Pipee hung back as Astha advanced towards the shrine flanked by huge donation boxes. A long line of devotees queued before the priest, clutching their offerings, boxes of sweets, coconuts, flower garlands, small thalis with tikka and incense. The priest, swift and practised, set aside their garlands and coconuts, deftly opened each box, dumped half the sweets in the bucket next to him, and returned the rest. The devotee then took a parikrama of the shrine, lingered in the courtyard and rang the bell while leaving.

If only I could feel like that, thought Astha, looking at the expression on some of their faces, coming to this temple would mean so much. Her eyes fell on the daan box. She opened her purse and took out five rupees, I wish I had something more in my life, I wish an end to this hollow feeling. She shoved the money in the box and rejoined Pipee.

'Do you not believe?' asked Astha as they passed through the inner courtyard, and down the steps.

'No,' she spat out. 'I believe in nothing. I hate religion. You wanted to see, and I am showing you.'

'I'm sorry,' said Astha, a little alarmed, 'that you are doing something you don't want to.'

The woman drew a breath, and touched her arm briefly, 'No, I'm sorry I was like that, it's nothing to do with you. Come, let's go to Kanak Bhavan.'

On the way, Astha hesitantly, 'If you hate religion, doesn't it upset you to come to places like these, where there is nothing but?'

'Oh, who cares how upset I get?' she said flippantly. 'I have to come. We are based in a slum, and this kind of field trip works very well to sensitise women to communal issues, which in moments of crisis get totally out of hand. Besides I don't like staying in Delhi much.'

'Why is that?'

'No particular reason. I live alone, I like to travel.'

Astha looked sideways at Pipee and encountered nothing but her hair.

In Kanak Bhavan a small guide greeted them.

'Five rupees, I show you.'

And for five rupees they saw the room where Ram slept, where Sita played her sitar, where they played chess, where they bathed, where they dressed, the cupboard where those clothes were kept, where Sita got ready to receive Ram in the evenings, where Kekayi did Sita's muh dekhayii when she came a bride into this house.

'Wasn't all this some thousands of years BC?' whispered Astha to Pipee, amazed that such anachronisms could be taken seriously.

'Nothing here is archaeologically or historically accurate,' whispered Pipee back.

The boy gauged what they were saying, though in English.

'Who knows what is real or not?' he said, smooth beyond his years. 'What matters is the feeling of devotion.'

Astha felt ashamed of herself, and tipped him ten rupees as they climbed down the narrow stairs, into the main courtyard below, repeating her earlier wish for something, she knew not what.

'I take it you are religious?' asked Pipee, observing the size of the tip.

'I gave because I want something.'

'He's not a wishing well.'

'He will do for one.'

'What did you wish for?'

'There are many hollows in my life, and I wanted them filled.'

Pipee fell silent, and Astha wondered about her empty spaces, with eyes like that, there could be many. 'Are we going to the masjid now?' she ventured as they left Kanak Bhavan.

Pipee sighed, 'We should have gone there first, but I always find it so depressing.'

'Why?'

'You'll see.'

They walked up Ramkot, the slight incline that led to the mosque. The way was lined with temples. Temples, houses, houses that doubled as temples, temples that doubled as dharamsalas, all needed for the lakhs of pilgrims that descended on holy occasions. Ramnavmi, Diwali, Navratra.

'It makes me sick the way Ram is being associated with Hindu–Indian–nationalism. It was terrible when the locks of the masjid were opened some years ago. The Muslims were not even given a hearing, considering this is waqf land. Millions of pilgrims poured in to see statues they believed were placed there divinely because God wanted his birthplace back. People will believe anything.'

'We did a play about it,' put in Astha.

'Really?'

'With Aijaz.'

'You knew him?'

'He came to our school. He put together a brilliant piece about the Babri Masjid. Then I never saw him again.'

'His life was short.'

'Yes. That's why I am part of this group.'

'The S double M?'

'Is that what you call it?'

'When I call it anything. I prefer never to think about it.'

'Why? Don't you think they do good work?'

'It's so elitist, and Aijaz was nothing if not one of the people. Now they sell art in his name.'

'I did something they sold.'

'You are part of their core group?'

Astha laughed dryly. 'Hardly that. I can barely make it to a few meetings. But the Manch was happy to have my canvas, I was happy to sell it, and the cause benefited, surely.'

'I wonder. Preaching to the converted. Working through songs, art, literature.'

'But that was what he himself did, I saw him, and he was very effective.'

'There is now such strong feeling about Hindu manhood, pride, valour, protection of the motherland, redressing the wrongs of history, that I wonder whether any street play, song or poster can make a point beyond general entertainment.'

'There were lots of people last night.'

'Of course they were there. They know how to promote themselves all right.'

'If you think like this, why are you here? Why did you bring your women?' challenged Astha.

'To attend the picnic,' said Pipee facetiously before lapsing into silence, leaving Astha to wonder how much to tread in these murky waters.

She turned her gaze to the bare feet of the women in front. It was not necessary to walk barefoot so far from the shrine, but for these women the very hill was sacrosanct, and their bare feet honoured a faith Astha could never have.

If she did, she would not be throwing money around, wishing for elusive fulfilment. Faith would do it. She too would walk barefoot up Ramkot not minding the stones, the heat, the germs, the piss of dogs, the shit of monkeys, the spit of people. Wearing no skin of dead animals to pollute the purity of the place, no leather, no shoes, no belt, no bag, no wallet.

By this time they had reached the top. The nicest thing about the mosque was its location. On the highest spot in Ayodhya, it overlooked the town, with its collection of spires, domes and houses crowded together. Beneath them swayed the trees, a mild calm breeze blew about, a breeze that seemed to suggest that there were many ways to worship.

In a mosque built in 1528 there was now a Hindu image. Was this not enough to make it a temple? Courts had declared that Hindus had the right to worship here. But now the worship had extended beyond the deity, so that the shape of the enclosing structure had become an obstacle to faith, and every barefoot pilgrim a warrior.

At the entrance they stopped to take off their shoes. Outside bhajans were blaring on loudspeakers, declaring that the name of god is more effective if all can hear. Inside, under the central dome, hardly visible under a mound of flowers, were the images flanked on either side by men in khaki armed with guns. In front of them a line of devotees streamed past, stuffing money into large donation boxes. Pipee refused to join the line while Astha, made uneasy by the guns, hurried past the little figure that had suddenly appeared on the night of December 22nd, 1949.

The two women walked down from Ramkot to a song shrieking from a cassette on full volume, 'We will go to Ayodhya / We will build Ram's temple'. They neared the main road and a waiting rickshaw wallah started cycling towards them. As he did so a policeman detached himself from a patrol group. His khaki clad belly hung over his belt, his truncheon swung from a thick hand. Leisurely he walked over to the approaching rickshaw wallah, grabbed him by his kurta, pulled so hard that the women could hear a tearing sound, forced him from his seat and kicked him. Once, twice. The grizzled rickshaw wallah looked around, smiled and slowly, quietly, began to pull his rickshaw away. Not a word was exchanged. The policeman walked back to his group.

'God! Did you see? How could he behave like that?' demanded Astha, her tone shrill and naive.

'Maybe he thought he was a Muslim,' shrugged Pipee.

'So?'

'So? I don't know. Perhaps the cops think Muslims shouldn't tread on this sacred soil. At any rate they generally don't come here. That man must have been desperate for customers.'

'And why shouldn't Muslims . . . it's a mosque as well. He should have hit him back.'

'And be beaten into pulp?' inquired Pipee. 'No, I don't think so.'

Astha stared at the ground moodily, and pulled her sari palla further over her head to protect herself against the sun.

'But why are you so upset?' demanded Pipee in her turn. 'These things happen all the time. Surely you know that.'

'He looked like Himanshu,' said Astha suffering into her sari.

'Himanshu?'

'My son.'

'Your son is so old?'

'Of course not. But that look – when he gets out in cricket for example – he is not very good, and when he gets out – that is when he smiles. Just like that.'

'Mother–son,' said Pipee somewhat gloomily. 'An obsessive over-protective phenomenon.'

Astha felt defensive. 'Hardly. I am careful not to smother him. He is the one who clings to me.'

'Despite yourself, you must be liking that.'

Somehow Astha didn't mind this comment from Pipee, it was so non-judgemental. 'I do rather,' she confessed, and then, 'he is the only one in the whole world who smiles whenever he sees me, no matter what.'

'Women. So pathetic in their hunger for love,' remarked Pipee sapiently, guiding Astha into a tea stall.

'Isn't there someone you love?' asked Astha seizing this opportunity, hoping Pipee wouldn't draw back, that it was not too early to be exchanging of themselves.

'I married for it,' said Pipee, and again that reserve. Yesterday it was 'I live alone'. Was she divorced, had her husband been unfaithful, or cruel, was it a problem of in-laws? How soon before she could ask?

They left the tea stall, and had stopped for a moment under the shade of a tree to exchange phone numbers, when a monkey jumped on Astha's back. The sudden weight, the shock of her sari being pulled from her shoulder, her own scream, left her collapsed with fright.

Pipee grabbed Astha and examined her arms, her back, her neck, pushing the hair to one side, looking minutely for any scratch the monkey might have left.

At last she drew her away from a crowd that was beginning to gather, curiosity gleaming in their eyes. 'It's all right,' she declared, 'no scratch, you won't need rabies injections.'

Rabies injections. This thought had not occurred to Astha, she had registered nothing besides panic and the fact that Pipee's arm around her had tightened for an unnecessary second.

It was getting on for five in the evening when they took separate rickshaws to go to their separate guest houses. Looking at the face before her, Astha said, 'Please keep in touch.'

The eyes crinkled. 'Of course. I'll be visiting my in-laws for a few days, they are not far from here. So sometime next week?'

'I'll look forward. I mean it,' Astha went on babbling, hating herself. Why did she always have to sound so stupid? And how come she was visiting in-laws when she was no longer married? Perhaps it wasn't divorce but death, and she so young and attractive, with her smile, her hair, her skin, her eyes.

The mouth folded inwards. 'Well, see you then.'

They smiled at each other and parted.

Back in the guest house. 'I see you have met Aijaz's wife,' said Reshana.

'No, I haven't,' replied Astha apprehensively.

'Pipeelika – his wife. The one you were talking to last night.'

Oh no. What must she have thought, why didn't she say, why didn't she guess, what kind of impression did she make – oh no, oh no, oh no. Aijaz. Aijaz's wife. What must it be like to be Aijaz's wife? Widow – widow, not wife. So that was why she looked like that, and spoke like that.

'It's obvious she didn't tell you,' Reshana continued. 'Just like her. Very strange woman. After his death she became totally neurotic. Wanted to own his memory. How can anyone do that? Aijaz was one of the people, if he was anything, but she resented everything we did to keep his memory alive, accusing us of all sorts of things. It was so perverse.'

'To have your husband die like that must be very difficult,' murmured Astha.

'It was hard for everybody, not only her,' shot out Reshana.

'But why didn't you tell me?'

'Me tell you? Why should I?' demanded Reshana annoyed. 'When I saw her with you, I imagined she must have introduced herself like any normal person. Besides she avoids us.'

'She did, she did introduce herself,' Astha was already defending Pipee.

Reshana looked at her, 'Then how come you didn't know she was Aijaz's wife?'

'She only said her first name, and that was so unusual I started commenting on it – oh, I don't know.'

'Huh. She never forgets she was his wife when it comes to the Manch. Always bad-mouthing us. I'm surprised she didn't try it with you.'

'She said nothing about the Manch.'

'Surprising. She usually does. Probably trying to impress you with her tolerance. Or maybe she is a little better now, I hoped so when I saw her in the audience,' said Reshana briskly packing her last item, her bathroom slippers, and then sitting on the suitcase to shut it. She was leaving by bus for Lucknow to do some fieldwork.

Alone Astha sat in a daze. She had met Aijaz's wife. She couldn't believe she had spent so many hours with her without knowing. She didn't think Pipee would phone her in Delhi, it now seemed too improbable. But she felt wretched, and in this mood passed the remaining few hours before leaving for the station.

'What is your train, beti?' asked the widow when she went down.

'The Sarva Yamuna.'

The widow sighed.

'It is not a good train?' Astha asked uneasily.

'It will be late,' said the widow.

'How late?'

'Two – three hours. Maybe four.'

'How can you be so sure?'

'It comes through Bihar. No law and order in Bihar. So the train is always late.'

'Always?'

'Without fail,' said the widow looking ghoulish and satisfied. 'These Biharis keep pulling the chain when and where they feel like it, getting off, getting on, so the train gets later and later. Simple.'

There was nothing Astha could do, but continue as she had planned. She was afraid of waiting at the station so many hours alone, she thought of Hemant who had not wanted her to come, and who might consider himself justified if she was dragged into a corner of a deserted platform and raped.

She gritted her teeth against her unreason, while the widow sent her gardener, Hanif, to call a rickshaw.

'Here is your packed dinner,' she said handing her the box Astha had forgotten she had paid for.

'Thank you,' she said and at nine-thirty departed into the still small-town night. The stars above were more brilliant than they ever could be in the polluted skies of Delhi.

The usual damp, stale, wet coal, urine station smells met her as she stepped onto the platform. She sat desolately on her suitcase and waited. Soon, it would be ten. Maybe the widow was wrong.

At 11 p.m. the train was announced to be three hours late, and the widow was proved right. The numbness that had been seeping into Astha during the past hour intensified. Mosquitoes big as flies buzzed around her. She slapped them off, and started walking up and down the platform. There were mostly people sleeping, covered from head to foot in sheets, shawls, durries or sacking to keep the mosquitoes away; shapeless bundles, unidentifiable as man and woman, the length alone indicating child or adult. Water pipes strung along the side of the track dripped through the hoses that were attached to each one.

She drank a kulhar full of sweet tea and went on walking up and down the long platform in a kind of daze. There were a few other passengers waiting, but most were the bundles scattered abundantly about. At the far end in the darkest corner of the station, the only sign of life, a bundle with an elbow raised, jerking frenziedly and rhythmically beneath the cloth, in an action Astha immediately recognised. She hurried back to the tube lights of the central platform, where amid the mosquitoes and the tinkling of water dripping onto rail tracks, she had another kulhar of sweet earth-smelling tea, and then waited, waited in one spot for the train to come.

*

Astha passed the night in the train restlessly. Not for her the easy sleep on the way out. Was it only two days ago that she had left? She thought of the meeting, the speech she had given, all the temples she had seen, the security around the masjid, Pipee protecting her from the monkey, thinking of rabies injections. She wished she had known her connection to Aijaz, she wouldn't feel so foolish now, but Pipee clearly hadn't wanted to tell, that much was obvious. If she had had the foresight to take her number she could at least phone and apologise.

Her thoughts turned to home. When would Hemant come back? When the work finishes was all he had said, maybe he would have called his mother and informed her. How would it be between them? Would he still be annoyed that she had gone away? Had he missed her?

Next morning, Delhi. Quickly she hired a coolie and jumped into a three-wheeler with her suitcase. She hadn't seen her children for two days and three nights, and now every thought was fastened onto them.

Vasant Vihar at last. She rang the doorbell, and there they were, her precious children.

Himanshu rushed to hug her, clutching a drawing in his hand that said *Welcome Home Mama.* Anuradha complained about the book she had to read in the holidays.

I am home, thought Astha. Emotion grabbed her firmly by the throat.

'Do you like my drawing?' shouted Himanshu, tugging her hand, feeling not enough attention had been paid to it.

'I love your drawing,' responded Astha automatically. She lifted it close to her face to illustrate her total concentration. 'Such peacocks, so colourful, and my, what a sun. And so many cars, you have done well with the cars. Are these blue streaks rain?'

Himanshu nodded.

'So interesting. My goodness, Himu, you've got everything in this drawing.'

'Didi said you wouldn't like it,' said Himanshu.

'Well, Anu doesn't know everything, does she?' replied Astha.

Himanshu beamed, and lost no time in informing his sister, 'Mama likes it. So there. You were wrong.'

Anuradha did not even have to think. 'She's saying that to be nice to you, stupid.'

'That was an entirely unnecessary thing to say,' Astha informed her daughter.

'You mean you are not being nice to him?'

'It's not that. I like the painting irrespective of whether I am his mother or not.'

Anuradha did not bother to reply, while Himanshu said nothing more about his art work.

'Have you heard from Papa, Anu? When is he coming home?'

'Don't you know?' asked Anuradha, puzzled.

'Of course,' said Astha quickly. 'I just wondered whether he was sticking to his original plans.'

'Well I don't know. Dadi might. Ask her.'

'I will. Now I'll just go up and see her, all right?'

As she climbed the steps to make sure no cause for offence would be found in postponed expressions of gratitude, or delayed news giving, Astha thought yes, indeed, she was home.

~

Hemant arrived next evening, smiling, genial and pleasant. Astha was relieved. Clearly their misunderstanding was a thing of the past. 'So,' he asked, after her questions about Bombay, 'the mosque still standing?'

'Yes indeed.'

'And Ayodhya? How was that? Did you see anything?'

'It was very nice,' said Astha, pleased at his interest. 'I met a girl. She showed me around.'

'What kind of girl?' smiled Hemant. 'You are no more than a girl yourself.'

'Oh Hemant, don't be silly, I am old. She is much younger than me.'

'Well, what kind of girl?' he repeated indulgently.

Astha changed the topic. 'The mosque is quite unremarkable, you know. It is old, but that's it. Half its beauty comes from the little hill where it is, overlooking the town. But it's full of policemen with guns, it's not possible to worship there, though people do – lots.'

'I told you there was no need for you to go.'

'I had to make a speech, don't you remember?'

'Why do you have to travel to Ayodhya to make a speech? It's not as though you were a religious leader, or a politician or a public figure.'

'But it is important for everyone to do what they can, to make things better, you have to try, whether ultimately it makes a difference is not in your hands,' said Astha earnestly.

'Well, I hope you are not going to indulge in more rabble-rousing.'

His fingers were twisting the ring he had given her so that her hand hurt. Hopelessness settled in its familiar place in her chest. He belittled her, yet if she pointed this out, he would deny it. It was better to stay silent.

Later they made love.

The ritual enacted before partings, after homecomings, this establishment of the marital tie, this coming together of flesh that had been sundered.

Or so Astha thought, until next morning, while unpacking his suitcase, she came across a condom.

She stared at it for a long time, its implications running through her head. What should she do? Leave it in the suitcase, throw it, or confront him? Who had he slept with, he who was never in any place for very long, it could not be that he was in love – or had a relationship – or maybe he did. Some woman might travel with him, how would she ever know? Maybe the distributor had supplied him with someone, she had read somewhere that women were often a part of business deals.

But why now? Was this his message to her? Was this why he seemed in good spirits? Why he had asked her about Ayodhya, and expressed an interest in what she had seen?

Finally she left the suitcase on the bed, the lid closed and buckled, the children should not see and ask what is this, the servants should not see and jump to unnecessary conclusions.

She waited till he came home. It was 9 p.m., he was late as usual. As usual he first poured himself a drink before settling down in the drawing room. The children were interacted with, while Astha moved between the drawing room, kitchen, and dining area, unable to sit anywhere, the condom firmly in her heart.

'How are things at work?' she asked after a while. Not that he ever discussed business with her. For that he had his father.

To her surprise he didn't brush aside the question. 'There is trouble in some factories in Noida, all the TV ones.'

Astha had to drag her mind to this. 'Are you worried about ours?'

Hemant got irritated. 'Obviously I am worried. Different unions compete for power over the workers, and we get caught in the middle. Everybody suffers but who sees that?'

'You pay a fair wage, the workers will realise that making trouble will benefit no one.'

'Even if they don't come to their senses, I can't pay more than I do. Five thousand for the men with overtime, and four thousand for the women with benefits. Paying four hundred and fifty salaries is no joke,' brooded Hemant, 'and these are the rates.'

'Then what is the problem?'

'The Communist Party Union tells them they can ensure they get more benefits and a higher wage. Well, let's see. So far they have not been able to make inroads.'

'Maybe nothing will happen.'

Hemant grunted, slowly sipped his drink, threw back his head on the sofa and closed his eyes. It seemed a bit difficult to bring up the condom in these circumstances, yet it had to be done. There were problems in her life as well as his.

'There's something in your suitcase,' she said. 'Perhaps you would like to take it out yourself. I left it on the bed.'

'Yes?' he said indifferently. 'What is it?'

'A condom.'

At this he opened his eyes. 'Ah, yes.'

'I take it when you travel you have sex, and that is why there are condoms in your suitcase,' Astha could barely keep her voice from breaking.

'As usual, your imagination runs away with you.'

'That is not an answer.'

'For your information, I don't.'

She didn't believe him, and yet the hurt eased a little. 'You carry condoms just like that?'

'Of course not. The dealer wanted to give me a girl, was very insistent, forced this condom on me, but I'm not that kind of guy, I left for the bar before the girl came. As you can see, it is not used.'

As a story it was thin, but yes, the condom was not used. Hemant got up and stroked her cheek. 'Even if you behave badly I love you,' he said.

Astha forced herself to be content with this. It was too dangerous to venture further.

VII

Pipee called a week later.

'I'm sorry, I'm sorry, I didn't know. You must have thought me horrible. I'm sorry,' Astha rushed to say.

'How were you to know? I didn't tell you. You could be the one angry with me.'

'Of course not, how could I be angry with you? You spent so much time with me, you showed me places you hate, you protected me from the monkey.'

'Hardly,' she laughed, 'I can't stop monkeys from jumping onto people, much as I would like to.'

'I have been waiting and waiting to tell you I'm sorry if I upset you in any way.'

'Well now you've told me. And you didn't upset me in any way – I'm over that kind of stuff. Don't worry about it.'

A pause. Then, 'You were going to show me your paintings.'

'Please, come over. I would love that.'

'Tomorrow?'

'Please.'

She had called, she had called, and for a moment despite the condom, and all the wretchedness of the past week, Astha felt a little lighter.

She looked at the work she was doing for the Manch, trying to prepare a readable memorandum that would combine historical accuracy with emotional appeal. It was proving uphill work. How could she make the nation care about the fact that no destruction of a temple had been chronicled in Babur, or in any other contemporary source, be it Abdul Qadir Badauni of the 16th centrury, or Goswami Tulsidas, in Ramcharitmanas.

Astha stared rebelliously at her writing: *The un-Islamic black stone pillars within the mosque are not proof that a temple was destroyed on the Babri Masjid site. As they are not load bearing, they were probably taken from a Hindu or Jain temple, ravaged by Shah Juran Ghori and brought for decoration. Seeing their location as a sign of contempt for Hindu feelings is a political interpretation.*

It sounded so uninteresting. Yet she had to go on sifting, sieving, fact from fact, fiction from fiction, and in the end not be sure of anything. It was lonely working on these pamphlets, it was not like painting where she required no mind to bounce her thoughts off. If only she had some of Aijaz's magic.

As she looked at what she was writing, her old hostility to words rose in her. She couldn't do it, she was a painter, not a writer.

'But it's not bad,' said Pipee the next day, when Astha showed it to her.

'Pedantic, dry and boring,' said Astha.

Pipee pulled in the corners of her mouth while Astha stared in fascination at the dents it made in her cheeks. 'Now don't bother so much, just finish it. No one will read it anyway. The Manch excels in preaching to the converted.'

'But it's for the nation.'

'Please. Give me a break.'

They went to Astha's work room. Pipee's eyes flickered over the canvases. 'I know nothing about painting,' she said. 'You must teach me.'

'There is nothing to learn. I've always responded to colours. It's words I find so slippery,' said Astha, the burden of *The Testimony of the Black Pillars* lying heavy upon her.

'How do you manage to fit so many people in?'

'It's something I learned from the miniatures. They are both very full and very detailed, I love that.'

'It must take for ever.'

'It does, rather. The one the Manch sold took almost six

months. Now I am getting faster, but still – I can't work on them as much as I wish.'

'You've got a pretty fancy set-up, it couldn't be that difficult. Doesn't your husband help you?'

'My husband spends a lot of time at the factory and he travels too, so he can't really help with the children. And the set-up . . .' her voice trailed off miserably. It was hard to explain her life, especially when she herself barely understood it.

'The usual female trap, it's all right, you are not alone, we all experience it in one way or another,' said Pipee putting her hand on Astha's and pressing it gently. 'So if you want to do anything of your own I guess you have to work your ass off. You are like an ant too. I shall call you Ant, I'm not sure I like this faith business.'

Astha blushed with pleasure, 'So we can be ants together.'

'Exactly.'

Anuradha and Himanshu stared at Pipee over lunch.

'Is that your scooter outside?' asked Himanshu.

'Yes.'

'How come you ride a scooter?'

'To get around. Do you think only men should drive scooters?' asked Pipee.

Astha felt embarrassed at her son's ideas, maybe she hadn't been sensitizing him to gender issues. She blushed into her roti, while Anuradha asked accusingly, 'How come you are called ant?'

'My father thought I should work like an ant for the good of the community.'

'And do you?'

Pipee smiled at the assembled mother and children. 'Sometimes,' she said, 'when I feel like it. I'm not a very good ant I am afraid.'

Pipee left after tea when Astha began to worry about her children's homework. Driving home on her scooter, she thought

I want to know her better, at least she doesn't remind me of Aijaz. Her house is quite near mine, that is convenient, I wonder if she realises she is attractive. Her marriage sounds horrible. I'm sure her husband is a jerk.

She thought of Astha's painting. She clearly had a political sensibility, which made her acquiescence in a traditional domestic set-up even stranger. Maybe she was just unawakened. And she loved her hair, it was so thick and curled around her face even when tied back, and her skin was so pretty, clear pink and white.

As for Astha who had shown such eagerness to know Pipee, how was she to realise that given certain circumstances, there was no aphrodisiac more powerful than talking, no seduction more effective than curiosity.

~

They began to meet more often. Astha was circumspect in revealing the amount of time she spent with Pipee. She knew it would be frowned upon as excessive. When the boundaries of what might be considered normal interaction passed, she started to lie. Thus an element of secrecy entered the relationship and gave it an illicit character.

They met on weekdays; evenings and weekends were out. Still Hemant caught a whiff of this new interest in his wife's life and was free with his disapproval. Since Pipee was a woman this disapproval was tinged with contempt, and the assurance of no real threat, indeed had Pipee been a man, Astha would have found it impossible to stray so far down the road of intimacy, or be so comfortable on it.

'Women,' said the husband emphatically after a somewhat long phone conversation the wife had had with her friend, 'always mind-fucking.'

Astha cringed. Mind-fucking. Not the excitement of the real thing. The organ penetrated, the ears, the weapon of penetration, words. Words, that left no mark but in the mind, where they mingled with others that had been used to describe someone else's past, till those experiences became your own, and you saw with other eyes, because you were no longer one person, but two. Listening upon listening, fucking upon fucking. In full view.

Then she grew angry. How dare Hemant be so derogatory. Would he prefer her to be like him, with condoms in her suitcase, which a friend had put there by accident? She refused to engage with him on any issue, he was capable of nothing but the very crudest understanding. Instead she related the whole to Pipee who said that men were so pathetic, so fucked up themselves, they only understood the physical, and in this way she felt soothed.

'Have you ever been in a relationship with a woman?' asked Pipee one day.

They were lingering at the café at the Tagore Arts Centre, after a lunch of kebabs and roti. It was late February, there were people sitting on the steps of the lawn next to them, on the walls white rose creepers were blooming. It was almost four, and the sunny spot they had originally chosen had long gone cold. A little boy was swabbing at the tables with a dirty cloth, a waiter was tilting the chairs against the tables, to enable the sweeper to clean properly. Pipee's voice had dropped to a murmur, Astha leaned forward to catch her words.

Astha felt uneasy and didn't answer.

'Well?'

She tried to laugh. 'I'm married,' she said.

'So? Are you telling me you are happy, fulfilled, and what have you?'

Unexpected tears came to Astha's eyes. Pipee was instantly contrite. 'I'm sorry. I didn't mean to make you cry.'

'It's all right,' said Astha wiping her nose on the edge of her sari palla.

'No, it's not,' said Pipee. 'If you are unhappy, it's not all right.'

Astha went on sniffing. 'I don't usually think about it,' she offered.

'Who would think about anything if they could help it?' said Pipee gloomily, 'God knows I have tried . . .'

There was a silence while Pipee drew squiggles in the rings of water left by their glasses on the table, and Astha watched her fingers. 'Have you?' she finally asked.

'Once. Met her in school, continued in college, on and off for three years. Eventually she got married. Much later I did too.'

'Oh.'

'What was her name?'

'Samira.'

'Was she nice?'

'Not often. She seduced me, and then when I fell in love, triumphed in that power. It was not so different from being with a man, though I am sure it can be.'

'Oh?'

'It is more a question of choice than people make out. That is what I believe at any rate. Besides sex is sex, don't you think? It is other things that become important.'

'Yes, yes – of course. Did your husband know?'

'I told him. But you know what men are like . . .'

'No, I don't think I do,' said Astha forlornly. 'I have actually only known my husband, and now I am not even sure of that.'

She thought of the condom again – would it go on coming up in her mind at every point of sadness in her life, she wondered. She could tell Pipee about it, but Pipee might think she was inadequate in her responses, or weak in her understanding, or a fool. For now she preferred to keep this wound to herself.

'Does your husband have affairs?'

'I don't know.' Then quickly, 'Did yours?'

'Well there were several women before we got married, I knew that.' Astha thought of the little gesture Aijaz had offered her, and now realised that it was in fact an invitation. 'I think he must have had an affair with Reshana Singh, the way she goes on. I know she thinks I am jealous, and maybe,' went on Pipee reflectively, 'I am.' She shook her head. 'There is no escape from jealousy, is there? We are all embryonic Othellos.'

'I know what you mean,' said Astha gloomily.

'Yes, well. I don't know why I am delving into the past today,' said Pipee, hauling her heavy bag onto her shoulder and getting up to go as the sweeper reached their table.

'Maybe so I can get to know you.'

'You're so pretty, Ant.'

'Do you really think so?'

They were sitting in Pipee's flat drinking beer before an early lunch. Pipee had made arrangements to go to work late, and now she pulled Astha by the hand and led her to the bathroom mirror.

'Are we going to do mirror, mirror on the wall / Who is the fairest one of all?' laughed Astha nervously. She often felt an underlying tension when talking to Pipee, as they swooped and dived among their lives, offering bits to the other to share.

'A modern version of it,' said Pipee putting on the light and pushing Astha's head gently forwards. 'Look.'

Astha tried to turn away, 'I don't like looking at my face, especially so close.'

Then she felt Pipee's hands in her hair, her clip undone, her hands framing the oval of her face. Lightly from behind she traced her eyebrows with her fingers, her nose, cheeks and mouth.

The two women said nothing looking at their reflections in the small water-stained mirror. 'See?' whispered Pipee.

Astha saw nothing, and abruptly left the bathroom. Later taking a scooter-rickshaw home, she felt lost and confused, the image of the two of them in the mirror often returning when she thought of Pipee.

*

One day, in Astha's house, a rare occasion. Pipee preferred to meet Astha anywhere else than in her house.

'So this is the marital bed,' said Pipee, surveying Astha's room, full of double bed. 'The marital bed in the marital room.'

'Like in most people's houses,' replied Astha, not particularly liking Pipee's tone.

'I know. It's how I used to live. Are you happy here? Do you have good sex?'

'Good enough, I suppose.'

'Don't you know?'

'Well he was my first, and only.'

'You're joking.'

'Not really.'

'What about the other two?'

'They were crushes. One I kissed a lot, with the other there were only letters.'

'Have you ever wanted more lovers?'

What could Astha say? She was living, the way people like her lived, where was the question of more lovers, or love for that matter?

Pipee stretched out her palm for Astha's hand. Gently she held it, fingering her thumb nail. Round and round the stubby nail Pipee's finger went, lightly tracing the pink part, the white part, the skin part. Astha looked at their two hands together, and inched a little closer to the woman on her bed.

Pipee took a firmer grip of the hand in hers, and turned it over, stroking the back of it, gently sliding her rings off, and putting them on her own fingers, manoeuvring her bangles off and slipping them on to her own more narrow wrist.

'I look so bare without them,' murmured Astha.

'All the better,' murmured Pipee even more softly. Her breath quickened, and she pressed the tips of Astha's fingers into her mouth, sucking each one gently before letting them go. Astha hardly dared breathe.

'What would your precious spouse say, if he saw us together now?' asked Pipee.

Astha swallowed and did not reply.

'Did you say he was a faithful husband?'

'I didn't say anything.'

'Is he good in bed?'

'I suppose.'

'If you have to suppose, he is not,' said Pipee severely.

Astha decided she knew nothing about love making, that she was inexperienced and stupid. 'What about you?' she responded in a low tone, 'You yourself have only had two lovers.'

'Yes, that's true,' sighed Pipee. 'But I'm looking for a third.'

'Why so silent?' asked Hemant that evening.

'Silent? Am I?'

'You need me to tell you that?'

'Sorry. I hadn't realised.'

More silence. What should she talk about? What had she talked about before silence came upon her? Their days, his day certainly. Now she made enquiries.

'I have managed to bribe our union leader this time, but bribing is difficult, the workers are watchful and suspicious, I won't be able to do it again.'

Astha hated it when Hemant talked about bribing, and yet the way he described it, it seemed necessary.

'Pipee came over today,' she said, changing the subject.

'That woman,' said Hemant.

Astha's heart sank. Things would be difficult if Hemant became violent about his dislike. She tried to change the topic again, but Hemant was having none of it. 'What did you say she did?' he continued.

'She works with basti children,' said Astha proudly. 'She helps them get through school, she gives them a sense of self-confidence, and strength.'

'Who finances this?'

'She's part of an NGO called Ujjala.'

Hemant grunted, 'One of those types.'

'What does that mean?'

'Take money from here and there, and pretend they are working.'

It seemed there was nothing Astha could say, and yet he wanted her to talk. She started on the children. That was always safe. It was what they were united upon, and it served its purpose now.

That night, Hemant started his sex routine.

'No,' said Astha, 'I don't feel like it.'

Hemant paused. This was the first time his wife had not felt like it. 'What's up?' he demanded.

'Nothing.'

'Then?'

'Then what? Do I have to give it just because you are my husband? Unless I feel close to you I can't – I'm not a sex object, you have others for that.'

Hemant relaxed. That old thing. He took her face in his hands. 'Sweetheart, why do you upset yourself over nothing? You are my wife, I love you, there has never been another woman for me, never. On business trips people don't understand commitments to wife and family, they assume their clients want a good time. If I had had sex, would the condom not have been used? You only tell me,' he whispered, his hands falling to her breasts and circling them in the way that was so familiar, kneading them, pressing them, as he continued, 'you only tell me,' then pulling up her nightie, and fondling her, 'does what you imagine have any logic?'

Without her willing it her body responded. Hemant became even more ardent. 'Baby, you are the only one for me, what's the matter, are you jealous?'

'No,' she said, trying to push him away, but it was of no use.

After the marital function had been performed, Astha got up to wash herself. Looking up from her wet and soapy hands, she caught sight of a sad and haggard face. How old she looked, and yet she wasn't old. She was thirty-six, but all the life seemed gone. She leaned over the sink, and examined her face more carefully, certain to increase her wretchedness. Around her eyes tiny wrinkles were beginning to form. She stretched her mouth in imitation laughter, and they became more pronounced. She stared at her nose and saw the blackheads there. Her skin looked yellow and sallow, when she put her head up to look at the folds in her neck more clearly, she could see the white line at the base of her scalp, where the new hair had come, and the dyed parts grown out.

Why should anyone love her, she thought hopelessly. She was so ugly. She thought of Pipee sucking her fingers. She looked at them, and put them experimentally in her mouth. They didn't taste very nice – of soap and sex. What had Pipee thought of them? And what would Pipee's own fingers taste like? What had Pipee seen when she had pushed her face towards the mirror? Certainly not what she saw now. Slowly she went back to bed.

Her meetings with Pipee increased. When she was alone in the home in the mornings Pipee dropped by on her way to work, she phoned her at least five times a day, short brief conversations, but which drew each of them firmly into the nitty gritty of the other's life. And the days when she didn't see or talk to her were days with something missing, and not even extra hours at the canvas could fill the vacuum Astha felt. She started to fantasise about touching her, imagined her hair between her fingers, her skin beneath her own, her hands on the back of her neck.

Astha frantically trying to reach an appointed meeting place.
'I'm sorry, I'm sorry, I'm sorry.'
'I was about to go.'
'I'm sorry. I couldn't help it.'
'What happened?'

'I forgot it was a bandh. Not a single scooter wallah agreed to come. Not one. They said they would be beaten up. I even offered fifty bucks.'

'Then?'

'In the end he took eighty.'

'Eighty! Three times! You shouldn't have paid it, Ant.'

'I had no choice. I would have given him anything.'

'He was taking advantage of the situation,' said Pipee sternly.

'What could I do? You were waiting, I kept thinking of that, but I was on the road, and there was no way to tell you.'

'Oh sweetie, it's all right. Now, forget about it. I thought you must be having a problem. I can't imagine where I'd be without my scooter.'

'I don't see why you haven't bought a car,' said Pipee later, as she was stirring her cold coffee. The meal had ended, and Astha was worrying about how she was to get home. 'One needs to be mobile. I learned how to drive a scooter, it was all I could afford, but with you it's different.'

'We have a car.'

'Hemant's.'

'Which I use.'

'Only when he doesn't.'

'He sends it back from the factory with the driver whenever I need it.'

'I'm sure he does, but you can be more independent with your own.'

'A car costs over a lakh.'

'You could hold an exhibition, and earn.'

'Not lakhs.'

'Ant, why are you being like this? Didn't you tell me your mother left you some money?'

'With Hemant.' And the old hurt comes to choke her.

'Hemant is not a monster. Have you tried asking him? Since ask you must.'

'He'll say whenever I want the car, I have it. Also I can ask my in-laws for theirs.'

'If Hemant can keep a car for his parents, he can keep one for you.'

'Well, I, the children that is, use it as well. For tuitions, classes, and stuff.'

'The point is,' went on Pipee patiently, 'if you had a car you would not have to do all this asking business.'

'I can't ask for a car for myself.'

'Why not?'

'Hemant says there is going to be trouble in the factory.'

'How long has this factory been running?'

'Ten years.'

'I imagine he has made enough money to buy you a car.'

'He is very generous to me.'

'Good. Now come let me drop you home otherwise you'll be cheated all over again.'

As they roared through the streets of Delhi, Astha leaned against Pipee, with her arms around her waist. Once or twice Pipee turned to ask, are you all right, Astha merely nodded, too happy to speak, even had the sound of the vehicle allowed it.

'But why? The car is there for you whenever you want it.'

'Please, Hemant. I am thirty-six. I need to be independent. I am always adjusting to everybody else's needs.'

'And the money?'

'We could use what my mother gave.'

'You know I have invested that for the children, and in five years the amount has grown nicely.' Hemant looked satisfied. Astha had heard all this before, heard when the bonus shares came, heard when the dividends came, when the debentures were bought, heard as it doubled, trebled, quadrupled. There was no question of touching it, she knew that. Only somewhere surely there was money she could touch? She said as much.

Hemant looked at her. 'Who is putting these ideas into your head?'

'Nobody,' said Astha offended. 'Does somebody have to tell me to want a car?'

'Mama, Papa is getting you a car?' Anuradha. Hemant had told her first.

'It is also my money,' said Astha suddenly angry. The children turned towards her, slightly shocked. Only prices were discussed in their house, never money, and certainly not whose money was whose. It was all common money because they were a family.

'Papa's money too,' said Anuradha quickly.

'Of course Papa's money too. But if necessary I will hold an exhibition to help pay for this car.'

Himanshu put his hand into hers. 'When I earn I will buy you a car,' he proclaimed. Astha tightened her hold on his thin interwoven fingers and stared at the overgrown nails, at the fine hair glinting blondly, at the sun exposed brown skin.

'And I will buy a car for Papa,' said Anuradha.

'But Papa and Mama are not separate,' said Astha, quickly. 'Whatever you buy will be for both of us. Don't I use the car we already have? It is not Papa's or mine. And now we will have a second car, besides the one upstairs, neither Papa's nor mine, but for everybody. We are a family with growing needs.'

~

It was the end of the term, before the summer holidays, and PTA day. Astha was in her children's school, trying not to stare at the fathers and mothers around her, united and content.

There was a whole list of teachers she had to see.

Himanshu had done badly in his mid-terms. He hadn't finished his papers, but really he knew everything. Astha was waiting to tell his class teacher this, something she had been saying since nursery. The teacher in turn would tell her that even so, he had to increase his speed, other children managed.

If he didn't, he was going to find it very difficult at the higher levels. Astha could predict the conversation verbatim, but these motions had to be gone through.

Anuradha was doing badly in science and maths. She didn't understand the method of explanation, and Astha had to find out why in a way that didn't compromise her daughter's intelligence, attentiveness, or abilities. Both her children were dead against her discussing any of their problems in school. Before she had left Anu had screamed, don't say anything, don't Mama, then in class the teacher says, so you are having difficulties, why don't you ask me during the lesson instead of complaining later, and the kids stare at me, as though I am a moron. Besides, I keep telling you, there is no *point* asking for explanations, they all repeat the same thing in the same way, only slower.

Himanshu had looked equally worried, you are not going to say anything to my teacher, are you, Mama? In class, she'll say something to me, she will get angry.

With the futility of it all firmly established, she waited in line after line to see various instructors, behind parents busy pumping them for the secret of success in that particular subject. She was going to be late for her meeting with Pipee, why had she, against all experience, allotted two hours to school? Now precious minutes were being wasted in the corridors of this huge and unfeeling institution.

The maths teacher, Mr Sharma, before whom there was a line half a mile long. Anu obviously not the only one having problems. After an hour of waiting, her turn.

Anuradha? Yes, a very bright child, but she should work harder, if she has a problem in following, she should ask me, I tell them, ask me, there is no excuse for not understanding. She should do one hour timed exercise every day, maths is only practice.

Astha pulled out Anu's mid-term exam from her bag, 59 out of 100. Mr Sharma's temper rose the moment he saw it, look at this, correct method, but a mistake in adding and the answer is wrong. And here, she has copied the sum incorrectly. How will she get marks? Crooked margins, untidy rough work. Careless, careless.

Astha stared at the paper, she understood nothing of it. Were Anu's crimes so bad? A crooked margin, a sum added wrong, another carelessly copied, did that result in 59 and feeling a failure?

Surely it doesn't matter if the rough work is not neat? she queried.

It is the attitude that matters, the attitude, thundered Mr Sharma.

In the face of this, further comment seemed redundant.

Finally, all the teachers met, the Vadera children ticked off in various registers, her participation in the learning process marked, her children's faults pointed out and noted, and she was free. Frantically she ran out of the school gates, she was over an hour late already. Pipee would have cooked for her, she would be wondering.

As she rang the bell to Pipee's apartment, she could hear footsteps coming towards the door. Her heart beat faster, explanations trembled on her lips. The door opened, and before her, the face, always in her mind, always indistinct, the long narrow eyes, the hair which sprang back wild and unruly, the voice she could drown in, the mouth that pulled inwards as she smiled, the little mole hanging under her nose like a dew drop.

There she was, and there Astha stood, and nothing else mattered. Silently Pipee motioned her in, took her bag, and closed the door.

'What took you so long? I was getting worried.'

'Sorry, Pip, I'm sorry, I couldn't help it, there were millions of parents, and the teachers took ages. I kept thinking of you waiting, I felt terrible the whole time.'

They were standing. Slowly Pipee put her arms around

her. She could feel her hands on the narrowness of her back, on the beginning spread of her hips. Gently she undid her blouse hooks, and her bra, looking at her face as she did so and slowly she continued, feeling her back with her palm, coming round up towards her breasts, feeling their softness, especially where the nipples were, feeling them again and again, in no hurry to reach any conclusion. They were enclosed in a circle of silence, the only sound, the sound of their breaths, close together and mingled.

In the small bedroom, Astha tense with nervousness. She was afraid, yet there was no going back. Sensing how she felt, Pipee took her time, touching every crevice of her body with her mouth. The sweaty patches of her armpits with small stiff hair beginning to poke out, the soft fold of flesh where the arm joined the torso, the hard bony part behind her ears, the deep crease between her buttocks, the hairiness between her thighs.

In between they talked, the talk of discovery and attraction, of the history of a three month relationship, the teasing and pleasure of an intimacy that was complete and absolute, expressed through minds as much as bodies.

Afterwards Astha felt strange, making love to a woman took getting used to.

And it also felt strange, making love to a friend instead of an adversary.

She returned home in a daze. As she neared her house, she succumbed to panic, she was a mother, nothing should disturb that. For a brief and guilty moment she wished she was like Pipee, alone and free, but she checked herself. A large part of her belonged to her children, that was how she lived her life. She couldn't imagine any other way.

She was a wife too, but not much of her was required there. A willing body at night, a willing pair of hands and feet in the day and an obedient mouth were the necessary prerequisites of Hemant's wife.

*

A few days later. 'Hemant should be pleased,' said Astha to her lover, 'he says women are always mind-fucking.'

They both laughed at the wife's revenge.

~

Astha was in love. All day she thought of her, visualising the turn of her neck, long, sloping, unornamented, the collar bones on either side of the small hollow at the base of her throat, the screws of her hair latticed, as she had once seen them against the dark, heavy, green of the trees of the Tagore Arts Centre. And her fingers, long and so narrow the bones showed, with stubby nails, and a snake ring, three silver bands, two small turquoise eyes, two black painted dots for a nose. And her eyelids, that fragile tender area where she wanted to press her lips, compressing them to the size of peas to enclose that space. And the mouth with its inward-turning corners, she could gaze at those dents for ever.

From time to time she brooded about her own sexual nature, but her desire for Pipee was so linked to the particular person, that she failed to draw any general conclusions. So far as her marriage was concerned, they were both women, nothing was seriously threatened. Meanwhile her best time at home was when she was fantasising about the one she loved without interruptions, lost in her thoughts, wallowing in her feelings.

All this made it difficult for her to focus on what was going on around her. She was able to forget she had another life only when she was absorbed in her painting or her children's homework, an echo of an earlier simplicity that now appeared to have some advantages.

Astha was surprised when Hemant noticed.

'You seem distracted,' he pointed out. 'What is it?'

She felt a flash of fear, but then an affair with a woman was not an easy thing for a husband to suspect. Caution drew her lips into a smile, and put a hood across her eyes. 'Nothing,' she said. 'What do you imagine?'

A look of dissatisfaction that it seemed must always be on one of their two faces, crossed his brow, giving her a momentary sense of control. She was not there. How right he was. But when had he acquired the sensitivity?

What about the times he had not been there, and the reasons had always been such that her own claims seemed selfish. Now sexually involved with another, she realised how many facets in the relationship between her husband and herself reflected power rather than love. Hemant had managed to ignore her because ultimately he filled his own landscape. That her discontent had been expressed in nuances that were minor, only helped him in his disregard.

In the days that followed, Hemant began to watch Astha. Let him watch, thought Astha, he who had not looked since the early days of marriage, was now looking and found that what he saw did not add up.

Her lies grew skilful. Her desperation and her need ensured that they tripped off her tongue, as though she had rehearsed them for hours.

Fed by right-minded parents, Astha had believed that never, ever must one lie. There was a Pinocchio lurking in her moral self, waiting and watching. Her nose would grow, her eyes cross themselves in vain attempts to hide the gruesome deed, her skin would turn yellow and pimples sprout all over her. Her inner ugliness would be reflected for all to see.

She had lied about the boys she had known, and each time she had been punished. They had left her, she had not deserved better.

When she married she had wanted to tell her husband about those boys, but she had been afraid he would not accept her, and that tiny seed, usually forgotten, was still inside, telling her she was unworthy. She had compromised by being excessively truthful; she knew her husband trusted her implicitly.

Now, she lied all day. The strongest thing in her was the most secret. Pipee encouraged her. Not for her the moral values of George Washington, the boy on the burning deck, Eklavya, Ram, Sita, Lakshman, those for whom words translated into codes of honour never to be broken no matter what.

'Of course you have to lie. They don't own you.'

'I know, but . . . I wish I didn't feel the way I did.'

'What way?' asked her lover very naturally, and when she didn't reply, very insistently, 'what way?'

'Oh you know,' Astha became vague. 'So much of the real stuff is with you, and since I can't talk about it with my family, it makes me feel pretty schizo.'

'Why do you have to talk about it with them? You talk about it with me. Are they your guardians or something?'

It was hard to explain. Pipee lived on a grander, more open scale then she did.

Meanwhile this grand and open creature was growing jealous of other claims. She had even wondered, to Astha's horror, when she was going to inform Hemant about them.

'He is not your owner, you know, he'll have to face up to his inadequacies.'

'No, no – I can't do that.'

'Why not?'

It seemed so unthinkable, how could she explain. 'Maybe I'm a coward,' she remarked thoughtfully.

'Oh dearest,' sighed Pipee, 'Don't be so hard on yourself. You've lived a certain way, you are used to certain ideas, you can't suddenly be different. If I am impatient with your situation, it's because I want you to be happy.'

She turned the other's face towards her, took out her pins and stroked her open hair, reaching into the scalp, in a way that reminded Astha of her mother oiling her hair every Sunday when she was young. She closed her eyes and sank against her, feeling as though she were in a warm bath. With Pipee there was no battering against something hard and ununderstanding, she was all warmth and intuition. She thanked God again for this love in her life, when she had thought all chance of love was over.

If God had given her love, there was no time supplement with this gift, so Astha often found herself wishing despairingly she could live each day twice, once with Pipee, and once on the ordinary plane.

She dreaded the occasions when her lives clashed, and was at no time more at the mercy of her circumstances than weekends.

One Wednesday Pipee said firmly, 'There is a gay and lesbian film festival this Saturday. I know, I know, Saturdays are difficult for you, but I want to go, and I think you should too.'

'But Pip . . .'

'Don't say anything. I want to see the films with you. Don't you think they have a special relevance?'

This was undeniable.

'Do you mind if I ask Hemant? Don't worry, he is bound not to come.'

Pipee made a face. 'Then why ask him?'

'He's going to be home this weekend.' went on Astha hurriedly. 'He will find it strange if I make a programme without him.'

'Let him.'

'He is beginning to complain.'

'Of what?'

'Oh, just,' said Astha, avoiding specifics. 'You know. He feels something is not quite right.'

'Well, it's not. It's time he woke up.'

'I wouldn't go so far,' said Astha quickly.

'You wouldn't, huh?'

'No. Everything is all right the way it is.'

'Don't ignore the obvious, Ant,' was all Pipee said.

'Go with you and Pipeelika Khan to a gay film show? Are you out of your mind, Az?'

'Well, I am going with her. You can for once come to something I am interested in.'

Hemant stared. 'I'm not interested in homosexuals,' he said. 'And I thought neither were you. But I'm learning something every day.' He held out his hand, and Astha slowly put her own in his. 'Stay home. We can rent a video. We haven't done that in a long time.'

It was not fair. It needed his wife's having an affair for Hemant to promise to see a video with her, something he knew she loved. Such an evening might have made her happy a year ago, now it seemed like blackmail.

'I've promised Pipee . . .' she said.

'So? Unpromise her.'

'Maybe next Saturday, but not this.'

A sullen look settled on Hemant's face. Astha could see resentment, and she felt sorry. But not half as sorry as she would feel if she didn't go, didn't sit next to Pipee in a dark hall, with their arms, hands, knees touching.

'Why can't we do this some other time?' she went on, 'often you have not been here for me. I think you should be understanding about one day.'

'I was busy, Az, I was establishing myself.'

'For ten years?'

'It takes that long, you knew that, you supported me.'

Their disagreements had the history of their marriage hanging onto them, and Astha had no time for this now. 'We can continue our discussion when I come back,' she said.

Hemant refused to respond, and Astha could think of nothing further to say. She didn't want to leave him like this, but he was giving her no choice. Quickly she put on the first sari that came to hand, grabbed a shawl and left.

It was only when she walked down the road to the scooter stand that she realised it was in fact a chilly day, and she was going to feel cold. Should she go back for a sweater? No, she didn't want to encounter Hemant again, better to freeze. She wrapped her shawl and palla firmly around her, and hoped it wouldn't rain.

The cold bit through her in the three-wheeler, and her nose began to run. She looked through her purse for a hanky – no, she had forgotten to bring a hanky as well. She bent down and wiped her nose on her petticoat.

At the community centre, Astha made her hesitant way into the hall. She was late, and it took her a few minutes to adjust to the darkness. She felt her sari being tugged, and there was Pipee leaning against the wall by the entrance, waiting. She sank down next to her, feeling exhausted after the battle with Hemant, looking with cursory interest at the screen, registering indifferently the men and women, speaking broad American about the discrimination they faced as gays. In between some social scientist gave his opinion, in between that there were clips of marches and demonstrations. Astha looked at the faces on the screen. All of them open, none of them living a life of lies.

Pipee's voice breathed through the craven recesses of her mind, 'We have to struggle for acceptance and the right to love as we feel. Don't you think so, Ant?' But try as Astha could, she could not connect to what she was seeing. Her own situation was different, though if Pipee didn't think so she would keep that information to herself.

In the intermission, Astha broke the news to Pipee as they were drinking coffee, 'I have to go.'

'Why?' she could hear the concern in Pipee's voice, feel her hand as it lay in the crook of her elbow. 'Are you feeling all right? Don't you find it interesting?'

'Anuradha has a test. It was difficult for me to get away today.' She didn't want to go into the whole Hemant thing.

At the sounds of domesticity, Pipee's face twisted slightly, but she merely said, 'Why can't the father sit with her for a change? Why do you have to do it all the time?'

'That's the way it is.'

'Go then.' She gave her a little push.

'Dearest, don't be offended, I'll make it up to you, I swear.'

'How will you go home?'

'Scooter,' said Astha dully. How did it matter how she got home? Maybe she should crawl to that shrine of marital and maternal bliss on her belly, or drag herself on her behind with the stumps of her legs sticking out straight out in front of her, pulling herself along with her hands the way lepers did, begging for alms around the crowded intersections of Delhi.

'Pipeee,' Astha could hear somebody shouting. 'Hurry up, the next film has started.'

'I'll call you when I get home.' She squeezed Astha's arm again, kissed her cheek, and vanished into the hall warm with its comradeship for her, cold with its indifference towards Astha.

'How come you are back so early?' asked Hemant in a jocular tone, as he saw her descend from the scooter, her ears red and her nose now running like a river. Without looking at him, Astha held out a hand and said, 'Hanky.' Hemant took out his own and gave it to her. She blew her nose, at long last, through the tortures of the day, she was able to blow her nose.

Then she looked at him. He was smiling. He thought he had won, and now was trying to be nice to her.

'Just like that,' she said.

'Gay and lesbian films not your cup of tea, huh?'

'Not at all. They were very good.'

'Then?'

'Then what? The hall was crowded, and I didn't have enough to wear, and I was feeling cold, and I came home because I didn't want to sit on the floor too long.'

Hemant looked disbelieving.

'Have the children had their lunch?' asked Astha.

'Yes, for all you care.'

It didn't bother Astha, his tone, nothing bothered her. She went inside, she was hungry, she had had no breakfast, and

238

she now ate some leftover lunch. Then she made herself a cup of tea, she felt a sore throat coming, and for now would think of nothing but her physical wellbeing.

That evening Hemant solicitously offered her a brandy for her cold. He talked of her painting, he talked about the children, he talked about her mother, his parents, he said maybe next year they would go on a holiday to America, by then the factory problems would be sorted, he worked very hard, and he needed to take it easy. And the car, what about that?

She, which car?

He looked hurt. The car she had demanded, had said she needed in order to be independent, he had arranged to get one in the company name.

In the company name. It was that easy after all.

What did she think of a white Maruti?

Astha's feelers went up. She could not remember when her opinion had been sought about a major purchase. Why was he being so considerate? Was he trying to buy her? True, she would be able to rush to Pipee's whenever she liked, in the car her husband had bought for her, but how was that going to make her feel? She didn't want a car, she realised, it would end up making her feel more guilty, and were she to express all this to Pipee she would say, but it is your car, why do you feel you have to pay for it with mind, body and soul, she could hear her voice even now.

'I don't know how to drive,' she temporised.

'I'll teach you, we can learn every Sunday,' he said, caressing her. 'We will be together.'

'Yes, yes, I suppose.'

'Try and sound a little enthusiastic, will you?'

'I am enthusiastic, why do you look for meanings in everything I say? They say husbands should not teach wives, the relationship deteriorates,' said Astha irritably.

'We'll see. I don't want to waste money on lessons.'

The car came. Hemant in fact had no time. In the end it was Ram Singh, the driver, who taught Astha in the colony lanes.

That summer Rajiv Gandhi was assassinated by a suicide bomber in Tamil Nadu during an election campaign. Political uncertainty meant that Pipee's work in the bastis grew more demanding and she could not see Astha much in the day. Astha felt her absence every minute, and when Pipee called her in the evenings, she went, but her home situation was such that the meetings had to be hurried, not more than an hour, not much for lovers, certainly not much for Pipee.

~

'Ajay has written. He is keen to sponsor me. He has been suggesting it ever since I finished my MA.'

'What?'

'A Ph.D.'

'You never told me.'

'It was before I met you,' said Pipee.

'How come you never mentioned it? And why are you telling me now?'

'Because his letter has come,' said Pipee in limpid accents.

Astha slid Pipee's hand from under her shoulder and looked at it. There was the ring, there were the bones, there were the long thin fingers. She placed their palms together, and thought it was an illusion, you could never be one with another, no matter how hard you tried. It was better to realise and accept that, life became easier once you did.

'Yes,' she said, 'you better explore doing a Ph.D. It's a good thing for the future.'

'Well let me see. It will mean leaving you.'

And Astha's poor heart rejoiced to hear she was important.

Driving home, Astha brooded over Ajay's letter. She was not stupid, she knew why Pipee had brought up the letter. She wants a full life, after six months she wants commitment, if I can't give it to her, why shouldn't she look elsewhere, but she didn't want Pipee to look elsewhere, she wanted her to stay with her for ever, as she was, as they were.

Resentfully she thought of Pipee's Ph.D. Suddenly it was a burning desire. Well, she knew why. She was saying if Astha had her children, she had her Ph.D., as though you could equate the two.

Astha: I have a fantasy, listen my love, and do not laugh. It is not much, I think it is not much.

I have a room, small but private, where my family pass before my eyes. It is very light, before me is a wall which divides the house, but I can see my children, that satisfies me, though to them I am invisible, that satisfies me too.

This room will be our room, you with me, living in harmony. Our lives are separate, different things call to us, different demands are made on us, but always that solid base beneath us, like two flies caught in a sticky pool they cannot leave.

'Sticky flies? You must be mad.'

'All right the image is bad. Still, you know what I mean.'

'You are a hopeless romantic. You want me and you want not to leave your old life. It's a nice fantasy, I wish it were possible. I also wish,' added Pipee after a little thought, 'that it had taken place in my house.'

'Does that show something?' asked Astha, wishing that she with whom she shared everything, was not quite so into analysis.

'Well, what do you think?'

'I think nothing. It was a dream, an idle dream, for God's sake, something I know can never happen.'

'But it can, don't you see, even in a dream you are in your precious Vasant Vihar. There are other places in the world, Ant, if you would only consider them. Instead you allow yourself to be shut up by that man, who neither knows nor appreciates you, and for what? I do not understand.'

'There are my children.'

'Your children don't have to be stuck in that house any more than you do.'

Astha's mind boggled. What about their school, their routine, their friends in the colony, their grandparents, their father, who whatever his faults, did love his kids? Maybe she was deeply conventional but for her the business of raising children had a set of dynamics that were the standard ones. That those dynamics did not include companionship and understanding was regrettable, but she had grown used to it. She saw herself as a bird pecking at a few leftover crumbs from the feast of life. She said as much. Pipee stared at her.

'I never thought of myself as a crumb,' she said dryly.

This drove Astha on to further explanations.

'I love you, you know how much you mean to me, I try and prove it every moment we have together, but I can't abandon my family, I can't. Maybe I should not have looked for happiness, but I couldn't help myself. I suppose you think I should not be in a relationship, but I had not foreseen . . . Oh Pipee, I'm sorry I am not like you.'

'What do you mean? Don't you want an honest above-board life?'

'You are being unfair.'

'When do you ever think of me? Always their needs, your needs, before mine.'

'That's not true.'

'It is. You can't see me in the evenings—'

'How can you say that? Just the other day I spent the whole evening with you, I went home at twelve, I told endless lies—'

'Who asked you to tell lies? I didn't. Don't you see, Ant, I want an end to all this deception.'

'My whole life is a fabric of lies,' said Astha sadly, 'you are the one true thing I have.'

'And you don't want to change it. That's the trouble with married people,' said Pipee gloomily, 'there are always others involved. Why did I think with a woman it would be different?'   ·

Panic rose in Astha. Tears came to her eyes, and she felt a headache coming on. All she wanted to do was drive back, shut herself in her room, and sleep till the end of time. She got up.

'What are you doing?'

'Going home, since you ask.'

Pipee reached out and pulled her dupatta. 'Don't you get it? That I love you, I want you, I miss you?'

'What about your other friends and your work?' asked Astha in a small voice.

'What about it? Work never kept one warm at night, and yes, I have friends, but they are not people I choose to be intimate with. Either I spend my time here moping, or I go out with them, talk, laugh, then come home to a flat which holds the moments I have had with you. It reminds me—' Here she paused, Astha looked tortured, and Pipee continued quickly, 'whatever it is, I don't wish to experience that kind of emptiness again. Sometimes I go crazy with longing, and I can't even pick up the phone.'

'You can.'

'I can't. I don't want to hear your husband's voice, I don't want to put the phone down if he picks it up, I don't want to share your life of lies.'

Astha thought that if husband and wife are one person, then Pipee and she were even more so. She had shared parts of herself she had never shared before. She felt complete with her. But this was not the time to say these things.

'I'm sorry, I don't mean to be harsh,' said Pipee contritely. 'Leaving a marriage, even like yours, could not be easy. I do feel that away from that house and those people you will be able to lead a fuller life. You have so much in you, so much to give, but take your time. Whatever you do it'll be all right.'

Astha turned towards her gratefully. That her lover should understand how she was feeling was enough. She sank down to the sofa into her arms.

It was dark before Astha got up to leave. With the thought of Pipee in her mind, the scent of Pipee on her body she moved trance-like towards her car, driving slowly and automatically down the roads of Delhi.

As Astha parked the car outside the gates of her house Anuradha came rushing out. 'I'm failing,' she gasped. 'You have to see my teacher. Where were you? I have been waiting hours and hours.'

'In what subject?'

'Maths.'

Of course. It had to be maths.

Anuradha was biting her nails. 'I'll fail the year, I'll fail the year, I'll fail the year, I'll fail the year,' she chanted in a frenzy.

'Can we wait for the results before you decide that?' demanded Astha.

'You don't care! Why can't I have tuition, all my friends have tuition, but you want me to do it by myself, because you did.'

'Anu, don't be unreasonable. When did I say . . .?'

'You did, and now you have forgotten. You want me to be like you. I am not, but you don't care.'

Anuradha stared at her mother, tears streaming down her young cheeks. Dear God, thought Astha, when did I say she had to be like me? When did I say she couldn't have tuition because I hadn't? When?

'Sweetie, can we talk about this later? I have just come home, I am tired, I don't remember what I said and when and why. If it is necessary of course you will have a tutor, but you also have to learn to do things on your own.'

Anuradha ran inside, scowling. 'I had to phone Papa, you weren't here, he said to wait till you came home, you would know what to do, you know the teachers, but what's the use? I have been saying I need tuition. No one listens to me.'

Astha walked in wearily. In the face of Anu's maths her own feelings seemed an indulgence rather than a necessity. They would have to wait, wait in the wings, wait on a more permanent basis.

After dinner Astha watched her daughter sit in her favourite chair and read unconcernedly. The lamp shone on her hair, highlighting its copper shades. Her socks lay untidily on the carpet, she was wiggling her toes in front of the heater, the light catching the lurid colours of her nail polish. Her troubles were over, her friend's tutor had been phoned, he was going to start from next week.

Astha sighed and took another sip of her tea. On the sofa next to her, Himanshu laboured over his homework, his notebook getting more and more smudged as he continually rubbed out what he had written, shredding bits of the page.

Her thoughts wandered, to the series she had imagined on mosques and temples in Ayodhya, Kashi and Mathura. Pipee had thought it was a brilliant idea, but there was no space in her head to execute any idea, be it ever so brilliant.

VIII

November 26th

Pip called. I want you to come with me for three weeks. Will you?

Where?

The Ekta Yatra, from December 10 to January 26. It starts from Kanyakumari and ends in Kashmir.

I thought of the Rath Yatra canvas I had painted for the Manch. Here was another journey, taken by another Leader.

What's this Yatra all about I ask her.

The usual. This Leader says he wants to unify the country.

They all say that.

Well, he is going to spread his message from north to south, east to west. I know it's a political stunt, yatras like this create nothing but trouble, but it's an excuse to be together. Will you come?

Of course.

(My heart is beating, my hands begin to sweat, of course I will come as though it is the easiest thing in the world, of course, as though I can get up and go anywhere I like, anytime I like, of course, because I love you, and at times love makes life simple because it demands you worship at its altar, dragged though you may be kicking and screaming.)

Good. Talk to you later. I have to work on this, her voice breaks in on my thoughts.

I put the phone down. Three weeks with her. My mind is whirring, how will I manage it, what will I say, but I have to go, I have to. She has never asked me to do anything so directly. Is this a test, I wonder?

Next day

With P. Why a Yatra? I ask. It's not like Ayodhya. You are not taking Ujjala helpers to sensitise them to communal issues.

I thought of this as a way to be together. Then she hesitated. I am learning the language of her voice, she was about to say something she thought might hurt me.

And?

She was silent.

Come on, Pip, tell me, though actually I don't want to hear. I want to stay with the pleasure of proof that she wants to be with me, but I force myself to ask because shadows between us are ten times worse.

She started talking of communal issues as an area of research, something that now interests her. (Due to Aijaz's death, I imagine.) With an interpreter she could get some field work done.

So she thought I might be upset because she is still thinking of her wretched higher studies.

Nice, I said enthusiastically, what a good idea.

She looked pleased, and then told me how she was arranging it. I waited for Neeraj's name to appear, which it did. I am sure Neeraj is pushing her towards this Ph.D. I hate Neeraj, though we met only once. She is fake arty, has a deep voice, smokes endless cigarettes, and of course has a marriage where her husband is deeply involved in all she does. He is a lawyer, and helps her when necessary, and in Ujjala it is always necessary. She looks upon Pipee as her protégé. Pip says she gets on her nerves sometimes, but she has been so kind to her, she can never say anything. I personally think she is insensitive and power hungry. I wonder if Pip has told her about us.

Neeraj's cousin is a journalist, she is arranging that we go in the accompanying bus. Pip has to produce articles for her newspaper (I am sure Neeraj thinks it will help her CV). The cousin herself is going to make an initial brief appearance. After a week or so we go to Bangalore, then to Shiksha Kendra.

Shiksha Kendra, her school, her past, her mother. I want to absorb everything to do with her, because it is her.

Next day
Dreading talk with H. Yet why should I be nervous, hasn't he travelled, it is my turn, but even as I think this, I know it is the wrong argument to use. I shouldn't seem to want justice, it will create endless arguments, I must seem to want his compassion, his magnanimity. He is doing me a favour, but I must also be firm, he is not going to be compassionate and magnanimous if he has a choice.

Yesterday. Pip, why can't the two of us go on a holiday for the weekend, why the Ekta Yatra?

I want more time with you. After this we will go on a holiday if you wish.

Night
Hemant could not believe his ears. What, go where? Do what?

Go on the Ekta Yatra, cover it for the Manch. (Since he has never taken much interest in the Manch, he doesn't know this is not the kind of thing they would do.)

Then he started. And went on and on. I was running off on a wild goose chase, neglecting my family and burdening his poor mother with my responsibilities. I had no sense of what was fitting for a woman, I hadn't bothered to ask him whether it was appropriate or convenient. Ever since Aijaz had died, and I had started being exploited by the Manch, and gone to Ayodhya, and met Pipeelika Khan, I had no sense of home, duty, wifehood or motherhood.

I said nothing. What should I reply to? The text or the subtext? How calm my relationship with Pipee has made me! There was a time when had he said half so much I would have started crying. Now all I said was I am leaving on December 8th, and will call my mother to help with the children, I didn't want to bother his mother, or even him.

This made him even angrier. 'Why stop at this yatra?' he

248

practically shouted. 'The Dalits have called a Nyaya Yatra, they want justice, some mill workers have called a Roti Yatra, they want employment, the Indian Save the Cow Federation has called a Cow Yatra, to prevent cow slaughter, every Tom, Dick and Harry is going to march up and down India demanding something. Join them all.'

Again I said nothing.

'Who will protect you? Suppose you get raped?'

He doesn't care how low he hits. 'Why would I get raped?' I asked after a moment.

'Anything can happen. All these yatras have goondas attached to them. You think everybody who is going is so moved by the desire to unite our country? Our country is better united by you staying at home, so that there is one less incident to cope with.'

Every day the papers are full of crimes against women. Yet I have to learn to not be so afraid. There are other women in this world. They live.

November 27th

When I told P. about the rape she got quite angry. Tell that sod to stuff his fantasies of rape up his ass. What does he mean by scaring you like this? It is his way of keeping you at home.

She takes what I feel, clothes it into words, and there it is, for us to look at, and for me to feel better.

Have to phone my mother tomorrow. Another session of blackmail and guilt.

November 29th

Finally phoned. She was all against my going, of course. Little does Hemant realise how much her thinking matches his.

She started out by blessings – from both God and the swami, swiftly moving to blame. 'I have been expecting your call. It has been a long time since I heard from you, but then I know how busy you always are.'

'I'm sorry, Ma.'

'Give my love to Himanshu and Anuradha, give my regards to Hemant,' she went on, messages too important to be left to the end.

'I'm going—' I started.

'With the family?' Sharp as a knife, when it comes to protecting their interests.

'Is that the only reason you can think of for going somewhere?'

'Then why are you going?'

'For an assignment.'

'With who?'

'By myself. Please come and stay here.'

'How long?'

'Three weeks.'

'Three weeks! Why are you leaving your family for three weeks?'

'It's an assignment, I told you. Assignments don't adjust themselves for my convenience.'

'Then don't take such assignments.'

'Ma, will you come or not?'

'I'll see. What does Hemant think?'

'Why don't you ask him?'

Let them both see together.

November 30th

Taking large supply of headache medicines, couldn't bear to have a headache even one day. Just imagine in two weeks, I will be away from pollution, stress, tension, strain, I will be rolling along in a bus, staring out of the window, sitting next to her, our bodies touching.

December 1st

Pip talks about nothing else but the Yatra, I thought education of slum children was her speciality, but it seems she is diversifying. She is full of this as a political ploy, the Hindu vote bank under the pseudo secular banner of national unity, the Rath Yatra last year, the increase in communal tension, the rise in violent incidents, the number of towns under curfew. And incidentally, one Leader trying to replace another by doing his own journey.

Maybe I can do another canvas on this Yatra – it will be fun seeing first-hand what it is all about.

P. has visited Neeraj's cousin twice. You also come.

No, you go. I shall see her on the trip.

When I am with her and others I feel marginal and excluded. It's stupid, I know, but what we have is so intense I can't bear for it to be diluted, I can't bear for her not to give me her full attention. This is not *good*, I know. Maybe if we were together all the time, it would be different.

But we are not because of me, not her, then I am the one who complains.

How do people have affairs? They seem very complicated businesses.

Next day
Told H. my ticket has come, hoping to involve him in my going. He demanded to see it. 'Why do you want to see it?' I asked suspiciously. 'I don't have it.'

'Why don't you have it?' he asked suspiciously in his turn. (The perfect marriage.)

'The Manch has it.'

'I want to check if it is all right,' he said.

'Don't worry, it is all right. But thank you for your concern. I know you want me to develop myself and stand on my own two feet.'

'Since my wife understands her duties so well, why should I worry?'

Ha, ha. Why don't we get divorced.

I hope my children aren't tainted by his idea of my duty. I don't want them to think I am abandoning them. What if they are taught that while I am away?

'In this day and age no child can think anything if their mother travels once in a blue moon,' said Pip.

I wonder.

December 3rd

As the time comes to go I am tense and anxious. I have never left the children for so long. I told them this evening I was going for three weeks, and I'll phone you every day – I promise.

'I don't care,' said Anu flicking her hair around. 'You can go. It doesn't matter.'

I wanted to slap her. It is so difficult to reach her in her adult mode.

Himu said, 'Go, Mama, we should learn to be without you.' (!) Sometimes he sounds so grown up.

I wish things didn't seem so muddled and confused. Nothing is sure except that I might be raped. I walked to the church nearby where it is usually peaceful.

'Teach me how to live, God,' I prayed, casting an uneasy eye at the Christ hanging bloodily before me. His own life had been short and violent, but presumably successful. 'I am not asking for happiness, but I would welcome some stability, so I need not run all over the place looking for love and confirmation. Give me substance, God, give me a life that has not been lived for nothing. And protect my children,' I added as I got up to leave.

I thought of Pip on the way home. She has her future plans, her study, Ujjala, Neeraj. Is there really a place for me in her life? Though even as I write this, I can hear her saying you have your painting, your children, your home. If there is neediness in love, is it more or less genuine? If you need, you want, you search, you cling. You reward the person you have found with all your feelings.

December 5th

My mother has come radiating disapproval. She considers

the whole trip unnecessary. She who has turned to God, while her daughter is running after human love, how can I reassure her?

December 6th
Yesterday Pip asked, 'Does Hemant think you are having an affair? Why else would he be so suspicious about your ticket?'

'I don't know. I don't care.'

'Maybe he indulges himself when he travels.'

I felt a tightness in my chest, and then annoyance. Why does she keep bringing this up? 'I don't know what he does. It could be, I suppose.'

'Most men do.'

'Do they?'

'Don't be such a child.'

I thought of all the late nights at the factory, the trips out of town, the extended trips to South East Asia, the condom, the many opportunities there must have been, but I said nothing.

'Sometimes one doesn't want to know. It's painful or inconvenient. But now you are not so dependent on him, now it is all right to see.'

'I suppose.'

'Does he suspect you are having an affair?'

'It's not the same thing.'

'Why not?'

'You're a woman.'

'And that makes you a faithful wife?'

'No. But it is different, surely.'

'What you mean is you don't feel guilty.'

What could I say to this? This love of mine would have not been possible had she been a man, and yes, I don't feel guilty.

'Would you mind if Hemant was having an affair?' she went on, probing.

'Of course not. He can do what he likes.'

'After all you do, don't you?'
'Yes. Yes, I do.'

Took the children and my mother to a restaurant in the
evening. A last outing before I left. They wanted dosas so we
went to Sagar. Hemant was working late as usual.

It was not a nice meal. I was not giving the children my full
attention; they felt it and began to fight. My mother fingered
everything unhappily. No doubt she was calculating the
owner's profits, seeing how the place was jammed with customers. But because she is so spiritually oriented she was
forced to remain silent. I couldn't wait to get home.

December 7th
Ma keeps saying in a puzzled way, why doesn't the Manch
send a man, it's not safe for a woman, what kind of place is
this, should I talk to them and explain the situation, you have
a family, maybe they don't have families, why isn't Reshana
going, why is she so keen to send you? Finally I lost my temper, and had to shout are men the only ones who can do
things, nothing is going to happen to me, will you stop talking
like this, you are making everything worse.

She continues in a different register, don't talk to strange
men, don't wear any jewellery on your trip, not even your
watch, be careful of what you eat and drink, keep on phoning.

I have to remind myself of my three weeks with P.

Later.
Am leaving shortly. More lies as to why they can't drop me
at the station, Reshana, Manch, gathering early, train leaving late. I want to leave before Hemant comes home.
Remember journey to Ayodhya, when the children came to
leave me at the station, and waited for hours with me, the
pre-Pipee time, the non-lying, looking for the key to happiness time.

Still later

At P.'s place we prepare for departure. We shut the windows, shut the fridge, leave two lights burning. I have had puris made for us and aaloo ki sabzi, along with pickles. We take all the fruit she has, plus water, glasses, steel plates, napkins, a knife.

We don't say much, but already I feel she and I are enclosed in our own special world. Is this feeling on call to those who are happily married?

This is what she is offering me if I leave Hemant, this togetherness. Dearest, is this why you were so insistent that I come? You have already proved your point, we don't have to get on that train at all, don't have to go to Kanyakumari via Madras, with my supposed Reshana at all.

I think we are ready she said. The taxi will come soon.

We lock up and go down.

December 9th, night

At last, Kanyakumari. The train to Madras took for ever, and from there a bus. Felt complete and peaceful the whole way; I think she felt the same. No wonder marriages start with going away, cutting off from the old, entering the new with a journey, just the two of you – even in an ocean of people – just the two of you. It seemed so wonderful, we kept looking at each other and smiling.

I am waiting for her to finish her bath, then we walk down to the beach. The Yatra starts tomorrow.

Later

The beach half a kilometre from hotel. We could see the gulls, smell the sea air. As we leave the hotel after tea, I babble, the tip of the continent, the tip of the continent. P. laughs at me, grabs my hand, and we run, our feet sliding in the softness of the sand. We run to the shore line, where we can see the waters of the Arabian Ocean, Bay of Bengal, and Indian Ocean merge, grey, blue and green. The sands are three distinct colours too, red, black and pale yellow flowing into one another. There is something about the sea, its smells, its sounds, you feel small but liberated. There it is before you, vast and eternal. My troubles felt trivial.

We were together, we were happy. We walked along the water, me with my polyester sari tucked high into my petticoat, handbag with our money heavy but safe under arm, chappals in hand, P. with her salwar rolled up, taking turns with the bag.

Little boys ran up and down hawking packets of the separate coloured sands. I bought some for Anu and Himu.

P. pointed out the Vivekananda Rock in the water. Apparently that is where Vivekananda stood one December a century ago and moved to great emotion by the sight of India across him, pledged to work for the upliftment of the masses and the unity of the country. The Leader of this Yatra is also big on unity and saving the country, still not unified; the masses, still not uplifted.

I stare at the sunset as though I had never seen one before. I felt every second of its sinking in my bones. I am scared. No one can be so happy and have it last. When am I going to pay?

Early morning, December 10th
We stayed awake the whole night. I kept telling Pipee she had to go to sleep, for me it was a holiday but she was here on work. She looked at me and said when will you learn anything, the whole thing was a way to be with you. She closed her hands over me, and I could scarcely breathe with the pleasure. I often find it hard to accept that she could desire someone like me, but when I am with her the doubts fade, and I feel strong and loved.

Muslim and Sikh relatives of martyrs who have died for the country are gathered here to hand the Leader the flag that will be hoisted in Srinagar's Lal Chowk, 47 days, 14 states and 15,000 kilometres later.

December 10th, night
The mood of last night completely gone. Five hours in the hot sun. P. was a wreck. If she arranged this trip to be with me, if I need this kind of plan to leave home, then we pay for our sins in sweat and irritation.

But we are together – no denying – would I have had the imagination to think of something like this? Why am I so passive, why can't I bristle with initiative, maybe this is what she hates about me.

Her Ph.D. rears its ugly head whenever I see her talk to someone or take out her notebook. She has already made contact with several journalists while I watch her.

The Leader was late, the auspicious moment came and went, and still we waited, sweat pouring down, 10,000 of us boiling away. Then finally the Leader spoke for one hour, then all the martyr's relatives spoke, then every Tom, Dick and Harry took his turn.

At 1.47 we started. The coconut was broken, lemons put under the wheels of the two vehicles made to look like a temple and a houseboat. South and north. Inside there are two rooms, storage, water tanks, etc. The Leader refused air-conditioning, he was taking this journey not for his comfort, but for the unity of India. We could have done with some air-conditioning, but then we are not leaders.

December 15th, night
We cross at least five villages or towns a day. Whenever I can I phone home from an STD booth. At appointed stops, the Leader emerges to the front of the houseboat he is riding in and addresses the people over loudspeakers. He indicates the flag in the Bharat Mata Temple perched on the bonnet of each vehicle. He tells them about the pride every Indian must have in his nation, the pride that has been trampled upon in the past. He announces that India is one, and that is the meaning of his journey. He declares that India will not tolerate terrorism in Punjab or Kashmir. He reiterates that no Indian can accept the separate

status given to Kashmir, that Article 370 of the Constitution is now irrelevant. He describes the water he is carrying with him, the water of all of India's sacred rivers; the soil he is carrying belonging to the birthplaces of India's noble sons. He allows them to have darshan of the vessels in which the water and the soil is kept. Amazingly they want to. They rush to touch them, to put tikka on them, to garland them. They also want to touch the Leader's feet, but this the security men do not allow.

At night we eat what has been arranged for us at the circuit house or dak bungalow, and fall into bed, weary as hell. Perhaps it is just as well we are so tired for we do not have a room to ourselves. All intimacy is confined to the bathroom. In the bus our hands enjoy a limited freedom, no one can see what we do, but still, was there an easier way to be together?

600 kilometres in 4 days.

December 18th

Who would have thought one state was so large? We are still in Tamil Nadu. We are visiting, glimpsing rather, all the temple towns in a cavalcade, flanked by two security jeeps, rifle butts poking out through the windows. The Leader has to be protected. The heat of the air is sharp, this is their winter, so strange to never be cold. From the bus window, the landscape flashes by, the greens and the browns brighter than the ones I am used to, with an occasional rock or hill. I think of the flat plains of the north, and I think Ah, the diversity of India. Soon I will talk like the Leader, of Unity in Diversity, of The Oneness underlying The Difference.

I fantasise about food constantly. The food provided for us is too hot, and I am forced to eat dry rice. Whenever I can I buy fruit for both of us. P. doesn't care what she eats, but if I go on with this stuff, I shall be sick.

Today she gave a banana I had kept for her to a journalist. I wanted to kill that woman. In the bus P. said, I didn't want it, and her stomach is upset. What could I say? I kept my jealousy to myself.

December 20th

We are now in Karnataka. Phoned children from an STD booth near the tea stall where we had halted, while P. finishes her cold drink. We then walk down the road bordered by red earth. The cacti on the edge come up to my shoulders. There are fields and fields of tomatoes, light green against the leaves, supported by trellises, or simply sticks. I can see women picking them. Green tomatoes wait in piles next to the road, for buyers. They are obviously reddened somewhere else. I remember my father used to like green tomato chutney, a recipe he taught my mother. My own children will never be able to think of my cooking, only Bahadur's. I don't care, I am too happy to worry about anything.

The Deccan Plateau. Hills popping out of the landscape. The bus weaves to and fro and I feel sick. I take Avomine, and drowse against P.'s shoulder. I love her smell.

Days merge one into another, the landscape changes, I too have fallen into the rhythm of the journey. My mind is stilled. At night we roll into beds that are provided for us at the circuit house or dak bungalow. How many more days before we can share a bed???

December 22nd

There are two buses following the Leader. One is security, aides and party workers. The other is publicity and journalists.

The woman who had a stomach upset continually hounds us. She is a correspondent for a paper based in Madras. Periodically, when the convoy stops, Pip and she disappear for their interviews. At these times I take out my pad and sketch. It will be a record of our journey when I return, and maybe a base for a canvas. I want to feel productive, that I did something besides stare besottedly at one woman all day. It's not easy being in love every single minute. Resentment creeps in, especially when the other person is talking to someone else.

Meanwhile we pass through Mother India, who impassively stares at this cavalcade of temple, houseboat, and gun-toting security men. Nothing is new for India. Doesn't the Leader say that again and again, India is our mother. Her qualities are patience, tolerance, love and resignation. Her rewards are that she is forced to suffer over Kashmir the recalcitrant child, Punjab the rebellious one. The father – i.e. the Leader – will not stand for this any longer. Time to take a firm hand.

How can we listen to this rubbish day after day? I complained to P. when she was looking at my drawing pad that night.

Only three more days before we take the bus for Bangalore. Then it will just be you and me, she replied, carefully examining each sketch. I am continually flattered by her attention and comments:

Are these scenes for your Ekta Yatra canvas, I like the houseboat and temple and the way you have captured these crowds, but isn't this a lot for one painting, and so on.

Living with someone interested in the details of your work is companionship at the deepest level. I long to create the canvas I have in my head so she can see it too.

December 24th
Bangalore at last! In the guest house of the Y. Our room, our bed, on which we spend hours. Maybe this is what good marriages are like. To be able to express what comes into your head, and know it will be understood as you meant it. To be more yourself because all of you is able to love in a way the other responds to.

She goes to sleep, and I pass my hand over her breasts. At first it had seemed odd, after years of being made love to by a man, to have one's breasts met by a similar pair, though larger. No wonder men like them so much. You can do much with a pair of breasts. These loose, hanging, swinging items, breasts, penis – objects of passion and anxiety. Stuff you can hold in your hands, squeeze, maul, make yours, like playing with clay – taking you back to your childhood.

The rubber trees are enormous and green outside, the bougainvillaea is blooming, it is warm, fragrant, pleasant, far from the cold of Delhi. Why can't I live here for ever with her, forget I have a life outside this room, this bed, these arms, this mind that sees me the way I am and loves me still.

She looks at my face, puts her arms around me, don't look so sad, we have each other, we are the lucky ones.

December 25th
Christmas.

She pointed out her grandparents' house as we passed by in a scooter.

'Can't we visit?'

'No.'

'Why? I want to see them. I want to see where you spent your childhood.'

'Well, you can't. They'll pester me to stay, and ask a lot of questions.'

I could make out a small house, a little garden and a huge tree, studded with white champa blossoms. Pretty, but I couldn't imagine Pipee in it, the antithesis of suburban.

'What was it like, growing up here?'

'All right,' she said non-committally. Getting into her past is sometimes a problem. Especially the death of her husband. She never talks about that.

Spent the day roaming Bangalore. Talking, talking to fill the time our lives were separate – oh this happened when I was here, didn't I tell you, and she said and he said, tell me, tell me how it was?

We laugh because we are together, doesn't matter where, or how, cemented by our nights and words together.

January 2nd, 1992
Back from a week at Pip's school. Idyllic place, with all the usual about idylls. Trees, millions of butterflies, thousands of

birds, lap of nature, the works. The most miraculous thing about the place, I had no headaches. Pip, no headache, I said every evening, and she smiled, the corners deepening, dimple appearing, eyes warming. My painlessness I offered as a gift, she accepted it as her due.

She showed me her butterfly tree, the walks her mother and she used to take, her classrooms, her library, she was even nostalgic about the din in the dining hall.

I had no idea P. was so involved in her school. The usual pangs with every teacher she threw herself on, with every old friend she talked about. This kind of jealousy, however slight, makes no sense. I think I need my head examined.

We stayed with P.'s mother. I slept on the divan in the big room, she with her mother in the bedroom. Her mother didn't say much to me, she is a house parent, besides being a middle-school class teacher and quite busy. Does she know we are lovers??? I ask P.

'I think so.'

'You told her?'

'She has eyes.'

So does my mother but even if I told her, I bet a thousand to one she would not believe it. I said as much.

'She has always known how I am feeling, that is the important thing.'

It seems Pip has the ideal mother-daughter relationship, just as she had the ideal marriage. I wonder how these things operate?

Pip organised a street play around interpretations of history. Among other things she used my pamphlet, *The Testimony of the Black Pillars*.

Last night we went to P.'s favourite restaurant in Bangalore, a great relief after school food, though to listen to P. it was manna from heaven.

(n.b. If I am jealous of every thing about P. that doesn't include me, perhaps I should not mind so much her attitude to my family.)

January 4th

We are leaving on the Karnataka Express. The Yatra has reached Gujarat, then it is going to Rajasthan, Madhya Pradesh, Uttar Pradesh.

In the evening P. said, I don't want you to go home.

What is she saying, it is almost a month, is this another test? Did I not pass the first one?

Stay with me a few days in Delhi, please. You can always go back to them a bit later.

I agreed, but for the first time, the thought crossed that perhaps P. was not always wholly reasonable. Maybe I should assert myself. (How?)

January 7th

We came yesterday. Took a scooter to her flat, stopping at the market on the way to buy provisions: milk, bread, eggs, fruit and vegetables. It seems strange to come to an empty place, no one waiting, nothing done. You have to do everything yourself the minute you come, clean, organise, buy, cook. If it is so tiring in winter, what will it be like in summer? But this is Pip's life, and she doesn't complain.

Pip has gone to Ujjala, I make the bed, dust, clean the cobwebs, cook lunch, and then haul out this diary to write.

I wonder how Anu and Himu are managing. I can't tell on the phone. Their school is opening today. Did they finish their holiday homework? Does my mother manage to get them up and off in time? Are they all right? They say yes to everything. P. says I worry to feel needed.

I feel disturbed here. Why isn't Pip coming? She promised to come quickly, she might have gotten caught up with meeting her colleagues, Neeraj probably, while I am here waiting. It was much better in Bangalore.

January 8th

Awful, awful. Couldn't sleep. Last night we fought. She left this morning without telling me where she was going.

What did I do, it was nothing.

'In a few days you will be gone,' she started over the dinner we had cooked together.

Oh no. 'Yes.'

'And then?'

'Then?'

'Back to the way it was?'

She was spoiling for a fight. I was determined to say nothing, but she went on, 'You don't really want to be here.'

'I do,' I said quickly.

She started withdrawing. Leaving a trail that I followed. 'Would I be staying if I didn't?'

She glared at me, pointedly left the table and began clearing away the dishes. Doesn't she realise what I go through because I want to be with her? I am in the same city as my children and I cannot meet them. Still she broods. Is this how she wants to spend our time in Delhi? To fight, sulk and turn away from me?

Why is she like this? I wish Aijaz were still alive, but then she would never have been interested in me. They had the perfect marriage, she hankers after that wholeness. What can I do? I live my life in fragments, she is the one fragment that makes the rest bearable. But a fragment, however potent, is still a fragment.

This morning I got up, made her breakfast, but she would not relent, continued cold. If she wants to punish me she certainly doesn't have to try very hard. I am in such misery, I don't care what I do. To be with her, yet distant, anything is better than that. She has left me alone here, God knows for how long. I might as well go home.

I wish I had the energy to hate her, but I don't. I feel sick.

January 9th

Home. They all exclaimed how thin I was.

I left without saying goodbye, or leaving a note. What will she think when she comes back and finds me not there?

January 13th

Jaundice. I vomit all the time.

P. is all right, then how come me? We drank the same things, but some germ from some water drop has lain inside me, waiting for me to be safe at home before moving in for the kill.

February 15th

What was the point? I can still barely eat. I look yellow and horrible. I smell.

I have travelled from P.'s house to my own via the tip of the continent, a long detour.

This is what happens when you leave your home. The in-laws, the mother, the husband, the servants all unite on this.

I feel exhausted.

My mother is still here because I am ill.

H. grates on my nerves. It's all my fault, does he never get tired of finding different ways to say this. He likes me to be ill and dependent.

P. comes to visit in spite of their hostile attitude.

I am sorry, she said, I'm sorry I left you like that.

I am sorry, I replied, that I didn't wait for you.

We talk of other things.

She told me there was a bomb blast attacking the Yatra in the Punjab, two people were killed.

Suppose it had been us?

Have I been struck by this dreadful illness because I left my home to be with the one I love? I feel so weak I can't get out of bed. When Hemant comes home and puts his heavy arm around me, I want to tell him everything just to see the look on his face. But then I'll have to cope with the rest of it.

My children draw pictures with huge Get well soon Mamas on them. I keep them by my bed and look at them often. Pip calls, concern in her voice.

I can't deal with my life. I want a safe place, a warm place, a loved place.

(n.b. Who doesn't?)

IX

Gradually Astha's bilirubin count came back to normal, as did her diet. Her mother departed for Rishikesh, yet she remained tired. When Pipee dropped by on her way to work, she did her best to be amusing and interesting. Pipee should not feel she was in love with an invalid, but it was so much effort, she almost wished she wouldn't come. Yet the days she didn't, she felt unloved and anxious.

Every morning she gazed piercingly and objectively in the mirror. She looked haggard, yellow, ugly and undesirable, she would perfectly understand if Pipee never wanted to see her again. When her lover left, she again checked the mirror, despite her better judgement. Maybe in the interim she had grown more beautiful, maybe Pipee had spotted something attractive that had missed her eye in the morning.

'I wish I didn't feel so exhausted,' she permitted herself to moan occasionally.

'It's only natural.'

'Yes, but it's so boring for you.'

'Let me decide that.'

A pause.

'How's your work going? How is Neeraj?' asked Astha to cover up the anxiety of the silence.

Everything was fine, Pipee assured her, as she got up to leave.

After these visits, Astha felt depressed and gloomy – why can't we be like we were during the trip – what's the point – I wish I were dead – while her family put her listlessness down to her fragile state of health.

Meanwhile tension in the house gathered. The workers of the factory went on strike, despite ClearVision offering fifty thousand rupees to the strike leaders, couched as temporary relief measures. It was clear that the rival union meant business, and soon another six TV factories in the area saw labour unrest.

These factory owners were not united. Meetings ended acrimoniously. They could not decide on an incentive package, though all of them felt that the demands of the union were unreasonable.

Every day that passed meant greater losses for the company, as well as an erosion of their market share. It was more than the owner could bear.

'Half pay,' Hemant fumed, 'we still have to pay them half their wages. Where do they think I am going to get this money if there is no production? The company will be ruined. Bloody fuckers.'

He spent his days running around looking for a solution, meeting lawyers, representing his case before the Labour Commissioner of Noida, trying to get the strike declared illegal. Meanwhile they were losing their share of the market at a time when there were over four hundred TV manufacturers in India.

Two months later the Labour Commissioner declared the strike to be a lock out. No work, no pay.

Triumph reigned in the Vadera household, it was seen as the silver lining in the dark cloud that had lain across their home.

The next day the manager's car was damaged, and every window of the factory broken. The number of guards were increased, but a few days later a fire broke out on the premises. It was detected before great damage could be done, but Hemant could not risk further vandalism and was forced to hire a private security agency, with instructions for twenty-four-hour surveillance. More money spent without any sales to cover the costs.

Despite being declared illegal, the strike continued. Too many workers, owners, factories were affected for there to be any immediate resolution.

Hemant developed chest pain. The doctors diagnosed hypertension, told him change your food habits, quit smoking, cut down drinking, exercise every day, and avoid anxiety. The early forties was a vulnerable time for men with stress.

Hemant was seeing the work of the past eleven years go down the drain, and he wasn't able to respond to this advice.

His parents went into damage control.

It was decided that as soon as school shut for summer, he, his wife and children would go on a holiday, and spend a relaxed time with Hemant's sister Seema in the US. When Hemant came back, they would work on the lifestyle-food habits-exercise thing. Meanwhile Papaji would manage things in the factory.

Astha told Pipee of these plans while they were having lunch at a restaurant in Connaught Place.

'How long will you be away?'

'I don't know yet.'

'I suppose you have to go?' asked Pipee a little hesitantly.

Astha remained silent. If only she didn't have to put her husband's health over the companionship of her lover. But not going was like getting divorced, a public statement of difference and separation.

'Look, it's not working out,' said Pipee suddenly.

'What is not working out?' asked Astha desperately.

'One should never have affairs with married people, they are the worst.'

Astha looked at the face she had kissed lovingly and in such detail at least a thousand times, and said resentfully, 'Why did you, then? You want to spoil what we have.'

'I had thought that with a woman it would be different—'

'So did I. With a woman—'

A silence fell, in which the air-conditioners fought audibly against the April heat. The glass on the windows let in blue-tinted light. At certain places the glaze had peeled and spots of glare came through. Astha dabbed at the breadcrumbs left on the table from their soup rolls. Pipee looked moody. 'You can tell me all about your nice little domestic holiday when you come back,' she remarked coldly.

Astha stared at Pipee anxiously, 'You know how it is. The workers are on strike, he has got high blood pressure,' then she stopped, hearing the words of a devoted wife in her ears.

Pipee concentrated on her empty glass. 'No. I don't know how it is.'

'You are independent,' said Astha bitterly, 'so you can talk like this.'

'And somebody is holding your hands, preventing you from being the same?'

'You need money,' flashed Astha, 'or do you think I should be independent on his money? Stand in the streets with a begging bowl? Live in an ashram like my mother? What about my children?'

'Your children, your children, don't hide behind them. Live with me. Bring them.'

That old thing.

'But no – you don't even try – Ant why don't you even try?' Pipee swallowed once or twice. 'Have an exhibition, do something on your own, or are you waiting for Hemant to give you permission?'

'You are not being fair.'

'Yes. Well.'

The anticipated vacation split Astha more decisively than anything else since she had got to know Pipee. There was her lover and her lover's feelings. But there was also the visas for the USA and the UK, the foreign exchange, the getting ready, choosing suitable clothes and shoes, the packing and shopping for presents.

With their holiday abroad Hemant and Astha joined the have-gone-abroad club, whose denizens created envy and ill-concealed curiosity about how much money they were going to spend, where had they got it from, even with the factory in trouble they can afford to go, they must have stashed it away all these years.

Many people took their proposed trip badly. The most immediate was Sangeeta who was there as usual for the summer holidays. She insisted on being part of the discussion and planning that revolved around itineraries, addresses of friends of friends, cheap fares, cheap central hotels, foreign exchange. Astha had to brace herself against the flow of her resentment and curiosity.

'One day I too will go abroad. Seema is always inviting me,' she said.

It has nothing to do with me, thought Astha, if she is angling for a trip let her angle directly. Sangeeta sighed, announced Poison was her favourite perfume and disappeared upstairs for the day.

Anuradha said now her friends would not be able to act so superior, she too could tell stories of abroad, and Himanshu said now he could have the latest in Nintendo and Sega, and could they please go to Hamleys.

'Hamleys? What is Hamleys?' asked Astha.

'A shop in London,' said Himanshu. 'Everybody goes there.'

'He is so retarded,' said Anuradha.

Astha hoped the trip wasn't feeding into her children's materialist desires.

Astha's mother was delighted. She wrote from her ashram: God bless you my little one and your family. Poor Hemant needs a break from all his troubles. You do not give him enough attention. Remember men have to bear the burdens of the outside world, home is their refuge.

Pipee retreated further into herself, getting ready for her summer, Shahjehanpur, Shiksha Kendra and Ayodhya, we'll compare notes when I get back, bye, no need to drop me to the station, have a nice time, call me on your return.

Astha felt Pipee's abandonment, but maybe she thinks I have left her, she brooded in the middle of the night, when the electricity went, and the couple lay sweating.

'I will be glad to leave this fucking country,' muttered Hemant.

'So will I,' muttered his wife.

Delhi, the trap in summer, with power cuts, water shortages, heat waves, dusty winds, and pollution emanating from all its pores. Not the garden city of their youths, but fourth, third, creeping up to second, now coughing and wheezing its way to first, yes, almost the first most polluted city in the world.

A trip abroad would be nice, no matter whom one loved and whom one left behind.

Finally the family took off on their cheap flight to Miami, Florida, with a stopover at London on the way back.

Hour after hour into the dark night they flew. Four abreast, in the central section of the plane: father, mother, daughter, son going to holiday on Western shores.

'Are you all right?' Hemant would ask from time to time. Astha nodded, her eyes closed. She wondered at the great silence concerning the discomfort of planes, the torture one had to undergo to get to the lands of milk and honey. Her knees were hurting in the small cramped space, her shoulders and back were aching, a headache was coming on, would she make it to the bathroom to throw up if she had to. Excuse me, I am sick, I have to throw up, madam use the bag in the pocket in front of your seat, ah, there it is, sorry, not at all.

The rest were enjoying themselves. Himanshu was absorbed in the child kit the airline had given him, Anuradha had her headset glued to her ears, and fiddled with the dials constantly. Hemant was nursing his drink, chewing with relish on the peanuts that came with it, tinkling the ice and the alcohol in his glass, twitching his toes in the airline socks, his shoes neatly stowed away under the seat in front of him.

He shouldn't be drinking, thought his wife, but she was in too much pain to comment or persuade.

They stayed for three weeks in Florida. Hemant talked incessantly of his life as a student, and how he had slummed it, how he had worked to earn a little extra money, how he had slept two hours a night, how the great American tradition encouraged self-reliance from babyhood, how you had to sink or swim, how the whole society was geared towards meritocracy, not towards blackmailing people by going on strike. Loafers wanting something for nothing were not tolerated here.

Seema and Suresh sympathised completely, never mind, you have family, family still means something, and they talked of here and there, there and here, till Astha felt her ears would fall off.

Three weeks crammed in their guest room, three weeks of Anuradha feeling jealous of everything that Sushma (the daughter) had to show her.

'School in the USA is like no school at all,' she announced to her mother. 'They get hardly any homework, they choose what they want to study. Her maths, I can do it with my eyes shut.'

'I am sorry, darling,' said Astha looking at her daughter's angry face.

'Why should you be sorry?' said Anuradha turning upon her mother, the easiest person in the world for her to turn upon.

'The system here is not so demanding, that's all I meant.'

'She thinks she is so clever, but she is not, Mama, I know much more than she does. Her handwriting and spelling are so bad, you wouldn't believe, but she doesn't care, and neither do her teachers. She says in the computer everything comes out OK, so what is the point? Imagine!'

'You are better off beti, you can write, you can spell, you can do maths, when you come here for higher studies you will be at an advantage.'

Anuradha looked mollified. 'I'll show her,' she muttered.

'Quite,' said Astha, 'and while you are about it, do remember that we are guests in their house, and that she is your cousin.'

'She has an American accent.'

'That is not something she can help, she only knows this country, poor thing.'

Mother and daughter smiled slightly at one another. Nothing is so much a bond as criticising relatives.

The marriage of Seema and Suresh was a source of great amazement to the brother and sister-in-law. Seema and Suresh constantly deferred to each other. Suresh cleared up after meals, ran the dishwasher, did the grocery shopping, mowed the lawn on weekends, and went to the park with his son to kick a few balls in the evening, almost as a duty.

'What has happened to Suresh,' wondered Hemant. 'He was never like this at home.'

'This is not home,' replied Astha.

'Poor chap,' went on Hemant. 'You should have seen him when he was just married. Boozing and smoking with the rest of us. Now he doesn't even touch a cigarette.' Hemant fumbled for his own packet and lit one, to further express his disgust.

'Perhaps it would be better if you took a leaf out of his book,' said Astha. 'Suresh looks just fine to me, at least he is not a source of worry to his family.'

'He is ashamed to look me in the eye,' declared Hemant, surrounding those very eyes with smoke.

The high point of their US holiday was a trip to Disney World.

'It's built on 27,000 acres. Acres of fun,' said Suresh, while Seema sketched the delights of the fairy tale park, water park, animal park, future park, past park, sports park. She spoke with all the pride of ownership.

They planned to drive to Orlando and spend three days there. The hotels were expensive, but to absorb such wonders money was necessary.

Hemant offered to participate in the driving, but Suresh did some more back slapping, this was America, not your India, where a visitor could drive without an International Driving Licence or indeed without any kind of licence at all, just a bribe.

Disney World, Orlando, Florida, USA.

Is such a thing possible in your India? There was no end to this question, as Hemant was forced time and again, to say no, such a thing was not possible in their India.

So organised, such crowds, such a money-making machine, such technological marvels, such fantasy, such going through tunnels, haunted houses and castles, such an onslaught of souvenirs, such marvelling, such eating of hamburgers, hot dogs, Kentucky Fried Chicken, tacos, and thick milkshakes. Around they wandered with those milkshakes which never seemed to end, sipping the cold sweet stuff through giant straws. Was there anything in this country that wasn't big?

Anuradha and Himanshu loved it, Hemant loved it, Suresh, Seema plus two kids, their millionth visit with Indian tourist and wonder seeker in tow, they loved it all over again. Even Astha managed to be caught up in what she saw and experienced. They were all children together, all Mickey Mousers in a Disney World.

Besides families everywhere there were couples embracing, couples walking with their hands in each others pockets, kissing, eating, conversing, laughing.

Suresh and Seema became even more of a couple here. They walked holding hands. For our benefit, or because they are on vacation, or because they have lived in America so long, or because they love each other so much? It was the last possibility that Astha could bear the least. Anything but that Hemant's sister should live in bliss while she lived in misery.

'I thought Disney World was for children,' she remarked to Seema.

Seema and Suresh both grinned at her.

'Arre, people come to enjoy,' said Suresh.

'Relax, have fun, spend quality time together,' clarified Seema for Astha's greater understanding.

'Well, wife,' said Hemant, the second night in the hotel, at his most affectionate, swept by emotion at having seen Disney World, and recorded it on a thousand pictures taken for the benefit of back home, 'it's been quite an experience, no?'

'Yes, it has.'

It was late, the children had fallen asleep, exhausted by so much pleasure and walking around. Hemant sat next to Astha, and put his arm around her.

'How's your head?' he enquired tenderly.

'OK.'

They sat on in silence. After a while Astha dislodged herself. 'I have to pee,' she said.

'OK,' said Hemant, getting up as well.

'What are you doing?'

'Coming with you.'

'Don't be silly.'

'What's so silly about it?'

It was easier to let him come, and Astha sat on the toilet seat, feeling a bit strange. It had been a long time since they had shared any intimacy.

'Go away,' she said at last, 'I can't pee.'

He ran the tap.

'Now?'

A small trickle. Hemant tore a piece of toilet paper and advanced his hand towards her legs. The trickle stopped. Her legs tightened. 'Please leave the bathroom,' she stammered.

'Why? I'm your husband.'

'So what?'

'So everything.'

'You think marriage is just sex.'

'Of course I don't. What do you want that I don't give you?'

'Interest. Togetherness. Respect.'

'Baby, I respect you,' said Hemant soothingly, 'you are my wife. As for togetherness, that's just what I want.'

'Why all of a sudden?'

'We are on holiday. This is what people do on holiday.'

'I don't want to. I am out of practice.'

'Well, let's get into practice,' said Hemant stretching out his hand again towards her legs.

'I am not able to switch on and off like you,' said Astha.

'It is not as though you were the most willing creature. Each time I try and come near you, you say you have a headache. A man is tired, he can't be doing the chasing all the time.'

'Is that what you call it, chasing? Not having sex on demand? There has to be something more between us. I have to feel it is me you want.'

Hemant looked baffled. 'Of course it's you I want. You are my wife,' he repeated.

'That's the problem. Anybody could be your wife.'

'What rubbish. I picked you, didn't I?'

'Picking is not the same as knowing.'

'Why do you always make things so complicated? You are my wife, that is enough for me, I would have thought it is enough for you. Or is it someone else?'

'Are you referring to my life or yours?' asked Astha flushing slightly.

'Come on darling,' replied Hemant, ignoring her barb, 'we are on holiday. I want this to bring us closer, as a family, as a couple.'

He had felt her distance, he wanted her back. There seemed to be no way out, unless she decided to leave the marriage there and then. Slowly she moved towards him. With sleeping children in the room they would of course have sex in the bathroom. He spread a towel on the mat and waited for her to undress.

On and on marched the holiday, relentless, inexorable, eating up money, energy, rolls of film, pushing them to cheap eating places, and suitcases that grew heavier by the day.

'Shopping on the way back, shopping on the way back,' Hemant kept saying but it didn't quite work like that. There were so many souvenirs, the Disney World ones alone filled half a suitcase. Besides there were the presents Seema and Suresh were sending back for the rest of the family, and clothes for everybody, so much cheaper in the States than anywhere else.

London. They were met at the airport by Hemant's cousin.

Astha had always liked this cousin. He had gone abroad to do well, since he couldn't do well in India, and ended up owning a shop in the suburbs of London. Just what this meant was only now becoming clear as they drove, drove and drove, and finally stopped in front of a house, which was a double storied, very narrow building, identical to the entire row on the street. Naked houses on a treeless street.

'Welcome to my humble abode,' said Jagdish, edging the car near the curb, and jumping out to take their suitcases. 'I'll see where Liz is,' he panted, lugging them inside.

Liz, the unenthusiastic wife. 'Hello, would you like a cup of tea?' she asked, and they could feel the indifference, and they could understand why Jagdish was being so effusive.

'Their house is so small, Mama,' whispered Anuradha, awed by such discomfort in the West.

'They don't have much money,' whispered Astha back.

The bags, the guests, and the host struggled up the narrow stairs, what a nice house you have Jagdish, well, it's all right, and they went down to have the tea that Liz had prepared.

One week in London, of learning how to take the Tube, of don't worry, Jagdish, we will take care of ourselves, no, no, please do not bother, Liz, we will manage, and Jagdish's reply, well, if that's all right then.

Every morning Astha got up and made sandwiches so they could save money on eating. They bought the ingredients and the drinks at the corner store, because Liz clearly did not understand the imperatives of Indian hospitality, and they didn't want to burden Jagdish's marriage further. They gritted their teeth and managed to not all bathe every morning, the house only had one complete bathroom.

There was some disagreement as to how they would spend this precious week. Astha wanted to see all the art treasures London had to offer, she was willing to go on her own while her family did whatever they wanted. But Hemant would not hear of this – we are here to be together – and as a compromise they spent a morning at the Tate, a morning at the British Museum, and then covered the famous sights of London in a couple of day tours. Many photographs were taken as proof of the good time they were having.

All this over, they devoted themselves to shopping. There had to be much looking, exclaiming, comparing, soul searching, and converting of currencies before they could buy.

'I must say London is a very expensive place,' said Hemant, as they emerged from Marks and Spencer, arms laden, a light rain falling, a cold wind blowing.

'I wish we didn't feel the need to buy everything we see,' moaned Astha, exhaustion reducing her to the desire to lie in front of the department store door, and be trampled to death by all the Indians rushing in and out, buying, buying.

Anuradha and Himanshu looked at her reproachfully. They could hardly contain themselves in this material paradise. Floors and floors of merchandise with Hemant the indulgent father. The trouble, thought Astha, was that she too could hardly contain herself when she saw the kitchenware, gadgets, art supplies, bed linen, children's toys, clothes, underwear, stationery. Was there anything that did not move her with the urge to possess? No, such shopping was not morally good, she felt her sense of perspective and focus vanish amidst its successful assault on her greed. It was just as well these trips were rare.

On the evening of their fifth night. 'There seems to be trouble in India,' said Jagdish, a held back pleasure edging the notes of concern. He was entitled to a revenge so small, that he was in the safe place, the sane country, something in return for his unsatisfactory house, job, career, marriage and neighbourhood.

Astha and Hemant looked at each other. At home trouble was part of the atmosphere, outside it assumed more sinister proportions.

'What's happened?' asked Hemant

'On the BBC. They are going to build the temple,' continued Jagdish.

Hemant relaxed. Oh, the temple. 'These politicians keep stirring things up,' he replied, uninterested.

While the family ate, Astha hung around the TV waiting for the news.

There it was. A brief visual of the Babri Masjid at night, floodlights beaming, sounds of bhajans in the background, thousands of kar sevaks surrounded by security forces, clearing the ground, laying the foundation for the temple, working, working, round the clock.

Things are tense in this ancient temple town, said the commentator, where a mosque stands on the site that Hindus claim to be the birthplace of the Lord Ram. While six thousand pilgrims work day and night, an estimated fifty thousand more have assembled here. The kar sevaks swear that this time they will rather die than stop. There have been protest marches by groups concerned with saving the Babri Masjid but so far the laying of the temple's foundation continues at a lower spot on the hill. The Prime Minister has called Hindu holy leaders to Delhi to discuss the issue.

How awful, thought Astha, what was going to happen? She wanted to go home. Her political self, her intelligent self functioned best there, here she felt isolated, saturated with things rather than thoughts.

What was Pipee doing? Each day she had been aware of her absence, yet she had enjoyed being with her family, enjoyed the comparative ease between Hemant and herself.

She dreaded what Pipee would say when she sensed this. As she tried to defend herself, I am married, she felt the betrayal Pip would feel, but by now betrayal was a second skin.

~

Astha had often imagined the breaking of her relationship with Pipee. What she hadn't realised was how slow the process would be, and in what infinitesimal stages.

There were differences, she thought miserably, but they hadn't seemed so important. This was no longer the case. After she came back they were clearly not in harmony.

'You won't like abroad,' remarked Astha to Pipee. 'It is awful.'

'Who would have thought it?' said Pipee dryly.

'You know what I mean,' said Astha impatiently.

'No, I don't. How could I? And anything is better than the things I saw.'

'What did you see?'

'For ten days total frenzy, policemen jeered at, control rooms smashed, loudspeakers blaring out prayers and bhajans – in such an atmosphere – pandemonium at the building site, and kar sewaks all over.'

'You mean you went to Ayodhya?'

'Yes.'

'But why? You didn't tell me.'

'Where were you to tell?'

'It might have been dangerous, Pip.'

'Oh Ant, one can't always be safe. It was no more dangerous for me than for all those other poor women there. Besides I wanted to go. I am thinking of a conference on how families are affected in communal riots.'

More PhD stuff, thought Astha. 'Well, how was it?' she asked.

'They are going to build the temple in the masjid area. That kind of energy, so deliberately stoked doesn't go away. It's only a matter of time.'

There was a silence. Pipee leaned back in her chair, and stared at the clouds that were running against the sky of her Vasant Kunj flat. Astha looked at her, she seemed so distant. She had felt closer thousands of miles away, thinking of her, writing to her.

Then Pipee said, 'Enough about Ayodhya. How was Disney?'

'Fine.'

'And you and Hemant?' she asked. 'How was that?'

Astha kept her face still. 'Also fine,' she said.

Pipee looked at her sharply, 'You have had sex with him,' she stated flatly.

Hemant's face rose before Astha's eyes, the moments in the bathroom, the appeal he would never verbalise, her own realisation that somewhere he still had the power to affect her. She felt her face going red.

'You've never really liked it any other way, have you?' persisted Pipee, her voice dry and hard.

'That's not true,' pleaded Astha.

'Yes it is. What you really want is your husband's cock.'

Astha winced and tried to retaliate. 'It's not that. You resent that I am not leaving him. You want a full-time partner. I understand that.'

'You would. It is what you have, after all.'

Astha was silent for a moment. If her husband represented more than just a cock, so much the worse, but how was she to explain to Pipee? It was better not to advance into these murky waters. She went on, 'It has nothing to do with us.'

'You went away with your family, that was bad enough, and I didn't say anything, because it's no use, and then you do this, why have me?'

Everything Pipee said was a distortion. Words were raising their ugly heads, and Astha could do nothing. No matter how hard she tried, she was not going to succeed.

Pipee kept that transgression in her heart and used it as a foundation for the separation she saw ahead. A good memory is always useful when something needs to be destroyed.

Pipee and Astha continued to see each other, but there was now a carefulness between them. For Astha everything became dull, the grass looked ordinary, the sky looked bleak, the paint on her canvas colourless.

A thousand times she said to herself, confront her, tell her you want it like it was, or not at all, but she was too afraid. Pipee might say not at all, then what would happen to her, worse than this, much worse.

Things would become all right on their own. Love would triumph, even in circumstances like these. Love had to, that was its nature.

But Pipee behaved as though love had had its day. Even moments of affection contained references to endings. Pipee to Astha, tucking her hair behind her ears.

'I'm so grateful to you, Ant, never forget that, no matter what happens. From you I got the energy to go on.'

'To do what? Leave me?'

'You really want to go into who left whom?'

Astha couldn't say she did. 'You see?' said Pipee. 'We both gave each other something. Let us leave it at that.'

Ashta couldn't say anything. Words made what was between them so small.

'And of course whatever happens, we will always be friends,' went on Pipee.

'Yes, always,' replied Astha gratefully, too inexperienced to know that that is what breaking up people say to each other to make it more bearable.

~

Meanwhile the strike was resolved after six months. There was a tremendous backlog to be made up, and a market share to be recaptured. Hemant made an effort to resume his previous pace of work, when the chest pains started again. The doctors were very severe, he was not paying enough attention to his health. Collapse was imminent if he continued smoking, drinking, not exercising, eating red meat and heavy food. Furthermore he had to try and control his levels of stress, a very modest working day was all his body could tolerate. Angina had to be taken as a warning, a serious warning.

The whole family was alarmed. His father insisted another manager be hired, money wasn't everything. As for Astha, a brief survey of the literature on heart disease established that permanent changes were required in their living habits. Diet – exercise, diet – exercise, there was no getting away from these pillars of health and longevity. It was up to her, Hemant was not going to change on his own.

Every morning she made sure they went for a walk. All those years ago, exercising and resentful with her parents, she was now doing the same with her husband, with feelings so much more complicated with the years that had passed. Was this where her life had led her, this the space she had travelled between those walks and these? Striding briskly to still the thoughts in her head, speaking to mask the feelings in her heart. She looked at Hemant, swinging his arms, concentrating on getting his heart rate up. Perhaps he was disappointed too, perhaps he had looked for something different in marriage. They didn't talk about such things, she would never know.

She changed her family's way of eating. She bought books on low cholesterol diets, she studied recipes demanding no fat and little salt. When the children complained they were compensated privately during lunch and tea.

Hemant was bad tempered about having to give up his favourite foods, but he had no choice. And if he had to eat porridge for breakfast instead of his usual green chilli-onion-tomato omelette, he could not complain, his wife was eating the hated porridge too.

Astha spent a lot of time thinking about herself. Was she a traditional wife as Pipee had alleged? She flinched at the idea, but she was certainly doing what devoted wives did, putting a great deal of effort into protecting their husband's insides. When she saw him tired, afraid, depressed at having to change, unprepared mentally for the betrayal of his body, she felt sorry for him, and wanted to help him live. She told herself it was for the children, but sometimes she wondered bleakly at the nature of the bond between them.

Hemant was touched by her efforts. Occasionally he would enquire, 'Well wife, how are you?' in a proprietary kind of way.

'Fine, fine,' Astha replied in a monotone. Hemant was not adept at noticing discrepancies between the apparent and the stated, and this quality was conspicuous now.

The monsoon came and went. The muggy days marched into October to become more human.

'I'm going to get an air-conditioner,' said Pipee. 'That is if my scores are so lousy I get no aid, and am forced to remain in this dump.'

Astha turned absolutely still. 'The PhD?' she asked.

'I give my GRE next month.'

Oh Pip, you didn't tell me and not telling used to be felt a deception between us, but I see no more, mourned Astha silently, as Pipee continued, 'I need a change.'

Astha made a heroic effort. 'Yes. I'm sure you do. In an academic environment you are bound to flourish. They'll love the work you do.'

Pipee looked at her and smiled, 'I'll miss you, Ant.'

Astha didn't believe her. Pipee went on talking, and Astha heard all the things she wasn't saying, her loneliness, her desire for steady companionship, the need for commitment.

284

They smiled at each other. Astha said she understood. They drank tea, they exchanged a goodbye kiss, they did all this before Astha ran to her car, buried her face in the steering wheel, and took a good, long look at the void she had desperately tried to plug through loving Pipee.

What would it be like to be painfully separate having known togetherness?

How would she live? But she had to, she had that rock of stability women had, her husband and her children.

Drearily she turned the ignition and let out the clutch. The car rattled and jerked. She had to start it three times in the two metres she backed it. The clutch seemed to be slipping, the car's servicing was long overdue. This knowledge had hovered on the edges of her mind for a long time, but the imperatives of her life had not allowed her to pay attention. No longer. Her life was made up of these things.

At home she threw herself into a frenzy of house cleaning. Every nook and cranny, every book, every mote of dust, layer of dirt, every inch of carpet, every remote cupboard high and low she attacked.

'Mama's gone mad,' Anuradha informed her father conversationally, 'all she does is clean. And she makes me polish and clean too.'

'You will thank me for it later, when you have your own home,' snapped Astha. Everybody looked surprised.

'Do you have a headache?' asked Hemant.

'No.'

'What is it then?'

'Nothing. Nothing.' And without her wanting or willing, the tears started pouring down her face.

Anuradha's face contorted. 'Why are you crying, Mama?'

'No reason, sweetie,' gulped Astha.

'Shall I get you your medicine?'

Astha continued to sob, while Hemant said, 'Do, Anu, there's a good girl,' and as the daughter ran off, he turned to his wife and said, 'Don't cry. You are upsetting the children. They will think something is really wrong with you.'

'Let them,' wailed Astha. 'Let them know mothers also can feel.'

'Az? Are you all right? Stop cleaning, if it upsets you.'

'You always say how dirty the house is.'

She sounded unreasonable to her own ears. Hemant sat quietly by. Anuradha ran back with the pills and a glass of water, dragging a worried Himanshu with her.

'She says you are crying,' he accused.

'It's all right, baby,' said the mother, swallowing the pills, though she had no headache. 'It's nothing really.' Himanshu stared at her, his face opaque. 'It's nothing, baby,' repeated Astha. The boy turned and walked away while Anuradha looked at him with contempt.

'He's so thick,' she said. 'He never understands anything.'

Into Astha's mind came a memory, dredged from her subconscious. Her mother coming from the bedroom, the bedroom that had been locked, unusually, for a whole hour.

'Why are you crying, Mama?'

'It's nothing.'

'How can you be crying for nothing?' persisted Astha.

'I am not crying. What gave you that idea, beta?'

Oh well, if she wasn't crying, then those couldn't be tears, nor could those be signs of grief around her eyes and mouth. They could go on being happy, everything in its place.

Astha was amazed at how much work Pipee devoted to applying for a Ph.D. She spent hours at the US Educational Foundation studying profiles of universities, their faculties, their requirements, the ones most likely to give aid, the cost of living in small towns, cities, East Coast, West Coast, balanced against the cost of living with Ajay if she got into his university, the cost of clothing in cold places, hot places.

'I can afford to apply to only five,' she said, looking at her finances, calculating how much for GRE, how much for application money, how much for postage. 'Though that is taking a risk. Well let us see. Maybe I won't get aid, or maybe I won't get a visa.'

She would talk of something else, and Astha would seize these flimsy possibilities, clutching them in her grip, where they lay mangled and inert, of no real comfort.

Who has seen tomorrow, she often thought, and this with tomorrow staring her in the face.

When she was with Hemant she felt like a woman of straw, her inner life dead, with a man who noticed nothing, with whom for that very reason it was soothing to be with. Her body was his, when they made love it was Pipee's face Astha saw, her hands she felt. She accepted the misery of this dislocation as her due for being a faithless wife.

Pipee's GRE scores were announced. She had got 23.4 on 24, and could now walk into any university she chose, or so her congratulators said. Astha hugged her, and felt she hadn't known misery till then.

'Oh, Ant,' was all Pipee said, but Astha could see how happy she was, how vindicated she felt with her score, how much further down the road towards the USA she was treading.

Then Pipee began to talk. 'You can join me for a bit if you feel like it.'

'Of course I'll feel like it.'

'No, I mean it, Ant. I know you'll be sad without me. You come for a holiday.'

'Sure.'

But they did not explore this topic further. Too much water had flowed under this particular bridge for it to be a comfortable one to tread on now.

It was December. The initial response from American universities was positive. 'I'm so glad,' said Astha looking at the face before her, and the shy glow on it. She re-read the letter Pipee had shown her. The University of Illinois had received Pipeelika Khan's application, and were acknowledging this. She would hear from them in the very near future. 'They have realised how bright you are,' went on Astha, thinking true love had no element of self in it, and she had better measure up.

'Not everyone thinks of me like you do, Ant.'

'Your application, your recommendations, your NGO work, your academic record, that paper you wrote and published, your GRE scores, why else would they reply so fast?'

'You're biased.'

'Not without reason, surely?'

Pipee laughed, and took the letter back, carefully folding it along the original creases, before sliding it into the browny-yellow envelope. Astha watched her.

'When will you finally hear?' she asked.

'Hopefully by January.'

Maybe by January a bomb would fall on Urbana Champaign and blow the university off the face of the earth, thought Astha, but what would be the point, there would be other places. The real act of leaving was in the decision, not in the departure.

'Maybe they won't give me a visa,' Pipee broke in on the pause. 'After all, I'm single.'

'Yes,' said Astha slowly, 'you're single.' How soon before she would find someone?

'You've not asked me what I'm going to work on.'

'Education of slum children, I imagine?'

'No. The politics of communalism and how it is represented. I am more interested in that now, maybe because of what is happening around us. It might also help me come to terms with things in my life. If you realise you are not alone . . .' She did not complete her sentence, and Astha felt more than ever removed from her life, from a pain so horrifying she bowed before it and shut her mouth.

'The only trouble is there are so many aspects, all of such relevance that it is a bit hard to choose a specific area,' went on Pipee.

For a moment Astha felt an intense stab of envy, not just for Pipee, but for anyone who had the possibility of a new life. She had to remind herself sternly that if she wanted, she too had choices.

X

By the end of the year, there was plenty of material being generated for Pipee's thesis. Kar seva had been stopped in summer on the condition that the Prime Minister solve the Babri Masjid problem in four months. Those four months were up with no solution in sight.

Thousands of kar sevaks were again being mobilised for what was termed symbolic kar seva, starting 6 December. The central government sent 135 companies of its security forces to Ayodhya and Faizabad despite the protests of the U.P. government, who claimed the law and order of their state was their responsibility.

'This time they are not going to give up easily, they have been stopped twice before,' said Pipee worriedly.

'Are you going?' asked Astha.

'Too much to do. I hope nothing happens.'

'The Babri Masjid has survived almost five hundred years. Why should something happen now?'

Meanwhile Ayodhya is witnessing the unprecedented influx of thousands of kar sevaks from all over the country. Religious leaders issue press statements declaring that religion is above politics, above nation, above courts and any restraining orders passed.

By 5 December the city has swelled by 200,000 kar sevaks, and there are not enough places to put them. Schools and colleges are declared shut, while the kar sevaks storm various institutions for accommodation. The area around the masjid is littered with garbage and human excreta. Food prices go up, the U.P. government declares they have in stock 8,000 tonnes of rice, 100 tonnes of sugar, 45,000 litres of kerosene, as well as an ample supply of life-saving drugs.

The BJP declares that no harm will come to the masjid, the kar seva will only be symbolic.

The Union Minister sends extra paramilitary forces to Ayodhya.

7 December, Astha's house. Headlines: A NATION'S SHAME there on the folded newspaper lying on the verandah, waiting to be read, digested, somehow understood.

Astha picked it up and stared at the front page. It was not possible, this could not have happened, but there it was:

A NATION'S SHAME: BABRI MASJID DEMOLISHED
Centre sacks Kalyan Singh's Government. 500,000 kar sevaks armed with pickaxes, crowbars, pipes and uprooted barbed wire barricades, attacked the disputed site yesterday. All domes collapsed under the onslaught. Between 11.50 to 4.50 the central dome collapsed. Between 2.00 to 4.00 p.m. the two side ones were destroyed. 50 people injured. Hundreds of kar sevaks carted away bricks, pillars, and large stones. BJP leaders urged restraint through megaphones.

Angry kar sevaks singled out photographers and foreign correspondents beating some brutally with sticks and leaving them bleeding on the road.

Curfew in many U.P. towns. Muslim MPs seek the Prime Minister's resignation. Muslim houses set ablaze. Kar sevaks not allowing fire engines in many places.

Army alerted in six states.

'They've broken the mosque,' she found herself telling Hemant. 'They have done it at last.'

'I know.'

'You know?' Astha stared at him.

'It was on the BBC last night.'

'Why didn't you tell me?'

'What was there to say? I didn't know you were interested.'

He was lying. She had gone to Ayodhya twice, painted the masjid at least five times, scripted a play about it, and he didn't know she was interested? This was his revenge for being concerned in things other than him.

She turned away, sickened by everything.

'I never knew you were such a Muslim lover,' said Hemant watching her. 'Do you know what happens to our shrines in Pakistan, Bangladesh, not only to our shrines but to Hindus? Why doesn't your precious Manch ever protest about that? Or any of your activist friends?'

'The fact that shrines are desecrated there, doesn't make it acceptable here. It's not a Muslim thing, it's a secular thing, a human thing.'

'It's a cowardly thing, a fool thing,' he said mockingly.

There was no point talking to him. Her one thought was to call Pipee, Pipee who felt like she did, with whom there would be no arguing at this moment. Quickly she dialled her number.

'Have you heard?'

'Yes. They've done it.'

'You were right.'

'What are we going to do?'

'What can we do?'

Both women fell silent, their own lives dwarfed by what was happening around them.

'Neeraj phoned. There's a demonstration on at the BJP office, we might as well go. It must have been planned, such a thing cannot happen without careful planning.'

'You said it was only a matter of time.'

'It was just a thing to say. I had no idea I would be proved right so quickly.'

'Don't cry, sweetheart. Come to the church crossing. I'll pick you up in half an hour.'

*

They talked little as they drove. As they came nearer Central Delhi they could see that the streets were lined with throngs of weeping men and women, dressed in black, faces covered. Near the BJP office, they were forced to walk, the whole area was cordoned off, lined with policemen, ready to lathi charge at any provocation.

Journalists were there, TV crew, academics and activists, all shocked and numb. They shared their information in broken sentences: paramilitary forces hand in glove with the kar sevaks – the police were helping – the leaders shouting on megaphones don't destroy the mosque – but pre-arranged that such messages to be ignored – many killed in the falling rubble – absolute pandemonium with 500,000 kar sevaks – the situation going to worsen – the government in U.P. had no political will to protect the mosque – only a matter of time before something like this happened—

They waited for one hour, two hours. Nobody came out of the BJP office to address them. Was there anybody there? They courted arrest, were put into waiting buses, taken to the local police station, kept for half an hour and sent away.

Three days later the United Left Front organised a march to protest the demolition of the masjid.

On the morning of 10 December Astha said to her husband, 'There is a march today.'

The husband said nothing.

Astha persisted with her information. 'It's going to be a tremendously big march. Traffic will be blocked around Red Fort and Connaught Place for hours. Do try and avoid those places if you wish to save yourself trouble.'

Nothing.

'OK?'

The husband saw a female bull charging from the distance and his body tautened. He lifted a wary face and looked at his wife. Astha carefully patted the tea tray cloth.

'I always admired your sense of proportion,' he said at last.

Astha raised her eyebrows and looked inquiring.

'Out in the streets, jostling with goondas, neglecting your family, all for some fool masjid you didn't even know existed before your great friend Aijaz chose to educate you.'

'It has nothing to do with Aijaz,' said Astha, choking on the rage she had kept inside her the last three days.

'Then his widow.'

'I suppose I have no mind of my own.'

'I didn't say that.'

'You meant it.'

'I refuse to talk to hysterical women,' said Hemant, 'especially when I have got a busy day ahead. Some people work, you know.' He got up and went into the bathroom, firmly closing the door.

When Astha reached the Red Fort her eyes were red with the hour-long cry she had had after Hemant left. Pipee saw her and linked her arm through hers, lacing her fingers through Astha's own clammy hand. 'Dearest, don't be this upset, it's terrible, but you can't afford to take it so personally.'

Astha nodded dumbly. Everything in the world was terrible.

A mild winter sun shone on the gathered marchers as they stood around waiting, while truck after truck of United Front activists and associates drove in.

The line started. It was so long that by the time it was Astha's turn, forty minutes had passed.

They marched out of the Red Fort into the middle of the road, blocking all traffic. As she walked Astha could see various people, Pipee included, handing out leaflets to onlookers, scooter wallahs, passengers in rickshaws, men scratching their balls, women holding children on their hips, women with plastic shopping baskets in their hands. Down the line the familiar slogans were shouted: *Down with communalism, down down; BJP down, down; False followers of Ram, you will never succeed; Mandir – masjid, all one.*

Astha was overcome with futility. Maybe Hemant was

right. What was the use of forcing motorists, passengers and pedestrians to listen to the voice of tolerance and peace? It had not prevented anything. Maybe the true victory of fundamentalism was the total despair of the secularist.

The line reached Delhi Gate, and turned right towards the Ram Lila maidan. Down another empty street with bad-tempered traffic gathered on the other side of the divide, and then the line poured into the Ram Lila grounds, to mill around a platform erected for the speakers.

One after the other they spoke, leaders from the Congress, from the Left parties, activists who had seen what had happened in Ayodhya. They expressed anguish, regret, sorrow, they issued warnings, predicted consequences:

What had happened was a betrayal of trust. Millions of Muslims would now feel insecure in their homeland. The assurances of the U.P. government had meant nothing, the assurances of the central government had meant nothing.

The law had been blatantly, openly flouted, what was going to prevent it from being flouted again? What was going to prevent the two disputed sites in Kashi and Mathura from going the way of the Babri Masjid? Was this a government or a passive instrument in the hands of thugs? Without delay the government should acquire all the land around the Babri Masjid.

It behoved every citizen in the land to be vigilant so that anti-communal forces did not gain ascendancy. How was it possible to demolish a masjid in broad daylight in little over four hours? And that too with home-made tools, pickaxes, crowbars, the implements of farmers and peasants. No, there was organisation and planning, there was the connivance of the authorities.

Various Leaders had been arrested, but was it all for show, like the security forces that were sent to protect the Babri Masjid, and helped in its destruction?

The nation and its people demanded answers.

It was late afternoon by the time Astha left. When Hemant came home he did not ask about the rally. And Astha was only able to sleep towards morning.

~

After the demolition:

Nationwide, 1,801 people were murdered in communal clashes in the next two months. 226 places in 17 states and 1190.18 lakh people were affected by curfew.

In Pakistan 240 temples were targeted by mobs.

In Bangladesh attempts were made to destroy 305 temples, 1,300 houses, and 270 shops belonging to Hindus.

In the United Kingdom 18 temples and cultural centres were damaged.

In Afghanistan 4 temples were attacked.

Over the next two months major riots broke out in Bombay. 41 areas were affected, 31 per cent of the deaths were caused by the police. Pipee decided she needed to gather first-hand material.

'Why are you going?' asked Astha.

'I have to go. Awful things are happening there.'

'I know. I also read the papers,' said Astha irritably, 'and that is why I wish you wouldn't go. It's not safe.'

Pipee looked at her for a moment, then gave a strange laugh. 'One has to do what one has to do.'

Astha looked bewildered.

Pipee ruffled her hair with a slow unsteady hand, 'Don't worry, I can take care of myself.'

She came back unharmed but terribly shaken. 'It's worse than you realise, the police are actually firing on the innocent, making false arrests, and refusing to register complaints. How can Muslims have any security or protection when the forces of law are among those who beat and kill? Go back to Pakistan they keep taunting, when were they ever in Pakistan, that they should go *back*? And nothing is done, nothing. What kind of country can these people feel part of? To be a Muslim here is a curse.'

'They started it,' said Hemant. 'After the Babri Masjid fell they were the ones who first took to stoning temples in Bombay. What did they expect, that this is the time of the Muslim rulers, where Hindus will sit down and not retaliate? Who set fire to the temple in Govandi? Who started throwing stones at buses, and police stations, and the BMC offices?'

Astha listened. If it was quite clear that there were many ways to regard what was happening, it was equally clear that she and Hemant held opposite views. Whose voice would be stronger remained to be seen.

The most effective way she had of making a statement was with paint, and she focused on that. It took her mind off her personal predicament, with such violence around her, her problems seemed small. She turned to brush and canvas to make her contribution to her country, she hoped it would be noticed. It was only a drop in a large, large ocean, but drops added up.

Pipee ended up making several trips to distressed areas. Work, she said briefly, and maybe, thought Astha, she keeps coming back because she misses me, though she knew Pipee would never say anything to this purpose. Once she had decided that they were going to break up, that was it.

She called Pipee over one day, and had the pleasure of her approval when she saw her canvases.

'They are strong and make a very effective statement. I can see how you have evolved, Ant.' So what if Pipee was leaving, at that moment Astha felt they could never be parted.

'They really are good,' continued the friend and activist, 'perhaps you can hold an exhibition on your own. It's time you emerged from the shadow of the Manch.'

Then she returned to her travels, so much is happening.

Astha noticed Pipee didn't ask her to join her even for a weekend. She would have gone anywhere if Pipee had only asked her.

~

It was in January that Pipee got the letter confirming her admission to the University of Illinois, Urbana Champaign.

'So soon, you have got to hear so soon, how wonderful,' said Astha over the phone, glad that Pipee could not see her face. 'They must really want you.'

'I don't know about that. The amount they offer will show.'

'When will you know?'

'Soon, I hope.'

Afterwards Astha scolded herself, this is the dress rehearsal for the real thing, why should I care, what is she to me, someone I loved, but we both have our own lives. She has chosen larger horizons, it's her life, this is mine. She told herself this firmly and repeatedly and was surprised that the information did not make her feel better.

Next morning she woke up with a headache. So, what's new, she asked herself, quickly swallowing a decongestant and a painkiller.

As the pills took effect and the pain receded, she drearily made for the spare room, to try that other cure, work. She pressed her turpentine rag against her face and breathed its sharp smells. She imagined it around her eyes, running under her eyebrows, through her temples, pushing all the throbbing in front of it, sweeping it away, throwing it out, so that it lost the power to affect, now and ever after.

It was a month before the axe finally fell. 'Oh, Pip, I'm so glad. How much are they giving you?'

'A full fee waiver, and twelve hundred dollars a month.'

'You deserve every bit of it. I hope you will be very happy.'

'Hey, I'm not going yet. And I want to see your exhibition before I go.'

'I'm doing my best.'

'I will get Ravi's wife to review it,' said Hemant. 'She is an art critic for *The Indian Express*. She probably knows others as well.'

'Thank you.'

'I'm sure they will be impressed,' said Hemant smiling at Astha.

Astha knew Hemant was being helpful because the Manch was not involved and he welcomed the breach between her and any activism, but she had been too long married to linger over the source of his appreciation.

Every morning, the children in school, the servants supervised, Hemant safe with his diet lunch in the factory, and Astha would shut herself inside her painting room. She needed to feel closed in and protected, if by nothing else than walls. There she was with shrouded canvasses, bottles of turpentine and linseed oil, tubes of colour lying in baskets around the easel, and grey rags stiff with dried paint. These were the tools of her trade, these were the things that established her separate life, touching them was comfort.

As her brush moved carefully over the canvas, her hand grew sure, her back straightened, she sat firmer on her stool, her gaze became more concentrated, her mind more focused. A calmness settled over her, tenuous, fragile, but calmness nevertheless. She thought of her name. Faith. Faith in herself. It was all she had.

Pipee too was working. She was looking for a tenant, getting her papers ready, packing away her books, winding up her affairs. She required no interaction with Astha in arranging these things.

There was a time when Astha's day revolved around being

available to Pipee. The children, Hemant and all her obligations were frantically juggled so that she could see and talk to Pipee whenever possible.

Now they talked, but it was on the surface, both of them reluctant to work at letting go of a connection that would naturally cease when Pipee left.

'I can't wait to see your work.'

'Come.'

'I'll come, I'll come. I'm going to Shahjehanpur. They have called me. I think I ought to go before I leave.'

'How come you didn't tell me?' quavered Astha, the weaker of the two, remembering the time when she knew what Pipee was going to do the second she thought of doing it.

'You are so busy these days.'

At this prevarication, for the first time Astha felt relief that in a few months she would not have to talk to Pipee anymore.

It was May. The amaltas trees were blooming. Every morning when Astha stepped onto the road, she was forced to step on fallen, perfect, clear yellow flowers, pale green buds, and scattered curving yellow stamens. She stepped on them because there was no way to avoid them, and the flowers forgave her by looking just the same.

This morning Astha was going to Vasant Kunj to pick up Pipee, despite her protests, to take her to the station for the train to Shahjehanpur.

As she drove her hands felt heavy on the wheel. How many times had she travelled down this road in hope and longing, and then rushed back dreading the demands and questions of her children, husband, in-laws. Where have you been, we were waiting for you, this that and the other happened, and you weren't here to fulfil your place in this house. Soon nobody would have cause for complaint, if there had been neglect, she would make up for it now.

In Pipee's flat, third floor, no fans or cooler because the

electricity had gone. 'How hot it is,' remarked Astha for something to say.

'Thank God, I'll soon be leaving,' said Pipee carrying a small suitcase and locking, then double locking the doors.

'Indeed.'

Pipee looked at her. 'I don't mean I want to leave you. You know that.'

At these words hope sprang up in Astha's breast. The eternal stuff, hope. She looked at it in disgust. Hope looked back coy and stubborn. It did not have to say anything. Its presence spoke for itself.

The suitcase thrown in the car, the two got in and started the long drive to the New Delhi Railway Station.

~

That summer was the hottest Delhi had ever known. The temperature hit the 40s and stayed there day after day. Astha only felt fresh enough to work in the early mornings. She now woke at 4.45, made herself a cup of tea, and was at her easel by 5.00. As a consequence it became necessary to sleep by 10 p.m. Every day she and Hemant fought about this.

'This is crazy, you are crazy, your life revolves around those canvases.'

How could she make him understand? Work was the only place she could forget everything, where she could become her mind, her hand, and the vision inside her head. At any rate she was sleeping badly, only by working hours every morning before the demands of the house took over did she know some peace. All this was not explainable.

'Only for a little while more,' she tried coaxing.

'You've been saying that for ages.'

'You were the one who encouraged me to hold an exhibition, you showed interest, you said you would speak to Ravi's wife.'

'But what's the big hurry? You can have your exhibition later, anyway winter is a better time.'

'I want it now.'

Astha was feeling too sick at heart to give being sweet and coaxing more than the briefest try.

The hall at the Tagore Arts Centre was rented for five days. There were twenty canvases in all. It was two years work, and from December on, she had worked almost every day. Six canvases were devoted to the Babri Masjid and different forms of protest, another six to various aspects of Pipee and herself, though she hoped they were so disguised no one would be able to identify the women. There were four of her children, and two of men she had modelled on Hemant, one of Mala and Bahadur. Basically my life, thought Astha as she, Hemant, and the children worked in the gallery, putting them up, placing them to the best advantage.

'Why is this so small?' asked Hemant picking up one the size of a sheet of paper.

'It's for Pipee to take with her,' said Astha. 'I made it small on purpose.' Then as Hemant said nothing, she continued, 'Do you think she will like it?'

The painting was an interior, two women sitting on a charpai. The patches of colour came from a red cushion, an open window, the white of a pillow on the bed, the bangles of one, the bag and chappals of the other thrown on the floor. The figures themselves were indistinct and shadowy, one had a drooping head, the other had her face turned away. The small canvas added to the sense of claustrophobia.

'It's kind of sad,' said Hemant.

Astha was always surprised when Hemant said anything she could remotely relate to. 'I suppose it is rather,' she said. 'Maybe she should only be surrounded by happy things in Illinois?'

'I'm sure she'll like it. Are these women you two?'

'Of course not,' said Astha quickly. 'They are imaginary. You can't see their faces. Could be anyone.'

'Hummm.'

The last paintings to be hung were the Babri Masjid series, six in all, ending with a bare hillock, a trishul and a saffron flag planted on empty earth amid scattered stones, a peepul tree hanging forlornly on one side.

'I hope it is not too obvious,' fussed Astha, knots gathering inside her from the stress of exhibiting, displaying, exposing.

'Not at all,' said Hemant. 'You need obvious symbols to say obvious things.'

Why is he being so nice to me, thought Astha. He even seems to have changed his political opinions. Is it because all the work is over, no more early nights, early mornings, is it because she's going in another two weeks?

'Mama, I'm going to give out the price lists,' said Anuradha firmly.

'Of course darling, I shall depend on you.'

Pipee had returned from Shahjehanpur, but she still had to get her tenant, and decide what to do about her possessions. She couldn't help Astha with the setting up of her exhibition, Astha couldn't help her with the disposing of her things.

'It is rather badly timed,' said Astha on the phone, 'but I am holding this exhibition for you, Pip. So that, before you go . . .' She stopped. She didn't need to finish her sentences with Pipee.

'I know, I know, Ant. I wish I could be more there for you.'

'And I for you.'

Privately Astha thought perhaps it was just as well, she couldn't bear to witness the disbanding of Pip's house, where they had been skin on skin, mind on mind with nothing in between.

And Pipee thought, it is just as well Ant is not here when I am packing to leave. I don't think she could take it, and I couldn't take her not taking it. I wish she hadn't come with so much baggage, but she did, and well, there it is.

The opening of the exhibition, 1 August.

Pipee said, 'I had no idea you had been painting so much. It's wonderful, just wonderful.'

All Astha could say was, 'Did you like no. 12? It's for you.'

Pipee looked at her, squeezed her hand, and after half an hour of hanging about, affectionately said, 'I have to go dearest, I will see you later.'

'So soon?'

'I have to. A tenant is coming to see the flat, and could come at no other time. I am getting frantic, I hope this one works out.'

Astha thought of the very long distance between Pipee's flat and the Tagore Arts Centre, of the rush hour traffic, of the hour it would take her to get back home, and decided she could only be grateful that Pipee had come at all.

'Bye, see you.' She blew her a kiss and was gone, leaving Astha to listen to what Hemant was saying and who he was introducing her to.

More than half the paintings sold. Astha made almost two lakhs.

'It is a good beginning,' said Hemant, quite the manager of his wife's career. 'Ravi said his wife is going to give it a positive review, and talk to some other art critics so they mention it too. Exposure is what counts at this stage.'

'You must mail me the reviews,' said Pipee. 'I'm sure they will be very good. I look forward to reading them.'

Oh, Pipee, don't talk like a stranger to me, I can't stand it. I only want to talk about how sad I am feeling.

But the wall between them was by now quite high, and from time to time they both threw another brick on it. They were doing this now.

'How is the tenant?'

'Just what I wanted.'

And so on.

*

'I will take you to the airport,' said Astha on the phone.

'Are you sure?'

'Please, Pip, don't be insulting.'

'I only meant what about Hemant, won't he mind?'

'Hemant will understand.'

With Pipee about to go, it was guaranteed that Hemant would understand anything.

The night of 6 August. The last time Astha would drive to Vasant Kunj. The weather was hot and still, it hadn't rained since the night of her opening. She parked, climbed the three flights to Pipee's flat, rang the bell, and contemplated the bars, bolts and locks on the wooden and screen doors. Last time, for the last time, rang irritatingly in her mind. Was there anything about this night that was not going to be drenched in significance? She wished it was over, that she did not have to go through it step by painful step, Pipee's departure from her life.

She thought of how they had both been ants together. And now Pipee was journeying eight hours to London, ten hours to Chicago, two hours by bus to Urbana, to be an ant somewhere else.

'Hi!'

'Hi.'

She entered. The flat was bare, with just the things Pipee had sold the tenant. The bed, the cane chairs, the small wooden dining table.

Astha sat down and looked around. 'What'll you do when you come back?' she asked. 'About bedding and stuff?'

'Oh,' Pipee sounded vague. 'Buy new, I guess.' Astha could tell it was far from her mind, her return, why was she hurting herself by looking for clues?

'Are you ready?' she asked.

'The chowkidar is coming. I have to give him the keys and he'll take down the stuff.' Pipee wasn't quite looking at her, and Astha realised she was making Pipee uneasy, the way she sounded, sad, heavy, teary. She said nothing more as she watched Pipee doing last-minute things.

'It's a good thing that weight is not important when you fly to the US,' said Pipee as the chowkidar staggered out first with one heavy suitcase, then another. 'They go by the number of bags.'

'Yes, I suppose.'

'Come, let's go.'

The long drive, their car one of a stream going to the International Airport late at night, all saying good-bye to people they loved. As Astha drove, she imagined the misery in the cars around her. Join the queue, Astha, join the queue.

The crowd at the Indira Gandhi International Airport was as usual overwhelming. Astha drove up the ramp to Departure, nosing through the cars, coaches, taxis, and thousands of people.

'I'll get a trolley,' said Pipee, jumping out.

'I'll get the luggage,' said Astha moving towards the dickey, and fumbling with the key. There was Pipee with the trolley, the luggage unloaded, there was a policeman waving her car away – no standing allowed, and Pipee saying go, sweetie – where will you park – it's so crowded, and Astha, wailing but I want to see you inside – they won't allow you – and the policeman – not moving towards any of the other parked vehicles on the ramp but threatening her with traffic violation – Pipee propelling her into her car – a last kiss, goodbye, goodbye, take care, and she was lost to the eye even before she had wheeled her trolley through the entrance door.

'So, she's gone,' said Hemant when Astha returned. Awake at that late hour and witness to his wife's face and eyes.

'Yes.'

'Was the plane on time?'

'I don't know. I didn't stay.'

'How was she?'

'Who?'

'Your friend, who else?'

Astha could not reply. 'I'm tired,' she said, 'I want to sleep.'

Mechanically she changed, brushed her teeth, put cream on, got into her side of the bed, pulled the sheet up, and turning to the very edge lay absolutely still. Motion of any kind was painful to her. Her mind, heart and body felt numb.

It continued like this for days. She felt stretched thin, thin across the globe.

Acknowledgements

Many people have been particularly kind in sharing information that I found invaluable. In this regard I would particularly like to mention Anshu Balbir, Mita Bose, Ranjan Dhawan, Jamal Kidwai, Vinay Minucha, and Jaya Srivastava. This book could not have been written without their help.

Masooma Ali, Sunanda Ali, Bharati Bhargava, Nidhi Dalmia, Nilanjana Dalmia, Christopher Fruean of Walt Disney World, Vijay Kapur, Vimla Kapur, Fauzia Khan, Angela Koreth, M. K. Raina, Maseeh Rehman, Saswati Sen Gupta and Jaya Sharma were badgered about numerous details, and responded with patience and generosity.

Jaya Srivastava, Sharmila Purkayastha and V. Karthika were generous with pamphlets and books I would not have been able to get otherwise.

Penelope Anderson, Janet Chawla, Katyayani Dalmia, Anuradha Marwah, Ira Singh, Ramya Sreenivasan, and Addison Ullrich contributed encouragement, interest, enthusiasm and criticism.

Anuradha Marwah helped in crucial ways during the final stages.

Julian Loose, my editor at Faber, bestowed a clarity and vision upon these pages that much benefited them. Heather Schroder showed faith in me by becoming my agent on trust.

Roma Bhagat Baraya helped with legal aspects of the text. Sanjeev Saith, my publisher at IndiaInk, was a model of patience and tact. His meticulous attention to detail was greatly appreciated.

Ira Singh's repeated readings and comments helped shape the characters. Her other contributions defy exact description.

Gun Nidhi Dalmia, my husband, was astute and reassuring in his reading of my manuscript. My hours at the computer would not have been possible without his support.

My children, Maya, Amba, Katyayani and Agastya were with me throughout in body and spirit.

During the research for my novel I consulted the following books for their spiritual commentary: *The Secret of the Kath Upanishad,* Swami Krishnananda, The Divine Life Society: Tehri-Garhwal, UP, India, 1974; Maharishi Mahesh Yogi on the *Bhagavad-Gita, A New Translation and Commentary,* Chapters 1-6, Penguin, 1967.

For the political events that form the background of the novel I consulted: *Ayodhya Imbroglio:* T. P. Jindal, Ashish Publishing House, New Delhi, 1995; *The Demolition: India at the Crossroads,* Nilanjan Mukhopadhyay, Harper Collins, 1994; *The People's Verdict:* An inquiry into the December '92 & January '93 riots in Bombay by the Indian People's Human Rights Tribunal Conducted by Justice S. M. Daud & Justice H. Suresh published by The Indian People's Human Rights Commission, August 1993; Pradeep Nayak, *The Politics of the Ayodhya Dispute,* Commonwealth Publishers, New Delhi, 1993; and *Cry the Beloved Country,* a PUDR pamphlet.

In section VI, the advertisement by Ramjanambhoomi Nyas (a non-political body affiliated to the VHP) in The Pioneer, May 11, 1991, has been taken from Pradeep Nayak, *The Politics of the Ayodhya Dispute,* (details mentioned above) p. 167.

The Hindustan Times was consulted on microfilm, accessed from the Teen Murti Memorial Library. I am grateful to the library for allowing me this facility.

The actual events leading to the destruction of the Babri Masjid have either been fictionalised or used in imaginative reconstructions.

This book went through several of its many drafts during a three month stint at the Universities of Kent and Stirling in the UK. I am indebted to the Charles Wallace Trust, India for granting me a fellowship to these places.